To Vince

"You made the brightest days from the darkest nights."

A Four
Treasures Novel

The Stone of Destiny

CAROLINE LOGAN

gob stopper

First published in 2019 by Gob Stopper

Gob Stopper is an imprint of Cranachan Publishing Limited

ISBN: 978-1-911279-50-1

eISBN: 978-1-911279-51-8

Cover & Interior Illustrations:

© Seasquint / Jay Madison © Lana Elanor

© Red Ink / Irina Trigubova © shutterstock.com / Katerina Branchukova

Map Illustration © Caroline Logan

www.cranachanpublishing.co.uk

@cranachanbooks

cranachan

The Isles of Ossiana

Vitovo Vinissa Venza Visenya

Vonsha

Nekheb

Kemet

Zau Raçote

Knidos

Thassos

Djanet

Aknosia

Islas de Amistad

Nenebus

Heaven's Gate

Piedra de Fuego Edessa

Ovest

Ononessa

Castillo de Plata

Panaiso

The Etivian Sea

Isla de Pulpo

Chapter 1

Ailsa tilted her head towards the sky and let the rain wash away the blood from her face and arms. The sun still had an hour before it would sink below the horizon. It had been a fortuitous day. Not only had she managed to get a fire started in the damp cave-mouth in less than two minutes, she had also stumbled upon a deer that had fallen to its doom over the cliff edge; its neck twisted. She had immediately set to work butchering it and stuffing the cut-offs into a clay pot. As she had worked, she couldn't resist cutting a few strands off the still steaming meat and eating them raw. Now all she needed was some fresh water and her tasks for the day would be done.

She sighed, inspecting the pieces of gore still stuck to the arms of her shirt. Maybe a wash would be useful too. Deciding to complete two jobs in one, she stepped back into the rock cave and tucked the pot of meat away into a natural alcove. Ailsa picked up an empty canteen and made her way to the beach, where a stream trickled into a waterfall just large enough to bathe in.

The steep cliffs led to creamy sand peppered with

wicked looking boulders. The sea was as fickle as love; sometimes an azure blue, more often a choppy, cold grey. Across the water lay the islands of Jay and Crait, which were clearly visible on a sunny day. Ailsa's favourite view came when the sun shone above the jagged peaks of Jay while the beach was darkened by clouds.

Ailsa had been living here long enough to know how to use the land to her advantage. She had wandered from place to place for five years after she had left her village, chased away each time, before finding her home here: a little bay far enough away from the rest of humanity for them not to bother her. No one wanted a *changeling* anywhere near them anyway.

She had sat watching the sleek seabirds dive into the water and named the little cove *Buthaid Beach*—using the ancient Eilanmòrian word for '*puffin*' and over the past couple of years, she had made it home. She trudged down the worn, grass path to the beach, trailing her hand through her small garden. She was not a gifted gardener, but the rain fell constantly, turning her stolen seeds into monster plants.

As she walked away from the headland, the rain died down and the wind picked up, tugging at her dark hair, sending it whipping over her face like seaweed in a wave. She sighed and pulled her cloak over her head; stopping the strands from misbehaving. With her hood up, she looked just like everyone else in Eilanmòr with

her ash brown hair, pale skin and silver-blue eyes—
save for the mark. A mark from the faeries to show
she was not human. Her fingers flew to the reddened,
painful-looking flesh below her eye. It was her skin—
her birthmark—that set her apart from others. Her skin
that told her neighbours she was not to be trusted or
tolerated. *Changeling* they had shouted after her. Her
mother had always shielded her, kept her away from
prying eyes, but that protection ended when her mother
died. Ailsa grimaced and continued down the path.

She reached the running fountain of water, holding
the canteen under the stream. *Maybe I'll heat some and
have a wash back at the cave*, she thought absently. It was
better to get most of the blood off first though. Bending
to wash her hands in the ice-cold water, she rubbed
them as quickly as possible. She was thinking of the tiny
tin of lavender and pine soap back in her pack, stolen
and saved for special occasions, when she heard the
screaming.

The scream started as a gurgling, then broke into a wail,
as a wave crashed on the large rocks further round the
beach. For a moment, Ailsa was still; crouching over
the narrow stream. If she stayed here and waited, she
would not be seen by whatever it was that was making

the noise. But the wailing turned to shouts. The words were foreign, but Ailsa knew they were a cry for help. Standing up, she shook her freezing fingers and licked her lip, tasting the salt in the wind. She took a hesitant step forward and felt for the axe she always kept at her side. Peering round a boulder, she surveyed the beach for the source of the shouting.

There, around twenty feet away from Ailsa's hiding place, was a young woman. Her scarlet hair was swept upwards by the wind, transformed into a crown of flames. Her eyes were wide with panic as she scanned the beach then back towards the ocean. She screamed again and it was unlike anything that Ailsa had heard before. Loud and piercing, it made her ears ache.

Ailsa scrambled up the rock to get a better view. Now she could see a little more of the scene, her breath caught in her throat. In the woman's arms, there was the body of a seal, a red rip marring its side. Blood covered the woman's legs and upper body. She choked back a sob, looking wildly around the beach again. This time, though, she raised her head higher and found Ailsa's eyes. She stared right at her, pleading and shouting, now in the common tongue.

"Help! Please help me!"

Ailsa's stomach rolled but she leapt from the boulder and sprinted over the rocks towards the woman, her boots flicking sand out behind her as she ran. The closer she got, the more gruesome the scene became. The seal looked close to death; the blood from its wound covering most of its body.

"Help him!" she cried when Ailsa got close enough. The woman's emerald eyes darted from Ailsa's face to the sea and back again like an animal expecting a predator to appear at any moment. Her breaths were coming in hiccupping gasps as she stroked the head of the seal, the only part of it that wasn't covered in blood.

Unsure, but willing to do anything to stop the woman crying, Ailsa slid her fingers around the seal's body. The woman resisted for a heartbeat before releasing the animal. It was still breathing and when she scooped it into her arms, it looked at her with glassy obsidian eyes.

"We have to get away from here," said the redhead, panicking even more now. "Hide!"

Ailsa was about to ask why when she saw them. Rounding the bend of the headland, a group of wooden longships sailed into view. The nearest was close enough to make out colourful carvings on the boat's side—and the men who were rowing fast towards them.

Her blood froze. Raiders.

"Run!" Ailsa shouted and, with the seal still in her arms, bolted back up the boulders. Its body weighed a ton, sending her off balance as she ran, slipping and sliding over the sand. She didn't need to turn back to know the woman was following closely, her pace hindered by her bare feet.

It was beginning to rain again as Ailsa reached a cluster of large rocks that marked the boundary between the beach and headland. She ducked behind the boulders, yanking the other woman down as quickly as she could. The heavy drops washed the seal's wound; it wasn't as bad as it had first appeared. Thankfully, the woman had finished with her damn screaming.

Their breathing came in thick pants as they stared at each other. From the beach, the sound of a boat landing hard on the sand reached their ears, accompanied by drums and urgent shouting. From what Ailsa could see, the group of boats had continued on, leaving only one vessel behind to inspect the beach.

Motioning to the other woman to stay quiet, Ailsa sank a little deeper into the hiding place.

Through the stones, they could see the boat and its inhabitants: three tall figures all wearing thick, oil-coated cloaks and carrying spears. One turned and looked in their direction. Ailsa's hair stood on end. Where she expected to see a face, there was just a skull: snow white against the tanned skin of the man's throat.

"What—" she whispered.

Her companion didn't seem surprised. Still staring at the raiders, Ailsa was shocked to see they each had a skull for a face.

"Masks," breathed the redhead beside her.

Avalognians, Ailsa realised.

The rain became heavier until it was thundering down from the skies. The warriors fanned out, sweeping the beach. It was clear they thought the woman had continued on somewhere else, because they sauntered around, swinging their spears at their sides. Two moved away heading for the other side of the beach but one stalked towards them. Ailsa gripped her axe in her hands and crouched down further, flexing the muscles in her shoulders.

She had heard stories about what Avalognian raiders did to their enemies. Not only did they travel from village to village, up and down the coast of Eilanmòr, burning houses, but if anyone survived the fire, they were either taken as slaves or slaughtered where they stood. Stories told of half-burned people, clawing their way out of their homes to freedom, only to be shoved back into the embers. More frightening still, sometimes they would be killed when they emerged, so their bodies could feed the hoard. Avalognians were cannibals, everyone knew.

A figure drew closer, stumbling over the shifting sand. He stopped, cocking his head and hesitating before pulling out a wicked-looking dart from a bag around his body. It was tipped on one side with a red feather, and poison, Ailsa guessed, on the other. Suddenly, he turned to look straight at their hiding place and Ailsa felt a chill as the skull's eye-holes seemed to settle on her. But behind the mask, she could faintly see two eyes.

Just a man.

With this realisation she blinked once. Twice.

Don't think. Act.

Then she stood and threw her axe straight at him. It spun, handle over blade, through the air before it embedded itself in his cranium.

From the moment the weapon left her hand, it moved in slow motion, as if in water. Ailsa watched, mesmerised as the body was thrown backwards, arching through the air. The handle of the axe shuddered from the impact, sticking out of his head like a horn. He didn't even have time to scream before he died.

Chapter 2

Dead. Dead. Dead. The word echoed through her mind, but she swatted it away like a fly before it could find purchase. She would need to wait until they were out of danger before she could pick apart what she'd done.

Ailsa moved from her hiding place to the body. The axe had cracked the mask, revealing a heavy brow beneath the blood. Black eyes looked blankly back up at her. She bent down and extracted the axe from his head, pulling it out of the wound with a sickening pop.

"Look out!" the woman from behind her suddenly shouted. Ailsa wrenched her gaze from the corpse to look back. She was pointing to the other end of the beach where the dead man's comrades were now racing towards them.

Dead. Dead. Dead. The word swirled round in her brain again, like a warning.

Ailsa steeled herself and strode forward, her weapon heavy in her right hand. A swift throw of the axe brought another Avalognian down with a glancing blow to his neck. It hadn't been a clean shot like the last one, but it was enough to send him tumbling to his knees, clutching at the wound as his lifeblood gushed down his body.

The third man was running for her with his spear Ailsa dodged his throw, but landed hard on her backside when he launched himself at her, taking her down.

Dark eyes stared out from the mask's sockets; he was so close that she could see his teeth were sharpened into points. A fist connected with her jaw.

For a moment there was silence as the force of the impact vibrated around her head. Stars burst in her vision, colliding together, before she was picked up and tossed to the side, the crash of the ground enough to clear her senses. She landed face first in the sand, the shingle scraping a path along her chin. Her assailant marched over to her, his body heaving with the effort of the fight.

Get up. Get up. Get up.

Desperation wound a hand around her neck and she wheezed as she pushed herself up. Scrambling, she found a rock at her side. With a roar, she rose and swung the rock round. It connected with the side of the man's head, with a sickening crunch. He whimpered before he crumpled to the ground, unmoving.

Ailsa exhaled and rubbed a hand over her face, willing her heart to slow again.

"Is that one dead too?" asked the woman, once again holding the seal to her chest, her voice wavering as she spoke.

"No. Just unconscious," gulped Ailsa. She used the toe of her boot to tilt the man's face and flick the mask away. To her surprise, it wasn't a man, but a woman. She rubbed her jaw while watching the warrior's chest rise and fall.

With a groan, she moved around the body to the feet and dragged the woman towards the boat. When she passed the man with the neck wound, she dropped the woman's feet and pulled out a knife, intending to deliver a cleaner death—but he was already gone. She sheathed the weapon in her boot and picked up her axe lying at his side. She hung it on her belt before continuing to the longboat, heaving the Avalognian behind her.

The woman she had saved followed her at a safe distance. When she saw Ailsa's intention, she carefully placed the seal down on the sand. It made a little bark of protest. Together, they lifted the raider and dropped her into the boat. Then, pushing the hull, they managed to cast it off into the sea. The strong waves rocked it violently before sucking it out into the surf like a thirsty beast.

Ailsa and the other woman both stood in the rain watching the craft bob on the open water for a few moments before turning away.

"Were they looking for you?" Ailsa asked. If she was going to have more Avalognians on her doorstep, it would be better to find out now.

The woman nodded. Ailsa thought she saw a hint of apology in her eyes.

For a second, she considered leaving the strange woman here on the beach. Why should she have anything more to do with her?

Because it's the right thing to do.

Ailsa groaned. It seemed like, for now, she would have to play hero.

"We had better go," she said, "Follow me."

Ailsa headed up the beach towards her cave. The woman picked up the seal with care and trailed after her. Ailsa fought to force the grimace from her face as she walked. When she reached the grass, she wiped both sides of the axe blade on the ground, cleaning off most of the mess. She did the same with her hands, watching as the dewy grass became coated with blood. Her heart gave an uncomfortable twitch in her chest, but Ailsa shoved the feeling down, focussing instead on the other woman. Ailsa led her up the path and into the shelter.

The fire was lower than before, but it still churned out a welcome bit of heat. The red-headed woman cradled the seal and sank down onto the cave floor, making a grateful sound in her throat. Ailsa gestured for the woman to move closer to the heat before throwing her a rag, the unease threatening to creep back up again as the stranger wiped her hands and forearms. Without taking her eyes away, Ailsa plonked herself on the floor in front of the embers. For a brief moment, her hands had moved to throw her axe to the side like she always did when arriving home, but something told her to keep her weapon close.

Danger was still nearby, whether from this woman or from raiders returning to find their murdered comrades.

They sat in silence, for which Ailsa was grateful. The persistent voice drummed louder in her head in the quiet of the cave.

Dead. Dead. Dead.

It never got easier, killing people. Ailsa had only done so twice before now, once when she had first moved to the area and a man had forced himself on her. He had stunk of sour alcohol and his eyes were glazed as if he wasn't entirely present. When his intentions became clear, Ailsa had pulled the small knife from her boot and thrust it into his gut.

The second time was when she had come across an older woman lying at the bottom of the cliffs further up the coast. Her body was broken and she was in so much pain that she begged Ailsa to put her out of her misery. Ailsa had hoped, as she thrust her knife into the woman's temple, that someone would do the same for her, if she ever found herself in similar circumstances.

She was pulled from her reverie when the woman placed a hand on her elbow. "Thank you. I was sure they were going to catch us," she said.

Anger bubbled up inside her. She had just killed people for this person. *What on earth was she doing on her deserted patch of land to begin with?*

Stranger still was the presence of the seal in her arms. Was it a pet or had the girl been trying to rescue wild animals? There was something about the way the woman stared at it, holding it almost like a child. *What was her story?*

"Your thanks aren't necessary," Ailsa ground out, backing up to the opposite wall. "But what is necessary is that you explain why I just risked my life to save a seal?"

Sad eyes met her own. The stranger cleared her throat and sat up a little straighter. *Was she a lady?* Ailsa had never really been around many females, but by the way she held herself, Ailsa guessed that the redhead came from a good family. Her clothes were all wrong though. She was wearing a loose, grey dress, more suited to a commoner. Although her red hair was wild, and her eyes were wide with youth, she had a certain poise that made Ailsa think she was older than she looked. Aside from the woman's curls, her most striking feature was the numerous freckles that speckled her face, neck and hands.

"My name is Iona." Her voice was still wavering in the aftermath of her crying. She gestured down at the seal. "This is Harris, my brother." She placed her hands in front of her and looked expectantly at Ailsa.

Ailsa's heart sunk at the word 'brother' as she tried to make sense of what the woman—Iona—had just said.

"Ailsa MacAra," she croaked out in response, offering a hand for the woman to shake. Iona's palm was soft, lending more credit to Ailsa's theory about her background. Ailsa wondered numbly if she should shake the seal's flipper too.

The girl just nodded and went back to stroking the animal's muzzle.

I've saved a crazy woman. She gave an exasperated grunt and set about building the fire back up again. She didn't think she wanted to ask about the seal until she was at least a little warmer.

Ridding herself of blood as best she could, Ailsa stared into the flames, thinking about what has just happened on the beach. The wooden longships were clearly searching for something. It was odd for the Avalognians to be so far south, though. There were no villages for miles; exactly how Ailsa liked it. *Why were they here?* She got the feeling that it definitely had something to do with this girl and her 'brother'.

She turned to ask Iona her questions but the words died on her lips. The woman still sat huddled near the fire but instead of a seal in her arms, there was a man. Or rather, the man's head, as he was quite a bit larger than the seal had been.

Chapter 3

The man's head, like the woman's, was covered in a mass of flaming red hair. He was completely naked but, thankfully, the fire's light did not reach his more intimate areas. He clutched his side where his skin was sliced, yet his cut was somewhat smaller than the seal's had been.

It was Ailsa's turn to scream, but the sound struggled to escape her throat.

"What the hell is this?" she cursed, holding her neck as she stared at the sight in front of her.

"I'm sorry," said Iona sympathetically, "*This* is my brother—"

Again, there was a twinge in Ailsa's heart, but she did her best to smother the feeling.

"—he didn't have the energy before," Iona continued, "But now that he's healed a bit, this is his human form. He's much easier to transport as a seal, so it was rather good luck," she laughed, gazing at the man in her arms and ruffled his curly hair.

"But I am much better looking as a man," he smirked, speaking for the first time. His voice had a mocking edge and his eyes danced with laughter, despite the pain that he must still be in from his wound.

When Ailsa looked at his side again, it resembled a weathered scar more than a slash. "You're *selkies*?" she breathed.

"Yes, dear," Iona said slowly, as if trying to soften the news.

Ailsa gripped her axe tighter. In the back of her mind, a little part of her was screaming. She should have known better than to help a strange, wailing woman clutching a bloody seal! From what she had heard about selkies, they would change from their seal forms into lovely creatures in order to lure humans to watery deaths, before feasting on them with their sharp, little teeth. But the two people sitting in front of her just looked sad and cold. *That could be a trick,* she told herself, edging away from the fire. Ailsa did her best to look like she was shifting for comfort, bringing her feet underneath her so she could jump up at a moment's notice.

"Are you going to drag me to the ocean and drown me?" she asked.

She wasn't prepared for the bark of laughter that the man, Harris, let out as he surveyed her.

"Calm down, lass. I believe you were the one dragging us away from the ocean," he chuckled. His side— miraculously—was now completely healed.

The screaming in Ailsa's ears went up an octave.

"I promise you we don't want to harm you," soothed Iona. She held her hands out in pacification. "You saved our lives and we are very grateful to you."

"Also," laughed Harris. "I don't know what stories you've heard, but I detest the taste of humans—too fatty and smelly, like sour milk." His mirthful eyes left hers to travel over her body. "Though you do look tastier than average," He wiggled his eyebrows at Ailsa. "Maybe I'll break my rule?"

"Behave yourself," Iona said, cuffing her brother on the ear.

Ailsa was too stunned to react. She still held her axe close to her body as she studied them.

"I'm confused and, honestly, I'm considering whether to fight you or run."

Iona smiled. "I'm sure that you could overpower us in no time. Please just allow us to stay the night. We won't hurt you."

At first, Ailsa had felt the need to protect this woman; she had thought her weak and in danger. Now she felt the roles had been reversed. Still, Iona seemed genuine and kind.

Ailsa looked at Harris, who pouted at her, eyes wide in mock pleading.

The brother on the other hand, she thought, *could do with a smack.*

"Fine," she drew in a deep breath and then fixed

Harris with the best glare she could muster under the circumstances. "But for all that's holy, will you please cover yourself up?" She chucked a blanket in his direction. He caught it, wrapping it around himself while he chuckled. Iona grinned gratefully at her and edged closer to the fire.

"Here, I have another," said Ailsa, throwing another blanket in the seal-woman's direction. Ailsa rubbed her hands together, in an effort to get some warmth into them. "You might want to change your clothes too, since they're wet from the rain and a bit manky from all the blood," she said, trying not to wrinkle her nose.

"Are your clothes wet?" Iona tilted her head and looked at her with large eyes. When Ailsa nodded, she chuckled. "I can fix that."

Ailsa wasn't sure what to expect when Iona lifted her hands. The water soaking her shirt and trousers sluggishly beaded on the surface of the fabric. Then, like rain in reverse, each drop of water rose into the air and hung suspended above her head. Iona did the same for her own clothes, taking most of the mess off with the liquid. Then with a twist of her hand, she hurled the water out of the cave.

"How did you—" Ailsa started.

Iona looked pleased by her awe. "Selkie magic. We can control water; well, the females can."

Ailsa turned to Harris, who didn't seem too put out.

"It's okay, I have other talents. Great looks. Good instincts. Nice hair. I can lick my elbow. Want to see?" He grabbed his right arm in his left hand and contorted his body.

"No, it's fine," Ailsa cut him off. He shrugged his shoulders as if to say '*your loss.*'"

Once all the water had left her clothes, Ailsa felt warmer. The fire's heat enveloped her skin, almost too hot. At exactly the same time, both women wrapped their blankets around their own shoulders. The selkie smiled at her and, after a moment, Ailsa returned the gesture.

It was beginning to get dark outside. Ailsa was suddenly exhausted, the adrenaline from the fight leaving her system. Her eyelids felt like they were being pulled down by heavy bags. She subtly grabbed her axe and pack, scooting to the side, so that she was a more comfortable distance from these strange creatures.

"If I go to sleep, will you murder me?"

"No, dear," whispered Iona, "I promise that you will wake feeling rested and with all of your body parts," Iona giggled. "I suppose that is the least we can do for you."

When Ailsa looked at her sceptically, she held her hands up in front of her.

"A selkie's promise can't be broken."

"I won't even have a taste until you are wide awake again," joked Harris.

Ailsa gave him a dirty look and sank into her nest of blankets. The siblings lay down side by side and fell asleep quickly. She stayed awake for some time, watching their bodies, waiting for them to attack her. Eventually, the gentle rise and fall of Harris's chest made her feel safe enough to risk closing her eyes. Still hugging her axe, Ailsa's body relaxed bit by bit and she drifted into deep oblivion.

Chapter 4

"N ever go into the woods by yourself."

"Why?"

"There are all manner of ghouls and spirits in the forest, child, ready to take you away."

The children sat cross-legged on the floor and stared at the old woman with a mixture of fear and excitement. This was the best time of the day, when their parents took them to the little cottage in the middle of town. None of them were sure if they were related to the woman, but it didn't matter. Everyone knew each other in their village; everyone was family. They all called her *Seanmhair*, Grandmother.

"Have I ever told you the story of the faeries, my loves?" The old woman's face crinkled into a smile at the sight of six eager faces, ready for the story. It was why they had come after all. She put down her mending and arranged herself on the chair, fluffing up the pillow behind her, ready to begin.

"Before you were born, before peace came to Eilanmòr, our people lived far apart and faced great dangers whenever they left their homes. No one went out at night, for that was the time that the faerie queen, Nicnevan, held her court."

The children at her feet pressed closer together. They loved scary stories.

The old woman continued. "Nicnevan was the most magnificent female in the world. She had hair golden like wheat and a laugh that could dazzle princes and beggars. But her temper was also great. For hundreds of years, she ruled these lands and punished those that disobeyed her, both human and fae alike." The woman fluttered her fingers at the children and they gasped in horror and delight.

"She was fond of the dark and the woods and the creatures that dwelt there. And so, these monsters were allowed to roam free between human villages and settlements, spreading disease and bad fortune, until one day, the good fae disobeyed her. They stole something very precious from her and she flew into a rage. She was so distracted by her anger that she did not notice when a mortal man crept into her court. He chained her to a willow tree with iron manacles and magic, trapping her. Faeries are weakened by iron, so Nicnevan could not use her powers on the man. Since then, Eilanmòr has been at peace.

"However, to this day Nicnevan is still out there, waiting to break free and seek revenge. Though the good fae have abandoned her, sinister monsters still serve the evil faerie queen. They wait in the forests and caves, ready to snatch any humans that come their way. If they find you, they will take you to Nicnevan and there you will be trapped with the nightmares of this world."

There was a collective shiver amongst the children and the old woman chuckled at them, eyes twinkling.

"Don't worry, my loves, they cannot get you here. The monsters fear light and warmth. The shield marks on our doors warn them off."

"But what about the good faeries, *Seanmhair*?" asked one of the girls, her shrill, little voice giving away her excitement.

"Don't worry, *mo leanabh*," the woman reassured the child, "they can still visit and give you sweet dreams."

Just then, a loud creak came from the cottage window and all heads turned towards it. The old woman's eyes immediately narrowed, filled with disgust.

A girl's small, heart shaped face peeked through the other side.

"Ailsa MacAra, leave this place now! Don't you be coming near these children!" barked the old woman, standing up. The face ducked away behind the window frame.

"What was that, *Seanmhair*?" asked one of the smaller boys, eyes round with surprise.

"That," huffed the woman, "was a little monster." She still stood, staring at the window, clutching at her chest.

"But it looked like a wee girl to me."

"Oh it looks like a girl, but don't be fooled," she warned as the children surrounded her skirts. The woman patted one girl's head, but her eyes never left the window.

"Eleven years ago, there was a young mother who lived in the next village. She had a gorgeous baby girl who fell ill and was likely to die. The mother nursed her baby for days but fell asleep, exhausted. When she woke, she found that her baby had been replaced by another. It looked almost identical to the child, save for a large, red mark on its left cheek. We told the mother to drown the monster, but I'm afraid she was already under its spell. She raised it as if it were her baby. That was the thing that was looking through that window just now. The mother died a few weeks ago; she probably had the health sucked from her by the little beast. Do not speak to it, children."

"Now, it is nearly time for your parents to collect you. Let's wait for them in bed, where we can get cosy. Don't worry, nothing can hurt you here." She ushered them through to the rear of the cottage. Before she blew out the last candle, she peered out of the window, but the tiny figure was gone.

The girl clung to the shadows at the edge of the village. She knew that tonight was not the night to try to stay;

she should return to the relative safety of the forest and wait until morning. Her mind was whirling with the curses that had been spat at her all day. As she walked, she gripped the chunk of cheese she had swiped from a table. Without breaking pace, she lifted the food to her mouth and nibbled on a corner. It had been worth it. So preoccupied was she by her first meal in days, that she didn't notice the faint echoing through the trees.

Crunch. Crunch. Crunch.

The sound got louder until finally her senses picked up that something was off. She slowed her steps.

Right foot.

Crunch.

Left foot.

Crunch.

The hairs on the back of her neck stood up.

She took two more steps.

Crunch. Crunch.

Was it the echoing of her footsteps? She stopped, holding her breath.

Crunch.

She didn't wait to find out who her mysterious stalker was. Ailsa dropped the cheese and ran. Branches whipped at her face and arms, but still she ran. Terror gripped her throat and she yearned for her mother. She ran and ran until her lungs burned and her muscles screamed at her to stop.

When she couldn't run anymore, she flung herself under a tree and sobbed.

This is the way of the world, a sharp little voice said in her head, as she cried at all the unfairness.

She wiped her eyes and stared at her tear-stained shirt. If she were to live, she would need to be tough. She would need to become the monster everyone thought she was. If they were scared of her, maybe she could use that to her advantage. She would get out of this forest. She would *survive*.

She stood.

This would be the last time that she cried.

Chapter 5

A large water droplet fell from the ceiling of the cave and landed on Ailsa's face, pulling her from her dream. *It must be raining again*, she thought, groaning and rolling over.

How many times had she had the same nightmare now? Was it not enough for the monster to stalk her waking moments but her dreams as well?

It can't get you here, she reminded herself.

The smell of fire drifted into her nose and Ailsa's eyes flicked open. Across the room, she could see a head of flaming, curly hair.

"Ah, you're up," Iona called out. Her voice was much too cheerful for so early in the morning.

"Am I?" groaned Ailsa. *Ah, I'm still insane. Perfect.*

The wind outside howled, just like the voice in the back of her head. Ailsa sat up. Iona had built the fire again but there was no sign of Harris.

"How did you sleep?" asked Iona, stoking the fire.

"Fine. Where's your brother?"

"Out, collecting breakfast." Iona continued poking the fire with a large stick and Ailsa scooted closer. If she was going to put up with the unwelcome intrusion, she may as well be warm. Iona gave her an encouraging smile, like she knew what Ailsa was thinking.

"So, I suppose you'd like to know why we were being chased by those raiders?"

"Well, I guess you could start with that, yeah."

Iona looked into the embers and her eyes grew hard. "We've always had a bit of a problem with the Avalognians. They think Selkie fins have curative properties, you see. They cut them off and use them as medicine." She scoffed. "Ridiculous. But lately we've been feeling like they've become more aggressive in their attempts to find us. Today, my suspicions were confirmed. Harris and I are in Eilanmòr on a mission and they seem to have caught wind of it. Or rather… someone told them and sent them after us."

"Someone asked them to kill you?"

"Yes. She does not want us to be successful in this particular venture."

"Who?" asked Ailsa, interested. The conversation was cut short when footsteps on the path announced the return of Harris.

He had borrowed one of her blankets to wear but being a lot taller, he had slung it around his hips like a kilt and an old rope held it together. His chest was bare, as were his feet, which were now covered in mud and sand from his walk. It was clear that he had just been swimming; his mop of scarlet hair was soaking wet and fat water drops travelled in rivers down his torso. In one hand, he was using his fingers to hook three fish by their gills. In the other, was her bucket filled with water. Ailsa was stunned by the sight. How could someone look so *wild*?

"Breakfast," he announced before striding up to his sister and shaking his hair all over her like a dog.

"Harris!" she screeched and threw a twig at him. It bounced off his chest and he threw back his head and laughed. Ailsa couldn't help but stare at the curls of red hair that dusted the place the twig had landed. He caught her looking and winked before tossing the fish down beside the fire. She scowled back.

"Making friends?" asked Harris before flopping down to the right of Iona. He set about creating a spit using the sticks littered around him.

"I was just telling Ailsa why we were being chased and why we are here." Iona picked up a fish and skewered it with a stick.

"Shh," Harris mock-whispered, "that's top secret." Iona rolled her eyes. The siblings seemed relaxed and happy.

What a dramatic change from last night, thought Ailsa. It was as if they had never been running for their lives. Indeed, she couldn't even see the place where Harris had been cut. She peered at his side, but the skin was blemish free. Harris snickered, having caught her looking at him for the second time. Feeling the need to explain herself, Ailsa pointed a finger at his side.

"You've completely healed."

"The perks of being a mythical creature."

"Sure." Ailsa nodded woodenly, not quite knowing how to respond, and turned to Iona. "So, do you want to tell me about this super-secret adventure you're on? Or will you have to kill me?"

"You are *obsessed* with us killing you," cut in Harris. One of the fish was cooked by now and he lobbed it at Ailsa who caught it in one swift movement, impaling it on a stick.

"Eat that and listen up," he ordered, then turned his attention to his sister. It seemed that she would be the storyteller.

"The King is dying," started Iona.

Ailsa sat up a little straighter. "I hadn't even heard he was sick—"

"You wouldn't; it's being kept a secret. Eilanmòr is surrounded by countries poised to invade. Avalogne in the North. Mirandelle in the South. You have rich lands that other countries could claim and many people they could sell. If an enemy found out that the throne was weakened. But there is more of a threat *inside* the country."

Ailsa's blood chilled. "What threat?"

Harris spoke from where he sat in the corner. "Nicnevan."

The way he said the name, it was like something foul had crawled into his mouth. The name rang a bell inside Ailsa's head, but she couldn't quite place where she'd heard it.

"Who is Nicnevan?"

"Nicnevan is the Faerie Queen. King Connall MacFeidh rules the mortals of Eilanmòr, but Nicnevan rules all the fae across the continent. Or rather, did. Twenty years ago, she was chained to a tree and her magic diminished. Since she was betrayed, she hates all humans. However, as long as there is a human on the throne of Eilanmòr, she cannot harm them. If she lifts a hand against one, she will feel all her power bounce back against her."

Iona leaned forward from where she was sitting. "It's why we are here, Ailsa. When the King dies, Eilanmòr will need to crown his son, Prince Duncan. But they cannot do that without the Stone of Destiny."

She blinked. "The Stone of Destiny?"

"It's a mythical stone," Harris explained, "that is always held by the Kings of Eilanmòr during their coronation. It helps protect them against evil forces. The last time a king of Eilanmòr was crowned without the Stone, he and half his army died in a cursed battle."

Iona barely stifled a whimper and Harris's eyes flicked

to her. The selkie girl bit her lip before nodding at her brother to continue.

"But more than that, it was used to bind Nicnevan to a tree twenty years ago. It is said that the Stone belongs to Nicnevan by birthright, but it turned against her because of her evil deeds. It helped her human lover restrain her and it provided greater protection to the royal family. However, at the time, it was deemed so powerful that it had to be hidden."

"By our lovely aunt. Who told only one person where she hid it before she died," interrupted Iona.

"Who?" asked Ailsa.

"Me." Harris winked at her and smirked.

Iona sighed before continuing. "We must retrieve the stone before King Connall dies, so Prince Duncan can be crowned while holding it, therefore gaining the protection against evil and, in particular, Nicnevan."

Harris plucked out the next cooked fish from the fire and took a bite.

"But here's the rub," he said around a mouthful of food. "Nicnevan has her dark little minions out looking for it too."

"Well," said Ailsa slowly. "I haven't really seen any faerie folk before you got here." Up until yesterday she had mostly passed it all off as children's stories.

Except for the thing in the woods.

"You're too far south. Nicnevan's influence doesn't

extend down here. Good fae tend to keep to themselves, so you won't have seen many of them either. But now that King Connall is weakened, her reach is extending. They'll be more active." Harris leaned back against the wall and surveyed Ailsa. "What we need is someone to watch our backs, be our guard."

"There's a village about two miles away?" offered Ailsa.

Harris gave her a devilish grin. "Oh, I don't think we need to go that far."

Ailsa frowned. "You don't mean me?"

"Sure. You're pretty scary as humans go. You brought down those Avalognians fairly easily."

She stared at Harris for a moment before barking a nervous laugh. "Are you joking? I'm not an assassin—I had to get good with a throwing axe or I wouldn't have eaten. You really think that I can protect you from faeries that are trying to kill you? They'd probably turn me into a doorstop before I could even pull out a weapon."

He chuckled. "You are severely overestimating their power. It's all tricks with faeries. Keep your wits about you and you'll be fine. Anyway," he continued with a grin, "faeries are told horror stories about women like you."

Ailsa shook her head in disbelief and turned to Iona who just shrugged. "I think you're perfect."

"It's funny," said Ailsa, "But I was sure this morning

when I woke up that I was the insane one, but it turns out both of you are off your heads. What makes you think I would want to come with you?"

"Nothing I guess," shrugged Harris, cleaning his nails. "Adventure maybe? The chance to see the world? Or maybe the chance to tear someone a new one if they look at us the wrong way?" He leaned forward and tilted his head. "Or maybe you'd like to be useful? Accepted? Maybe you'd like to have friends?"

She felt the blood creeping into her cheeks. *Who does he think he is?*

"You are an idiot," growled Ailsa.

"Please?" said Iona, "I know it's a lot to ask, but we would be incredibly grateful. Just until we get to Dunrigh. You'll be paid."

Ailsa paused. If she could make a bit of coin, she could buy up some stores of food or even some materials to make the cave a bit more comfortable.

"How much?" she asked suspiciously.

Iona's eyes had lit up. "You can name your price. You would have the thanks of not only our family but also the royal family of Eilanmòr."

Ailsa ran a hand through her hair and stared at the back wall.

"Could you just give me a moment?" She still wasn't sure if she could trust these people, or their story. They'd proven they were really magical creatures—she was fairly sure they couldn't have faked Harris's transformation or the rapid healing of his wound—but it was much more likely that they were swindlers who would slit her throat and rob her blind, than nobles on a quest for a mythical stone.

Harris and Iona returned to eating their fish, but she knew that they were waiting for her decision. She kicked a pebble with her toe. The last time she had been near a town or city, she had been driven out by a mob because of her face. However, that was when she was younger and weaponless. Wouldn't it be gratifying to see not fear, but respect, on their faces? The bodyguard of foreign dignitaries? She rolled the idea around in her head, testing it. They did say she could name her price.

"*Urgh*. Fine. But if I have to put up with that one—" she jabbed a finger at Harris, "—talking half as much crap as he has so far, then I want the right to stuff something in his gob to shut him up."

"Done," said Iona while Harris pretended to look hurt.

Ailsa stood up. "When are we leaving?"

"Whenever you like. The day is young, though, and we're in a bit of a hurry."

"Fine, let me pack some clothes and food. And Harris?"

"Yes?" He tossed his fish bones into the fire.

"I think you should go scavenging for some clothes first."

"Am I too revealing?" He covered his chest with his large hands in mock modesty and laughed. "Well, I certainly wouldn't want you to get all flustered now."

"You'll be the one getting flustered when I throw my axe at you."

He grinned. "Ooh, I do love a strong woman."

Ailsa scowled and stalked outside to grab some supplies.

Chapter 6

It turned out that one of the raiders was around the same size as Harris, and while the sleeveless shirt was a little revealing, it would do for now. Unfortunately, the boots he had stolen seemed to be a couple of sizes too big. Altogether, with Ailsa's blanket and the Avalognian's shirt and shoes, he looked a mess. A cold mess. Harris didn't seem to mind, which made Ailsa wonder if he might be cold-blooded.

While watching Harris raid the dead bodies, Iona helped Ailsa collect some food from her garden. *If I'd just had more time, I could have cured the deer meat,* Ailsa thought to herself.

"You know, I never asked," said Ailsa, "Why do you have clothes, but your brother doesn't?"

"I was a bit more prepared, you see," answered Iona. "He wasn't supposed to come onto land with me. He was supposed to escort me to Eilanmòr, then tell me where the Stone was. But then the Avalognians came. I thought it would be better if we stuck together."

"So, you packed your dress?"

A faint blush tinged the girl's skin, sweeping down

from her hairline. "Well, when we turn back into our human form, we have on whatever we were wearing when we turned into seals."

Useful, thought Ailsa. A sudden thought occurred to her and she had to try her best to keep in her laughter. "So, Harris was naked?"

Iona cleared her throat, a smile playing on her lips. "Better not to ask with that boy."

Ailsa left Iona to finish picking berries so she could pack. In truth, she didn't want either selkie watching her pick through her meagre belongings. She strode to the back of the cave and pulled out a spare pair of trousers that she had stolen from a young fisherman a while back; he had decided to take a swim and charitably left his clothes over a tree. She packed these along with a shirt, her lavender soap and another knife in a leather satchel she had found. She turned to go, but then paused. On a makeshift stone shelf was a modest box where she kept the few possessions she had managed to hold onto from her childhood: her mother's comb and scarf and a tiny doll made from sticks and cloth, held together with string. She carefully removed the box and deposited it into her bag.

"We'll need some form of transport," called Ailsa as she walked back down the path towards Iona.

"Don't worry. There are horses waiting for us about two miles up the road."

Ailsa raised an eyebrow. "You planned to wash up here then?"

"A beach further up, but yes, more or less. I spent some time in this part of Eilanmòr when I was younger..." Iona stared off to the sea. Her eyes swept over the beach. Ailsa waited, expecting more from the story but she appeared to have lost track of their conversation. She was oblivious to her brother sauntering back up the path. When he reached them, he gave Iona a little shove, ending whatever memory she had been reliving.

"Okay, brave and fearless bodyguard, better lead the way."

Harris picked up her bag and gave her a nudge too. She snatched it back from him and set off, hearing the swish of grass behind her as he and Iona followed. She turned right along the barely visible coastal track. She made an effort to stay a little way ahead of her companions, allowing them to converse in whispers as she took in the view.

The last time Ailsa had been along this road, she had been cold, starved and persecuted. The pattern had always been the same. She would find a barn or old building to squat in for a few nights, eating leftovers someone had thrown away, or killing a rabbit. Really, she had been a help to the farmers who were always trying to rid themselves of the pests. They always seemed to think she was a bigger pest, though. Some villagers would send her on her way with a loaf of bread and a warning not to come back. Others would give her a black eye or a swift kick as a parting gift. No matter whether they were sympathetic or aggressive, the message was always the same: *changelings were bad luck and should stay away.* And so now, at nineteen years old, Ailsa had been scraping by—alone—for five years.

Two years ago, she had been building a fire in a ruined cottage when some people from the nearby town had arrived and thrown a bucket of water over her and the glowing embers. She had risen without a word, collected her pack and then made her way to the road. As she passed, she had bared her teeth at one of the men. He had jumped back in fear. She smiled now at the memory. That fear had saved her countless times since. No one wanted to see if the stories about faeries stripping flesh from the bones of grown men were true.

She had set off that evening, heading further south than she had ever been. Holding her chin high the whole way, she walked all night. About forty minutes from the nearest town, she had come across *Buthaid Beach*. It met all her prerequisites for a good home: no people, plenty of food and *no forest*.

Now she was leaving. Would the world have changed in two years? She doubted it. But she had changed. She was stronger, faster and smarter. *Would she be less frightened?* At least now she knew that she could justify the fear that men felt when they saw her. In fact, she supposed she looked even more terrifying now.

Though maybe Harris was right. Maybe by escorting her two companions, she would be seen differently. She was useful. Maybe someone would see how well she had protected them and would offer her a job?

Don't think like that, Ailsa chided herself, *you'll make sure they don't get murdered, then go back to where you belong. No one is going to think you are useful.*

The trio marched on in silence, listening to the crash of the waves against the shore. The path wound like a snake across the grass, rising over the hills, leading to the top of some cliffs before turning inland towards the nearest settlement. With one last backwards glance, Ailsa left her home, sure that she would be back before the month was over.

Chapter 7

The village was little more than two houses and a farm, but it looked empty.

I wonder what happened to the owners, Ailsa thought, shuddering as she peered in the abandoned windows. It reminded her of another house she had found in a similar state a few years ago. *His house should only be another twenty minutes away.* She shivered from the cold, dark memories.

Seemingly oblivious to the oppressive loneliness of the place, Iona seemed cheered. "Look!" she cried, pointing to the back of one of the dwellings. As they approached, Ailsa could see two horses tied up loosely in a garden. The horses were grazing in rings around the stakes where they were secured. Some hay had been laid out for them under the cover of an old shed roof, the siding of which had blown off long before.

Iona approached one of the geldings to stroke his nose, while Harris poked his head into the structure.

"They've also left us some food, money and clothes." He held up a bulging, brown leather bag.

Ailsa eyed the chestnut horses with trepidation. "I've

never ridden a horse before."

"Don't worry, you can ride with one of us." Iona looked between Ailsa and Harris. "I think you better come with me. Wouldn't want you two fighting and scaring your mount."

"We wouldn't fight, would we, Ailsa?" He grinned and sidled up to her. "We're best friends!" He moved to slip an arm around her shoulders, but she squeezed out of the embrace.

"I think I'll ride with your sister."

"It makes more sense anyway," said Iona placing a saddle on her horse's back. "We'll weigh less than if Ailsa joined *you*."

"Yeah, because your horse will be lucky if he can carry that fat head," muttered Ailsa, but she looked off innocently when Harris narrowed his eyes at her.

"Ailsa, give me your knife." He stalked over to her and held out a hand.

"Why in *Beira's* eye would I do that?" she exclaimed, peering up into his face.

He smirked and leaned in. "What if I say please?"

"What if my knee found the place between your legs?" Ailsa smiled sweetly up at him. "Or do selkies even have anything to damage there?"

He choked on an incredulous laugh.

"Please, stop fighting! Ailsa, may I have your knife? I think I better cut a slit in my dress so I can ride."

"Well that's why I was asking." Harris shrugged his shoulders and lowered his voice. "And for the record, you have nothing to worry about when it comes to what is between my legs. If you're still curious, I can show you any time you like." He winked suggestively at her and stepped away. Ailsa made a particularly unladylike gesture then gave the blade to Iona, who quickly cut through her skirt.

Finally, they were ready. Iona swung up into the saddle and reached down to help Ailsa, whose heart was thrumming with nerves. She did her best to hide her shaking fingers by winding them around the other girl's waist.

"How far do we need to travel?" she gulped when she was finally secure.

Harris pulled himself into the saddle of the other gelding in a graceful move. Ailsa had to clench her jaw to prevent it from popping open.

"The King is in his castle in Eilanmòr's capital, Dunrigh. It's a full day's ride to the North." said Iona, patting Ailsa's hand in reassurance. "We'll stop at an inn tonight and continue our journey tomorrow. We should arrive around four in the afternoon."

That doesn't sound too bad, Ailsa thought. Maybe she'd even be back home within the week, if they let her ride the horse back.

Chapter 8

I never want to ride a horse again."

Five hours later, Ailsa unhinged her arms from around Iona's waist and collapsed off their mount. She was not used to riding and the journey had taken its toll. Her thighs were burning and she was freezing. She tried to walk, but stumbled and, to her distaste, Harris had to catch her.

"Whoa, there." He hooked an arm around her back to take some of her weight. "Looks like you could use a rest. Or a beer. Or both?"

When Iona had mentioned an inn, Ailsa had been uncertain. It had been a long time since she was around a crowd of people, and the last time she had been chased away. But the squat little building was the most lovely thing she had seen for a long time. Harris led her through the door while Iona paid a young man to take their horses to the stables around the back.

Immediately, they were hit by the pleasant smell of baking bread. The tavern had an interesting array of mis-matched tables and chairs that had been scavenged over time. Old, bare flagstone slabs covered the floor and the walls, giving the impression of being underground. The roaring fire in the middle of the room combatted the cold that seeped in through the stones nicely. A band played a lively tune in the corner and many of the inhabitants were already rather merry. Iona caught up with them and together they squeezed through crowds of revellers until they found a table at the back, on a platform to the right of the bar. For a while they scanned the pub for possible threats, but no one seemed remotely interested in them.

They must be used to strangers here, since the road is so close by, Ailsa thought. Still, she finger-combed her hair over the left side of her face and lowered her head.

"Let's have some fun," smirked Iona before dancing off to the bar. "I'll get some food for us too."

Ailsa flexed her calf muscles and winced. *Thank the Gods the chairs are padded.*

"Having a good time?" Harris enquired, steepling his fingers together.

She hunched over the table and looked murderously at the other people while she scraped her nail along a blemish in the wood. She could feel a knot forming in her backside and it was making her grumpy.

"Clearly," answered Ailsa, leaning back in her chair to survey him, wincing as she moved. "Why are you so cheerful? There are people hunting for you who would very much like to kill you. And you're sitting across from someone who would like to do the same thing, depending on how annoying you're being," she continued, pointedly.

"Ouch," Harris laughed, his eyes scanning the room. When he saw her watching him, he let out a huff and ran a hand through his hair. "I can't be scared all the time. How would I get anything done? Besides," he grinned, "I have you to protect me. And may I add, how lucky I am to have such a beautiful bodyguard."

"Shut up," growled Ailsa. "It's not funny."

"What isn't?" Harris looked confused.

"It isn't funny to call me beautiful. I'm obviously not," she said, gesturing at her mark.

"That—" He leaned forward, "—does not stop you from being beautiful. In fact, it makes you interesting, which is actually better than beautiful." He smiled like that was the end of it.

Was that a compliment? In truth, she was wholly unconcerned with whether someone found her attractive or not. When she was younger, she had wondered if she would be pretty without her mark. She had nice eyes, but she had a heavy jaw and one of her bottom teeth was crooked. However, any trace of vanity ended when she was trekking through mud and wondering where her next meal would come from. Being beautiful was for princesses in castles. If threatening was all she achieved with her appearance, then so be it.

You had wanted Gris to think you were beautiful, a voice whispered in her head. She cursed inwardly. Some things were best forgotten.

Frowning, she turned to watch Iona sashay back to their table, carrying a cloth-wrapped lump under her arm and three mugs of ale.

"Here," she announced, setting down the drinks and then handed them the object. Inside was a freshly baked rosemary loaf with cheese on top. Harris was the first to tear a chunk off and scarf it down. His eyes almost rolled up into his head in pleasure, prompting Ailsa to grab a piece herself.

"Thanks," she murmured, taking a swig of ale after her first bite. The beer was decidedly disgusting, like liquid, citrusy, goat's cheese, but eating the bread helped her choke it down quicker.

"Would you believe that someone at the bar just proposed to me?" Iona laughed.

Why am I not surprised? The redhead was truly exquisite all curves and long legs. Ailsa doubted that any of the men in the inn would even notice her, especially since she was about a head shorter than Iona. Not that she wanted them to look at her.

Urgh, a day around Harris and I've become as vain as he is.

"Oh no, sister," he said, grabbing Iona's tankard from her hands. "Mustn't drink too much or you won't be your glorious self tomorrow. Wouldn't want King Connall to see you all haggard." He fluttered his eyelashes at her.

She gave him a haughty look. "Don't worry, *brother*. I always look glorious." She went to snatch the drink back, but he held it away. She narrowed her eyes and when he didn't relent, she grinned and flicked up her finger. Immediately, the beer in the flask leapt out and splashed him in the face.

Ailsa couldn't help the burst of laughter that escaped her. *Selkie magic*, she supposed. She clamped a hand over her mouth as Harris wiped his face. Iona, taking pity on him, flicked her finger again and the liquid from Harris's face fell back into the glass.

He grinned and pushed the drink back in front of her. "Fine. Do what you want, Your Highness. But if you make a bad impression tomorrow, you've only got yourself to blame."

Iona stood up and deftly swapped her tankard for his. "I don't want face juice."

With a groan, Harris pushed his chair back and went to the bar to retrieve a replacement for himself. Ailsa looked sideways at Iona as she took a drink. She debated about whether she should ask personal questions or not, but in the end her curiosity got the better of her. "So, you're a queen?"

Iona wrinkled her nose as she popped another bit of bread into her mouth and chewed. "I wouldn't say queen..." she said, swallowing. "We don't have a royal family like Eilanmòr. It's more of a democracy."

"So that would make you..." Ailsa pressed.

The other girl tossed her hair over her shoulder. "Ambassador for Foreign Affairs."

"Affairs is right," muttered Harris, sliding back into his seat. For his comment, he received a smack to the back of the head.

"And what about you?" said Ailsa, turning to him.

He raised his tankard in his sister's direction. "Brother of the Ambassador for Foreign Affairs."

"Court Jester," Iona clarified with a wink.

For a while, Ailsa listened to them cheerfully bickering. Seeing the siblings together, she wondered if it would have been like that with her own brother. Memories of tears and empty, searching hands danced before her eyes, making her stomach drop.

Don't think about the day he was taken, she chided herself. *There have been too many ghosts haunting me tonight.*

She blocked out their playful squabbling and attacked the bread with her teeth, watching people come and go around the room. For a moment, she swore that she saw a tall figure peeking in through the windows, but he obviously decided to try elsewhere for a drink because he never entered the bar.

After drinking her beer, Ailsa was starting to feel

sleepy and her body hurt less than before. She stretched out her legs and rolled her shoulders with a grinding *crack*.

"Do we have rooms?"

"Yes, they were already booked for us when I asked the bartender. They're just up the stairs." Iona nodded to the steps in the corner. "You can have a room to yourself. Harris and I will share."

"Thanks," yawned Ailsa and went to pick up her pack.

"Here, let me help you," said Harris, swiping it from her. She harrumphed but was too tired to argue. Together, they climbed the wooden staircase and found the rooms, side by side.

"Will you be okay by yourself tonight?" He looked at her with genuine concern before handing her the bag. "I know it's been quite a lot to handle."

"Yeah, I'm fine," shrugged Ailsa sleepily, "Just a bit sore from riding. To be honest, I'm trying not to let myself stop and think too much. Being here, it's bringing back a lot of memories. One day at a time though, right?"

"Want to talk about it?"

She fought the urge to snort, he was just trying to help. "I'm your hired muscle, right? I'm supposed to worry about you."

He nodded. "Thanks, Ailsa." Harris ran a hand through his copper hair, parting the strands and making them glow in the faint light. "I know my sister appreciates having someone around to help. I'm not the best with a weapon myself, so it's comforting to know we have you with us." He looked away and shrugged. "I know I joke around, but I am glad we met you."

Ailsa blinked up at him. *Was he being nice?* She made a non-committal noise and opened the door to her room.

"Oh, and Ailsa?" called Harris, who was now walking back down the corridor.

She stopped and turned back to look at him. "Yes?"

"If your ass is still hurting later, I'd be happy to massage it for you." He winked and carried on down the stairs.

Ailsa huffed and slammed the door shut behind her, earning an annoyed thump from the guests in the room above. She blew out the candles, wrenched off her clothes and slipped under the sheets. *He was absolutely infuriating.*

Two more days, she thought, *then I'll be on my way back home.*

It already felt like ages since she had left the beach, bringing unwelcome memories and thoughts to the edges of her mind.

Think of something else. What will I spend my money on? Ailsa started to imagine every bag of sugar and every type of seed she'd buy with her pay. But it had been a long time since she had been in a proper bed and not long after she'd visualised heaving sacks of oats and spelt, she drifted off to sleep.

Chapter 9

In her dream, Ailsa could see a golden-haired woman with a crown of branches. The woman held out her arms.

"Come to me, my child," she whispered.

When she didn't move, the woman's face became angry. "You'll never escape." Behind her, four large wolves appeared with glistening fangs.

Ailsa turned and ran through the forest, the wolves hot on her heels. She could feel their breath on the backs of her calves. Suddenly, there was a thud and the sounds of pursuit ended abruptly. She stopped and waited. Then she heard it.

Crunch.

Crunch.

Crunch.

Throughout the woods, the footsteps echoed. Ailsa turned to run again but realised her feet couldn't move. When she looked down, they were encased in mud. It shifted around her legs as if alive; creeping up her skin and clothes, gnawing and sucking. Her heart beat wildly in her chest as she struggled to wrench herself free.

I'm going to die, she thought as she sank further into the ground. She tore at the dirt in front of her face, scrambling to find purchase. Her breath came out in desperate sobs but the mud continued to crush her body in a vice grip. As it pinned her arms, she looked up for someone, anyone, to help her.

That's when she saw them.

Two large, red eyes glowing from between the trees.

Ailsa woke with a gasp, and sat up to remove the blankets that had become tangled around her ankles. She'd had the same nightmare many times before; the blonde woman was a new addition, though. She had probably seen her in the inn somewhere. Ailsa leaned against the headboard and allowed herself to wake up fully.

Although the dream left her with a residual feeling of terror, she felt strangely hopeful. Today, they would be travelling to Dunrigh. She had often wondered what it looked like but had decided not to risk venturing too near in the past. Ten people and a goat in a wee village she could handle. Thousands of men and women, packed closely together, watching and gossiping? She'd have been hounded in the streets if she were lucky. At worst, a mob would have lynched her on the spot. Regardless, she was curious about Dunrigh. There must be something worthwhile about the city, if so many people decided to stay there?

The mouth-watering smell of bacon drifted up to her nose through the crack under the door. The light peeking in through the little window told her that it was just after dawn. No doubt it would be a grey, dreich day, as usual.

Ailsa heard a faint whistling sound coming from Harris and Iona's room next door. Unsure of who or what was making the noise, she rose to investigate.

The siblings had not locked their door, either in carelessness or anticipation of her visit. Inside, she found a narrow room, a twin to her own. The fresh smell of sea salt and citrus wafted about the room. Hers probably smelled like sweat; she hadn't bathed last night.

Iona must already be downstairs. Harris, however, was still fast asleep and seemed to be the source of the whistling.

He snores? Ailsa grinned to herself. She'd have to file that useful information away for later. Stepping fully inside Harris's room, she closed the door quietly behind her. Leaning against the door, she studied the unconscious lump in the bed.

He'd managed to find an undershirt and trousers to sleep in. His messy hair curled around his face, which had formed an unpleasant expression: his mouth was hanging open and drool was pooling onto his pillow.

It was still hard to believe that only yesterday she'd

witnessed Harris change from a cute, injured seal into the slevering man that slept before her. She wondered, not for the first time, how his transformation actually worked.

Then, thinking about how infuriating he had been the night before, she stepped around the foot of the bed, creeping quietly across the rug-covered floor. Peering down at his sleeping form, she couldn't contain her smirk.

Beside the bed, a glass of water sat on top of a side table. With nimble fingers she lifted the tumbler from its place and held it in one hand.

Let's test some theories.

Ailsa dumped the water on his face.

Harris thrashed and, still half asleep, let out an almost scream. He wiped the water off his face, spluttering in surprise.

"Sorry, Harris," said Ailsa in a honeyed voice, mischief glinting in her eyes. "I just wanted to see if you would turn back into a seal." She backed away from the bed.

He squinted groggily around the room until his eyes fixed on her.

"YOU!" he growled, sitting up. He would have looked menacing, Ailsa thought, if not for the hair plastered to his forehead and the lines his pillow had left on his cheek.

"Obviously, I was wrong." Ailsa's attempts to stay out

of his reach failed when Harris dived towards her with a wail of fury and they thudded to the floor.

"Let me go," she protested. "I'm sorry I got you wet!" She tried to escape his grasp, but he held on strong.

"Here, you can have some," he grumbled, shaking his hair at her. She grunted and pushed at his chest, but he just grinned wickedly.

"You deserved it, you wretch."

"Don't dish it out, lass, if you can't take it."

"What in the Hag's name is this?" Iona shouted, appearing at the door. She towered over them with her hands on her hips, glaring down at their entangled bodies.

It was Harris who started giggling first. With one look at the hair streaked across his face, Ailsa let out a quick bark of laughter. With a gasp, she covered her mouth with her hand. She got up, adjusted her clothes and then marched from the room.

"See you at breakfast," Ailsa threw over her shoulder.

What the hell was that? Ailsa thought. She would need to be more careful. She couldn't afford to start liking her new companions—and that was a very bad idea. *Because when you like people, they have the power to hurt you.*

When Ailsa was young, other than her brother, Cameron, she'd only had a few friends. He had alternated between playing the doting older brother and wanting nothing to do with her. The best days had been when he let her tag along on adventures with his friends. The neighbourhood children were talented at sneaking away from their parents and didn't have the same prejudices. Ailsa had spent her summers wandering around the woods, playing bandits and maidens with a gang of youths, long before the forest embodied her fears. The children knew their parents disapproved of Ailsa, but this had only made her friendship more appealing. They used to hide her round the back of their cottages and feed her treats like a pet. Then, when they played their games, she was always a lovely, good, faerie princess or a wicked pirate queen with her motley crew of cutthroats and scoundrels. Cameron had loved to parade her around them.

But it all came to an end the spring her mother died. Then Ailsa became a wandering orphan: an outsider not tolerated by the villagers. Afraid she would hurt him next, her brother had been taken away and sent to live with distant relatives. She still remembered the sorrow in his panicked eyes as he was led away from the cottage, kicking and screaming her name.

Later, towards the end of that summer, Ailsa returned to her house to find the door kicked down and the walls smashed. She gathered up her belongings, including a few of her mother's trinkets, and moved on to the next town.

Even now, she couldn't bring herself to think of the

only other time she'd had a friend. *He* didn't deserve to be remembered.

If you start to care, you'll be disappointed when they leave. You can only rely on yourself.

They ate a quick breakfast before departing on their horses. Ailsa had also stolen a towel from the inn, cut it up and wedged it down her trousers, around her bottom. It provided a little cushioning, allowing her to remain on the gelding for the rest of the day. The trio even ate lunch in the saddle in order to make good time. The sun appeared from time to time between the clouds and the day remained gloriously dry.

Meanwhile, Ailsa tried in vain to contain her growing excitement, as Iona and Harris chatted about the delights of Eilanmòr's capital as they travelled.

"The whole place sings with music. It's great for dancing."

"I hope we have a choice of clothing when we get there. They have so many colourful dyes."

"You have to try the curry, it's imported from Visenya. It was my favourite the last time we visited."

"When were you last in the capital?" Ailsa couldn't help asking.

"We were both invited for the King Connal's

coronation, around twenty years ago."

"Harris was just a boy." Iona held up two hands to show how small he had been. "I was long since grown."

Ailsa tried her best to reassess Iona's age. She thought the selkie was at least as old as her, but now she was obviously much older.

The redhead simply shrugged. "Selkies live longer than humans and age slower. Anyway, I'm excited to see how it's changed!"

An hour later, they caught their first glimpse of Dunrigh. The buildings spread like ivy across a hillside in the distance and, at the top of the hill, sat the castle. Flags fluttered merrily in the breeze from the grey, stone towers. One large pine tree could be seen growing within the castle walls. Ailsa had the feeling the tree had come first due to the sheer size of it.

"How long now?" she asked, chewing on her lip.

"Another two hours," shouted Harris exuberantly.

Ailsa groaned and gripped Iona's waist tighter. She was counting down the minutes until she could get off this blasted horse.

Chapter 10

An hour later, they came across houses, dotting the surrounding countryside like little cakes with straw frosting. The buildings were sunken with age, gravity slowly crushing them down over time. Ailsa felt the return of a familiar unease at being so near *civilisation*. However, there didn't seem to be many people around, for which she was grateful.

The reached a creek, water cackling loudly over the stones, and Iona pulled their horse to a stop.

"I think I'll make myself look a wee bit more presentable before we reach Dunrigh."

Ailsa didn't know what she was talking about. Her copper hair was tied away neatly at the side of her head and she could smell nothing from her other than the pleasing scent of fresh lemons and sea air.

How must I smell by now? The horse under her gave a whinny as if to say: *Like me.*

They dismounted and Ailsa grabbed her soap from her pack. Wanting some privacy from the selkies, she limped off a little way until there was a bend in the burn, her steps hindered by the pain in her thighs. She scrambled down onto the bank, pleased to find she was mostly hidden.

Unclipping her cloak from around her shoulders and placing her axe on the ground, Ailsa debated whether to undress further. She wasn't terribly worried about how clean she was before getting to the capital, but the ice-cold water looked so inviting. The thought of numbing her aching backside in the stream was enough to bring a groan to her throat.

She stripped down to her undershirt. A cold breeze made her shiver and she amended her plan of a bath to a quick dip. The leaves in the nearby trees swayed softly and she found herself checking the spaces between them.

Too far apart, she told herself. *It can't get me here.*

She had pulled out the towel and was unbuttoning her trousers when she heard a sound, like the snap of a twig. It could have been any woodland animal, but Ailsa's hair stood on end. She had the distinct feeling she was being watched.

"Harris?" she called. Her voice was met with nothing but silence. "I'm going to have a wash. Go away." Again, there was no reply.

She waited a few heartbeats, wondering if it was her imagination or something else.

I still feel eyes upon me. Was it the male selkie? She had thought she could trust him.

Finally, with a huff, she redid her buttons and picked

up her axe. She wasn't getting undressed around any depraved fae. As soon as she picked up her weapon, she heard another twig snapping and the sound of footsteps moving away.

Scared him off, she thought with a growl. *That'll teach him to spy on girls.*

Still, she couldn't shake the feeling that, somehow, it wasn't Harris who'd been watching her.

She shrugged back into her blouse, foregoing the bath for a splash of water on her face and neck. The droplets tickled as they ran down inside her clothes, rinsing away some of the sweat that clung to her skin. She was adjusting her cloak back around her shoulders when she heard a shriek.

It was far away and short. She would have mistaken it for a bird's call if she had not heard something similar a few days prior. Her hands gripped her axe tightly as she waited to see if she would hear it again.

One beat.

The scream was quieter this time but unmistakable.

Ailsa dashed up the bank and onto the grassy slope where she had left Iona, Harris and the horses. Rounding the bend, she met with a sight which made her heart skip a beat.

Harris was restrained by a burly man, a knife to his throat. The blade had edged so far into his skin, that Ailsa could see a long wound oozing bright, crimson blood. Bald and tall, the man had a scrape on his jaw and the skin around his eye looked swollen. It seemed that Harris had landed a few punches before being captured.

Iona was struggling in the hands of another, smaller, man. They were splashing water around as they grappled down in the stream. The man was grinning grotesquely, as if the fight was a game they were playing. He had a strong jaw and a clever nose, with inky black hair brushing his shoulders.

The two bandits clearly hadn't realised she was there. Iona kept struggling, until the smaller man swept her legs out from under her. Iona landed on her hands and knees in the water and he grabbed her roughly to him in a way that told Ailsa exactly what his plans were for the selkie woman. Harris snarled, but the sound was cut off by the knife sinking deeper into his throat.

Rage, white and blinding, froze Ailsa where she stood. Blood pumped loudly in her ears and thunder crackled somewhere deep down in her stomach. Another shriek from Iona finally set her in motion, descending on the two men like a wrathful tempest.

She lunged at the bald man first. Harris widened his eyes when he saw her, unable to produce more than a choking sound. The bandit didn't have time to turn before she swung the butt of her axe into the side of his head. He let out a groan and staggered backwards from the blunt impact, dropping the knife, freeing Harris.

Dazed and bellowing, the man charged at her, his steps off balance from the blow. He made to grab her but she managed to shove him to the ground. His shocked eyes briefly met hers before she swung the backend of the axe down in the exact same spot as before, this time rendering him unconscious

One down.

She turned her attention to Iona and the vile bandit she was struggling against. It was obvious that she had been holding back in worry for her brother's life. Now that Harris was free, Iona had slipped the man's grasp and stood defiant in front of him. Raising her arms wide, she raised the water from the stream upwards. The man merely blinked in shock at the magic whirling around him.

Ailsa was sure that if Iona had glared at her the same way she was staring down the bandit, she would have turned and ran. However, the handsome man, his mouth gaping open like a fish, was not as smart as Ailsa. With a guttural yell, Iona sent all the water surging in his direction, down his nose and throat. The man clutched at his neck as he drowned. He sank to his knees, yet Iona did not relent. His eyes bulged out of his skull and he scratched at his chest, lungs clearly burning. Finally, his movements quelled and his lifeless body flopped back into the shallow river.

Iona let her arms fall, panting heavily as she surveyed

the corpse in front of her.

"By the Gods," Ailsa swore.

Harris ran down the bank to help his sister out of the burn. The wound on his throat had already closed and the blood down his neck was starting to crust. When he reached Iona, she jumped slightly before letting him lead her back to the horses.

"What happened?" Ailsa asked.

Harris raked a hand through his hair before answering.

"They jumped us. Told us to hand over any gold we had. When they saw we had none, they got violent." He reached out and clasped her shoulder. "Thank you, Ailsa, I don't know what would have happened if you hadn't turned up."

"I do," said Iona, tears starting to trail down her face.

Ailsa averted her eyes from the crying selkie and reattached the axe to her hip.

"We better get going before the other one wakes up," she grunted, grabbing the horse's reins.

Iona shakily swung herself into the saddle, but as Ailsa moved to do the same, her foot found something half hidden in the grass: the unconscious robber's knife, still covered in Harris's blood. She bent down and picked it up, wiping it clean before adding it to her belt. When he roused, the man wouldn't have a weapon to threaten anyone else with.

"Are you going to be okay?" Ailsa murmured to Iona when she was behind her in the saddle.

The selkie girl nodded and squeezed the hand Ailsa wrapped around her waist.

"I'm so glad you came with us," she replied.

Ailsa nodded, keeping her features neutral, but inside she was thrumming with pride.

Perhaps I'm not so useless after all.

They urged the horses into a trot, determined to leave the men and the stream behind. The bouncing gait did nothing to help the pain in Ailsa's rear, but she gritted her teeth and thought of the food and soft beds waiting ahead.

Chapter 11

Dunrigh was surrounded by a thick, stone wall but was made all the more imposing by the two creatures flanking the city gates. Made from granite, a massive unicorn and stag reared up on their hind legs. Ailsa guessed they were about thirty feet tall, from hoof to horn or antler. As they approached, the trio had to crane their necks to see the statues.

A troop of uniformed men and women greeted them at the entrance and Ailsa immediately pulled out her axe. They were guards of some sort, with swords hanging around their hips, flat caps and the same muted purple tartan on each of their wool kilts. Iona put a hand on Ailsa's shoulder and stepped forward.

"Greetings, ladies and gentlemen. I sent word ahead. I am Lady Iona of Struanmuir. The Royal Family is expecting me."

Much to Ailsa's surprise, the men parted to reveal a young, golden-haired woman adorned with a white flower crown. She was leaning heavily on a walking stick and when she limped forward, her green velvet dress revealed her leg ended before her foot. *She's pretty,* thought Ailsa, *even with the purple circles under her eyes.*

"Lady Iona, Lord Harris," she greeted them with a graceful curtsey. "I am Lady Moira, the King's niece and emissary." Her gaze flicked between the two, without pausing once on Ailsa. "Please, follow me and I will take you to the castle. His Highness is most anxious to see you."

The girl flipped the train of her dress around and started off in a quick shuffle towards the streets. The guards ushered them forward, making a loose circle around them.

Ailsa let Harris pull her along behind him. As soon as she had seen the men, she had thought about turning around and leaving them here. Her job was done, wasn't it?

As they entered the gates, she pulled the hood of her cloak up so that it obscured the left side of her face.

Just get in and out without causing mass hysteria, then you can go home.

The city was a flurry of activity. People everywhere leaned out of windows and doorways, calling to each other. Their group passed through a square where musicians played fiddles and children danced by spinning each other with opposite arms. Ailsa noticed that some of the younger boys weren't really dancing but spinning violently, trying to fling others off their feet.

On leaving the square, they crossed into a narrow

lane filled with fruit and vegetable sellers and carried on into the main town. The streets were set out like a grid, but this was where the uniformity of the city ended. The buildings were a mix of wood and stone, a few towering tall with many storeys, while others were squat little shacks. Wooden walkways ran between the towers, some covered and some not. While many of the older houses were grey and brown, the newer ones had been painted in bright colours, from greens and yellows to blues and purples. There seemed to be a competition for gaudiness of décor, too. Several merchants flew pennants while others covered their storefronts in hundreds of flowers, as if the very buildings were being taken back by the forest.

The straight streets all led upwards as they continued into the city. A few were so steep that iron railings ran along the sides of buildings to aid travellers in their ascent. Ailsa's thighs howled in protest as she urged herself forwards.

I am never getting on a horse again.

Finally, the entourage emerged from the maze of streets into the fresh air of the hilltop. Away from the dense city, a cool breeze caressed their faces and the sun kissed their faces through a gap in the clouds.

In contrast to the disordered jumble of the city, the castle was a sturdy, symmetrical construction made of granite. Flags of jolly purple and green flew from the battlements. As they drew closer, Ailsa could see vines creeping up the stone walls and on either side of their winding path, bluebells grew wild and unchecked. Ailsa thought it was magnificent.

Two round look-out towers sat at the front of the palace; between them, a pair of gates of opened, beckoning them into the inner courtyard. The pine tree Ailsa had spied earlier stood in the middle, covered with ribbons fluttering in the gentle wind.

Lady Moira followed Ailsa's stare and smiled, finally acknowledging her third guest.

"That is the Peace Tree," she said in a lilting voice—Ailsa was sure it was forced. "Originally, Eilanmòr was split up into various clans. The tree was planted when the warring clan leaders came together, in this spot, to unite the island and make our country whole. The story goes that Eilanmòr will stand strong so long as the Peace Tree remains standing. This is why the castle was built around it."

"And the ribbons?"

Lady Moira rolled her eyes, clearly enjoying being asked, "Bit of superstition." She shrugged. "If you tie a ribbon to the tree, then one of the ancient clan leaders will hear your prayers. If you're worthy, they might even grant you a wish."

"I guess the colours of the ribbons mean something?" asked Ailsa as she bit her lip.

"Yes. Pink for love. Blue for health. Green for prosperity. The purple ribbons are for wishes for our country. Those are usually used in times of crisis. There are fewer of those at the moment because no one is aware of the King's condition yet. When he dies, white ribbons will be added to the tree as the people pray for his soul."

Iona fixed Harris with a stare and frowned. "What colour of ribbon should I use if I want my brother to behave himself?" He stuck his tongue out to show his sister he wasn't willing to do any such thing.

"Yellow," answered Lady Moira with a smirk. "Though if I were you, I'd be tying a red ribbon to the tree."

"What does red mean?" questioned Ailsa.

Lady Moira paused. "It's supposed to bring you luck in all endeavours."

They reached a pair of ornate wooden doors emblazoned with the MacFeidh coat of arms—the unicorn and stag. Lady Moira nodded her head and the doors were pulled open by two guards stationed on either side.

"Come," she commanded and they followed her into the entrance hall.

Chapter 12

Ailsa sucked in a deep breath, which she tried to cover up with a cough.

Elaborate pillars held up an impressive vaulted ceiling, decorated with animal carvings; badgers, foxes, unicorns and squirrels spied down at them. From the foyer, five doors led to rooms on the ground floor and a grand staircase rose steeply on the opposite side of the room. But what caught Ailsa's attention the most were the people; they were everywhere, running between doors, heaving tables down the stairs and dusting picture frames. It was like being inside a beehive.

Lady Moira gave a stately wave of her hand. "Welcome to Dunrigh Castle. You must be weary from your journey —your chambers await. Servants will see to it that you are taken care of. If you require anything further, please let me know." Lady Moira gave them a quick bow and limped through the nearest door.

A group of women rushed in and ushered them up the stairs, As they ascended, Ailsa studied the ceiling and noticed a seal tucked away in a corner. Beside it, there was a maiden with flowing locks. She wondered if one of Iona's relatives had been the inspiration for the fresco. Before she could wonder aloud at the carvings, they reached the first floor.

"I guess I'll see you later then?" Harris chuckled before a particularly bawdy set of young women grabbed his arms and led him through a huge door, slamming it shut. The rest of the group could still hear the cackling as they were led further down the hallway.

The women who escorted Ailsa and Iona were much more reserved. Whether it was because they were more serious, or they felt they had got the short end of the straw, Ailsa couldn't tell. One kept surreptitiously glancing at Ailsa's face, so she ducked her head, feeling safer in the shadows of her hood.

Iona and Ailsa were shown to a spacious chamber, adorned with gold chandeliers and velvet carpets. Before they could admire the furnishings, the chambermaids promptly pushed them towards the adjoining bathing room where two copper tubs of steaming water sat waiting.

Iona, in a graceful flourish, stripped herself of her dress in full view of the servants. Ailsa tried not to stare at the selkie's naked body. Despite the hard day's riding, she looked like a nymph from a painting, with her red hair in loose coils and her freckled skin slightly flushed from the heat. When one of the girls approached Ailsa to help her with her clothes, Ailsa hissed at her and hugged herself.

"Please, Ailsa, you'll feel better for it," pleaded Iona, stepping into a bathtub. She reached over the side of the tub, hovering her hands above the various lotions and oils, selected an orange bottle and poured its contents into the water.

Ailsa debated with herself, giving the chambermaids a sideways glance. They hesitated, casting terrified looks in her direction. With a harrumph, she detached the axe from her waist and dropped it to the floor with a *clang*. She didn't bother hiding her grin when the girls jumped.

Once she had removed her clothes—without assistance—Ailsa dipped a toe into her own bathtub. It had been so long since she had bathed in a full-sized tub. She sank down into the foam and purred.

"You scared our helpers away," Iona remarked, though she didn't sound too dejected.

Ailsa closed her eyes and settled into the relaxing liquid. "I'd rather not have an audience."

Iona laughed. "You'll get a reputation, no one will want to come near you!"

"Good," said Ailsa and started cleaning her hair with some divine shampoo that smelled floral and spicy.

"Well I, for one, am not that easy to scare off," replied Iona, flicking water at her. "So you'll just have to deal with me."

"We'll see," Ailsa sighed, ducking her head into the bubbles.

Chapter 13

To Ailsa's horror, it seemed that the servants had complained about her behaviour, because when they came out of the bathing room, there was an older, rotund woman who looked like she would not be so easily spooked. The woman glared at her, before pushing her into a chair so that she could begin on her hair. Ailsa gripped the chair arms as the woman worked out the knots.

"Ooh," cooed Iona from behind her, "it seems that we have been left a choice of dresses!"

"Dresses?" groaned Ailsa.

Iona hit her on the arm. "Play along and don't ruin my fun."

Ailsa could hear Iona moving around and the rustle of fabric behind her. The servant was doing her best to brush her hair over her left cheek and make it stay there, so she folded her hands into her lap in submission. "Are you excited to see the King and Princes?" she asked Iona.

"Yes and no," she replied slowly. "I'm usually a little worried whenever I meet Eilanmòrian royalty." She skipped into view beside her. Ailsa couldn't deny that

Iona looked stunning in her pale blue dress. Wave-like embroidery swirled around her bust and down her arms. The neckline was respectable, but the dress hugged her body snuggly, revealing luscious curves.

"Why are you worried?" Ailsa stared at her sceptically. She glanced at herself in the mirror nervously. The servant had left most of her hair unbound, though she had braided some of it back behind her right ear to show off that side of her face; the other side remained in shadow. While she knew the woman was trying to be kind, it just made her more self-conscious.

Interrupting her thoughts, Iona sighed. "Go on, go and pick a dress." They swapped places and Iona settled herself regally on the seat. "I'm worried," she explained, "because I have some history with the royal family."

Ailsa shot a quizzical look at her and moved to the wardrobe.

Iona cleared her throat. "I may have had a... *friendship*... with the king's father." Ailsa's head whipped round from the dresses to look Iona in the eye through the mirror. *How was that possible?* The servant also looked like she was having difficulty processing this, before she schooled her features into a neutral position again.

"And when exactly was this?" Ailsa asked, frowning.

Iona just shrugged and looked wistfully into the mirror. "Around fifty years ago."

The woman, clearly confused, abruptly stopped doing her hair; Iona motioned for her to continue. The servant did her best to hide her anxious fingers from the selkie, but Ailsa could see the woman was as shaken as she felt.

Ailsa knew that Iona was older than she looked, but she hadn't been expecting this. She stared incredulously into the back of Iona's head. "You're looking good for your age."

"Remember," sighed Iona, "selkies age differently. It was before the current King was born; before his mother even arrived from Crait. He was handsome, funny, and liked to paint, especially coastal views."

Ailsa sensed the selkie's sorrow and realised the tale did not have a happy ending.

"What happened?"

"He had to return to court. He would have taken me with him but… On our last night, I looked at the sea and I couldn't leave. So, I returned home. I knew he didn't regret it; it was beautiful and brief and when it was over, he was crowned and presented with a new bride he later grew to love."

Iona closed her eyes. "When I was here last, Alasdair had just died in a terrible war and his son was being crowned. It was strange for me, seeing his resemblance in King Connall." She paused for a moment, caught up in her memories. "I know that they know who I am, who I was to his father. And it always makes me feel a little uncomfortable." She seemed to reprimand herself, then quirked her lips up, her whole face brightening with the smile. "But I *do* look good for my age. Maybe I'll snag a duke or a knight this time?"

Ailsa grinned, glad that the mood in the room had lightened. "You sly seal."

Iona just blushed and smoothed out her dress. The maid looked like she was about to keel over, but she continued to weave a tiara into Iona's hair.

Turning back to the wardrobe, Ailsa snickered to herself. She really was glad to have met Iona, despite the circumstances.

"What about you?" asked Iona. "Any love interests in your past?"

Ailsa gave her a long look. "It's hard to have a love interest when you are routinely chased out of villages." She stared at the piles of silks and tulle. Her lips grew thin. "Though there was one, a soldier." Her heart sank in her chest as images of strong arms and sombre eyes resurrected themselves from her carefully buried memories. But Iona confided in her, it was only fair.

"His name was Gris, he was an Edessan warrior."

Iona's eyes grew wide. Edessan warriors had all been exiled or killed when a neighbouring kingdom had conquered the country. Dangerously intelligent, their skills were honed from knowledge and studying strategy.

"He found me half-dead after being beaten by a

farmer," Ailsa continued, shaking her head. "He's the reason I'm still here; he taught me how to hunt. how to defend myself…"

"What happened?" asked Iona softly.

Ailsa's lips made a hard line. "I thought he liked me. Why else would you spend weeks teaching a girl how to throw axes, giving her food and letting her sleep in your home? Turned out, he just felt sorry for me. Said he was much too old for me," she sniffed, her cheeks feeling hot. "I'd told him I loved him. After that, I couldn't face him, so I left."

Ailsa flexed her hands, which had curled into fists. "It's fine, I didn't actually love him." She jutted her chin out. "I'm better off by myself anyway."

Her last statement met with silence. When she looked up, she realised the servant had left the room. *I wish I hadn't revealed so much*, thought Ailsa. She rolled her shoulders as if she could somehow shift the weight of the memories she carried.

"Of course, you can look after yourself." Iona's quiet voice drifted over from the chair where she still sat. "But you're wrong about being better off—you need friends." She smiled tentatively at her through her reflection, but Ailsa just returned her attention to the dresses.

She didn't need to think about stupid men with stupid, sad eyes. She needed to figure out how she was going to survive this evening. If she could fit in, hopefully she would make it through the night without more humiliation.

Which dress would be best? She selected one and pulled it on.

"Is there anything I should know when we meet the King?" she asked, changing the subject. She didn't like that Iona hadn't said anything in a while, but she could see the selkie was lost in thought, gazing at her own reflection in the mirror.

"I'm sure you will be just fine," she said. "Though you are our hired muscle, so I guess it would be best if you could look capable of defending us."

"Right, bring the axe then?" said Ailsa as she fiddled with the buttons on the gown. There were way too many buttons on it; she huffed, trying to do them up.

"Maybe we'll get you an ornamental sword or something?"

"That's okay," said Ailsa, "I can look menacing without weapons."

Iona finally turned in her chair and let out a bewildered bark of laughter.

"Pink?" She quirked an eyebrow at Ailsa.

Ailsa looked down at herself. She picked the dress because she'd seen another girl downstairs wearing a similar one in purple. The chiffon fabric cinched her waist but then draped over her hips to the ground in a way that allowed it to swirl around her legs as she moved. She'd never had the chance to choose what to wear; most of her clothes had been swiped from a scrap pile or washing lines.

She lifted her chin and looked Iona in the eye. "I like pink."

Iona chuckled. "I'm not arguing with you. You look just as menacing in cerise as in black."

Chapter 14

Once Iona had finished poking and prodding at Ailsa, they met Harris out in the hallway. Ailsa was stunned to see that he was capable of looking so cultured. He'd dressed in a plain ghillie shirt, a navy, velvet waistcoat with tiny shell buttons, and a blue and green tartan kilt; a tan leather belt held his kilt together. However, he still wore the boots he'd stolen from the Avalognian.

Ailsa sniffed surreptitiously. He had the same sea-salt smell as his sister, but she could also detect the fragrant aroma of something sweet, like fresh peaches. Her mouth watered involuntarily and she swallowed hard.

"Enjoy your bath?" she asked, remembering the ridiculous servants that had led him away.

"Not really. As soon as I reached the bathing chamber, I realised I was to be washed by a rather brutal looking man by the name of Mungo." He screwed up his freckled nose. "He scrubbed me within an inch of my life. At one point, I couldn't take it anymore and I transformed into seal. Oh, he did not like that," he trailed off, chortling.

"That's not nice, Harris!" admonished Iona, her hands

finding their way to her hips in a gesture reminiscent of a mother telling off a naughty child.

This didn't deter Harris, who grinned from ear to ear while taking her arm, leading her down the corridor.

"It was quite funny really," he mock whispered. "Mungo fell into the tub trying to catch me. There were soap bubbles everywhere—even in his beard!"

Iona made a huffing sound behind them, but Ailsa couldn't help giggling at this. "When did you turn back?"

"About the time he shouted for his aunt—who, by the way, is the head housekeeper and the scariest woman I have ever met—and they threatened to chuck me back to sea where I belong. No fun, these humans." He nudged her playfully with his elbow. "No offence."

Ailsa grinned. She could just imagine the chaos he'd caused. It made her infinitely fonder of the seal-man, since she was feeling so mutinous towards the household staff herself.

At the end of the hallway, they were greeted again by Lady Moira, a tired expression gracing her face. She had changed into a satin, lilac dress with long, billowing sleeves.

"Lady Iona, Lord Harris. Please come this way. I will take you to the King." Descending the stairs, she briefed them about what to expect. "He is extremely sick. It's like he's aged forty years in a few weeks. Please don't say anything about the way he looks. The healers have tried all they can, but it seems that he is bleeding on the inside. It will only be a matter of weeks, I think. He's stubborn, so no doubt he'll try to hold on longer." As they reached the bottom, Lady Moira peered hesitantly around the entrance hallway. When she was happy no one else was around, she spoke again in hushed tones.

"He is ready for death but wants to live long enough to see the Stone of Destiny returned. Though we, of course, want to see his suffering end, Prince Duncan has remarked that he would be happy for it not to happen *too* soon. He is about to become a father any time now and would like the King to be able to meet his first grandchild."

Ailsa felt a stab of sadness. If what they'd said about King Connall was true, he had been a benevolent and fair leader who'd tried his best to eradicate poverty in Eilanmòr. In the last twenty years, he had travelled to other countries to negotiate trade deals and alliances, including a peace treaty with Mirandelle. The King had ensured there was a steady shipment of salt from Visenya, which had allowed many people to store foods that would have otherwise rotted.

The trio was ushered through a heavy door to the left and then through a labyrinth of halls. It was gloomy and cramped; Ailsa instantly got the impression they were underground. Sconces held torches but they glinted dimly and she found herself unsure of her footing over the uneven flagstone bricks. Dozens of paintings and tapestries showing ancestors of the royal family lined the walls. She stopped when one caught her eye.

The painting was unlike the others, with their dark backgrounds and regal poses. It was also much smaller. It showed a beach scene with two sitting figures painted beside an elaborate sandcastle. The man was leaning back on one hand, relaxed and wearing his shirt half undone. He had a look of total contentment on his face. The other figure was a woman, leaning over the castle, holding a spade. She seemed to be in the act of adding another turret. When Ailsa looked at her face, her stomach gave an unpleasant turn; like she'd jumped and was falling longer than she had expected.

"Iona," she managed to croak out, "this looks just like you!"

The other girl came closer, squinting at the canvas. "Well, it seems that it is me. I thought he'd got rid of that."

"The story you told me earlier... about the King's father..."

"Yes, that's him, Prince Alasdair." Her voice was tight and she cleared her throat, continuing in a soft voice. "This was before his coronation. it was painted when we lived in our little cottage by the beach. About a month later, he was summoned back to Dunrigh and I decided to stay."

"He was handsome."

The King's niece chimed in, "The painting was restored to the gallery when Queen Saoirse died. He said that he wanted both of his great loves remembered."

Iona became glassy eyed as she stared at the painting. "I had thought to return to Eilanmòr when the queen died, but then Alasdair died in the Battle of Inshmoor against Mirandelle. Cursed, they called it. Remember how Harris and I told you about the last king who had been crowned without the Stone of Destiny? They couldn't find it in time for Alasdair's coronation. People say that's why he and half his army died in that battle." She cleared her throat. "Half of Mirandelle's army perished too. The war ended and Connell was crowned, holding the stone. I had always wondered what would have happened if I had been quicker." She reached up as if to touch the former king's youthful face but stopped before brushing the canvas, lost in decades of ponderings. Finally, she heaved a sigh and faced Lady Moira again.

"Well, best be off to meet the future, instead of becoming tearful about the past."

They carried on and finally, when Ailsa thought they must be back out under the city, they arrived at a wrought-iron gate. Two guards opened it and revealed a cathedral-like greenhouse. The juxtaposition between the cramped tunnels and the soaring heights of glass left her blinking in wonder. Towering foreign and indigenous plants stretched up several storeys. When she looked through the glass ceiling, she could see the turrets of the castle. This structure was behind the palace, away from the town. They had a clear view of mountains and a loch in the distance.

Still they walked further, coming to a narrow door which seemed to lead outside. Instead, it opened on to a much smaller glass chamber into which many people were crammed, all facing the centre.

"Please excuse us, everyone," called Lady Moira in clipped tones. "I have brought the ambassadors to speak privately with His Majesty." Immediately, the crowd dispersed: a line of people filing back out the way they had come. Once gone, only the King's niece, Ailsa, Iona, Harris, a couple of guards and a fragile figure atop a bed remained. Lady Moira regarded Ailsa in blatant displeasure, as if she wanted her to leave too, but eyeing the selkies, she seemed to think better of it.

There was a moment of awkward silence before the bedridden figure raised a hand.

"Please. Come closer."

Iona and Harris moved towards the King's bed, but Ailsa stayed back. She attempted to shrink behind the guards as much as possible, but it was hard in the cramped room. She pressed herself against the glass and let it cool the skin of her palms. Only the king's head was visible from this position and for that she was glad. He looked ghastly enough. She didn't want to see what was below his neck. His face was pale with bruise-like circles under each eye. His nose was completely blackened and rotting; a thick sheen of sweat glistened on his forehead.

He murmured to the two siblings but, due to the shape of the room, his low voice carried to Ailsa's ears.

"The ambassadors from Struanmuir. It's been a while since I've seen faerie-folk and even longer since I've seen a selkie."

"Your Majesty." Iona dipped into a curtsey and Harris bowed.

"Please," the king croaked, "There is no need for formalities. When a man is on his deathbed, he is equal to all others, for all men die." He paused and Ailsa could hear his ragged breathing. "Although, some die quicker than others. How does it feel, Lady Iona, to see me so withered, when the last time you saw me, I was a young man in his prime, straight-backed as I sat on my throne for the first time?"

"Beneath it all, you're still the same young man, Sir."

"Am I?" A wheezing cough overtook him but he continued. "That young man was so full of passion for the world. I, however, want nothing more to do with it."

Harris took a step forward. "What happened to you?"

"The life has been sucked from my body, leaving merely a shell." His voice got louder and his head trembled with the effort. "My soul has been scooped out of my insides and left me raw and bloody." Lady Moira gestured for them to stand back.

Harris ignored her and knelt beside the King.

Concern lacing his words, he asked, "But what did this?"

The King closed his eyes and shuddered, like a fit of some sort. Suddenly, his eyes snapped open and he lunged for Harris. The monarch barely made it off the bed. Harris leapt back and Ailsa felt a wave of horror wash through her as she realised the King was chained to the bed frame. He writhed around and gnashed his teeth together, cursing at them. Finally, after a few minutes, he slowly gave up, the fight draining out of him. He gripped the mattress and wailed, tears pouring down his face.

"Please, just let me die. Let me die."

Lady Moira patted Iona on the back softly. "I think we should leave His Majesty alone now. We won't get much sense from him for a while."

"What happened to him?" she demanded, her gaze never leaving the King as they moved towards the door. Ailsa quickly followed. She didn't want to be left alone with the demented man.

"Prince Duncan will tell you." This was all Lady Moira said before signalling the attendants to go back into the room. One was carrying a jar of liquid and a needle. "He has asked to meet you during the ceilidh in the main hall." She steered them back across the large greenhouse and through the cramped portal to the tunnels.

"Where are we going now?" asked Harris, half of his attention focussed on the paintings again as they made their way back along the corridor.

"I'll see you back to your rooms while the guests are still arriving. Dinner will be served for you there. Once you've eaten and are ready, I will return and escort you to the hall."

Ailsa was glad to be gone from the little glass room, but the King's contorted face still haunted her. She was pleased to hear the buzz of the entrance hall again. The King's sick room was like a tomb and she didn't want to be around when he got his final wish.

Chapter 15

When the trio arrived back at their chambers, a spread of Eilanmòrian delicacies lay across a table in the lounge area: venison and lamb steamed on enamel plates, blackberries and spring fruits sat beside a pitcher of golden wine. A servant poured some glasses for them and Ailsa caught a hint of sweet strawberries from the drink.

Harris lifted a lid to reveal something black. "Hmm. I don't think I've ever tried this before." He grabbed a spoon and helped himself. "It's delicious!" he said, mouth full, reaching for more.

"It's blood," muttered Ailsa, loud enough for him to hear. He immediately spat it out.

"What!"

"It's congealed blood. Or blood pudding." She popped a bit in her mouth and grinned in satisfaction as the colour drained from his face. "It's peasant food. It seems to have become popular among royalty, though."

"That's disgusting." He grabbed a raspberry and threw it in his mouth to get rid of the offending taste.

Ailsa just shrugged and helped herself to a plate.

"When you kill a pig, you should use up all of it. You can't be picky when you're starving." She grinned darkly. "I would have thought that, as one of the fair folk, you wouldn't be afraid of a little gore in your food?"

He shuddered. "Give me fish any day."

When they'd eaten their meal, Iona stood up from the table and announced she would change for the ceilidh. *What? It's only been a few hours since we last dressed*, thought Ailsa.

"Go on without me," she sighed, lounging back in her chair. "I don't think I can bear more womanly fussing today."

Iona left the room, with a swish of her skirts.

"Shall we retire to the couch?" asked Harris, yawning as he rose from his place. "I think I need a nap after eating all that food."

"Well, you didn't need to eat so much," she chided but followed him over to the comfier seating in the corner. From here, they could look out the window, where city lights were starting to be lit. They stared out into the view in companionable silence. Ailsa's mind drifted back to King Connall. From the look of him, she would be surprised if he lived long enough for Harris to go on his adventure to find the stone.

"What do you think happened to the King?" she asked in a subdued voice.

He braced his arms on his knees before answering,

still looking out the window. "I don't know for sure, but I have my suspicions."

"What?"

He turned to her then and raised his eyebrows. "Not what, who."

Last night's dream came to mind and she shivered. "You think it was the faerie queen, Nicnevan?"

"She's tortured men before and everyone knows she has no love for humans, especially royal ones." He ran a hand through his hair, pulling at the russet strands. "The only problem is, Nicnevan is supposedly chained to a tree somewhere up north."

"And the King was attacked on an island south of here," Ailsa finished for him.

He considered this for a moment and then spoke, choosing his words carefully. "Could be... she's found some... help."

Ailsa's pulse thundered under her skin. "Are there a lot of other fae that could do this?"

"Rumour has it that she has horrible demons under her control."

Ailsa bit her lip, trying to contain her questions. Being here like this, being *told* things, it was fast becoming an addiction. She felt giddy with it; like standing on the edge of a dark pool, she had glimpsed things, terrible and magical, swimming just beneath the surface.

Finally, she whispered, "Like what?"

"She rules all fae kind but favours her Unseelie Court: the wicked faeries." He leaned closer, and Ailsa felt his body—his warmth—on her bare arm, just as his voice froze her in place. "Haven't you ever heard stories about evil creatures? Or felt the hair at the back of your neck stand on end when you're in a dark room or the forest?"

Red eyes, crunching footsteps...

Ailsa felt like she was being swallowed by the sofa her heart beat frantically. *Does Harris know what lurks in the forest?* The thing that had stalked her since she was twelve. *Was it one of Nicnevan's monsters?* She tried to swallow but her throat was dry as bone. Oblivious, Harris carried on with his theories.

"I'd bet that Nicnevan decided to attack when she thought King Connall was weaker." He snapped his attention to Ailsa's face and grabbed her hand. "If Nicnevan has allies, it is even more essential that we get the Stone. Before, I thought that it was just a safety precaution, but Prince Duncan must have his suspicions too."

Her pulse still pounding in her ears, Ailsa held up a hand. "Sorry... *We?*"

"You're coming with me."

Ailsa's lip curled. "Since when?" She supposed she had been enjoying this strange adventure, but she wasn't ready to take the plunge into the monster-filled waters.

"Come on, Ailsa, you're involved now." She couldn't

bear the disappointment in Harris's voice. "This is your country, aren't you worried?"

Needing to move, Ailsa stood and paced by the window, looking at the city sparkling in the darkness below.

"To be honest, I might as well live on a different continent. It all seems a bit detached to me. You said yourself that the further south you go, the fewer faeries there are. Plus, I don't know these people and they sure as hell don't like me. Why should I risk my life?"

Ailsa felt the air shift as he came to stand behind her. The glass reflected Harris's outline with his hands on his hips. The similarity between him and his sister was striking. *Am I the naughty child now?*

His voice was low and gruff as he leaned in close to her ear. "If Nicnevan rises again and takes over Eilanmòr, you won't be able to escape the hell she will unleash. *Anywhere.*" Harris grabbed her shoulder and spun her round to face him. "She wants revenge, Ailsa, and she won't stop until the whole kingdom—maybe even the whole world—is decimated."

She considered this, doing her best to look anywhere but at his face. Despite what he'd said, Ailsa was sure that if she didn't go with him, he'd find someone else to help. She casually stepped back from the selkie. He joked around a lot but underneath that guise, he was determined and committed. Plus, he was cunning, which would be an asset during his mission.

Her thoughts deserted her when his hand, still holding her shoulder, squeezed her gently, bringing her closer again. She felt a little thrill of something shoot through her.

"Please, Ailsa. I want you to come with me. There's no one else I'd rather have watching my back."

She scoffed quietly. "You hardly know me." Her voice broke on the last word as she answered.

"I know enough." His eyes warmed. "I see who you are, even if you don't." Ailsa found herself wanting to lean into his smile, as if drawn the heat of a crackling fire on a cold day.

"And who's that?" she whispered.

"A hero," he said, simply.

Doubt had its claws in her mind, plaguing her every thought. *But what if I'm not?* Ailsa looked over her shoulder, towards the lights in Dunrigh. Although the sun had set, twilight still illuminated the land. As if responding to the doubt within her, a gust of wind whistled through the castle turrets and surprise drops of rain splattered against the window.

Harris gently lifted her chin towards him and stroked the back of her shoulder with his other thumb as they studied each other. For the first time, she lifted her gaze fully and stared him straight in the eyes. In the lamp-lit room, his pupils were large, eclipsing a bit of his irises.

Flakes of gold embellished their sea-glass green and they glinted in the semi-dark, betraying the magic hidden inside.

His hand grazed her fingers, breaking the spell she had been under.

Harris cleared his throat. "Think about it."

Ailsa nodded.

Needing to change the subject, she stated, "Your sister should be ready."

"Right." He winked. "I better go and see how long we've got until the ceilidh starts." He left the room and Ailsa couldn't help but feel disappointed, though about what she was unsure.

Ailsa was about to knock on the door that led to the adjoining chambers, when Iona burst through it wearing an even more spectacular dress than before. Ailsa suddenly understood that Iona had been attempting to appear demure before the king. The gown she now wore was strapless and emerald green. The cut of the dress left the front significantly shorter than the back and Ailsa could see the heeled sandals Iona was wearing and several inches of bare, freckled legs.

"That dress—" she started, gaping at the flesh on display.

"I know," squealed Iona with excitement. "It's gorgeous!" She twirled, giving Ailsa a view of the plunging back. She halted in front of Ailsa again, peering down at herself and shifting her hips. "Though maybe it's a bit much."

"Well," breathed Ailsa. "You might freeze to death—"

"Not the dress, silly girl. The shoes!" She clicked the heels together. "They won't last long at a ceilidh. I'm sure I'll have them off after a few dances. But they're so pretty!"

Ailsa swallowed. "Iona, no offence, but you're showing a lot of skin—"

The selkie clicked her tongue. "That's the point. I don't want to trip over my dress when I'm dancing." She met her eyes and sighed. "You Eilanmòrians are so prudish. It's not like I'm naked. All of the vital parts are covered." She smirked. "If I were a seal right now, I'd have even less on."

"You'd also be covered in fur."

Iona just sauntered confidently to the table and poured herself another glass of wine. Ailsa absently plucked up a blueberry and popped it into her mouth. The berry was sweet and sour and made her cheeks pull inwards. Ailsa was worrying about being prudish and overdressed when Lady Moira appeared at the door again, Harris hot on her heels. The King's niece was wearing the same dress as earlier but had a comically shocked expression plastered on her face.

"Lady Iona, you look—"

Iona cut her off, smiling graciously. "It doesn't matter how I look; I feel fabulous!"

Harris didn't seem to notice the difference in his sister's attire.

"Right, come on you two. The hall has filled up and I want to join in on the dancing before we have to talk business." He stepped aside to let the women pass, choosing to rest a hand on the back of Ailsa's elbow.

Does he think I can't make it down the stairs? She let him keep his hand there all the same.

Chapter 16

*T*he hall looked like a giant, luminous pond with hundreds of rainbow fish gracefully swimming around. The floor, a polished blue-grey stone, glittered in the candlelight. Pillars bordered the round room with curtains partly drawn across shadowy alcoves in between. Ailsa wondered how many of them were being used for clandestine business.

In the centre of the room, women in long, bright dresses and men in swishing kilts danced together in perfect synchronicity. She vaguely remembered the steps to some of the dances, but resolved not to join in. It was much easier to look threatening when she wasn't being thrown around in time to a jig.

The piper, drummer and fiddler were playing a quick-paced reel, while the harpist sat in the corner, waiting on his turn. A tiny woman stood in the middle of the group on the stage, singing in ancient Eilanmòrian, her voice high and angelic.

Lady Moira hobbled away, murmuring instructions to servants as she went. The remaining trio chose a round table next to the stairs, Ailsa watched, mesmerised, as the dancers weaved in and out in a blur around each other.

"So, what do you think?" asked Iona, squeezing Ailsa's knee through her dress.

Ailsa jerked her leg. "It's... erm... big," was all she managed. There were just so many people.

Ailsa sank into her chair and lowered her head, wishing dresses came with hoods. The song had ended and couples dispersed, seeking refreshments and rest. Ailsa's mind flew to memories of angry village mobs.

Harris interrupted her thoughts by leaping up as another song started.

"This one sounds good, Ailsa. How about it?" His feet tapped along to the beat of the music, betraying his impatience.

"How about what?" she asked, melting further into her chair.

He planted himself right in front of her, forcing her to look him in the eye. "You *know* what. Be my partner."

"No thanks."

"Do you want to be remembered as a spoil sport?"

Ailsa pressed her lips together. "Absolutely. Nothing would give me greater pleasure than to stay in this chair while you make a fool of yourself."

He groaned in exasperation, turning away from her. "Sister?"

"I'd like to keep my heels on a little longer, Harris."

Iona pointed her toes to show the elegant arch of one of her feet. "Go find someone else to babysit you for a while," she said, waving him away.

He made a big show of pouting. "Fine, but don't come crying to me when no one else asks you while I'm having fun." With that, he bounded into the colourful crowd.

Harris was wrong about their lack of dance partners. Song after song, men appeared at their table asking for their company—or, rather—for Iona's.

"It's because you're glaring at everyone who even looks your way," Iona offered quietly after she declined the invitation of yet another dejected youth.

"It's because they're worried I might eat them for my dinner."

Iona scoffed. "That's ridiculous. You're clearly full of black pudding."

"It's ironic really," said Ailsa. "They think I'm a changeling, but really you're the ageless, supernatural being. I bet you could take a good chunk out of them if you wanted."

"Oh no," Iona smirked, showing her delicate teeth in a way that Ailsa knew had meant to be threatening, but came off as dazzling instead. "We only eat *drowning* men. Though, if I'm peckish, there's a deep fountain in the gardens."

Harris was with another partner and, instead of the slow, graceful dance the rest of the crowd were performing, he was dragging her along by the hand as he raced under the outstretched arms of the other couples. However, the lady he was with didn't seem to mind: she chuckled while her slippered feet slid all over the floor.

Ailsa pulled her eyes away from Harris and fixed Iona with a sideways glance. "Do selkies actually eat people?" *Is it worrying that I don't really mind if the answer is yes?*

"Just a rumour." Iona flashed her teeth again. "I prefer salmon."

Ailsa clicked her tongue. "Pity," she replied, doing her best to seem blasé. She sipped her drink. "You know, you can go dance if you like."

"I'm fine here just now. My brother is being so entertaining."

But Harris had stopped dancing and was now staring quizzically at the other side of the dancefloor where there seemed to be a disturbance unfolding.

Ailsa and Iona stood on tiptoes to get a closer look. Iona, with her greater height, managed a little better and she relayed what was happening to Ailsa.

"It looks like someone is enjoying himself a wee bit too much," she laughed. "He must have had too much wine."

Just then, the crowd parted, and Ailsa could see a young man with a thick beard who was dancing with anyone who would go near him. He wore a creased, collarless shirt and kilt of the purple and green royal tartan. His eyes crinkled as he laughed and danced. Linking arms with a partner, he would spin her—or him—as fast as he could, just like the boys she had seen earlier in the city. Far from being put off by this, many guests were lining up for the privilege of becoming his next partner or copying his style a little further away. Every now and then, the man would swing one of them so violently they would be thrown out from the turn, arms flailing, only to be caught by an onlooker. Some spectators had expressions of disdain at the scene, but others were obviously having the time of their lives.

Harris jogged over to stand beside his sister. "Who is that?" he asked, a little breathless.

"That," Iona answered, "would be the prince."

Ailsa barked a laugh. "*That* is who you're trying to give the crown to?"

"Shh!" Iona cautioned but no one was paying them any attention. Everyone was fixated on the young man. She continued in a half whisper, "Remember, King Connall's condition is a secret. And no, that is Prince Duncan's younger brother, Prince Angus."

"Well, whoever he is, he's a genius!" crowed Harris and with that, he strode off to join the melée. In no time, Harris was near the front of the circle, clapping along.

"If he breaks his neck, it has nothing to do with me," huffed Ailsa. "I delivered you both here safe and sound. Now he's on his own."

The two girls remained at a safe distance.

The music quickened and Prince Angus lost his latest partner. Harris took the opportunity to jump in front of him. The prince grinned and offered Harris an arm. Instead, Harris grabbed both of the man's hands so that their arms were crossed and started to spin him around as the tempo of the music increased once more. Hoots and whoops came from the crowd. Guests called to Prince Angus to knock the stranger down. The two men whirled so quickly they became a blur of dark and red curls. Ailsa was grateful that Harris's kilt was heavy. Nonetheless, it threatened to fly up and reveal more than she cared to see.

The music reached its crescendo until, with a final note on the fiddle, it ceased and the two men lost their grip and were flung onto their backsides. They both landed, laughing, and the crowd cheered.

Prince Angus stood and offered Harris a hand up before clapping him on the shoulder. They made their way over to Iona and Ailsa, with arms loosely around each other's shoulders.

"Do you ever wish that you could fast forward through the next few minutes?" muttered Ailsa as they approached.

Iona gave her shoulder a light pat of sympathy and greeted them. "That was some wonderful dancing."

"Well, feel free to join in on the next one," boomed

Prince Angus over the music, smiling from ear to ear. This close, Ailsa could see that the man was around her age and much too unkempt to be a future king. He had the distinct carefree bearing of a younger sibling.

"Sister, Ailsa," cut in Harris. "May I please present Prince Angus, second son of King Connall of Eilanmòr. Prince Angus, this is my sister, Iona, and our guard, Ailsa."

The man bowed gracefully. "It's a pleasure to meet you, but please, it's just Angus. No need to put on all that pageantry for a second son." His grin was open and warm. "So, you have a guard?"

Ailsa groaned inwardly, sure he was about to make a joke about her looking incapable, but he merely squinted at Harris.

"I thought you'd be able to look after yourself. Want me to teach you some combat skills?"

Harris clapped him on the back. "I don't need to be able to defend myself when I've got Ailsa."

Angus paused and looked her up and down. "She does look like she's thinking of stabbing me. A good trait of a guard." He held up his hands. "No offence."

Ailsa shrugged but felt pride swell in her chest.

Suddenly, the prince's eyes lit up. "I love this song!"

He rushed back to the dancefloor, whooping and grabbing the hands of two blushing women on the way.

"That," said Harris solemnly, "Is the man I'm going to

marry one day."

This earned him a slap around the head from his sister. "Please remember he's a member of the royal family. Don't make jokes—"

He lifted a palm to his brow and closed his eyes in a mock swoon. "Don't *you* joke about my feelings. I have found my soulmate. Ailsa, tell her she cannot keep us apart."

Ailsa made a show of playing with her nails, pausing only to shoot him an annoyed glance. "Keep me out of this. I will say one thing: if you and Prince Buttercup over there do decide to tie the knot, I'll start following Prince Duncan around with my axe."

Harris stopped his melodramatics and looked at her, perplexed. "Why would you—"

"Because if he died, Angus would be king." She shoved his shoulder. "And there is no way I'm having *you* as my queen."

Iona let out an unladylike snort of laughter but quickly regained control as a rather frazzled Lady Moira appeared beside them.

"Lord Harris, Lady Iona, would you please follow me. Prince Duncan would like to see you now."

We're about to finally meet the heir to the throne, thought Ailsa as she followed the two selkies. *I just hope he doesn't dance like his brother.*

Chapter 17

Lady Moira escorted them behind a large tapestry of the MacFeidh stag. It obscured an antechamber in which many people, dressed in their finery, were sitting around a long table. A man at the centre rose. He was unmistakably Prince Duncan. Like Prince Angus, he was bearded, though his hair was a lighter, golden brown. He wore the MacFeidh tartan but in the form of a great kilt, the fabric arranged regally around his body and over his shoulder. His body had known hard labour, possibly even battle, and he stood, sword at his side, as if he was coiled to spring to attack at any moment.

Lady Moira dropped into a low curtsey. "Your Majesty, may I present—"

He held up a hand and almost growled, "Please, Moira, it's still '*Your Highness*.' Currently, I remain just a prince. No need to throw too much respect at me before my father has died."

She hesitated, "Of course, Your Highness, I just thought, with your father being ill—"

"Ill, but not dead yet." He sat back down. "You can continue making your introductions."

"The ambassadors from Struanmuir, Lady Iona and Lord Harris." Giving Ailsa a furtive glance, she mumbled, "and... friend."

Harris clearly wasn't having that because he extended an arm, his voice booming across the room. "Your Highness, may I please introduce our guard, Ailsa MacAra." The other people around the table began to whisper amongst themselves.

The Prince shifted in his seat and fixed his eyes upon her. "Well, Lady Ailsa I—"

"Just Ailsa. I'm no Lady." She lifted her chin.

A grey-haired man, two seats down from Prince Duncan, spluttered and rose from his chair. "Excuse me, young woman, do not interrupt the Prince when he is speaki—"

"Never mind that, General Fraser. It seems everyone is being misaddressed tonight. I don't particularly care about manners as long as I know I can trust the girl to protect our emissaries."

"You don't mean to allow her to sit in on the council meeting?" asked the General incredulously, his face growing red.

The prince considered her for a moment and then leaned forward on a forearm. "What say you, Lord Harris? Is she trustworthy?"

"Absolutely."

"Well then, this girl may join us, if it is agreeable

to her. As she already knows the situation, there is no reason to dismiss her."

The general's moustache twitched. Others around the table seemed to be disgruntled but didn't voice their concerns.

"Please. Sit." Duncan gestured to the three chairs in front of him. Servants stood behind them and pushed the chairs in as they sat.

Look at me now. She could scarcely believe she was coming face-to-face with the man next in line for the throne of Eilanmòr. To his right sat a stunning young woman with ebony hair and bright, bronze eyes rimmed with long lashes. She rested her hands on her very pregnant belly. Lady Moira took the chair to his left but kept her head ducked. The other nobles clustered around the table seemed to be a mixture of relatives and military.

"I might as well start from the beginning," Prince Duncan began, his voice clipped. "My father was returning from a visit to Mirandelle when he became sick."

"So the Mirandellis poisoned him?"

His jaw twitched. "What poison could do that to a man? No, they had left Mirandelle a couple weeks prior and were exploring the islands to the east using my father's ship. They had been skirting around the island of Nerebus—"

"The Island of the Gods?" Iona interrupted.

Oh great, thought Ailsa, *not just faeries but Gods too.*

Prince Duncan nodded solemnly and continued. "He decided to go for a longer trek through the forest. My father and a group of sailors were gone for a few days when the crew grew worried. They sent a search party and found them only fifteen feet away, just inside the forest's boundary. Three lay dead, with two survivors: my father and a cabin boy. All were covered in patches of dead, blackened skin, like you saw and had many broken bones. It was like the life had been sucked out of them. The crew asked my father and the boy what had happened but neither said a word."

Harris leaned forward, his fingers steepled in front of his mouth. "Was it an animal?"

"Maybe, but they would not speak of it." The prince scratched his beard, taking his time to select his words. " One night, the cabin boy pulled himself to the side of the ship and heaved his broken body into the sea. He didn't even try to stay afloat. He drowned before anyone could rescue him. My father tried to do the same a night later."

Prince Duncan's lips twitched and he took a steadying breath. "Everyone was watching him carefully. They had to restrain him with rope. Upon arriving back to the capital, he was speaking and appeared to be recovering, but still wouldn't tell anyone what had happened. '*An evil*' was all he mentioned."

"Has he attempted to kill himself again?" questioned Iona.

"No, he says he wants to die, but that he must wait till the Stone of Destiny is found so that I am protected. I put him in the greenhouse to try to cheer him up, but to no avail. I just hope that he can hold on until Vashkha has our child." The regal woman beside him laid her fingers on his shoulder and he took them into his own. The love between the prince and his wife was unmistakable. Ailsa shifted uncomfortably in her seat at the subtle, yet obvious, show of affection.

"Is there no hope that he'll heal?" Iona said, her words full of sympathy.

Prince Duncan flexed his hands. "The healers believe he's bleeding on the inside, where his bones have been broken."

Harris scrunched up his face in thought. "There used to be magical healers long ago. I suppose you would call them angels, but they were part of the faerie race. They would turn up to heal the wounded after battles. When the war between Eilanmòr and Mirandelle ended, they disappeared."

The other man nodded. "We tried looking again, when Father returned, but they're long gone. Our only choice is to keep him comfortable in his last days. I know that he'll find peace when you return with the Stone."

Harris nodded swiftly. "We'll find it."

"What are your plans?" The prince leaned back and took a sip of his wine.

Harris straightened, all business. "My sister will stay here to help while we go up north."

"You're not taking this girl, are you?" spluttered General Fraser.

Harris lifted his chin, his gaze defiant. "I have asked Ailsa if she would come with me, yes," he admitted in a clipped tone.

The general was now even redder than before. Ailsa thought that, with his large ears, he looked like a boiling teapot.

"Isn't there someone else that can go?"

"No, there's not." Harris glared fiercely at him.

The general turned beseechingly to Duncan. "If I may, Your Highness, I do not think it's a good idea. Let me send a few of my men to accompany Lord Harris. They'll be more trustworthy—" Ailsa bristled, but Harris clapped his hands down on the table. He looked livid. "If you insult my friends then you insult me, sir!"

The sour man glared contemptuously back at him. "My men are trained and ready to sacrifice themselves for the cause—"

"I don't need a pack of overzealous idiots looking to die for King and Country with me!"

General Fraser looked ready to boil over. "We don't

need a *Changeling* betraying us and taking the Stone to Nicnevan!"

Prince Duncan held up a hand and silence fell immediately. However, it was his wife, Princess Vashkha, that spoke.

"What silly superstitions you Eilanmòrians have." Her voice was sharp and heavily accented. "In Visenya, such marks show the child has been blessed by the Gods." She rubbed her belly soothingly as she spoke, making the jewelled panels in her dress twinkle as she passed a hand over them. "If the girl accompanies you, the mission will be a success."

Ailsa stared, completely stunned by the kind words of the princess. *Maybe I should have moved to Visenya.*

Duncan paused for a moment, glancing from face to face before raising his chin. "It has been announced that my father is hoping to pass his crown to me soon, though the rumours say that he wishes to retire. The simple act of the coronation will not be enough to protect me. They do not realise how precarious the situation is. We need the Stone." His eyes were as hard as steel as he stared them all down. "If this girl accompanies you—"

"Your Highness," Harris cut in, "She has the advantage of knowing the situation, being good with an axe and is without friends or family to confide in."

Great, thought Ailsa, *being an orphan finally pays off.*

Harris folded his arms and then threw the general

a cold look. "I won't be bringing any of your men with me. Ailsa will accompany me." He looked at her apologetically, "But only if she agrees."

Now they were all staring at her, waiting for her reply. She thought of her beach back home and how easy it would be to slip back and forget about this whole adventure. Ailsa was sure she could even ask for any supplies she wanted. But the general's words stirred up an old rage within her. Everywhere she went, she was met with the same prejudice, except from Iona and Harris. Hadn't she wanted to prove herself?

She gave General Fraser a wide smile. "Count me in."

Prince Duncan stood up, rigid-backed and resolute. "I don't care how you get the Stone, as long as it's done quickly and discreetly. Lord Harris, I trust your judgement. Please take the time you need to prepare and take whomever you wish."

Ailsa followed Iona and Harris's lead, standing from the table and curtseying to the Crown Prince and Princess. Together, they were just about to exit the antechamber when the prince spoke again.

He seemed a little more vulnerable, his eyes revealing a bleakness within. "But Harris? Don't fail."

The selkie bowed and answered earnestly, "That word doesn't exist in my vocabulary."

Chapter 18

*Y*ou'll need to be as stealthy as you can. Which is why there will be no horses, I'm afraid." Iona was speaking rapidly, her mind clearly whirring with calculations.

They had returned to their rooms before the ceilidh was over, intent on discussing the plans for the journey. Now that Ailsa had made the decision to join Harris, she felt a bit more keen to be involved.

She hugged her arms around herself as they walked. *I'm going to regret saying this.* "No horses? Do you want this to take forever? I mean, I'd prefer to walk but…"

Harris shrugged. "Better to be done slowly than not at all." His expression became dark, like a maelstrom on the sea. "I can't believe that man. Does he even realise that I sat on my first war council when he was still swinging a practice sword?"

War council? She'd have to file that away for later. She glanced at him from the corner of her eye, watching warily as a muscle ticked in his jaw. She'd never seen Harris this irate before. "You know, I really don't mind if you think there would be someone better suited to the journey than me."

"I am not having one of General Fraser's blundering halfwits with me when I'm trying to be covert." He wiped a hand down his face as if to rub off some of the fury. "At least I know that you can handle yourself. And to be honest, you'll be far better company."

Ailsa didn't want to admit it, but she was secretly pleased he had so much faith in her. Being trusted was like a powerful drug. It made her lightheaded. If she wasn't careful, she might get addicted to this friendship. She considered the word: *friendship*. Had things really changed so much in a few days? She felt a bubble of laughter rise at how unlikely it was but one look at the rage simmering on Harris's face had her pressing her lips together.

"This situation has, however, raised the stakes a little more." Harris stopped outside their rooms.

Iona placed a hand on the doorknob but turned back to face her brother, her voice unconvinced. "How could the stakes be any higher? The fate of the whole world is resting on your ability to find the Stone and bring it back to Dunrigh safely."

His face was deadly serious. "If we fail, I'll have proven General Fraser right. And if there's one thing I won't be able to stand if the world falls apart, it would be the self-satisfied smirk on that asshole's face." He headed into his own chamber, slamming the door shut behind him.

"So, no pressure, Ailsa." Iona rolled her eyes and

opened their door. "The fate of Eilanmòr and my brother's fragile pride is at stake."

Ailsa said nothing as she went to wash her face in the basin. For once, she couldn't agree with Harris more.

Chapter 19

The next morning, Ailsa awoke to sunlight on her face. It was such a rare treat in Eilanmòr that it made her feel more cheerful than she had been in a long time. The soft, warm bed and Iona's shallow breathing from the other side of the room, were like a quiet, soothing melody telling her she was safe. She laid back and tried to match her own breathing with Iona's.

Breathe in. *Things will get better.*

Breathe out. *You are trusted.*

Breathe in. *Harris needs you.*

Breathe out. *But what if you fail?*

The last thought came unbidden but ruined the peace she had felt moments before. Her legs twitched as she thought about the enormity of the task ahead.

Harris is relying on me to get him there and back with the Stone. But if I fail, the whole country is at risk. Why did he ask me to go? I can barely walk around the countryside by myself without getting attacked. Maybe I should say I can't go? She groaned under her breath. *But then General Fraser will be proven right.*

The first drops of rain had pattered against the

windowpane. Ailsa sighed and stretched; her body still ached from the journey to Dunrigh and now she would be hiking through the wet and cold again. She swung her legs out of bed and shuffled to the door. The plum, silk nightgown she wore clung between her legs, making walking awkward.

Perhaps I'll feel better after some food, she thought, stepping through to the lounge.

"Oh, good morning!"

She stopped rubbing the sleep from her eyes and snapped her head up to find Harris bent over a pair of packs. He was dressed in travelling clothes and looked like he had been up for hours.

"I thought I'd get a head start." He tilted his head as his gaze slowly glided over her body. A faint blush dusted his freckled cheeks, but his eyes were sparkling with mirth.

"Could you not have done this in your own room?" She surreptitiously crossed her arms in a bid to cover up. This was the least dressed she had ever been around a man.

"Not when the bacon was delivered over here." He took a bite of breakfast and continued with his mouth full. "Plus, I wanted to catch you as soon as you got up. I was thinking… you'll get pretty bored with having only me to talk to."

She laughed. "Bored isn't the word… infuriated…

annoyed… irked… exasperated…"

He raked a hand through his copper mop of hair, avoiding her eyes. "I get it. Anyway, I was trying to think of some ways to lower the tension—"

She raised an eyebrow. "You could just be, you know, *less irritating*—"

"Impossible," Harris scoffed. "Anyway, I came to the conclusion that you might need a break from me every now and then."

Ailsa nodded her head slowly. "I agree."

"But it would be dangerous to split up."

She narrowed her eyes. "Yes…"

He persisted, his tone nonchalant. "So, we should bring someone else with us."

"Well, I'm not too sure about that." Ailsa frowned. "You don't mean one of General Fraser's men?"

A wave of indignation crossed his face. "That pompous fool? No, that would be too cruel of me."

Ailsa's patience was wearing thin. "Who are we bringing then?"

Harris grinned. "He's a trained warrior and quick on his feet."

"Sounds perfect."

"Plus, he's very loyal to the crown."

"Okay…" She wasn't entirely sure where this was going.

"Easy on the eyes… marvellous dancer…"

The blood drained from her face. "Wait! Not—"

"That's right, Prince Angus!"

Ailsa balled her hands into fists. "Harris, this is ridiculous."

. "But he would be a huge help," reasoned Harris. "He can take care of himself, too. I've also heard he's extremely skilled with a sword—"

She growled in frustration. "I don't care if he can close his eyes and do a jig while singing *Mairi's Wedding* backwards. He's not coming!"

He shrugged. "Well, I already asked him and he said yes."

"Harris! I am not a babysitter," seethed Ailsa. towering over where he crouched. "He's going to be more trouble than he's worth."

Harris stood in a fluid motion and stared down at her. "He'll look after himself. Besides, we're risking our lives for his family. Why shouldn't he help?"

"Just because you have a big fat crush doesn't mean I have to be happy about this."

Harris stuck his tongue out at her and grabbed one of the packs to continue packing.

Great, Ailsa thought, plucking a sausage from a tray on the table. *Why did I say yes to this insane journey? Oh, that's right, because someone complimented me and turned me into a puddle of drool.* She threw herself into one of the chairs. "Such an idiot."

"Did you mumble something, Ailsa dear?" Iona called from the bedroom door. She emerged wearing a robe and a sleepy smile. "Why are you wearing nothing over your nightgown? You'll freeze!"

"Shh sister," admonished Harris, his voice joking and light again. "Ailsa was just giving me the motivation to not die on our quest, lest I never see a pretty woman in a negligee again."

Ailsa launched the rest of the roll she'd been eating in his direction and smirked smugly when it hit him squarely in the temple. "Pig."

"Are you almost ready to go?" Iona asked, pouring herself a cup of tea.

"Nearly," replied Harris, brandishing a coil of rope. "Just have to pick up a member of the royal family and we will be on our way."

Iona looked surprised. "Prince Duncan is joining you?"

He grinned. "Even better—Prince Angus. Ailsa thought it would be a lovely idea to have another trained fighter around to watch my back. She's so thoughtful."

Iona shot a questioning look at Ailsa.

Ailsa answered with a growl of fury. "I swear, Iona, I will leave your brother and bring the Stone back myself if all I have to hear is how much he is in love with Prince Perfect."

"What did I do to deserve such a compliment so early

in the morning?" Angus strolled into the room in black travelling clothes. He caught sight of the two girls and instantly averted his eyes. "Oh, sorry. I didn't realise you were all still in your nightclothes."

Ailsa marched up to him and poked him squarely in the chest. He began to back up, but his ankles bumped into the wall behind him.

"Listen, if you're coming with us, then you have to keep up. I can't look after you."

He swiftly nodded. "Don't worry, you can count on me."

Ailsa huffed and speared Harris with a dirty look.

"We'll just go and get ready," Iona soothed as she pulled a raging Ailsa towards the bedroom, but not before Ailsa snatched another sausage. She savagely tore into it while she scowled at the two men over her shoulder. Angus was already checking what Harris had packed, whispering with him as the door swung closed.

Chapter 20

Two hours later, Ailsa was waiting to depart at a humble entrance behind the castle. She kicked a stone and tapped her fingers impatiently on her arms, surveying the darkening sky and listening to Angus say his goodbyes. Lady Moira was straightening his jacket and swamping him with advice. He kept fidgeting like an overexcited child, and watching Harris, who was teaching a kitchen boy how to do a handstand. Meanwhile Iona, who was becoming increasingly annoyed with Harris, was attempting to speak with him about the journey. He squinted at her from where he balanced upside down as she spoke.

"And please, Harris, don't forget to stay away from the coast as much as possible—stand up when I'm talking to you!—because the Avalognian raiders are probably still out there—"

"Urgh, wind your neck in, Iona. We'll be fine!" At that moment, Harris fell landing on his backside. He rubbed his rear with both palms and the boy beside him snickered.

"Maybe I should go with you," Iona muttered,

wringing her hands. "If Nicnevan is really out there, then—"

"I can handle it." He gave the lad a smirk and then snapped his fingers behind the boy's head and revealed two apples, pretending to have magicked them into existence. Harris began to juggle the fruits in the air in front of Iona.

She clicked her tongue. "Harris, you're not exactly the most careful. How is your side anyway?" She gave him a cool look. "You know, where you were injured swimming to Eilanmòr? Or how about your neck, where your throat was almost slit?"

"Quit nagging me," he groaned, dropping one of the apples. The other, he caught between his teeth, biting down. He produced another apple, which he held out for the kitchen boy who grabbed it and darted off merrily.

Harris chuckled, then turned to face his sister. "Look, let us get on with this and you do your job here. Just in case we're too late with the Stone, we need you at Dunrigh to help Prince Duncan."

Iona squinted sceptically but nodded anyway. Angus had also finished his conversation with his cousin; she threw up her hands in surrender and gave him the sword she had been clutching. He beamed and fastened it to his belt before giving Lady Moira a swift hug.

Ailsa lifted her pack onto her back. Although they'd packed lightly, it was still heavy. She buckled it around her waist to distribute the weight evenly on her hips, then traipsed over to Harris and Angus.

"Do you think he'll come and say goodbye?" Angus asked Lady Moira.

"He's probably busy, cousin." She put a hand on his arm, but just then the doors banged open and Prince Duncan strode out. He took the steps two at a time, coming to a halt in front of his brother.

"Duncan," Angus beamed.

The Prince's face was severe as he greeted his brother.

"Angus," he boomed, "this is paramount." Duncan placed a hand on his brother's shoulder. His tone was clipped, formal. Ailsa shifted her weight uncomfortably as she witnessed the exchange.

Angus straightened and set his jaw. Gone was the playful, young man from the previous night. Here was a soldier, standing to attention.

"I know, I will not let you down."

Ailsa wondered if Angus's upbringing had always been like this: always serious around family, hiding away his true self. For a moment, she felt sorry for him. While the time she'd had with her mother and brother had been short, it had been full of laughter and love.

"It is also important that you stay safe." Duncan's face relaxed, and just like that, Ailsa was no longer looking at a future king and one of his knights, but at two siblings. Angus's shoulders loosened. He offered the Crown

Prince a hand, which Duncan shook.

"Good luck."

"Thanks." Angus broke from the embrace. The future king ascended a few steps and Ailsa took that as their cue to *finally* set off.

Harris blew his sister a kiss and then two guards escorted the three travellers to a gate, overgrown with ivy. Ailsa was glad they didn't have to go through the city with crowds of people gawking at them. She glanced over her shoulder at the group of waving people. The weight of the responsibility with which she had been entrusted felt more cumbersome than her pack. Next to her, Harris and Angus paused in front of the barrier.

"Well, here we go, I suppose," quipped the selkie, his voice wry.

They waited as the soldiers pulled open the gate, ripping the weeds away, then stepped out into the country beyond.

Chapter 21

The bluebells grew in patches on this side of the hill and the path was much steeper. Ailsa glanced at the two men, who were quiet for once, both staring at their feet as they descended.

After twenty minutes of silence, she became concerned. While she would have preferred a quiet, blissful journey, it felt almost unnerving that the two men weren't chatting inanely. Sighing, she eyed the brown-haired royal.

I'm going to regret this.

"So, Prince Angus," she said, thinking hard for a topic of conversation, "have you ever come this way when leaving the city? It seemed like the gate hadn't been used in a while."

"Actually, I haven't left the city in years." He took in the rolling hills ahead of them and scowled. "And please, if it's going to be *Prince* Angus for the rest of this journey, I may need to plug my ears."

Ailsa tilted her head towards him. "I hope you know that there will be no other special treatment."

"Thank the Gods!" He rolled his shoulders and grinned.

"When was the last time you left Dunrigh?" asked Harris, grabbing the stalk of a plant as he passed, peeling off the leaves.

"When I was a child, I used to go hunting out here with my father and brother, but that all stopped when I was fourteen."

"Why?" asked Ailsa, curious.

Angus's lips pressed into a hard line. "I ran away."

Surprised, she stared expectantly, waiting for him to continue. He let out an uneven breath and rested a hand on his sword hilt.

"I wanted to become a soldier. Turns out that if people know you're a prince, they hold back. So, I went somewhere that would treat me like anyone else. There was a training camp about half a day away with a reputation for brutal—but effective—teaching. I managed to stay hidden there for three weeks before Father turned up." Angus gave a short laugh. "I was sure he was going to take me home, and I would have been glad for it. When he found me, I had a broken nose, blisters all over my sword hand and I was covered in bruises. They used to do this thing where they'd get all new recruits to hold themselves on the rafters of a barn for an hour. If you fell, then you'd land in a huge pile of cow dung and they'd make you sleep outside like that." He scratched his beard thoughtfully. "I fell every day on the first week. Manure does keep you surprisingly warm though," he chuckled.

"Did your father punish you for running away?" Harris glanced at him with concern, and hooked his thumbs through the straps of his pack.

"In a way, yes. He made me stay. Said that if I wanted to be a soldier, I could bloody well see it through. I was there for six months in total." He kicked a stone ahead of him on the path. "Best six months of my life so far."

Ailsa choked. "Are you nuts?"

"Well, after a few weeks, I made some friends. They made it bearable. Soon I wasn't falling in crap or breaking bones; I was doing *well*."

"Bet you had all the ladies falling at your feet when you got back home!" Harris laughed. Angus's cheeks pinked slightly as he ducked his head. Harris's smile was wide as he nudged the other boy with his elbow before pulling an apple from his pocket and biting into it with a wet crunch.

Ailsa pursed her lips and appraised the prince. "You actually know how to use that sword then?"

Instead of answering, Angus drew the weapon, flipping it into the air in one smooth motion. He caught it behind his back and bowed to her with a flourish. It was impressive given the incline, if a bit showy.

"Not just a pretty face." He winked.

"Doesn't mean you can actually use it," Ailsa grumbled, walking ahead. Perhaps she had underestimated him;

he was clearly able to look after himself. If Harris had Angus, why did she need to be here? Had Harris realised she couldn't defend him? Was this his way of getting some real muscle without hurting her feelings?

Angus's eyes fell on the weapon at her side.

"I bet you can use that axe." He reached towards it but dropped his hand at Ailsa's low growl. With a chuckle, he asked, "What is it called?"

"What is it *called*?" repeated Ailsa skeptically. She heard Harris snorting a laugh behind her but refused to acknowledge him.

"Yeah. What have you named it? I call my sword *Saighdear-Saorsa*, Freedom Fighter." He hoisted his sword again, allowing the light to illuminate the inscriptions on the blade. "If Eilanmòr is ever in danger, I can use it to defend my country." He returned the weapon to his belt. "So, what do you call yours?"

Ailsa fought hard to keep her annoyance under control.

"The axe is called *Axe*," she finally replied.

Angus wisely kept his mouth shut for the next half-hour.

The trio rounded a bend at the bottom of the hill to find another, smaller mound. Ailsa's muscles throbbed slightly up the incline but she just huffed and kept her head down.

"Well, there's the road," Angus remarked once they'd reached the mound's apex. She lifted her gaze as he pointed off into the distance.

Ailsa sucked in a breath as she scanned the horizon. The vast land that stretched ahead was dizzying. From their vantage point, she could see the glen carried on below them for many miles. The path wound like a grey river as far as their eyes could see. Sparse trees dotted the landscape, but purple and yellow heather dominated. Modest, rolling knolls ran alongside the path but great, jagged mountains bordered the glen, like teeth. Far off, silhouetted between a gap in the bases of the mountain, a thick forest grew like clumps of hair. Ailsa couldn't shake the sudden vision that they'd be walking along a tongue into the mouth of a waiting beast.

"How long did you say it would take?" Her voice came out a little shriller than usual.

Pausing for a moment, Harris pulled out a map from his pack.

"Here." He held it out to her casually as he chucked his apple core off into the bushes.

Ailsa scanned the swirling characters for a moment, chewing her lip, then shoved it back to his chest.

"You do know I can't read, right?"

Harris's mouth popped open. "You can't?"

Angus gave her a pitying look that she itched to wipe off his face. Instead she just shrugged.

"Just *when* would I have learned?" *We weren't all raised as royalty.*

"You mean you can't read *at all*?"

She tried her best to rein in her temper and said patiently, "I've never really needed to."

Harris's head looked like it was about to explode from shock. "You need to now."

"No, I don't." She gritted her teeth. "You can read it to me."

Angus came to stand in front of her, blocking out the view of the glen. "I can teach you, if you'd like?"

Ailsa glowered as she felt the rage rising in her chest, making her lip curl. "I'm not interested." He stepped back at her tone, hands up in surrender. She turned her attention back to Harris, who was watching her face, an unreadable expression in his eyes. "Just tell me how far I need to walk with the pair of you."

His brow wrinkled as he studied the map himself. "Five or six days, I think. Then it's a boat ride over to the Isle of Faodail. That's where the Stone is hidden."

"Then we need to get back, of course," Angus added, and Harris grunted in agreement.

Ailsa nodded and Harris returned the map to his bag, hefting the pack onto his back. With a sigh, he started back down the path.

Five or six days? She groaned inwardly. After adjusting the ties on her own bag, she continued after him, with Angus by her side.

At least I'm not on a horse.

Chapter 22

*F*ive hours later, the sky deepened to a thunderous grey and torrents of water pelted them as they struggled on. They had just managed to reach the base of one of the mountains and were now making their way towards some ruins a little farther down the road. The slow pace was excruciating. Although her body was hard and muscled from hunting, it had been a long time since she had actually hiked and it seemed that the young prince was in the same poor shape. He still managed to chatter as they went, giving Ailsa a pounding headache to go along with her sore feet.

"Do you have any brothers or sisters, Ailsa?"

"No." *Not for the past five years.* For all she knew, Cam could be dead. Her heart ached with the same old pain and anger.

"Family?"

"No."

"Friends, then?" His chipper tone grated against her skull.

"No. I don't like people."

He paused for a moment, as if absorbing this fact or

debating whether to push her further. The temptation was obviously too great.

"Why don't you like people?"

"I just don't, okay?" she growled back at him.

He chuckled. "But why?"

"Because."

"Why—"

She whipped around to face him fully. "Quit it! Maybe I don't like people because they ask too many questions."

His eyebrows pinched together. "Come on, Ailsa, we've got a long road ahead of us. I want to be friends wi—"

"Urgh, enough, Angus." She carried on up the path, putting as much distance between them as possible. She didn't look back to see if he'd been hurt.

Harris jogged up to her, his cocky grin irking her. "Ouch, it's like you just kicked a puppy. How do you live with yourself?"

Ailsa just snarled, and booted a pebble ahead of her, imagining that it was Harris's head.

The selkie lowered his voice. "He's right, you know. We've got a long way to travel together, so it would be good if you could play nice?"

Her ears burned as she stalked ahead; Angus remained silent as he followed behind. Harris, however, entertained himself by counting out 100 steps at a time and then throwing a stone as far as possible down the path. He muttered as he went, counting every time his left foot hit the puddled trail.

"... fifty-six... fifty-seven... fifty-eight—"

"Will you please stop!" Ailsa yelled in his direction as she pulled her hood more securely about her face. Lightning streaked across the sky, illuminating the serrated peaks around them.

"Problem, Ailsa dear?" asked Harris innocently.

Her eyes sparked with irritation, marching back to poke a finger into his chest.

"It's bad enough we've been walking through this same glen for hours now without a change in scenery, but if I have to listen to you count to a hundred one more time, I swear I will go mad." As she said this, a clap of thunder sounded nearby. Beside her, Angus jumped but tried his best to turn it into an intentional skip.

Staring back down at Ailsa, Harris's lips curled into a smile. Ailsa could tell he was about to tease her again, but he was cut off by another flash of lightning. He laughed once and she growled, the sound mixing with the answering rumble from the skies. His mouth parted in a silent gasp as recognition flooded his gaze. It felt like Harris was regarding her differently now, as if he had suddenly uncovered a secret.

"Interesting..." he muttered under his breath.

"What is it now?" As she turned away from him in frustration, she lost her footing and her boot plunged into a particularly deep puddle. She shook her foot out and scowled. As if to herald her misfortune, the lightning flashed again, rumbling accompanying it a scant half-second later.

Harris seemed to gauge her profile, then shook his head absently.

"Looks like the storm is on top of us now, we'd better hurry to those ruins and see if we can shelter there for the night."

"Agreed," mumbled Angus.

It took the trio another half hour to reach the abandoned structure. While most of the roof had caved in, there was still a bit left around the hearth. Out of the downpour, Ailsa quickly set to work making a fire with some cracked wooden shelves she found in a corner. Angus and Harris removed the bedding from the packs. The castle had provided sleeping bags, wrapped in oiled and dried sacks, which had kept them from becoming sodden. Once Ailsa got the fire going, they each took turns peeling off their waterlogged clothes.

While Ailsa was changing, Harris distracted Angus by turning into a seal. She heard the moment that he transformed because Angus let out an excited squeak.

"I've never seen a selkie fully changed before!" he squealed, amazed. A second later, he cleared his throat in embarrassment.

Ailsa rolled her eyes as she tried to undo the buckle

on her trousers. "I'm sure you've seen a seal though? It's just the same."

"No, it's different," he replied. "I know that he's Harris, not a dumb animal—"

"Same difference." She pulled on a clean shirt and poked her head out from behind a crumbling stone wall. Angus was crouching just within the cover of the roof, while Harris rolled about in puddles.

"Look!" said Angus. "He's so cute."

The seal stopped splashing and rolled towards them. Since his flippers weren't strong enough, he had to move using his stomach in a sort of belly-roll motion, with his flippers extended out to the side.

He came to a stop at Ailsa's feet and she scoffed. "You look ridiculous."

Then it was Harris's freckled face, pouting at her. He got to his feet and stuck his tongue out at her.

"Took you long enough. My turn to get changed. Go close your eyes."

She made a rude gesture but turned away from the selkie all the same.

Finally, they had all donned new clothes and were now cosied in their rolls.

"I'd go catch us something to eat but I'm not going back out again," Harris huffed, fishing around for an apple in his bag.

"*Could* you catch us something?" Ailsa questioned.

She narrowly missed the wet sock he flung across the shelter.

"How dare you question an apex predator!"

She scowled back at him and nibbled on a piece of cheese she had packed.

"Well, we could toast some of this bread on the fire?" Angus had taken a modest loaf from his bag and ripped it into pieces before skewering them on some twigs. They crowded around the hearth in silence as the bread warmed.

After a while, Ailsa noticed that Angus kept shooting her furtive glances. He would open his mouth to speak, then close it again, thinking better of it.

The third time it happened, she turned her face fully towards him and growled. "What?" He immediately returned his gaze to the fire, looking sheepish.

Harris raised a brow. "I think that Angus has been trying to start a conversation with you, but you are too terrifying to attempt it."

She showed all her teeth in her smile. "Good."

Harris leaned into Angus and murmured conspiringly, "She just pretends she's all scary. I swear she has a fluffy, gooey centre, my friend."

Angus gave him a look like the very thought was ridiculous. "She also seems to be in a rotten mood, which you are doing nothing to help with."

Harris just grinned merrily. "Nonsense. Ailsa is

feeling much better, aren't you?"

She pulled her sleeping bag over her head to block them out and muttered, "No."

Harris frowned. "Could we talk to nice Ailsa please? I know she's in there."

She took a deep breath in and squinted out from beneath her blanket. "Fine. What would you like to chat about?"

Angus's lips turned up tentatively. "I was wondering where you learned to throw that axe?"

She scowled. *Of all the things…*

"I just… learned," she lied. "If I didn't hit something, I didn't eat."

"Have you ever killed someone with it?"

Harris nodded eagerly. "Oh yeah, she made this really cool shot—"

She cut him off with a long, hard look. "I can defend myself if need be. Is that what you were wondering?"

"Oh, no. Sorry. I was just thinking maybe you could show me sometime?" Angus watched her like she was a venomous snake. "I've never used a throwing axe before."

She considered this for a moment, stunned. He kept throwing her off with his kindness. Weren't all royals puffed up with delusions of self-importance?

He wants me to teach him? She deflated. "Yeah, fine."

It was hard being around people again. She was so used to being alone, she'd forgotten what it was like. Just when she thought she had them figured out, they would surprise her.

Ailsa was left gloriously alone while Harris recounted the tales of his past adventures on land. It seemed he had been a bit of a wicked youth.

Angus was a good listener, she noted, always asking questions about the story, never cutting in with his own experiences. Once she had finished with her food, she snuggled down deeper in her bedding and listened for a while, too. In this tale, there was a princess, or a lord's daughter at least, and a faerie, a ghost and an enchanted flagon that filled itself with beer. Harris clearly liked to embellish so she wasn't sure how much of it was true. She truly hoped there were no wyverns or sea serpents in Eilanmòr at least; although, nothing would surprise her now.

The next story was about a deer he'd met who was actually a farmer's son, cursed by a wicked faerie. Ailsa's eyes drooped as his soothing voice recounted how the boy's true love had changed him back by tying a lock of her hair to his antler. She didn't hear the end of the story as she sank into a dreamless sleep.

Chapter 23

The storm had moved on by the time they woke the next day. The clothes they had left out had dried somewhat but were still uncomfortable to put on. The cold from the damp cloth seeped into their skin and they shivered for the first part of the morning as they ate a meagre breakfast and packed up their camp.

Branches littered the path all along the glen, making it an arduous task to step around and over them. *The storm must have worsened,* Ailsa thought, carefully avoiding the puddles along the ground.

Though the walk was much more pleasant without the rain, it did have the effect of making Angus and Harris more talkative. Last night's conversation had opened a can of worms; Angus was insatiable in his quest to find out more about her.

"So, Ailsa, where are you from?"

Honestly, it's like having a pet I never signed up for. "A village east of here."

"And do you still live there?"

"No, I live further south."

"There's not many people down there."

She gave him a level stare. "I like it that way."

Harris smirked at her from Angus's other side.

Unperturbed, he carried on cheerily. "Do you ever go back home to visit?"

Her tolerance quickly reached its limits. "You know what? Why don't we just walk in silence for a bit, okay?"

The selkie snorted but didn't comment.

Angus deflated a little, his lip pouting of its own accord, but shrugged. "Sure, if you like."

The quiet lasted for ten minutes before he was blethering away again to Harris.

"What is Struanmuir like? Is it deep underwater? What do you eat? Is it just selkies that live there?"

Harris just laughed good-naturedly at the onslaught. "Struanmuir is magnificent, but a bit boring. Not like your human towns. It's actually not underwater at all, but you have to swim underwater to get to it."

Angus was in his element. "How does that work?" he asked excitedly, his eyes lighting up like two blue beacons.

"It's inside a series of caves, on a stretch of land just to the south-west of here," Harris explained. "You have to swim under the sea to reach the cave opening."

"It's not very big, then?"

The selkie shrugged. "It's big enough. The main cave is over half a mile wide and as tall as your castle. Enough to fit a town inside. That's where we do most of our business." As he spoke, his hands animated the scene. "There is a series of little holes in the ceiling and my ancestors hung up mirrors to reflect in light from outside. When the light reflects off the water, it looks like we are under the ocean."

"So that's where you live?" pressed Angus.

"Some selkies live in the connecting caves. But remember, most of the time, we're seals. We live in the sea."

The prince sighed. "It must be wonderful to float around."

"It is. To be a seal is to be free." He stretched his arms out in front of him and mimicked moving in an ocean current. Angus laughed as he swam around in front, encouraging the other man to do the same.

They circled back around Ailsa, who scowled as they came nearer. Harris stopped when he got behind her and mock-whispered to the other man.

"We do have to watch out for sharks sometimes though…"

Angus chuckled and whispered back. "Especially grumpy sharks?"

"Yup," Harris laughed. "Especially the ones that stomp around glowering and carrying an axe."

Ailsa glared back at them from over her shoulder. "You know I can hear you, right?"

"Oh no!" shouted Harris. "She's seen us! Swim away!"

They tripped over each other as they ran past, splashing through the puddles in the road.

"I swear to the Gods, you two, I will leave you somewhere while I go and retrieve the Stone—alone," Ailsa shouted. *I guess this is what I get for agreeing to one of Harris's ideas.* She knew they were just trying to pass the time. She smiled ruefully and plodded on.

At midday, they found a sheep with a broken leg, which Ailsa quickly slaughtered for lunch. The meat had been properly roasted on the fire Harris and Angus had built, and they all tucked in. Ailsa licked the fat dripping down her fingers with relish while Angus sang a bawdy tune, which had Harris rolling around, laughing. His voice was surprisingly good. *A soldier and a musician?*

All too soon, it was time to head off. The road ahead meandered on in an endless ribbon, the view monotonous.

Ailsa pulled on her pack and groaned. "I have decided to rename this valley to the *Glen of Sorrow*."

"Really?" asked Harris. "I think the *Glen of Suffering* would be better."

"I would give anything to the Gods if they just gave me something else to look at." Angus nodded in agreement. Harris huffed. "I've already sacrificed my feet—which are covered in blisters—I'm not giving them anything else. I fear they shall drop off at any moment."

Angus grinned. "Well, I think you got your wish. Look!"

Ailsa's head snapped up and her heart sank.

"A forest?" A wave of cold washed over her from head to toe. *No.*

Harris nodded. "Yeah, it covers a few acres."

Oh Gods...

She swallowed, her mouth suddenly dry. "Isn't there another way to go?"

"Not unless we want to head back the way we came," he responded warily.

For a moment, Ailsa considered this, biting her lip, weighing up the options in her head. Neither choice was appealing—but she knew she didn't want to go into the forest—not even with Harris and Angus.

"We are not turning around, Ailsa." Harris turned to face her full on. "*What* is wrong?"

"I really don't like forests." She dipped her head, trying not to look at the shadowy spaces between the trees in case she saw something staring back.

"Are you *scared?*" He placed a hand on her shoulder.

Her face became hot. *Why did she even come with them on this journey?* "No..." The shame wrestled with her fear, making her feel worthless. "Maybe."

His eyes softened. "Look, we'll be fine. We'll protect each other." Seeing her mortification, he hardened his jaw. "It's the only way. You can do it."

Ailsa hesitated, scanning the trees in front of her as they swayed slowly with the wind. From the corner of her eye, she saw Angus reaching out with his hand as if to touch her too, but, thinking better of it, returned it to his side. She gave a quick huff and squared her shoulders. *Some guard you are.* "Okay. Let's get this over with."

Together, they stepped over the threshold of trees. Ailsa held her breath as if she were plunging into an ocean. *One foot in front of the other*, she chanted to herself.

Harris led the way into the woodland, walking slowly now, with Ailsa and Angus in tow. He wound his way between the trees, touching each one as he passed.

Ailsa kept her head down, focusing on Harris's footsteps. Though her eyes itched to scan around the dark, she was fearful of what she would find staring back at her. She pulled her axe from her belt, telling herself it was just something to do with her hands.

You can do this, she repeated with every careful step. *You are too old for monsters. You're not a little girl anymore. You are what others fear.*

But the trouble with monsters was that they were all much older and much more terrifying than she was.

Chapter 24

They had been traipsing through the woods for an hour when they saw the first sign of people. The trio came upon a small clearing, where a ring of delicate, white flowers surrounded a huge standing stone. The boulder had been righted and covered in intricate symbols.

Angus approached hesitantly. "Are these faerie symbols?"

"No, they're human," supplied Harris. "They think that these runes will protect them from the fae."

Ailsa cleared her throat before speaking up. "I remember the doors in my village having similar ones."

Harris shrugged, looking unimpressed. "Whatever keeps people happy."

"They don't work?" asked Angus. It felt frustrating, knowing so little about faerie kind. Why had he never been told any of this? *I bet Duncan would know.*

"Not unless you picked up the stone and bashed them about the head with it," answered Harris with a laugh. He seemed so at ease for being so far from the sea. Angus felt a pang of jealousy which he immediately admonished himself for. *It's no good envying others. If you want to be that way, just act like it. Fake it till you make it,* he thought wryly. He puffed up his chest and followed behind the selkie, being sure to keep Ailsa in the middle so she would feel safer. He knew how debilitating it was to be afraid.

Harris whistled a tune and Ailsa swung her axe as they walked. Her eyes were always alert and focussed in front of her. Angus sensed she was listening intently.

Once they could no longer see the clearing behind them, it was Harris that gave a start.

"What is this?"

He was trailing his hand over the trunks again, but the one he was touching had something on it. When Angus came closer to investigate, he realised it was a scorch mark.

In the shape of a hand.

"Well, that's suitably creepy," said Harris. his voice still cheerful. "Don't worry, it looks pretty old," he attempted to reassure Ailsa.

From the corner of his vision, Angus could see she was not convinced.

"What do you think caused it?" she whispered. Her gaze darted wildly around the trees, taking in all the shadows.

"A few months ago, some people came to speak to my father about fires being started in the woods." Angus lifted a finger and traced the burn mark thoughtfully. "They said they had been caused by a demon and asked him to send someone to kill it. My father told them it was probably some youths attempting to scare everyone and sent them away with some donkeys they could use to transport water if the fires got too close to their village."

"Which is probably why this handprint is here." Harris pushed them on, away from the tree. "Just some kids trying to scare travellers."

"How exactly would they do that?" questioned Angus. He received a glare from Harris, who looked pointedly over at Ailsa. Her face had become ashen and she was unconsciously hugging her axe and wringing her hands.

"Right," said Angus, taking a deep breath. "Probably kids."

The sooner they left this forest, the better.

Chapter 25

Ailsa was feeling more tired than terrified after yet another hour. It wasn't that she felt reassured, she just couldn't stay uneasy any longer. This had been the longest she had ever been in a forest without the red-eyed creature appearing. *Maybe it had died?* She was still rather tetchy though.

Angus bumped his shoulder against hers. "Let's play a game."

Ailsa could think of nothing worse, but seeing Harris's warning look, she reined in her frustration. "Is it called *Everyone-Shuts-Up-and-Leaves-Ailsa-Alone?*" she asked with steely eyes.

Angus pursed his lips. "No, the day will seem quicker if we talk—"

"Not likely," she muttered.

Undeterred, Angus pressed on. "So, what you have to do is, make up a rhyme about a person we know and Harris and I have to guess who it is."

"We've only just met," she grumbled. "How many people can we make rhymes about?"

Taking her question as cooperation, he beamed. "We

have a few people in common. Harris, you start."

The selkie thought for a second and then gave her a wink. "Okay. There was a girl who moaned all the time, though her axe skills were simply sublime. She thinks that I'm hot, and likes me a lot, but she isn't impressed by my rhyme."

"No," Ailsa protested, reddening all the same. "I'm not."

Clearly enjoying the fun, Angus's grin grew. There was also a wicked glint in his eye that made her wonder if he was making things awkward on purpose.

"Right, Ailsa, your turn," he snickered.

She narrowed her eyes. "Nope. Not going to happen."

"Please," he pouted, sidling up to her and, in an unexpectedly bold move, wrapping an arm around her shoulders. He squeezed her tightly, causing her to suck in air. The prince smelled like the outdoors: cedar and some type of herb. It distracted her and she missed half of what he was saying. Unfortunately, he seemed to still be pleading with her to join in.

He gave her another squeeze and implored sweetly, "I'll give you a title?"

A quick bark of laughter escaped before she could stop herself. "You can do that?"

Angus grinned guiltily. "Not really." He let her go and she immediately missed the warmth his arm had provided. "But I can promise all-you-can-eat cake when we return."

She turned to Harris, but found that he was not smiling. Instead, he was instead watching them with a with a look Ailsa couldn't quite place.

"Urgh, fine," she relented, catching the selkie's eye and sticking her tongue out at him before continuing. "There once was an annoying prince, who constantly made me wince. I don't want to play, so please go away. You and Harris both talk utter..." She chewed the inside of her cheek in concentration, searching for a rhyme. "Mince."

Harris's lips twitched, but it was Angus who threw his head back with laughter. "That's good, Ailsa, well done. Now I'll go." He scratched his beard in thought before making a noise of triumph. "There was a boy who turned into a seal..." he began, reaching around to clap the other man on the back, "and really loved eating fish for a meal. He was a huge flirt, and did not wear a shirt—"

"Such a shame he had no sex appeal!" finished Ailsa smugly.

"Hey!" Harris grabbed at her but missed as she dodged out of the way. "I'll have you know I'm very appealing."

"You know, Ailsa, he's right," laughed Angus. "As a seal, he *is* adorable."

"He should stay that way more often, then," she teased.

Harris sniffed in mock indignation. "Shut up," he said. "Or I'll no longer be your friend."

"Angus, you're a genius!" said Ailsa. "All it took was some poetry to get him to leave us alone!"

Harris turned on them then, hands on his hips, doing a good impression of a nagging mother—or his sister.

"You two need t—" His head snapped to the side, his body suddenly rigid. "What was that?"

Angus rolled his eyes. "Don't try to trick us, Harris."

"No. I heard a noise. It sounded like a crunch, behind us."

Ailsa's laughter died in her throat and she went still.

It couldn't be. Not now.

They remained silent as they listened. The wind whistled through the treetops and the birds chirped somewhere overhead.

"There's nothing—" Angus began, but cut off to stare at the forest behind them.

Then Ailsa heard it; the distinctive *crunch* that always echoed her footsteps whenever she stepped into a forest.

"Move," she breathed.

Chapter 26

Angus could tell that Ailsa was extremely frightened. Even Harris looked unsettled. Although unaware of what the potential danger was, Angus knew these woods. He'd spent his youth hunting game in here; the things that could harm them tended to stay out of the way. Just as he was about to joke about squirrels, he saw Ailsa's knuckles turn white as she gripped her axe handle fiercely.

"Just keep walking," Ailsa spoke quietly but firmly, clearly pushing down her fear. "Faster." The trio remained in a tight line but quickened their footsteps.

Why is she so scared? The hair on the back of his neck stood up when he looked behind them. It was like his body could feel danger, even if his mind was still attempting to understand.

"What is it?"

Ailsa's blue eyes were wide, piercing. "This is why I don't like to go into the forest."

His face contorted with confusion. "Because of a crunch?"

"There's something following us, Angus," Harris

murmured from the front. The selkie was taking her fear seriously.

Ailsa's voice cracked as she urged them on. "Just walk faster."

"Look, over there—" Angus pointed through the trees to a loch sparkling in the fleeting evening light. "Just there, at the water's edge. There's a boat under that bush, maybe we should get out of the forest for a bit."

He hesitated for a moment at the thought of spending the night on a cramped boat, but Ailsa was already sprinting to the shoreline. As he followed, he heard Harris's thundering steps behind him, echoed by another presence.

Oh Gods, it's real.

It wasn't the thing chasing them that scared Angus, but the realisation that Ailsa—this brave, indomitable girl—was terrified of it.

The boat was little more than a wooden dinghy, but it looked sturdy. Ailsa pulled on it desperately. When Angus and Harris reached her, they joined her in forcing it through the muddy banks to the loch.

"Don't you think it belongs to someone?" asked Angus. He was all for getting away from whatever monster stalked them, but stealing was something he liked to avoid in general.

Ailsa's lip curled as she snarled, "I swear to the Gods, Prince Dope, that I will leave you here to be eaten."

"Fine!" He gave the dinghy a hard shove, launching it into the water. They waded in up to their knees, pushing it further in. "Let's go." They both hopped in while Harris steadied the little craft.

"Hurry!" cried Ailsa to Harris as she scrambled for the oars.

"I'll give us a boost." With a splash, Harris became a seal again. He nudged the boat with his nose, propelling it into the middle of the loch.

"That's it!" Ailsa shouted to him, keeping her eyes on the selkie. "You did it, Harris!"

Meanwhile, Angus scanned the trees for their would-be attacker. His heart stopped for a moment. There, in the gloam of the forest, he could see a pair of red eyes, then the boat rounded a bend and the eyes disappeared from sight.

Close call, he thought as he fought to calm his breathing.

It seemed that Ailsa had been right.

Chapter 27

arris swam beside the boat for a while, nudging it whenever they needed to change course. The loch water was black with silt and plants and Angus wondered if the selkie could even see anything under it. Angus had always been a little afraid of water. It was something about *the unknown*. When he'd been younger, he'd always tried to avoid swimming beyond the shallows. Of course, when the officers had discovered this fact during a training exercise, he'd been forced to spend a day chained up to a dinghy in the middle of the sea. He'd baked in the sun, terrified of what was lurking underneath him, but at the end of the day his unit returned and found him defiant and uneaten. He still didn't like deep water, but he was much better at hiding it.

He glanced sideways at Ailsa in the fading light. She had been huddled up at the opposite end of the boat for the better part of two hours, scanning the trees compulsively. Angus had left her to it. He knew that if he had attempted to comfort her, she'd have bitten his head off.

Angus wondered what caused her to act that way.

Panic borne from such a deep fear gnawed at your insides, leaving lacerations on your being. How long had she been running from her monsters? How many wounds did she carry?

Soon the sky dimmed as night pressed in and Harris gracelessly heaved himself into the boat before turning back into a human.

Ailsa grimaced. "Wouldn't it have been easier to shift before getting in?"

Harris wedged himself in between the two of them. "This way my clothes are mostly dry."

"Looks like this loch goes north for quite a bit. I guess we could just stay in the boat until we reach the top—" Angus was about to continue when he noticed Harris wasn't really listening. Instead, he was staring intently at the Ailsa.

Nothing new there then, Angus mused.

"Ailsa, what *was* that?" The selkie finally asked.

She bit her lip, a gesture Angus had come to realise meant she was trying to keep her emotions under control.

"I don't know," she murmured. "Ever since I was a girl, there's been *something* in the woods, following me." Her voice broke on the final word and she set her mouth in a grim line.

Harris carried on, his voice soft. "These woods? Is this where you came from?"

"No, *every* wood. *Every* forest. Sometimes even groves of trees. They aren't even connected. And when I'm away from the trees, it's gone. Somehow it always finds me, even if I'm across the country." Her voice was weak, now, and tired. It seemed like it pained her to ask her next question.

"What if it follows me all the time, but I just can't hear it unless I'm in the forest?" she whispered. Harris reached out to comfort her and she let him, leaning into his body.

"Today was the first time I could feel its presence," said Harris. "There hasn't been anything hanging around you before."

Angus scanned the forest suspiciously but there was no sign of the red eyes from earlier. "Can you still feel if it's there?"

Harris gave a nod. "It's away from the shoreline, further into the trees. It's moving away."

Angus heaved a sigh of relief, watching the shadowy bank. "Well, at least we're safe for now."

Ailsa cleared her throat. "You two should get some sleep. I'll take first watch and let my clothes dry a bit more." Ailsa scooted away from Harris and ran her hands through her hair in an effort to compose herself.

Angus studied her profile as he got more comfortable in the boat. He sensed it was rare for Ailsa to fall apart as much as she had. He placed his pack under his head as a makeshift pillow and crossed his arms over his chest. The boat rocked gently in the breeze, yet he couldn't sleep. He longed to comfort Ailsa too, but he knew their relationship was tenuous at best. A creak from the other side of the dinghy told him that Harris was awake too.

"Harris, do you think it wants to kill me?" she whispered.

"I don't think so," the selkie murmured back. "Don't worry, I'll protect you."

Angus could feel the tension as Ailsa quietly snapped, "I can protect myself."

Harris chuckled, immune to her sour mood. "Of course you can, lass, but I'll watch your back nonetheless."

They became silent again, and soon Angus could hear a gentle whistling snore from the middle of the boat.

Ailsa was still tense and stiff at the bow of the craft. She hugged herself tighter and gazed at the night sky. The reflection of the twinkling stars danced in her eyes, the moonlight turning her skin pale like ice, her expression just as cold. If he were to write a melody based on the moment, it would be melancholy and sorrowful, played on a single fiddle. He fell asleep imagining the notes, letting the music carry him to unconsciousness.

Chapter 28

The boat bobbed steadily northwards, a soft wind gently jostling the water surrounding them. The day was brighter than yesterday, and the trio allowed themselves to drift peacefully.

Around midday, Ailsa's stomach started rumbling which prompted an overdramatic Harris to announce that he would find her some food, lest she starve. With that, he leapt from the boat, transforming before hitting the water with a *plop*.

When he resurfaced with his catch, Ailsa tutted in annoyance. "Fish? And just how are we supposed to cook fish on a wooden boat?"

The seal stared at her, its large black eyes unblinking, before tossing the fish into the air, then catching and swallowing it in one gulp. With another splash, he disappeared back under the water.

Half an hour later, a sharp tail slap alerted the duo to his return. This time, Harris was floating on his back, with a blackberry branch on his stomach.

Angus seized the branch and they tucked into the food. With the few crackers left from their packs, the berries were quite good.

During their meal, Harris floated beside the boat, periodically flicking his tail so he would spin in circles. Every now and then, he would thrust their craft in the right direction. Ailsa had moved to the stern, sitting with her back against it, trailing her hand over the water. The seal sniffed her finger and licked it playfully. She sighed and scratched him under the chin.

"Becoming quite cosy, aren't you?" Angus laughed from his new position at the front of the boat. She scowled and withdrew her hand, earning a quick splash of water. Harris blew some bubbles and ducked under the surface.

"What's the deal with you two anyway?" asked Angus, giving her foot a nudge.

She shrugged and stretched. "Well usually, he's an utter pain in my backside."

His lips pursed under his beard. "Not what I meant, Ailsa."

She blushed and lowered her head. *Meddling prince.* "I know what you meant," she replied in a clipped tone, "We're friends."

Angus folded his arms across his chest and regarded her with mirth dancing across his face. "Sure. Or maybe he likes you." He gave her a half smile to show he was joking… mostly.

She pouted. "Who says I like him?" she said, turning

her focus to the forest again.

She'd been scanning the trees for the last few hours. They were almost to the top of the loch, which meant they would have to go on foot again. *Had the monster left?* She gave a rueful sigh as she remembered how utterly boring and *safe* the glen had been.

There was a movement off to the right of the boat and Harris's whiskered face appeared over the side.

"Look," said Angus, directing her attention to the end of the loch where they could see the end of the water and the beginning of the treeline.

"Let's help him move us," Ailsa suggested as she grabbed an oar. Together, they managed to make it to the northern bank before sunset. Sweat poured down Ailsa's back, making her shiver in the evening cold.

The trees had thinned out. The gaps between them were lit up by the sinking sun. Nothing was hiding amongst them, but Ailsa still ordered Harris and Angus to fan out, checking the area to be sure. Once they had all paced out a hundred yards, the two men re-joined Ailsa where she stood on top of a large slab of bedrock, jutting out from the grass.

The land ahead sloped gently upwards and it was clear they would be soon passing over more heather-covered hills, thankfully devoid of trees. Bubbling burns snaked through the earth on either side of them, their sounds mingling with the songs of the birds.

"Do you want to keep going?" asked Ailsa as she gazed up the path. The wind blew bitterly, even through the wool of her cloak. She hugged her arms tightly against her body.

"We're running low on food and our clothes are a bit damp." Harris crouched down and plucked a buttercup from beside their boulder. He eyed it absently before picking the petals off. "Let's stay here tonight, I don't fancy going much further today. A bit of rest will do us some good."

She nodded. "Agreed."

"Wait," Angus cut in, "Are you sure you'll be alright here? I know it's the edge of the forest, but if that thing comes back—"

Ailsa's heart lurched involuntarily but she squared her shoulders. "We'll be fine." It never followed her away from the forest. *That I know of*, she amended, biting her lip.

"I don't sense anything." Harris straightened, contemplating the horizon. "Except hunger. We need some food."

Ailsa lifted the axe from her belt. "I'll get it. I want a chance to kill something."

He smiled at her. "That's the spirit." Passing by, he touched her ear and she gave a slight start. He chuckled as he walked away to find some firewood, Angus following him. When she lifted her hand to the place his fingers had brushed, she found a tiny, pale yellow flower tucked behind her ear. She placed it back where it was and trooped off to a thicket of bushes to catch dinner.

Chapter 29

The hunt was fruitful; she managed to catch a fair-sized capercaillie, which Angus began to prepare upon her return. Harris stole some of the grey tail feathers Angus had plucked and inserted them into his hair, creating a silvery crown upon his scarlet curls. When the bird was ready, Harris took it from the prince, stuffed it with some wild garlic he'd found nearby, and skewered it with a spit above the roaring fire.

"This is going to be the best thing you have ever tasted," he crowed. "Better than all of that fancy castle food."

Angus returned from one of the streams, having washed his hands of blood. "Actually, we've had capercaillie before—"

"Shh, he thinks he's a master cook." Ailsa flicked him on the knee as Angus came to stand beside the fire. "Just let him have it. As long as I don't have to cook, I'm happy."

Angus shrugged and grabbed a large stick from the ground beside him. He circled the campsite, twirling it around. "How are we doing for time?"

Harris clicked his tongue, concentrating on rotating

the bird. "I don't think we're too behind; maybe a few hours at most."

"Hopefully there won't be anything else out to kill us." Angus thrust forward with the stick, swiping it through the air like a sword. His motions were calculated and practised. "Though the boat was probably faster." He stopped his exercise and stared at the vegetation under his boot. "Do you think we'll make it back in time?"

Ailsa exchanged a glance with Harris. *Would they be back before the King died?*

The selkie lowered his voice and poked at the embers with a twig. "I'm sure we will. He's waiting for you."

"Yeah… You're right," Angus mumbled. He raised his branch again but didn't commence his drills again.

Ailsa pulled off her cloak and stood up from her spot beside the fire.

"Hey, Angus? Would you teach me how to do that?" She gestured to his makeshift sword.

His body relaxed. "Yeah, sure. Grab a stick."

Ailsa took her time selecting a decent, straight one from underneath one of the scattered trees. Once she'd chosen hers, she stalked back towards him swinging the branch from side to side.

Harris watched from his position by the fire, clearly delighted by the prospect of dinner and a show.

"First rule," Angus stated, "Don't swing your sword around like that. It's too showy and your opponent will likely hit it out of your hand."

She eyed him, doubtful. "But you did it."

He rolled his eyes. "I was *trying* to be showy. In a real battle, you keep your sword at the ready in front of you."

Ailsa stopped swinging with a huff and held the stick out in front of her with both hands.

Angus nodded in encouragement. "The trick is to stay balanced. Keep a wide stance—not that wide—and you won't be knocked over. Plus, you'll have a lot more power for your own attacks."

She widened her legs and crouched lower, just like she would if she was about to attack with her axe. He drew closer, tucking his left arm in and swinging his branch down slowly on hers.

"Typically, you would have a shield in one hand and your sword in the other. You bring the sword down on your opponent like this. Don't worry too much about where you aim for. Get in as many hits as you can. That way you'll injure them before they can attack you."

Ailsa shifted her stick to her right hand and struck at his shoulder. He sidestepped out of the way before it could impact and retaliated. They did this, back and forth, until she managed to land a blow to his arm.

"Good," Angus nodded, breathing hard. "Now try to drive me back."

Ailsa narrowed her eyes and went in for the attack. She knew she was fast, but she lacked his skill. She compensated for this by throwing her energy into quick, sharp *thwacks*. Angus blocked each one with his own branch or his left arm. Frustrated, she whirled faster, hoping to tire him out. Every movement was reflexive; she didn't have time to plan strategies. She just let her body move. Still, Angus dodged and ducked. Finally, she drove him back to a tree, causing him to stumble over one of the roots just enough to let his guard down.

"Ha! I've got you!" She lifted her sword high in the air, ready to bring it down on him. Before she could do so, he took advantage of her unguarded body and brought his stick up to poke her chest with the end.

He chuckled. "Sorry, not today. You're dead."

"Urgh." She threw down her branch, fuming. "I hope you know that in a real combat situation, you'd have an axe caving your head in by now."

"I don't doubt it," he snickered, getting to his feet.

"What is this?" Harris called out. "Here I am, slaving away over a hot fire, cooking your dinner and the two of you are rolling around in the dirt?" He scowled at them as they approached.

Ailsa flopped down to the ground with a sigh, relishing the combination of cool air and hot flames. "Angus was just showing me all his weaknesses so I can kick his ass next time."

Harris clicked his tongue. "Ah, but you wouldn't need to know how to swordfight if you just learned some tricks from me." He grinned. "I'm more of a stealth attack sort of person; they never see me until it's too late." He made a few quick hand movements to back up his claim. Ailsa thought it just made him look like he was having a fit.

She raised an eyebrow. "Harris, you are the least sneaky person I know."

He tapped his nose. "Maybe that's what I want you to think. Maybe I've been secretly watching you for a while now," he said, leering at her.

"Creep."

"He travels by belly roll, Ailsa," Angus cut in, grinning.

"I extremely doubt it."

Harris just raised his nose haughtily in the air. "My awesome intelligence and outstanding wit make me an excellent travelling companion."

Now both Ailsa's eyebrows were raised. "Sure."

They tucked into the capercaillie, which was surprisingly tasty. They sat in silence as they ripped the meat from the bones, the juices dripping down their chins and splattering their clothes, not that it made much difference because they were so filthy anyway. Once sated, the trio reclined on their packs and let the heat of the fire melt away the evening chill.

Angus turned to the side, unable to move very quickly because of his fullness. He had a bit of ash smeared on his cheek, but Ailsa felt too lazy to say anything about it.

I'm sure I look a mess, too.

Angus sat up, suddenly rummaging about in his sack. Finally, he lifted a hand, producing something from the bottom of his bag.

"Oh. I forgot I had this. My cousin stuck it in as I was leaving." He removed the cloth with a flourish and held his hand out for Harris and Ailsa to take what was inside. She reached over and found a thick, sticky biscuit.

"It's a honey waffle." She took one and the package was passed to Harris. She sniffed at the treat and closed her eyes. The smell was sweet and floral. It brought back so many memories that she couldn't breathe for a minute.

"Ailsa, are you okay?" asked Angus.

She opened her eyes and nodded. "Yes. It's just... honey reminds me of my childhood. My mother used to keep bees and we would collect honey to sell." She sniffed again at the biscuit, then took a little bite. Her mouth filled with the smoky, saccharine flavour.

Harris moaned in appreciation as he munched into his own. "That must have been great as a kid. Endless sweets!"

Ailsa nodded in agreement. "It was. We used to put honey in everything. In the soap, in the candles, you could even put honey on cuts so they wouldn't become infected."

"Did you ever get stung?" Angus asked around a mouthful of biscuit.

She chuckled. "Yeah, a few times. It's okay after the

first one though. Visitors would come and watch my mother collect the honey. They thought it was amazing how she was immune to the stings, but really, she was just used to it."

"Your neighbours must have liked it; not every village has something like that."

She bit her lip. "Our neighbours wouldn't touch it, not with me around. They thought I would give them a disease." Ailsa looked down at the treat in her hands, suddenly feeling full. "My mother had to go to nearby towns without me. She'd be gone for days at a time, but she'd tell our neighbours that if they came near me, I'd curse them. We were on our own for the most part, my mother, brother and me."

Harris stopped his chewing. When she met his gaze, his eyes were unreadable. "You said you had no siblings," he accused.

Her jaw clenched and she dragged her eyes from his to stare to the flames.

They sat in silence for a moment, until Harris made a noise of impatience in the back of his throat. It almost sounded like a growl. The sound pulled her from her thoughts, though the memories of her past life—a *better* life—still swam before her eyes.

"His name was Cameron. When my mother died, a woman… took him, sent him away. I haven't seen him since." She heaved in a deep breath. "It was the worst time of my life."

"What happened to your mother? How did she die?" Angus asked in a gentle voice.

"Ever since I can remember, she'd had health problems, but they'd come in bouts. Muscle weaknesses, tiredness. Then, one winter day, it got much worse. She'd spent hours working outside in the freezing cold and then she couldn't get up the next day. She was coughing and had a fever, but worst of all, she couldn't control her muscles.

Then, one morning, she woke up and she couldn't see. Over the winter, her sight came and went. She developed slurred speech, she'd sometimes forget who I was. A few doctors came by and even a couple of the villagers. They made me go into the other room while Cam looked after her. Then she got *sicker*." Her voice had wobbled on the last word and she took a moment to steady herself before continuing.

"A cold. She got a *cold* from one of the villagers. It had been passing between them and one of them had been coughing when *they* came to visit. She was already so ill…" Her expression hardened. "Everyone said that I gave her the disease because I was a changeling. But really, they did it.

"I managed to stay in the house until the summer, but they eventually chased me out. I haven't been back since." She wiped a hand over her face. "I was fourteen."

"I'm so sorry." Angus placed a hand on her shoulder. Surprised by the contact, she flinched but he did not let go. "I know it's not the same, but I lost my mother too. I know how it feels, at least."

"Thanks." Ailsa pinched the bridge of her nose to try to dispel the stinging in her eyes and gave herself a mental shake. She had told herself she would never talk about this with anyone and here she was, spilling her guts. She hardly knew these men. Now they were staring at her with pity. Trying to deflect their attention, she shrugged and forced a half-smile.

"Anyway, I think we need cheering up. Harris, tell us a story?"

He scrutinised her for a beat before grinning mischievously. "Well, how about the time I was betrothed?" Harris leaned back again on one of the packs and crossed his arms over his chest.

Angus couldn't hide his surprise. "You were betrothed? To whom?"

"A very appealing lady selkie, I'll have you know. She had handsome whiskers."

"So why didn't you get married?" Ailsa asked.

He sighed, throwing his arms up in the air. "She said some fisherman trapped her on land. You see, if someone puts gold on a selkie, they have to stay with that person until it's taken off."

She fought to appear uninterested. "So, he kidnapped her?"

"Oh, I don't know. Looked like a wedding ring to me." Leaning forward, he fixed them with a teasing look, eyes twinkling. "And she seemed pretty content to leave it on."

Ailsa couldn't help but scoff. "She ran away from you?"

He brought a hand to his chest. "Ack, my heart has never been more wounded."

"More like your pride," she sniffed, fixing him with a wide-eyed stare. "Or did you love her?" *What if he did?* Ailsa wondered if she was being too mean, interrogating him like this.

"No, no. It was really for the best. It was a political engagement." He shrugged. "I had actually met her only once, when my mother dragged me to the fisherman's home to rescue her. There she was, all curled up with her husband's head on her lap and a dog at her side, looking like the cat that got the cream." He chuckled. "My mother was furious but, in the end she had to give in. The girl had the gold after all. When she took me home, my mother threatened to find another girl for me, but I think she's mostly forgotten about it now. Too many important female selkie things to think about, like saving the world or making friends with Eilanmòr's royal family." Having successfully distracted Ailsa, he turned his attention on the prince. "So, Angus, has your father ever tried to sell you off? Isn't that what second sons are for?"

Angus ducked his head and snorted. "Yeah. Once."

Ailsa raised a smile. "Who to?" *A noble woman? A princess?*

"My brother's wife."

Ailsa's mouth dropped open at the same time as Harris whistled, a look of disbelief etched on his face. Angus played with his beard as his cheeks reddened.

Sensing that he was going to have to elaborate, he groaned before continuing. "Right. At the time, our countries were on friendly terms, but my father wanted to make the alliance stronger. He sent my brother to Visenya to escort Princess Vashkha back to Eilanmòr. Duncan told me later that he knew he wanted to marry her as soon as she strode onto the boat, carrying her own luggage. When they returned and told my father, he just shrugged and said it didn't matter which one of us she marries, as long as it was done within the month."

Harris reached over and patted Angus's knee. "We have that in common then: jilted grooms. Were you mad at your brother?"

Angus ducked his head again. "Relieved actually. She wasn't exactly my type…"

"Was there someone else you liked?"

He regarded them from lowered brows, his blush deepening. "Yeah. It was at training camp. We looked after each other, worked together, fought together. Eventually I realised I liked him."

"Oh." *Him*. Ailsa did her best not to look at Harris. She didn't want Angus to feel like they were judging him if he caught them exchanging glances.

Angus continued, his cheeks now quite scarlet. "Of course, when training ended, we had to leave each other. I tried to convince my father to take him on as a guard, but he caught on pretty quickly to the reason behind my request."

"Was he okay with it?" asked Ailsa.

Angus sighed. "He told me that he didn't care about my... *preferences*... as long as I did my duty. I wasn't his heir, so I guess he thought it didn't really matter. When my brother's wife became pregnant, he eased up a bit more."

"But what about the man?" she asked, concerned.

"I don't know." His voice became wistful. "He's probably still living with his family. I think that when my brother becomes king, I'll try to find him. Who knows, he might have forgotten about me. He might have a wife of his own by now..."

Ailsa's heart broke a little at that. Not only did Angus have the disapproval of his family to contend with, he might have to deal with losing his first love because of it. She would never understand people who took something as pure as love and made it into something shameful.

Harris had been quiet throughout the exchange. Finally, the selkie leaned forward and flashed Angus a grin. "Well, plenty more fish in the sea, I would know after all." He winked. "When this is over, Angus, you and I can go out on the town. I'll find you a man." The prince sagged a little in relief and turned to Ailsa. "What about you?"

She shrugged. "Oh, I'll help too. I wouldn't leave you to Harris's bad taste."

"Thanks," Angus chuckled.

Harris stretched and yawned loudly, ending the conversation. "Well, I think I would like to go to sleep now, so no snoring, you two."

Ailsa harrumphed in disbelief, but Harris had already tucked himself into his bed roll. She sighed.

"I think I'll stay up for a bit, keep an eye out." *Someone needs to.*

Angus pulled out his own bedding. "Well, wake me up in a few hours and I'll take the next watch."

"Then Harris can take the last one," muttered Ailsa.

A disgruntled huff came from within Harris's blankets. "Fine, but someone else better be making breakfast."

Chapter 30

"Just admit it, Harris. You are lost."

They had been wandering around for a full day and a half. An imposing, rocky headland had blocked the road and Harris had decided it would be quicker to climb it rather than hike around it. Ailsa had spotted a carved sign stating that this particular path was called the 'Devil's Staircase' but that did not deter Harris. When they'd reached the top, their chests heaving, they had realised what lay beyond was a confusing maze of caverns and ridges. They had done their best to navigate through them but whenever they thought they were descending; the ground would start to slope up again. Now they had come to a flat stretch of earth with a scorch mark Ailsa was sure she had seen before.

"Oh, ye of little faith," Harris scoffed. "I have simply, momentarily, misplaced our whereabouts." Harris's voice was confident, but he was chewing his bottom lip savagely.

Ailsa gave him a withering glare. "You had better find them again."

He threw down his pack, grumbling. "You know, we

got in that boat for you—"

"What? There was a monster chasing us!" She dropped her bag beside his and poked him in the chest. Angus just slumped to the ground, content to let them bicker.

"Chasing *you*," Harris mouthed.

The look she gave him promised retribution. He stepped closer and grabbed her hand.

"I'm sorry." The warmth of his palm against hers was enough to dispel the anger that had been building up. "I *am* worried we're lost," he admitted. "We're tired and it doesn't help that we're going around in circles." He kissed the back of Ailsa's hand, making her stomach do a strange flip. "I'll go and scout ahead if you two want to make some lunch?"

She took in the surrounding boulders and foliage, suddenly aware of the sparse trees.

"Fine. Don't take too long, though."

He curled a finger under her chin, turning her face back towards him. His eyes were gentle as he lowered his voice. "It's gone, Ailsa. Don't worry." Louder, he said, "Angus, you'll protect our bodyguard here if any beasts come stumbling out of the trees?"

"Sure thing. Leave it to me," he answered from where he sat, although he lessened the sentiment by yawning.

"Urgh, I don't need protection," she growled, snatching her hand away. She stalked over to Angus but did not sit down. Harris grinned at her before trekking over the next hill. Ailsa stuck her tongue out at his retreating back, the action calming her nerves.

Stupid selkie, getting us lost, then insinuating that I—

Her thoughts were interrupted by a hand on her knee. Angus sighed. "You know, Ailsa, we were just teasing. Do you want to practise your sword fighting while we wait for Harris?"

She blew out a breath. "Yeah, fine."

They parried back and forth for a while; Angus shouting encouragements and Ailsa trying her hardest to whack him with her makeshift sword.

It was getting easier to drive him back. She lunged with her right leg as she brought her sword down. Angus dropped, barely missing the blow, and kicked at her legs. She jumped and twisted to the side, meeting his wooden sword with hers as he attacked her. Breathing hard, she thrust out with the branch and caught him on his left shoulder.

"I did it!" she shouted, triumphant.

"Well done," he chortled and stood up, leaning on his own stick. "You're improving rapidly." He dropped his practice weapon and rubbed his stomach. "I'm starving. Let's eat. I've still got some of those eggs you found earlier."

Ailsa followed him to the middle of the small clearing. *Something doesn't feel right.*

"You didn't… let me win… did you?"

"Of course not." He rummaged around in his pack and produced a flintstone. "You did great."

She crossed her arms as she watched him. "Hmm. It seems like you just wanted our fight to finish so you could have lunch."

He *tsked* at her and set about building a fire.

She clenched her teeth for a moment and then moved a few feet away. "I think I'll keep practising. Next time, I want to be sure I got you."

"Fine by me. Don't forget to keep your elbows bent. You were locking them a few times during our spar."

She went through the drills he'd taught her; swinging her stick to her left shoulder, across her body, to her right shoulder, then thrusting out, over and over. The smell of eggs wafted over from the campfire, but she refused to acknowledge it, instead concentrating on her technique.

All too soon, Angus called her to eat, so she finished the sequence and dropped the stick before flopping down on the ground in front of the fire.

"You're doing better. When we get back to Dunrigh, you should do some training with the castle guards." He used a knife to unstick one egg from the heated rock he'd been using as a frying pan and slid it onto a tin plate before handing it to her.

She pursed her lips. "They probably wouldn't want to train me. In case you haven't noticed, I'm only nineteen. Plus, people have a tendency to think I'm going to devour their souls or something." Ailsa poked at the yolk, making it burst. "Besides, I don't think I'll be staying long once we retrieve the Stone."

He shrugged and scooped up his own egg. "Well, you're welcome to. And they'll do anything I tell them."

She groaned, in part from the thought of that and partly from the delicious taste of the egg as it hit her tongue.

"That would be even worse. They'd hate me more if you forced them into it."

"Fine, *I'll* just have to continue training you. Then we'll have a huge tournament, and I'll place all my bets on you, and you'll make me lots of money."

She cocked an eyebrow at that. "Because no one else would bet on me?"

He sighed. "It's not my fault if people underestimate you. You should use it to your advantage."

She nodded slowly. He was right about that, but she wouldn't be sticking around long enough in Dunrigh for anyone to find out. When she raised her eyes again, he was looking at her expectantly. She smiled, close-lipped, unwilling to shoot down his offer just now.

"Only if you share your winnings with me."

"We have a deal." Angus grinned and she noticed that he had a few bits of egg in his beard. She almost told him but decided it would be a small punishment for how trying he could be.

She finished off her lunch before stretching and standing from her spot, cracking her back.

"I think I'm going to go wash. I must be smelling a bit by now."

"No more than me." Angus lifted an arm and sniffed audibly to make a point and her lips twitched. Going back to his lunch, he continued, "I'll let Harris know when he comes back to stay clear of the stream."

"Thanks."

Ailsa started to stride away from the camp before remembering the soap she'd packed. She found it at the bottom of her bag and lifted the scented bar to her nose. It had been a few days since she'd washed but it felt far longer. Thick black mud coated the underside of her nails and when she rubbed her skin, her hands came away with blobs of dried sweat.

The sound of flowing water led her away from their campfire and through a dense patch of coconut-scented yellow flowers. The twigs dragged across the bare skin of her arms, making her shudder.

She kept going, wanting to put as much distance between herself and Angus as possible. They had learned a great deal about each other last few nights, but she didn't feel like being caught with her clothes off, even when she knew he wouldn't be interested in looking. There was also the matter of Harris and his whereabouts.

Although, she thought, her cheeks heating, *I'm not*

sure whether I'd be all that upset about him finding me. She admonished herself immediately for the thought. *He is a massive flirt, don't get carried away.* But sometimes, the way he looked at her, or found an excuse to touch her... *Don't think about it.*

She stumbled into a shady glade, and the hair on her arms stood to attention. Something was watching her. She scanned the bushes, waiting. *There*, a movement. She tensed to run as her eyes tracked the moving shape. But instead of red eyes, she saw the ears and upper head of a horse.

It looked at her, clearly startled, before turning and disappearing through the shrubs. She called out to it and rushed after it, pushing branches to the side and doing her best to avoid twisted roots.

I wonder if it belongs to someone? If it's a wild horse, maybe I can catch it and we can use it to carry our packs, just until we get through the rest of this glen.

She broke free of the large thicket as she came to the bank of the river, but the horse was nowhere to be seen.

Idiot. She kicked herself for not being quicker as she scanned the trees around her, suddenly realising she was not alone.

Chapter 31

A man stood, knee deep in the river, plainly in the process of washing himself. He was shirtless and bent over, cupping water in his hands. He straightened when he saw her and shook his hands dry.

"Sorry," she mumbled, backing up. They had been walking for days now without seeing anyone, so she had assumed the horse was lost or wild. She scrabbled for something to say while he stared at her blankly. The man was taller than her, with russet hair and hooded, almost golden eyes. He was easily the most handsome man she had ever seen or would *ever* see again. This realisation heated her cheeks.

"I was just following a horse. It must be yours…" He kept staring at her and she trailed off, squirming under his gaze.

If the horse isn't his, I must be imagining things. When he didn't reply, she tried again.

"Who are you?" she asked, her heart hammering. In answer, he slowly raised a finger to his mouth.

Maybe he can't talk, she thought, *or maybe he's crazy. Run or fight?* She estimated the distance she would have to run to get back to Angus.

The man licked his lips and Ailsa's eyes were immediately entranced by the movement. He moved to the side of the stream, swinging his hips as he walked, and paused a few feet away.

"Listen, I don't know who you are but—" She couldn't finish her sentence; he pouted at her before bringing a finger to his mouth again.

Giving her a half-smile that made her feel warm inside, he leisurely moved his gaze from her eyes down to her chest, which seemed to snag his attention for a moment, before descending further. He eyed the axe at her waist and sauntered forwards with a smirk.

At the back of her mind, Ailsa knew she should be getting angry, but there was only white noise in her head. She gawked at the stranger as he approached.

Once he reached her, he raised a hand to cup her cheek and peered into her eyes. He still smiled fiendishly as he lazily brushed the side of her cheek with his thumb. His smell was deep and purely male: amber, pepper and musk.

Ailsa's breath hitched in her throat. The world felt like it was spinning and she swore she could hear drums beating.

Or is that my heart?

She felt there was something—or someone—she was forgetting but as he slowly moved his face in to whisper—

no *bite*—her ear, *Oh Gods*, she lost track of the thought. His other hand lingered at her hip as he ghosted his lips from her ear down her neck. She arched into him.

What am I doing? She couldn't bring herself to move away. She'd never been touched by anyone like this; although, in the past, she'd imagined what it would feel like.

His fingers brushed against a sliver of exposed skin on her stomach and her entire being became centred on that touch.

Why do I want more?

Slowly, he moved behind her, trailing his fingertips across her skin. He shifted her hair to the side, kissing her cheek before nipping her ear again. Her skin felt so sensitive and her heart hammered to the beat of phantom drums.

A scared little voice whispered in the back of her mind that something was wrong, but it was quickly squashed when he blew on the flesh he had been biting. Whoever this man was, she wanted to be his: body and soul.

Ailsa closed her eyes as he moved a hand up her torso from her stomach. She arched again, back bowing. The stranger chuckled softly under his breath.

He pulled her to him with a strong forearm, still rubbing circles around her torso.

Burning.

She was burning alive.

With another tug on her ear, he let her go and she felt the absence of him like a new wound.

Suddenly, he faced her again and offered his hand while backing away. Ailsa's heart leapt into her throat as she took it. She had wanted this so long ago with… *What was his name?* It didn't matter.

She looked at his lips as he languidly licked them again. She wanted to kiss him, wanted to taste him, touch him.

She felt like she was wading through syrup as she followed his pull. At the back of her mind, she registered that her feet were frigid, but she ignored it. He smirked at her as he moved back and pulled her with him. Then he winked before tugging her waist flush against him.

She felt the solid planes of his muscles against her whole body. He looked in her eyes before dipping his head, barely a breath from her lips. Far off, she thought heard her name being called, but she ignored it. It wasn't important right now.

He captured her bottom lip between his teeth. She closed her eyes in anticipation. His hands roving over her body, leaving chills in their wake. She was hot and freezing all at once. He licked her upper lip and she tilted her head back.

She felt a wave of cold surround her.

Why was she so cold?

Her lips clamped shut but he painfully gripped the

back of her head and kissed her, willing her to open. She grasped at his arms and struggled to get away. She couldn't breathe. She had to stop. His touch was ice. Ailsa felt panic bubbling in her stomach. She hit a bicep with her fist and pulled her face away from his, gasping for air. But there was none.

Only water.

She looked back at his face and saw the stranger leering back at her through the murky liquid. She kicked her legs out but found them tangled in weeds. Looking up, she realised that they were at least four feet below the surface of the river. She struggled to push herself up, but her arms tightly banded around her body. She looked at the man who was laughing, bubbles of air escaping his mouth.

She had no air. The need to swallow took over and immediately her lungs were searing. It was agony. Her eyes flew back to the surface and she desperately kicked and punched, but her limbs were leaden.

Slowly the world began to fade. *This is how I die.*

Faces of the people she would be leaving behind passed through her mind as she frantically fought to resist oblivion. There were so few: her brother, Iona, Angus, Harris.

Goodbye.

The surface rippled and a shadow passed in front of her face. Suddenly she was released and pulled up through the current. As strong hands held her under her arms, she caught a glimpse of the man, rage evident on his face, before he morphed into a strange, horse-like creature.

Miraculously, her face broke the surface of the water and she was hauled onto land. A fist thumped her back and she threw up the water. Her lungs were on fire as fresh air gushed in.

"Hold on, Ailsa," called a voice, but it was far away. She leaned her forehead into the ground and saw no more.

Chapter 32

In her mother's arms, she felt safe. The faint scent of honey lingered in the air and she breathed it in. Mama loved beekeeping and would often put the heather honey into her dishes. Honey in porridge was Ailsa's favourite. Whenever Ailsa was especially good, she would be allowed a piece of honeycomb to suck on.

Comforting hands stroked her back as she was lifted and carried towards the door. The hammering was getting louder, and she wished they would go away so she could sleep.

Her mother pulled open the door and a cool breeze flew in, tickling Ailsa's neck. Goosebumps sprouted on her arms, even under the wool blanket.

"I told you to go away," spat her mother. She held Ailsa a little tighter.

"Look, she has it with her," sneered one of the visitors. Ailsa craned her neck to look at them. There were four around the door but another fifteen stood a little farther away, beside the fence.

"Now, Heather," began one of the men beside the door, "we are just worried about the safety of yourself and the village. You know this is not natural."

"She is my daughter."

"No, she is not! Your daughter died, Heather." Ailsa listened intently and rubbed her mother's shoulder. She knew that they couldn't be talking about her—she wasn't dead. It was all very confusing, and she still felt sleepy. Her eyes wandered to the back of the room, where Cam had risen from his seat at the table, his body alert but his face unsure.

"What do you want me to do? She's a little girl. It's not her fault she was left with me."

"Please, just give her to us," said a woman on the other side of the door. Ailsa peered at her and realised she had her arms outstretched towards her. She clung to Mama tighter, feeling afraid. She didn't know what these people were talking about, but she sensed they wanted to take her somewhere.

Cameron had crept up to the door and now stood with a hand on their mother's arm. Ailsa looked down at him and he gave her a wee smile, pressing his thumb into her bare foot for comfort.

"What about your son, Heather?" the woman asked, her voice quiet. "Don't you care if she hurts him?"

Ailsa glanced at her brother again. Why did these people think she would hurt him? His lip curled as he watched the crowd. He stroked her foot and she felt his hand shake against her skin. They were frightening him.

They were the ones who might hurt him.

"For the boy's sake, please, let her go," the woman whispered.

Suddenly Mama pulled her away from her shoulder so she could look into Ailsa's face. Her mother appeared frightened but as they stared at each other, Ailsa saw a steely resolve enter her eyes. Finally, Mama hugged her tightly to her chest and tucked Ailsa's head into the crook of her neck.

She heard Mama's voice ring out sharp and commanding, "Leave. Now. You will not have my daughter."

She heard people departing hesitantly. Her mother went to close the door and Ailsa caught a glimpse of one older woman still standing on the porch.

"You too, mother," said Mama.

The old woman stood her ground and pointed at the child. "Kill her, Heather, before she kills you." Then she turned around and limped off, supported by a cane.

Mama slammed the door and carried her back towards her bed. Cameron followed behind silently, twisting his fingers through his blonde hair.

Instead of putting Ailsa in the little cot, her mother placed her under the covers of the larger bed and climbed in after her, along with Cam.

"Mama, who were those people?" Ailsa asked, glancing worriedly towards the door.

"Hush baby, they won't hurt you. Just some nosy neighbours."

"They wanted to take me away!"

"I won't let that happen," said Cameron fiercely from where he was tucked under their mother's arm. He was only two years older than her, but his boyish face was determined.

Tears filled her eyes. "They said I'm not your daughter."

"Of course you are, love. Look." Ailsa's mother lifted her chin until she was looking into her face. She smoothed Ailsa's brown curls away from her eyes. "See? Same hair as mine. Same eyes." Ailsa lifted a little hand to touch her mother's hair. Then she raised her eyes to Cameron's own, wide-eyed and blue like the ocean.

"My little family." Her mother squeezed them tightly to her.

"You don't have a mark," Ailsa murmured. She didn't like hers, it looked wrong on her face.

"You were blessed, baby, by the faeries. Some people don't understand, but I know that one day, this mark will help you." Her mother blew out the candle, plunging them into darkness. After a while, her brother's soft breathing filled the room and she slipped into a comfortable sleep.

Chapter 33

Ailsa awoke in an unfamiliar room and was immediately alert. She was warm and dry, and she knew that this hadn't been the case before she had lost consciousness. A grey glow shone through the curtains on the opposite wall. She attempted to lift her head up from the soft pillow when she felt a twinge of pain in her chest and throat and gave up.

"Ailsa!" cried a voice from the foot of her bed. Harris's ginger curls blocked out the daylight and she sighed, relieved. At least she wasn't alone.

He peered down at her, concern pinching his face. "How do you feel?"

"Like my lungs and throat have just been scrubbed by a dish sponge," she croaked. Speaking was painful, like sandpaper was rubbing against her throat, but she persevered. "What happened?"

"A kelpie."

She squinted at him wordlessly.

He kept his eyes glued to her face as he explained. "A kelpie is a water fae, usually found at river crossings. They lure their victims into the water before they drown and eat them." He sat down on the edge of the bed and took her wrist in his hand; she felt his warmth pleasantly envelop her.

"They can turn into any form most desirable to their victims," he continued, stroking her skin with his thumb. "Usually a horse for a weary traveller, an abandoned child for a passing mother..." He clicked his tongue. "Your neck has a huge bruise."

Her hand flew to her throat, where the skin felt as tender on the outside as the inside.

When Harris was satisfied she wasn't about to combust, he asked, "What did it appear as for you?"

Blood rose to her cheeks. She pulled her wrist away. *How embarrassing! Does this mean that what I most desire is... a man? Pathetic.*

Harris cut through her shame. "It's okay, Ailsa," he said, giving her a strange look. "When I saw the kelpie it appeared as... a beautiful maiden... with ash-brown hair and a sparkling dress." Instantly she felt better, though her cheeks felt hot still.

It must be normal then, she thought.

"What happened to Angus?" she rasped.

His expression hardened. "Once he'd gotten his fat head out of the clouds, he ran for help. He managed to buy a few donkeys from a farmer to carry you and our things." He stood and moved to look out the window. "Since then, he's been hiding from me."

She grimaced at his back. "Why?"

"Because I'm bloody mad at him for not watching out for you," he growled. "After what happened in the forest, I thought he'd be a bit warier—"

"Don't be mad at him, it's not his fault."

"You could have died, Ailsa!" He whirled on her, anger darkening his features. "Not fifty feet away from him."

She folded her arms over her chest in protest. She wanted him to know she was annoyed with him, but her words weren't quite conveying the right message. "You can't watch me all the time," she whispered. "Besides, aren't I supposed to be *your* guard?" *Stupid selkie.*

Harris reluctantly shrugged his shoulders. "I'm still mad. I'll let him suffer for a bit."

"You're just worried. I'm fine though, see?" She gesticulated.

His face softened a little and he bobbed his head.

"Get some sleep. We'll need you back at full strength soon so you can go back to saving our asses." He pushed off from the window ledge and patted her head. It made her feel like a dog. "Stay safe please," he whispered to her, before striding to the door. He gave her a parting wink then closed the door with surprising care.

She didn't understand why he was blaming Angus for something that clearly wasn't his fault. Angus didn't have any special powers. He was just as human as she was.

Maybe he would've been more to blame if he'd been fae *himself* and had sensed the kelpie…

With sudden clarity, she understood. Harris wasn't truly angry at Angus. He was angry with himself.

Her head was starting to swim so she closed her eyes again. The allure of sleep was too much to resist. As she drifted off, she drowsily wondered about Harris's own version of the kelpie and what it meant he wanted.

Chapter 34

It turned out that the two men had managed to drag her all the way to Kearnaharra, about half a day from the western coast. They'd brought her to a little inn on the edge of town, which was moderately empty and infinitely cosier than the one Iona, Harris and Ailsa had stayed in on the way to Dunrigh.

To her confusion, Harris did not return to check on her. Instead, when the sun was going down, Angus appeared at her doorway, holding a tray of food. The hair on his head and beard was matted, sticking up at odd angles, and his clothes were wrinkled, like he'd been attacked in his sleep. He avoided looking at her as he entered, and instead stared miserably at the meal.

"I'm so sorry," he began before Ailsa cut him off.

"It is not your fault!"

He shook his head wretchedly. "If I had been with you—"

"You probably would have been drowned, too. I'm sure we humans are more susceptible to fae trickery than, say, selkies." She stared pointedly at him and he deposited the tray on her lap, sitting beside her on the bed.

"If you had died, I never would have forgiven myself," he muttered, gaze still on the steaming stew. His eyes were starting to glisten with unshed tears.

Oh no, she thought, *I do not need a prince wallowing in self-pity. How long had he been like this? Since she'd lost consciousness?* She needed to snap him out of it.

"Well I didn't, so stop moping," she snapped, grabbing a fork and digging in. "If you really want to be useful, then you can get me a drink, Your Highness." When he gaped at her in disbelief, she flicked a pea at him and it hit the side of his nose.

He let out a stunned croak of laughter. "When you're better, you'll regret that. One drink coming up." He mussed her hair with a big hand before heading back through the door, looking a bit more cheerful.

Ailsa slept fitfully that night. She dreamt of visiting the King and finding not him, but a crippled and dying Angus instead. He reached towards her, flesh peeling from around his nails, and she backed away to the edges of the cramped glass room.

As she moved backwards, she thought she hit a wall, but it was Harris. He looked down at her sadly, before exiting through the only door and locking it. She could still hear his voice through the glass as she banged on it.

"I'm sorry, Ailsa, it's just better this way," he shouted and then he walked away from the chamber.

A moaning sound came from behind her and she whipped around to find that Angus was huddled over, wrapped in his blanket. She approached cautiously to help him but when he looked up, the blanket fell away to reveal her mother. She was covered in the same sores as the King.

Ailsa woke suddenly, gasping. It was still night, and the wind whistled eerily outside, accompanied by the tell-tale patter of rain. Just once, it would be nice if it were dry all day. She rubbed her face with a hand and rolled over to go back to sleep.

She almost screamed when she realised that there was someone in the chair beside her bed, until her brain registered Harris's rhythmic snoring. A gap in the rain clouds allowed the moon to illuminate his sprawling form. He had one leg on the dresser beside her and, in the dark, he looked ghostly white, grey freckles spattering his cheeks. The only colour, as always, was his vibrant red hair, chaotic even in slumber.

When did he come in? she wondered, pulling the blanket up a bit higher to dispel the cold. She studied him for a while as he twitched in his sleep, examining the curve of his mouth and the wings of his eyebrows that, even asleep, had a mocking arch.

She had been travelling with the selkie for a week now

and she still knew little about him. So far, she knew he had been engaged, he had a sister and... he'd saved her life. There had been other pieces of information she had gleaned as well. The way he talked about his family told her he wasn't well respected in their matriarchal society; he was more used to playing the fool than having any real responsibility. Something also told her that the success of this mission was much more important to him than he was letting on. Could it be that Harris, who seemed to fit in effortlessly, was trying to prove something as much as she was?

Then there were his feelings. She had almost thought he'd been jealous when she hung around Angus. Now, though, he was being a right idiot, blaming Angus for her brush with death. His emotions were all over the place. She could never quite work out who he wanted to be: the immature trickster, the concerned friend—or something more.

Ailsa studied him as he slept. His hair dangled over the side of his head, revealing even his ears were freckled. The sight reminded her of a story about an enchanted faerie, cursed to sleep for a thousand years.

In the dimness of the room, she couldn't tell whether he had his eyes opened or closed. With a jolt, she realised that she couldn't hear his light snoring anymore. She stared at him for a moment more, her heart banging against her chest. A scene played out before her eyes, where she called out into the night and he answered, rising from his place at the end of her bed to join her.

She shivered and closed her eyes, doing her best to go back to sleep.

Chapter 35

There was a loud, dull noise coming from the main room. When Ailsa went to investigate, she found a young man playing the bagpipes. She'd woken that morning to find Harris gone, but a mug of tea steaming was beside her bed. As she descended the stairs, she still felt the aches in her muscles from the attack. One particularly weathered step caused her to pitch forward, painfully twisting her shoulder as she gripped the bannister, dragging a groan from her lips.

The noise alerted her companions and she immediately had two sets of strong hands helping her down the remaining stairs.

"You two are worse than mother hens." She clicked her tongue at Angus and Harris. Her throat was still in agony and all her words came out as croaks. Harris had told her yesterday it made her voice sound husky, but she wasn't sure that was a good thing.

The youth with the bagpipes gave them a quick glance, before heading out the door. Ailsa was glad not to have an audience as they half carried her across the room towards an enormous fireplace.

"You're injured, lass. We need you fighting fit again as soon as possible."

Urgh. It wasn't as if she had died. Reining in her frustration took most of her will power.

Gritting her teeth, her voice somewhere between polite and a growl, she said, "Well in that case, I think you should get me some breakfast."

Angus dropped her arm. "I'll do it. You sit down and relax." He raced through a corridor to the left, from where the faint smell of baking bread was emanating.

Ailsa sighed and let Harris support her. "He's still trying to make it up to me."

He glowered, his hand gripping her arm a little tighter. "Good. He almost got you killed."

"No, he didn't," she objected. "Stop exaggerating. Are you planning to forgive him any time soon?"

His face remained stormy. "I'll keep him on his toes for a bit longer."

"Like kicking a puppy," she muttered, repeating his words from a few days prior.

He stuck his tongue out but helped her into an armchair beside the fire.

When Angus returned, he was somehow balancing three plates of bacon and eggs. A portly man followed behind him, carrying a copper pitcher.

"Ailsa, this is Gibby," Angus explained. "He owns the inn."

The man wore a flour-dusted apron and a friendly grin. "Very nice to see you up, dear. When these two walked in with you, you looked half-dead. Gave me and my girls quite a fright."

"Thank you for letting us stay," Ailsa mouthed around a bite of breakfast. It was the best thing she had tasted since leaving Dunrigh.

"Don't worry about it." He set the pitcher down and patted his belly. "Least I could do for a young lady in need… and royalty."

Angus's eyes bulged, cutting around the room. "I don't want everyone to know."

"How many people are there around here?" asked Harris, frowning.

"Well, there's my three daughters, plus the rest of the village." Gibby held a meaty fist over his heart. "Don't worry, lad, I won't go blabbing when people start to arrive."

"Arrive?" Ailsa asked, uneasiness creeping through her. "Do you have more guests?"

"No, but we're having a ceilidh tomorrow night. It's *Bealltainn*, the Beginning of Summer. We usually throw a party to celebrate."

"It's wonderful," exclaimed a lanky, blonde girl entering the room. She carried a tray of tankards made from cow horns.

The innkeeper looked apologetic, his face growing

red. "Sorry for the interruption. This is my youngest daughter, Flora."

"Oh good, you're up. Are you feeling better?" Flora bounced on her feet as she spoke, giving Ailsa the distinct impression of an over-excited rabbit. She even twitched her nose at the end of her sentences. Ailsa watched as the mugs rattled around on the tray without toppling over.

"Mostly," she replied, a twinge making her grimace as she settled back into the cushions of the chair. Aside from her throat, her body wasn't feeling that bad but there were still a few too many aches and pains.

Flora hopped forwards and deposited the tankards on the table beside the jug. "If you're recovered enough, you should come to the ceilidh."

"Oh, I—"

"There will be a band. And dancing. And a bonfire. And lots of young farmers." The girl filled the cups as she chattered, her words coming faster with excitement. Ailsa caught Harris's eye and suppressed a smirk.

Lifting a tankard, Ailsa said, "You probably don't want me there. I'm not usually popular at parties."

The girl tilted her head. "Because of your face?"

"Flora!" admonished her father, his cheeks going beetroot.

His daughter simply laughed. "Don't worry, we're not as easily scared up here. We have bigger monsters than changelings to worry about."

Gibby looked like he was about to faint. "Flora, these are paying guests. They are not paying to be insulted."

"No, it's okay." Ailsa didn't want to get the girl into trouble. Chances were that she would forget about inviting her soon enough. It wouldn't hurt to at least pretend she was going. "Thank you for inviting me, Flora. I'll think about it."

"Don't you think you should stay in bed? You need to rest," Harris murmured, crouching down beside her.

She turned to him, incredulous. "Since when are you turning down a party?"

He scowled, the freckles condensing on his nose as he wrinkled it. "*I'm* not turning it down, I'm telling you that you can't go."

"Oh? *Can't?*" she repeated, her face becoming thunderous.

He rocked back on his heels. "Shouldn't," he corrected quickly. "Probably."

She narrowed her eyes, before turning to a beaming Flora. She would show him.

"Count me in. Can I borrow a dress?"

The girl squealed and clasped Ailsa's hand. "We'll have so much fun! I'll dig out a few things and leave them in your room."

Harris folded his arms in front of him, regaining some of his nerve. "Well, if you're going to be dancing tomorrow night, you should rest."

"But I've slept for almost two days," she protested.

Angus sat down beside her and gave her a wink. "Better let him coddle you, Ailsa. Or he might not let you go."

It was all she could do not to leap out of the chair and strangle them both.

"I'd like to see him try."

"Please. I'll read to you," Harris said, in a wheedling voice.

True to his word, once they finished breakfast, a large book was placed in Ailsa's arms before she was lifted from the chair. One of the selkie's arms went under her knees, the other around her back, somehow trapping her arms in the blanket he'd thrown over her. It was just as well, Ailsa thought, because she would have gladly taken the opportunity to claw at his face. She glowered at his winning smile as he carried her back up the stairs.

Chapter 36

Ailsa spent the rest of the afternoon wrapped up in her cocoon of blankets, listening to Harris read ghost stories. She wasn't sure if this was the right reading material for nursing someone, but she was glad it wasn't a book of faerie tales. She'd had enough of those for a while.

"It is said that if you walk over his grave, his ghost will appear and challenge you to a fight. If you stand your ground and accept, he fades away without harming you. However, if you refuse, he will chase you through the glen and you'll never be seen again."

"I liked that one." She watched his fingers as he flicked through the next few pages. "Are ghosts real, Harris?" She felt stupid for asking but she wasn't taking anything for granted anymore. Plus, it was much easier to talk about ghosts when it was the middle of the day and she was cosy in front of a fire.

"Never met one, but I don't see why not," he answered absently while choosing the next story. "Everything else is real."

Ailsa hugged her blankets tighter. "Useful to know.

Next time, I'll make sure there are no spirits around before I take my clothes off."

"Those naughty ghosts!" he chuckled. "To be fair, I know that if I had to spend eternity walking this earth, I'd want to see women in states of undress—"

She gave him a shove with her foot. "You'd be a poltergeist. As annoying in death as you were in life."

"That's it," he said snootily as he opened the book to a new page. "I'll haunt you forever. Now hush, I'm going to read you a sad one."

He waited until she settled back then cleared his throat dramatically.

"A few hundred years ago, the Lord of Kelliedun's daughter—"

"Does she not have a name of her own?" Ailsa cut in.

"Fine," sighed Harris. "Her name was… Mildred. So, Mildred was walking through her garden one day when she met a young man. I suppose you want a name for him too? Well, he can be Hamish. Anyway, Mildred met Hamish, the gardener, tending to the tiny, ivory blooms that grew between the larger plants. Seeing her, he cut off one of the stems and gave it to her.

'Such a fragile flower,' she remarked.

The young man nodded. 'When winter has killed everything, this flower still grows; the only flower to grow. It gives us hope that spring will come again. Though it is small, it provides beauty where otherwise there is none.'

Touched by the man's story, she visited him again the next day, and the day after that. After a month of meetings, he produced the wee blossom again. 'My love is everlasting, like this flower. Will you marry me?' he asked."

Ailsa scoffed. "After a month?" She was having quite a lot of fun interrupting Harris's story, mainly because he was getting increasingly annoyed.

Serves him right.

Harris gave her a withering look. "It's romantic," he stated before continuing with the story. "The girl—*Mildred*—immediately said yes and went to tell her father. But he refused the marriage when he found out that the boy was a simple gardener. He told her the boy was just looking for money.

When Mildred looked for him again, her mother told her that Hamish had left. But really he'd been imprisoned in one of the towers. The girl knew that her love would never leave her, so she decided to wait for him all night in the garden. There was an early frost that evening, and when they found her in the morning, she had frozen to death, clutching a tiny, ivory flower.

When the boy learned what had happened, he jumped from the tower, hoping he would be reunited in death with his love.

Now the two haunt the castle, the girl's ghost in the gardens and the boy in the tower. It has since been abandoned. They say that if the garden is tended to again, and the white flowers bloom, their souls will finally be at peace."

She blinked at him as he put the book down. "That was depressing." Now she didn't feel like joking.

Harris placed the book on the small table beside them. "It's supposed to be a poignant love story, Ailsa."

"Do people like stuff like that?" she asked, wrinkling her nose.

"Yes, people are usually moved by tales of tragic romance."

"Why do people like to be sad? What's the point? Life is already sad enough."

He fixed her with an unreadable gaze, which had her shrinking back into her pillows. For a moment, he just stared at her. Finally, he wiped his hand over his face.

"Maybe it reminds them not to waste what they have." He met her eyes again. "To fight for love."

She squirmed under his watch, feeling uncomfortable. Whenever he looked at her like that, she felt out of her depth.

"Maybe I'd better get some sleep. I'm still not feeling great."

"Yeah, we need you fighting fit for the dance floor." He scoffed, leaning down then, over the bed. Her heart pounded. For a moment, she thought he was going to kiss her. Instead, he tucked a stray strand of hair behind her ear. "Sweet dreams. If you need anything, just let me know."

"Thanks," she whispered. He flashed a half-grin before leaving her alone in the candlelight.

Ailsa thought briefly about calling him back in. For *what*, she couldn't admit to herself. She picked up the discarded book and flipped it open at the picture from the last story.

Chapter 37

I like it." Ailsa twirled slowly in her borrowed dress, giving Flora a better view.

From over in the corner, Angus lifted his head from examining a fiddle the band had left and gave her a nod. "You look lovely."

"Pfft." Harris's lips curled. He lounged on a plump chair beside the main fireplace, one leg thrown over the arm, chewing on a chicken leg. A spread had been laid out for the guests and he'd promptly plundered it. He gnawed on the meat aggressively, throwing glares at everyone in the room. It seemed he hadn't slept well the night before, having to share a room with a sleep-talking band member. Harris had become even more sulky when Angus had mentioned to Ailsa that there would be plenty of young men at the ceilidh, suggesting they 'help each other.'

"What is your problem?" Ailsa stopped her spinning and stuck her hip out. His eyes followed the movement before rolling towards the ceiling.

"I just don't think the dress suits you."

"Why not? It's nice." The gown she'd borrowed was

crisp and white, with delicate sleeves that floated around her arms and fluttered when she spun. The skirt began just under her bust, fanning out in a tumble of lace, barely brushing the floor so she was free to dance. Flora had also given her a pair of slippers which were slightly too small.

"You look too—" His lip curled as he tried to find the right word. "Pure," he finally grumbled.

"What is that supposed to mean?" Her voice rose an octave and she bit the inside of her cheek in frustration. *Is he trying to pick a fight?*

"I don't know," he answered, glowering. "Maybe I'm too used to you looking murderous. I think I prefer that, actually."

"Enough," Angus chided. "Ailsa, you look wonderful. Tell him to go *boil his heid*." The prince beamed, happy with his impression of a common accent.

"Fine. I'm taking *this*," Harris stood, snatching another chicken leg, "And *this*." He grabbed his tankard of ale. "I'm going to get ready."

"Don't bother coming back till you've cheered up." Ailsa yelled after him as he stomped up the stairs.

"Men," chuckled Angus, "I'll never understand them."

When Harris knocked on her door later, she almost

slammed it in his face. But he had brought her a pastry by way of apology and her growling stomach convinced her otherwise.

"I think people are starting to arrive. Do you want to come downstairs?" he asked. He had borrowed a kilt from someone and it was a little too short, showing off his hairy knees. The freckles on them caught Ailsa's eyes for a moment until he bowed and she had to worry about his modesty.

"If there are guests, it means I get to start eating, yeah?"

Harris held out an arm for her, his eyes twinkling. She gave a sigh. It was too hard to be peeved with him for very long.

"Where's Angus?"

"He wasn't in his room, so probably at the party already?"

"Have you made up then?"

"Yes," he grumbled. "I'm sorry, Ailsa." He stopped her at the top of the stairs. His eyes baleful as he continued, "I just don't know what I would do if I lost you."

She shrugged, willing her cheeks not to colour. "I'm sure you would get over it. You got on fine before you knew me…"

His hand cupped the side of her face. "I didn't know what I was missing." He stared at her a moment, before breaking into a grin. "Right, let's go. Food. Beer. Dancing."

Arriving in the main hall, they found the band already warming up and the chatter from the guests filling the room up to the rafters. Drinks flowed and eyes were bright.

"There must be at least a hundred people."

She spied Angus in the corner and gave him a wave. He smiled and continued to chat with the musicians as he eyed a fiddle one of them was holding. The man laughed and clapped Angus on the back before handing it to him. He grinned exultantly and lifted it to show her that he was joining the band for a while. Ailsa's affection for the man bubbled into a laugh. It was nice to see him happy after all his worrying.

Ailsa angled her body so it was behind Harris's as they looked for a place to sit. With every step, she felt eyes upon her, but there were none of the usual uttered curses or shouts. Her ears burned in shyness as Harris led her through the throngs towards a table at the back. The people at the neighbouring the tables glanced at them nervously, but Harris didn't even seem to notice. Ailsa sipped her beer quietly and kept her hair curtained over her face.

After a while, he gave her a nudge. "Want to dance, oh fearsome one?" he asked, not taking his eyes off the crowd.

"Not right now," she said, expecting Harris to relax back into his chair. When Ailsa glanced back at him, she saw that he was becoming restless.

"Are you okay if I go up?" he said.

"Oh, yeah, I'll see you in a bit."

He grinned as he rose and, without looking back, strode to the dance floor. Immediately, he was surrounded by enthusiastic partners. He spun each woman eagerly, swinging energetically in time to the music.

Ailsa knocked back the rest of her pint.

Chapter 38

Within an hour, the floor was packed with bodies. There was little room to do the steps, so the dances had become a writhing, uncoordinated mass. The sun had properly set now, generating shadows in the corners which some people were already making use of. In response to the rising temperature indoors, the front door had been flung open to reveal a few stars peeking out in between wisps of cloud.

Flora perched on a tall stool beside the fireplace, with two older girls that could only have been her sisters. They waved when they saw Ailsa looking, she nodded back and sank further into her chair.

Harris danced with almost every woman in the building. He was certainly popular. As she watched his progress across the dancefloor, Ailsa had been stuffing her face full of sweet cakes. A couple times, he'd caught her eye and attempted to excuse himself from the throng, only to find another young lady begging him for a turn.

And, of course, he couldn't *refuse*. Ailsa swigged her drink bitterly.

She should never have agreed to come to the ceilidh.

Shouldn't they be back on the road already? The sooner that they reached got the Stone, the sooner she could be back home. How could Harris be enjoying himself at a time like this, when Eilanmòr was counting on them? She longed to be moving or doing something useful.

The musicians paused for a short break, shouting to the crowd to bring them food and ale. Angus appeared in front of her, breathing hard.

"How are you doing?"

"I'm having a *fantastic* time."

He frowned at the sarcasm in her voice and at the empty plates piled beside her chair.

"Have you been sitting here alone all night? Where's Harris?"

"Off having fun."

He pulled up a chair beside her. They sat in silence for a while, watching the crowd mingle and laugh. Finally, Ailsa mumbled something incomprehensible under her breath.

"What was that?" Angus asked. She knew it was a bid to get her to talk. *How does he know me so well after a week?*

She huffed and spoke a little louder. "I said, I don't understand that man."

Angus nodded. "He is a mystery."

"One minute, he's watching over me in my sleep and the next... it's like, if there's another woman in the room he forgets all about me."

"Not to mention," said Angus. "He gets jealous every time I speak to you, although I think after our heart-to-heart the other day, he's less concerned." They watched as Harris picked up one of the girls he was speaking to, showing how strong he was. The females around him tittered and the one in his arms went bright red.

Ailsa sighed. "I just wish he would make up his mind. Are we friends? Does he just like to flirt with me?"

Angus leaned closer to her. "The question is: what do you want?"

She threw her hands up. "I don't know. To be honest, if he wasn't making me feel like he liked me, I don't know if I would have thought about it." She studied Harris's profile for a moment, taking in his straight nose and mischievous smile. "I guess I do think he's attractive."

Angus grabbed her hand. "Harris is my friend and I like him a lot. He's the sort of person you could have a lot of fun with, who'll always have your back and try to do what's right. I just think he's easily distracted. Maybe for the right girl, he'd stop fooling around but I'd say, guard your heart. You're special, Ailsa, and if a man can't see that, he doesn't deserve you."

She dipped her head and closed her eyes. "Thanks, Angus. You know, I think this is what still having a brother would be like." He wrapped an arm around her shoulders and gave her a hug. They sat like that for a while before he finally pulled away.

"Look after yourself," he murmured. "The band are looking for me and *someone* is coming to speak to you."

She straightened in her chair and watched as Angus strode towards the stage again, meeting Harris in the middle of the room. The two men patted each other on the shoulders as they passed. Angus took up his fiddle and joined in the next song. Harris weaved his way towards her.

He sat down beside her, still scanning the dancers as they cheered.

"Having fun?" asked Ailsa sullenly. With a pang, she missed Iona and her large high heels. At least she hadn't abandoned her at the last party they'd attended.

He fixed her with a grin. "You need to learn to relax, Ailsa." He was sweating from his lively dancing, his white shirt plastered to his body.

"I brought you a drink," he said, laughing like it was a secret joke. She snatched the glass from him and downed the liquid in one go, coughing as the wine hit the back of her throat. Harris let out a gasping laugh. Ailsa handed the glass back to him, avoiding his gaze. His face sidled into her line of sight as he tried to make her look at him.

"Dance with me?" he asked with a pout.

Still playing one of his games.

"I'd rather not," she grunted. "In fact, I don't even know if I can in this dress. It looks pretty but it's a bit tight. And hot." She pulled at the long flowing fabric angrily.

He knelt in front of her, brushing the skirt of the dress with a finger. "You look amazing."

"But you said earlier—"

"I know, and I'm sorry. You're... stunning," he said, most of his flippant tone gone. Ailsa couldn't help the blush that crept up her cheeks.

Stupid idiot, she thought. *I should know better than to be tricked by his words like the other girls in this room.*

She harrumphed, doing her best to appear vexed. "I am not dancing; there are too many people. Besides," she crossed her arms, "Your friends will be back soon to coo over you."

Harris frowned at her, but the wicked glint was back in his eyes. Before she could protest, he had swept her up over his shoulder.

"Harris!" she screeched. "This is no way to treat a lady."

"Just as well you aren't one, then," he snarked. "Come on, I have a solution to our problems." He carried her out of the building as she half-heartedly punched his back. They emerged into the cool night air and, for once, it was not raining.

Ailsa stopped struggling as he led her further away from the building. One of his hands brushed her bare ankle and she gasped. He seemed to pause in his steps, before striding over to a patch of grass. Harris slid her out of his arms, her body gliding against his until she reached the ground. He held her waist with one hand and offered the other to her.

"Dance with me?" he repeated, eyes twinkling.

She considered him for a moment, her heart beating to the rhythm of the music. It *did* feel nice to be outside and she *had* been watching him dance for so long now that she might as well try it. Perhaps it was the wine, but she was starting to feel giddy and forgot all her aches and pains. Finally, in a show of bravado, she rolled her eyes and slipped her hand into his own.

When she kicked her shoes off to the side, his face split into a beaming smile.

Without warning, he began spinning her to the reel. Her limbs flailed clumsily at first as she tried to follow his lead. His steps were light as he swept her round in circles and she caught his familiar scent of sea salt and citrus.

He leaned down to whisper in her ear. "Just enjoy yourself."

The grass between her toes tickled delightfully, the sensation strange but welcome. Their bodies moved to the beat of the drums and she let Harris's hands and instinct guide her. She grinned back at him as they turned and skipped.

He picked up the pace until the world around her

turned to stars and all she could focus on was his face.

Round and round and round.

Harris's coppery curls danced across his forehead in the breeze and she watched as one strand fell over his eyes which crinkled in amusement.

Still they twirled.

Underneath her skin, she was alive—electric. She felt bewitched, although she was sure that Harris wasn't using magic.

The band played on and Ailsa noticed between spins that the party had also moved outside. The musicians watched through a window, also thrown open to the cool summer night. Angus gave her a wink when she spotted them, his hands deftly flying the bow over the strings of the fiddle. A few couples joined them in spinning, but most were content to watch and clap in time as the dancers twisted and swung each other around.

Harris nodded to the band and the tempo grew inexplicably faster. Now they were spinning and weaving between the crowd. Some of the other dancers were lifting their partners into the air and Harris gave Ailsa a mischievous grin before hoisting her above his head too. When he set her back down, her legs wobbled in a thrilling way and her head felt full of fluttering insects.

Her heart drummed wildly against her ribs as they flitted back and forth. Other revellers filled the air with tremendous whoops and she couldn't help but breathlessly join in.

The melody changed and the male dancers in the room dropped to their knees while the girls lifted their skirts and spun about them.

Harris held his hands out to her as she danced in front of him, kicking her legs out. He gazed up at her admiringly. "Dance for me, Ailsa."

Just as she pulled him to his feet, so that he could spin her again, the music stopped. Everyone let out a shout and then stood breathing in deep gulps of night air.

"I... don't think... I'll ever recover... from that dance!" laughed Ailsa, bent over, panting.

"I told you that you'd have fun," snickered Harris. He held his hand out to her. "Let's go and sit down!" He led her away from the celebration and flopped down onto the grass. On the other side of the clearing, people had started to pile sticks for a bonfire. The smell of pine drifted from them as they handled the wood.

Harris and Ailsa sat side by side, breathing heavily. They lay back, viewing the stars through the branches of the trees. In that moment, Ailsa felt like she could fall into them; like she could jump and fly between them, skirting galaxies and twirling around planets, like she had in the dance. She stretched her arms above her head and pointed her toes, grinning at the night sky.

"Enjoying yourself?" asked Harris. He nudged her side playfully, then rolled over, resting his head on his hand.

"I suppose I am now." She shrugged. "I've never danced like that. I've sneaked into parties before, but I always kept to the back, well away from anyone who could recognise me."

"That's a shame." Harris ran his other hand through his hair. "You'd love the parties in Struanmuir. Everyone comes along and when you dance, it's without effort. The current swirls around you in time with the music and carries your body." He looked over dreamily to the side. "You simply let yourself drift."

"It sounds wonderful, but I'm afraid I would drown," Ailsa said, nudging his foot with hers.

"I would look after you. I wouldn't let you drown. As long as you held my hand, you wouldn't die." At this, his hand closed around her own tentatively. "You could breathe the water as we do." He rubbed his thumb over hers in slow strokes.

Ailsa couldn't prevent the blush that crept into her cheeks. "What happens when I have to let go?"

"Don't," he replied simply.

When she risked a glance at Harris, she saw that his eyes were examining her face. She watched as his gaze slid from her hair, down to her eyes, her cheeks and finally to her mouth.

"Anyway, you didn't look like you wanted to let me go earlier," he smirked in his usual manner. Ailsa's head still felt like it was floating as she stared back at him.

Before she could regret it, she rolled on to her side and pecked him quickly on the cheek. She leapt up to return to the revelry, leaving an incredulous Harris behind on the grass.

Chapter 39

Upon returning to the party, everyone was taking a break from dancing to listen to a group of men singing. The innkeeper's daughters waived Ailsa over to where they sat around the fire, sharing large bottle of whisky. She sank down beside them gratefully, some of her earlier tension dissipating as she found herself amongst people she recognised. After an hour, the bottle had been drained of half its contents. Ailsa had been sneaking only tiny sips, but she still felt lightheaded. The sisters asked very little of Ailsa, instead chattering about their own lives and dreams. She was glad for it and felt surprisingly relaxed.

The eldest's name was Lorna and she had a man in the King's army. Kirsty, the second oldest, was a painter and, when not helping around the inn, made a little money selling wee pictures painted on rocks she found nearby. Flora wanted to be a nurse. She was only sixteen, but she would soon be travelling to Dunrigh for her apprenticeship.

Every now and then, she scanned the room for Harris. The selkie was entertaining a group of young ladies in the corner. He caught her looking and gave her a wink and a huge toothy grin. Her bad mood from earlier had completely evaporated as she waved her hand in his direction, then continued to drink with her new friends. *Perhaps*, she thought, *I should cut back on the drinking.*

"Who wants another dram?" shouted Gibby. "I've opened some of my twenty-year-old malt!"

Oh well, can't say I didn't think about being sensible, she thought as she lifted a tumbler to her lips.

A couple of hours later, Ailsa had her head on Lorna's lap as the girls mumbled incomprehensibly along to a song.

"I believe you are drunk, young lady," Angus chastised in a mock fatherly voice. Harris had joined him and was leaning on Angus's shoulder for support.

She stuck her tongue out at him. "I'm not drunk, you are."

Both men laughed. Harris seemed as inebriated as she was. He kept trying to pick up other people's drinks before Angus snatched them away.

"Honestly, you two," chided the prince. "It's as if this is your first party."

"Second," she slurred, "And I like this a lot better than your stinky castle."

"Ouch," Angus replied in exaggerated offence.

Harris wobbled on his feet but reached for her hand. "Right you, time for bed."

"Bed, eh?" Ailsa wiggled her eyebrows at him, giggling. He threw his head back and belly-laughed before picking her up. She shrieked in protest.

"Well don't come crying to me when someone gets hurt," mumbled Angus. They both ignored him.

"Remind me to get you drunk more in future." Harris smiled down at her, carrying her through the thinning crowd.

"You didn't get me drunk; I did that all by myself."

"I started the process, so I'm taking credit."

Harris stumbled up the stairs, kicked open the door to her room and threw her down on the bed. Her bounce made the springs in the bed creak loudly. They both tried and failed to keep their laughter down. Between fits of giggles, she managed to scoot over, and he laid down on the bed beside her. Their sniggering quieted after a while and they stretched out in companionable silence.

The bonfires shone through the window, casting a flickering orange-gold glow on the opposite wall. Ailsa stretched up her hands to catch the light, creating a shadow. Her arms danced back and forth, making shapes as they listened to the fire crackle and the faint laughter from lingering partygoers.

"Did you have a good night?" Harris asked quietly after a while, turning his body to face her and propping his head up with a hand.

She nodded. "I loved the dancing." The room shifted before her eyes. He reached over and stroked the arm she still had on the bed.

"Me, too. I think when we get back to Dunrigh, we should be thrown a party every night as saviours of the realm."

"And I would like a new dress for each party."

He watched as she brushed a hand down the lace of her gown.

"How decadent."

"Maybe. Not as decadent as the desserts they will serve." She groaned and smacked her lips together to make him laugh but, for some reason, he remained quiet. She eyed him in confusion and found him staring at her mouth.

He cleared his throat but didn't remove his eyes.

"Or the imported wine," he continued. "You know, once they hear about the bewitching Heroine of Eilanmòr, there will be queues of suitors outside the castle gates—"

Ailsa gave a snort. "Not likely."

He grinned. "It's true. You'll never want for a dance partner again."

She was starting to feel hot and light-headed. "I suppose I'll have to save a dance for you."

"You'd better." Harris said, leaning in. "Or *maybe*, I

want all of your dances."

He pressed a kiss to her shoulder, and she felt a flush sweep over her body like a tidal wave.

"You'd break the hearts of all the other girls wanting to dance with you," she whispered, thinking about the women downstairs that had been all over him.

"I'm sure they'll get over it." His lips travelled up, until he pressed a kiss into the hollow of her throat. She moaned when he found the sensitive place below her jaw.

"Ailsa," Harris rasped, "I want—"

Her stomach gave a lurch.

"Oh no. Harris—Stop!"

His eyes widened and he pulled back. "Sorry Ailsa, I was just—"

"It's not that. I'm going to throw up." And with that, she ran from the room, barely making it to the bucket where she lost most of her dinner, and her dignity along with it.

Chapter 40

The world was spinning so fast she wasn't sure if she could hold on. Somewhere nearby, she heard a droning noise that had likely woken her up. Ailsa tried to pick a spot on the ceiling to focus on, but she saw double of every knot and swirl in the wood.

"Well, well, well." A voice reverberated around the room. She turned her head slightly to take in Angus's silhouette in the darkened doorway.

"It seems you two had fun last night," he chuckled, gesturing to the lump on the mattress beside her. She whipped her head around and instantly regretted it twice over. Once, for the sickening pounding in her temples, and again for the shock of finding Harris laid out beside her, snoring into a pillow. From what she could see of his shoulders and upper arms, he was naked from *at least* the waist up. She cautiously turned her face back towards the ceiling, trying not to move any other body part.

"Seems like I'm going to have to wake up sleeping beauty over here."

"Angus," she croaked, "Tell me now and keep it short.

241

Why am I in bed with Harris?"

"I don't know, the last I saw, you were being carried up here by Harris. Shall we find out?" He rocked back on his heels before launching himself at the bed. "HARRIS! WAKE UP! WAKE UP, WAKE UP, WAKE UP!"

The selkie jerked up, banging his head on a bedpost. "What the hell, Angus!"

The covers had fallen off him in the tumult and Ailsa was glad to see Harris was wearing trousers.

Angus stopped jumping and fixed an innocent, boyish smile to his face. "I just thought you would want to know that it's time to wake up."

Harris growled and flung himself at the other boy, but Angus bounced out of the way. Harris grabbed one of Angus's ankles and tugged, causing him to tumble onto the bed.

Ailsa's head gave a nasty twinge. "When I can move again, I'm going to kill the both of you."

Angus snickered. "Sorry."

"Urgh, I feel like crap," groaned Harris, rubbing his head as he lay back down. "I think I may actually be dead."

Angus *tsked*. "Look, I brought you both water." He pushed two half full glasses into their hands, which they both attempted to sip from without lifting their heads too high.

"This is all your fault," moaned Ailsa to Harris,

rubbing her temples.

"What a couple of babies." Angus grinned and bit into an apple. "Wow, it really reeks of alcohol in here."

If she hadn't felt like the room was spinning, she would have lobbed her boot at him. "How are you okay?"

He smiled, mouth full of fruit. "I was sensible."

"Well, at least I feel better than he looks." She was about to nod her head at Harris but thought better of it. "Though, I still don't remember how I got to bed…"

Harris glanced at her. "I carried you up here."

"Nope, complete blank."

His mouth twisted and he was silent for a moment.

Did I say something to him last night? She'd been angry with him at the beginning of the party after he had abandoned her. *Maybe I gave him an earful when he tried to put me to bed?*

"It's your own fault you had to look after me. If I'd had my own way, I would have sat in the corner and sulked all night."

"Urgh, this is what I get for showing you to have a good time," he moaned. The selkie rolled himself out of bed and pressed his forehead to the cold floor.

"I didn't make you drag me into it. And I didn't *make* you drink that much, either."

"You did. Poured it down my throat," he sighed.

"Oh? And I suppose I made you lift your kilt to all those girls when they asked you what was beneath it?"

"Oh, no…"

"Not that I saw anything, but there was an awful lot of giggling that erupted from that corner of the room. What do you think, Angus? I reckon they weren't impressed."

Harris sniffed. Then, without speaking, he poured his glass of water on his head. Immediately, his skin shifted and there was a seal on the floor instead of the redhead.

"I think Harris is in a huff with you," laughed Angus. The seal just snorted and rolled onto his back.

Ailsa stuck her tongue out at Harris's seal form and leaned down to poke him in the side. "Harris, I can see your chubby little belly ripple."

The seal flapped a flipper in her direction as if to say, 'Piss off.'

She poked him again, and giggled. "Blubber-butt." He snapped his pointed teeth in her direction.

Angus fought to suppress a chuckle. "Ailsa, don't poke Harris. Harris, don't sulk."

She flopped back onto her pillow. "I don't think I'll be able to travel today."

"It's fine, you're still recovering anyway." He picked up Harris's empty glass. "You'll feel better if you get up though. Fresh air will do you both some good."

After some more squabbling and a couple of bacon sandwiches, Angus managed to get Harris and Ailsa up and out of the inn. The sun hid behind wispy clouds, for which Ailsa and her head were grateful. Angus led them to the top of a small hillock, where they reclined, enjoying the light breeze. The ground was mercifully dry and the springy grass cushioned their bodies as they gazed up at the clouds, concocting stories around them.

"That one looks like a rabbit running away from a fox." Harris pointed up at a puff to the left. Ailsa followed his finger, only seeing a blob.

Angus pointed to another. "That one looks like a shoe."

Ailsa made a noncommittal noise. "Okay, I've got one," she said flatly, "That one looks like… a cloud."

Harris clucked his tongue. "No imagination."

She nudged him in the side and stretched. "Go on then, tell me a story."

"Okay. See that cloud up there? It's actually a brave young man come to save a princess in the tower over there."

Ailsa sighed. "Can't it be a brave young woman?"

He shrugged. "Sure. So, she gets to the tower, but it turns out a troll is guarding it."

Angus waved an arm in the air. "The troll asks her to play a game of chess."

Harris nodded. "Yes, and she wins."

Angus laughed. "She has so much fun with the troll that they become best friends and decide to kick the princess out of the tower so they can live there together."

Ailsa chuckled and inched her way over towards the

prince, so that she could rest her head on his stomach. He looked at her with surprise but smiled and rubbed her temples. It felt so good that she quietly moaned. Harris cleared his throat, but she was enjoying herself too much to be embarrassed.

She decided to continue the story. "The brave young girl does the hunting while the troll carves garden gnomes."

Harris was watching the path of Angus's fingers now, as he slowly massaged her head. Harris nudged her foot with his and smirked, but it did not reach his eyes.

"But nearby villagers hear about the troll and come to the tower to kill her."

Ailsa sat up from her position on Angus's stomach and grabbed a stick nearby. "The brave young girl fights them." She poked him lightly on the chest and threw another stick towards him, eliciting a snicker. Angus rose so that he was crouched with the stick held out like a sword.

"'Don't you dare touch her,' said the girl." Ailsa thrust her twig towards him. "'She makes great pancakes!'"

"No, we must kill the foul beast," Angus bellowed, smacking her quickly on her rump with his own branch. She cried out and he grinned. "Take that." They turned to find Harris gawking at them. The prince grabbed her stick and thrust it under his armpit.

"Oh, no. I am wounded." Angus collapsed to the

ground, tongue lolling out.

Ailsa folded her arms and came to stand over him. "That's what you get for trying to kill innocent trolls." She flopped back down beside Harris who was frowning slightly. Angus pulled himself up from the ground, leaning on his elbows.

Harris raised an eyebrow. "Feeling better?"

"Oh, yes. Best cure for a headache is killing pompous knights."

Angus gave them both a long look, then sprang up quickly. "I'm going to go and get us some food and water," he exclaimed cheerily and ran back down the hill to the inn.

They were silent for a while, watching the clouds float by. Ailsa pulled her knees to her chest and glanced sideways at Harris. He had his face screwed up and turned towards the sky, yet his eyes seemed glazed.

"Seems like you and Angus are getting friendly," he said.

Ailsa shrugged and wound her arms tighter around herself. "I guess he finally wore me down."

Harris scratched his chin, where there was some short stubble growing. "Well I'm glad, I suppose, though a bit jealous." She looked at him quizzically and he shrugged. "Of the head rub he gave you." He folded his arms across his chest and stuck his bottom lip out. "Maybe I should be crabby and get my head rubbed."

She shoved his shoulder and smiled. "You seem pretty crabby right now. Would you like me to?"

His mouth popped open, then he narrowed his eyes, unsure whether she was joking. She met his stare and he nodded slowly. "Sure."

Ailsa scooted round so that she could pull his head onto her lap. He watched her warily for a while, until her gentle stroking made him close his eyes and sigh.

She swirled her fingers over his brow and thought about how much had changed. A week ago, she had been alone, with no one in the world. She'd been happy about it too. But now, she actually cared about Harris and Angus. Angus was naive and far too upbeat sometimes, but he was also kind and selfless. At some point, she'd stopped being annoyed by his happiness and had started to look forward to it.

Harris, on the other hand, was becoming more of a mystery the longer she knew him. She had thought he was frivolous and conceited, but then he'd stood up for her in front of the prince's men. He had rescued her from the kelpie and had been furious at Angus on her behalf, even though it hadn't been his fault. He had read her stories and made her tea. And last night's dancing… Although, he *had* abandoned her for the first part of the night, dancing with every other girl in the room.

She simply could not work out what he wanted. Sometimes she thought Harris liked her. Other times she wondered if it was just because she was convenient. A fuzzy memory of his lips being awfully close to hers as he put her to bed came unbidden to her mind.

Continuing to massage his temples, she cleared her throat. Since they were alone, maybe she could get some answers.

"Harris, I think we need to talk about last night."

She waited with bated breath for his response. Would he tell her he liked her? Or would he make a joke about things as he always did?

The silence stretched on, so she peered worriedly into his face. "I mean, when you brought me to bed, did we—"

A loud inhale stopped her sentence in its tracks. After a beat, he snored deeply, oblivious to the world.

She sighed and eased back onto the grass, careful not to jostle him, folding her arms beneath her head.

Probably for the best anyway, she thought. She still wasn't sure how she felt about *this*. She wanted answers, but when all was said and done, he'd be off gallivanting around Dunrigh while she went back to her beach. She would be better off not bringing it up again.

Why do I feel so disappointed?

Harris and Ailsa had snoozed in the grass for most of

the afternoon. Angus had brought them food, but upon finding them asleep, had thought better of waking them. Now they were starving, so Gibby and his daughters made them a feast to eat while they lounged in squishy brown chairs. Most of the food was fried.

Lorna brought out the last dish, a cheesy dip that smelled heavenly, and they tucked in, relaxing before the fire.

"So, will you be spending more time with us?"

Angus snagged a piece of chicken. "We'd better set off in the morning. That is, if you're feeling better Ailsa?"

She groaned around a mouthful of potato. "Aside from the pounding head, yes."

"How far do you have to go?" asked Flora, while she nibbled daintily on a piece of bread.

"We're heading to the Isle of Faodail," Harris answered.

Gibby paled. "Why would you be wanting to go there?"

"It's important," said Angus, leaning forward to grab another spoonful of potato.

The older man let out a long whistle. "It had better be. Few go to that island and make it back alive. Those who have vow never to return."

Harris stretched his legs out. "I've been before. It was fine."

The innkeeper squared his jaw. "How long ago?"

He shrugged. "Twenty years?"

Lorna tossed her hair impatiently over her shoulder. "The disappearances have been more recent than that." All three girls had stopped eating and were now staring at them with the same concerned look as their father. Ailsa wondered whether they were being superstitious or had a reason to be so worried. In her experience, superstitions were often borne from genuine fears. "They say there are monsters on that island," Lorna finished in a whisper.

"Some people would consider present company to be monsters," Harris responded darkly.

Kirsty raised her chin. "I would have thought that you would want to be more careful since Ailsa's narrow escape."

Harris's only reply was a crunch as he took a huge bite of pastry. The sound of his chewing echoed around the silent room.

Gibby finally shrugged and grabbed a plate of haggis. "Well, I suppose you're going to go anyway. How do you plan to get there?"

"Swim?" Harris suggested. Ailsa sniffed in answer. No way was she swimming across the sea.

The old man clicked his tongue. "My cousin lives on the coast, tell him I sent you and he'll let you borrow his boat. It's a rowing boat but it'll get you there." Angus smiled. "Thanks, Gibby."

His face grew serious again. "Just look after each

other, will you?"

Harris slid a hand to Ailsa's knee and squeezed it. "We will."

Chapter 41

After a quick farewell to Gibby, Lorna, Flora and Kirsty the next day, they set off again. Ailsa's throat had healed and there were barely traces of the bruises that had decorated her skin. Still, she rubbed the skin as they walked as if to erase the mark quicker.

The sun shone brightly and, for the first time in weeks, Ailsa did not feel the prickle of an impending downpour on her scalp. Eilanmòr was a completely different place in the sunshine. Clear skies turned ponds and lochs a glorious sapphire and they could see squares of farmland etched like patchwork on the earth. Sparkling faintly on the horizon, like shards of pale green glass, was the ocean. The trio could even see a row of snow-capped peaks to the north-east, beyond the sea.

"Snow in summer?" Ailsa studied the distant mountains curiously.

"That's a different country. Monadh," said Harris absently, "it has a… strange climate."

"It used to be part of Eilanmòr," Angus's gaze was also trained on the mountains, "until the sliver of land that connected us cracked and fell into the sea. Since then, they've had unusual weather."

Harris let out a bark of laughter. "More like supernatural!"

Ailsa raised an eyebrow to say: *Well you'd better continue or I'll hit you.* He sighed and rolled his eyes, eliciting a low growl of warning from Ailsa.

Stupid know-it-all selkie.

"The south of the island is mostly flat rainforest, humid and hot. But when you reach the foothills of the mountains, the temperature plummets and the forest… stops. I've only gone as far as the edge, but you can see that nothing grows there anymore. It's as if life just ends. No one really knows much about the interior mountain range. I've only ever swam around it or seen it from afar."

Angus readjusted his pack, glancing again at the jagged peaks. "Some of our people lived there, before the islands split and tried to venture north. But the weather changed suddenly and none returned; their families decided to move back to Eilanmòr. The people who live there now actually came from a country in the far east. They don't venture further than the forest boundary."

She could almost see it, two different worlds clashing together. She imagined stepping from jungle into a winter wonderland and shivered. "What made it that way?"

"The original inhabitants seemed to think it was the work of the Gods," replied Angus.

Harris's face shadowed. "I've heard different."

"Nicnevan?" Ailsa asked.

"Witches."

"Witches?" she scoffed. "Those are real, too?"

"Well…" His mouth twisted and he glanced at her sideways. "I don't think I've ever actually seen one."

Angus gave Harris a friendly shove. "It's just superstition, Ailsa."

"Like selkies?" Harris questioned with a bite of sarcasm.

They had no response to that.

The sun beat down upon their backs, warm enough to coax them out of their wools and leathers. The sweet smell of late summer flowers wafted on the breeze as they walked. At one point, Harris bent to pick one, a lilac-coloured bloom, and offered it to Ailsa. Angus stuck out his bottom lip before he, too, was presented with a flower. They both tucked the blossoms behind their ears.

Weary but enjoying the fresh air, they walked most of the day. With every step, they were closer to the ocean and Gibby's cousin's village. Perhaps he would give them a place to stay, in addition to letting them borrow his boat.

Harris, leading ahead, was the first to give a shout. Ailsa and Angus raced up the hill to join him, aghast at the sight below.

It was not the ocean, so close and sparkling that had

their attention. Their eyes traced a path, which curved down the slope until it reached the village below.

Or what was left of one.

Smoke billowed from the carcasses of buildings clustered together. It looked like the fires had been burning for at least a day.

A wave of horror coursed through Ailsa's body.

Her feet carried her swiftly towards the village, soot making her cough as she neared. She heard the footsteps of Harris and Angus behind her, their presence a welcome comfort.

Was this Gibby's cousin's village? What had happened here?

Without a word, they spread out. Ailsa, carefully climbed over the smouldering wreckage, ducking her head into homes, attempting to find any survivors. The first house was filled with suffocating, black smoke. The furniture had been consumed by the fire and all that was left of the main room was an empty shell.

The next building was missing a door. At first, it looked as if it had burned away, but as Ailsa explored inside, she noticed that the hinges were at odd angles and huge splinters littered the floor.

The door was kicked down.

Whatever had happened here, there were no bodies. She'd expected to find the charred remains of people, but the buildings were empty.

Where were they?

Angus called for them from the other side of the settlement. When she reached him, his silhouette was opaque against the sun, which looked blood red through the smoky haze. He was kneeling in the mud, wiping at something buried there.

"I think I know what happened." His voice was sombre as he held up an arrow. The end of the shaft had been tipped with a red feather, although it was coated with soot.

"Raiders?" Harris questioned from behind.

They stood in silence for a moment, absorbing the scale of destruction. How many people had been in this village? Where were they now?

"It's likely they've either been taken as slaves or sacrifices." Angus stood from his crouched position and chucked the arrow to the ground in disgust.

"Is there anything we can do?" Ailsa asked. She thought of the Avalognian skull masks and shivered. She didn't fancy crossing paths with raiders again.

"Not unless we have an army," said Angus.

"We'd better look for this boat," said Harris, kicking the dirt. "But be careful. They could still be close by."

Their small group spread out again, and after a half hour of searching, they found a rowing boat behind one of the lower buildings. The sun had all but set by the time they'd hefted the craft down to the beach and readied it for the next day. Sweat poured down Ailsa's back.

They were quiet as they walked back up to the edge of the village. They stopped a good distance away, still in sight of the boat, but with enough respect for any ghosts lurking around. A combination of sorrow for the smouldering community and the uncertainty of the next day, had them setting up camp in silence.

They'd just set out their packs, closer than usual, when Harris's head snapped up.

Ailsa followed his gaze. "What is it?"

"Shh. I heard something."

They peered into the darkness, holding their breath. It had been a cloudless day, but now a thin blanket of mist blotted out most of the stars. The sound of distant waves crashing over the shore was all Ailsa could hear. This close to Angus, she could almost feel the adrenalin radiating from his body as he coiled in anticipation.

Snap.

A twig cracked to their left. They swung round, Ailsa and Angus unsheathing their weapons.

A flare of flame in the dark suddenly blinded them. Their hands immediately shielded their eyes and Angus gasped in surprise as their surroundings were illuminated.

Further up the slope stood thirty men, all wearing light armour and carrying rapiers.

Chapter 42

Ailsa didn't dare take her eyes off the soldiers for one moment; she could feel the tension rolling off her companions. She gripped her axe tighter and curled her lip.

One of the men strode forward until he was little more than ten feet from them.

"Identify yourselves."

Harris raised his chin. "Why should we? Who are you?"

The man gave a chuckle. "I have more men—and more swords. You first." His voice had a slight accent that Ailsa couldn't place.

"Just three soldiers. I'm Harris, this is Angus and Ailsa. We're from Dunrigh."

The man swaggered towards them, clearly enjoying the situation. "I am Chester Scarsi, Captain of the King's First Battalion."

"But not the King of Eilanmòr?" said Angus, raising his chin proudly. He still had his sword raised.

The man smirked. "No. King Merlo of Mirandelle."

"What are you doing so far north, Captain?" asked

Harris, a muscle twitching in his jaw.

Scarsi placed his hands on his hips, inches away from his sword. His clothing was far too colourful for a soldier, Ailsa thought. His jacket was a bright, cobalt blue with a green trim. And was that velvet? She tried her best to keep her snort inside. He looked like a peacock.

"Just visiting the delightful countryside," he replied. "We accompanied the King's emissary to Dunrigh for the coronation, but we wanted to sail around instead of waiting." He beckoned his comrades forward and they sheathed their rapiers at their sides. They wore drab beige clothing, better suited to an army.

A peacock surrounded by peahens.

Angus barely masked a grimace but lowered his own weapon. "Will you be attending the coronation yourselves?"

"We wouldn't miss it. We'll be sailing south in the morning."

One of the other men stepped forward. "Please, come and share our food with us," he offered.

Scarsi's eyes darkened. "What a splendid idea, Lieutenant," he ground out. "Let's get to know each other… if you are indeed King Connall's soldiers."

The troop led them up and over the neighbouring hill until they reached a campsite. One of the men gave them each a plate of meat and some ale, while Scarsi stalked to the other side of the campfire. Most of the soldiers eyed them curiously. One or two shot them hostile looks as they sat down. All were young men, which was strange considering they were supposedly the first battalion.

Perhaps they don't let older men into military service, pondered Ailsa.

Scarsi, however, was a stocky man in his mid-thirties with a broad chest and hunched shoulders. Aside from his ridiculous clothing, the man screamed violence; not the regimental fierceness one would expect from a soldier, but the reckless savagery of a bar fighter. One of his ears was cauliflowered, like he'd had it punched one too many times. His face was angular below his close clipped beard and his eyes were calculating as he watched the trio get comfortable in front of the fire.

"So," Scarsi cocked his head, "What brings you so far north?"

Harris held out a hand to forestall Angus's reply. The selkie narrowed his eyes. "We heard that there had been some Avalognian raiders spotted on this coast, so we were sent to investigate."

Scarsi smirked. "On foot?"

Harris shrugged. "Well, they would have spotted us out at sea."

"Did you see what they did to the village?" asked Angus.

"Yes," said the captain. "In fact, when we arrived, we saw them picking up the last of the villagers."

Angus stood, rage turning his face ruddy in an instant. "They were *alive*?"

"You didn't try to stop them?" cried Ailsa.

Scarsi inclined his head. "Yes, they were alive. Captured." His voice became deathly quiet. "And I didn't fancy having my men join them." He spread his hands out with a rueful grin. "We were grotesquely outnumbered, I'm afraid."

Or just too selfish to help.

"Have those Avalognians been making a habit of this?" he asked Harris. "They don't usually go as far south as Mirandelle."

"Some. We've had a few attacks on isolated villages. But nothing like this."

"Barbarians. Surely you'll send soldiers to handle it?" He widened his eyes dramatically. "Or are your outer towns unprotected?" Scarsi's smooth voice did little to hide the threat belying his words.

He's wondering how easy it would be to attack Eilanmòr.

"Don't worry," Harris smiled back at Scarsi, mimicking the delicate way the captain played with his words. "We'll be doubling the protection of the coastal villages in the future."

"Wonderful." He threw his hands up as if to claim his fears had been assuaged. "Of course, you have your fair share of worries inland too, don't you? I'd say you have an infestation of fae. Mirandelle could always help you out with that."

Angus stepped in now. "Not all of the fair folk are malicious." He purposefully avoided looking at the selkie beside him.

Scarsi took his time folding his arms, making a show of his well-defined muscles. "Well, the offer stands if your new king requires it. I'm sure Mirandelle and Eilanmòr could become great allies." He clapped his hands, making Ailsa jump a little. "Now, come have some deer. Neroni here slayed it this morning."

Harris nodded politely but did not smile. "Thank you; you're very kind."

Captain Scarsi was thankfully silent for the next hour. His soldiers were infinitely more pleasing to speak to. They even offered some of their wine, which Ailsa only sipped lest she have a repeat of the headache from the day before.

Lieutenant DiMarco seemed genuine enough as he asked Harris and Angus about themselves. When he attempted to speak to Ailsa, she glowered at him until he gave up.

She did not trust these people, even if they seemed friendly. The truce between Mirandelle and Eilanmòr was tenuous at best. Before King Connall had been crowned, the two countries had been at war. Now their visits were… tolerated.

Why exactly had this regiment come so far north when

they were supposed to be escorting their ambassador? Regardless of what Scarsi had said, they'd be idiots to believe his '*visiting the countryside*' excuse. The question was: what were they scouting for up here? The Avalognians had recently raided a few of their smaller islands; could the Mirandellies be planning an attack on the raiders? The northeast coast of Eilanmòr was a perfect place for them to watch their enemy, but it was also a perfect place to investigate Eilanmòr's weaknesses.

Her two companions seemed to be enjoying themselves well enough. Harris was chatting to the Lieutenant while Angus made himself comfortable amongst the regular soldiers. She supposed he was used to them after his brief stint at training camp. She noticed that one man in particular, with long eyelashes and closely shaven stubble, was leaning into Angus as he spoke. A blush crept up Angus's throat under his intense gaze. The soldier seemed to check himself, leaning back and casting a furtive glance at his captain.

Content to leave her friends around the campfire, she stretched and rose from the log she had been sitting on. She needed to relieve herself and intended to go a fair distance before doing so, in case any prying eyes followed her.

As she strode away from the fire, picking her way over fallen branches and clumps of dirt, she pondered their next move. While it was nice to share a meal and some warmth with the soldiers, she'd feel much better if they camped far away, on their own. However, nothing could bring her to camp in an abandoned house in the village. It would feel too much like digging up a fresh grave.

The glare from the fire dwindled, replaced instead by the soft glow of the crescent moon above. In the darkness, the few stars escaping the cover of light clouds shone brighter, burning like the twinkling lights of a distant village. Her heart ached as she took them in.

With a heavy sigh, she found a boulder to sink behind, cursing the anatomy of men and how easy this precise task was for them.

Once finished, she rose, closing the buttons on her trousers. Maybe when she returned, she wouldn't have to wait long before she convinced Harris and Angus to leave the soldiers behind. After a few days socialising, she felt drained completely of energy. Her mind wandered back to her pristine beach, timeless, untouched and breathtakingly beautiful.

Soon, she'd be back home.

She thought of the way Harris had smiled at her that morning.

Perhaps she would stay in Dunrigh for a bit first.

As she rounded the boulder, she heard footsteps approaching. Not the dreaded *crunch* that constantly haunted her whenever she was in a forest, but a slow shuffle against the ground. Cautiously, she peered into the dark as she picked her way across the dewy grass.

"Nice night for a stroll," Captain Scarsi's voice rang out in the dark.

Chapter 43

Keeping her back straight, Ailsa continued towards the campfire, until she passed him under a gnarled old tree, just on the edge of the flickering light. Scarsi was leaning against the trunk, his arms crossed over his chest in a relaxed, arrogant, posture.

"I wouldn't wander too far," he grinned, his white teeth flashing in a shadowed face. "You never know who's going to be out there with you."

Ailsa sneered, though she wasn't sure he could see it. She tried to inject enough hostility into her voice so that he would get the right impression. "I suppose you were coming to protect me?"

"Just thought I would stretch my legs. I saw that you'd left and I thought you might enjoy some company."

"Well, I'm just heading back now."

"Stay a little. It's not often I get to talk to a pretty woman."

"Maybe you should have stayed in Mirandelle then," she growled.

His grin momentarily dropped from his mouth; he clearly did not like being spoken to like that. His eyes glinted nastily, gliding over Ailsa in appraisal.

"So, why exactly are you here with those two?" He pointed towards where Harris and Angus were being entertained, his smirk widening. "Or are you *with* one of them?"

She gritted her teeth. "No, I'm a soldier."

"Sure you are, pet."

She squared her shoulders. "I'm actually their bodyguard."

"*Well*," he drew the word out salaciously, "I've got another body you could guard." Her skin crawled as she felt his eyes creeping across it. She began to stalk back to the ring of logs when he threw an arm out, stopping her path.

"Oh, don't be like that. Come on, pet, I'm just being friendly."

She turned to face him head on, the stench of sweat and recently consumed wine hitting her fully. "Well, I'm not interested in being your friend."

"Ouch, that hurt." He held a hand over his heart and stepped closer to her, trapping her against another tree. "But you don't need to be my friend for us to have some *fun*." She couldn't see his features in the dark, but she could hear the leer in his voice. "We're all alone here." He released her then, backing up until he was against the old tree behind him. When his heels knocked against the trunk, he slumped down to the ground, stretching out his long legs. "Everyone else is having an enjoyable time, why shouldn't we? Now be a good girl and come sit on my lap."

She pushed off from her tree, coming to stand in front of him.

"If you were twice as smart, you'd be a fool." Turning away, she growled in a tone she hoped would end their interaction. "Now back off. I said no."

A low, menacing chuckle stopped her in her tracks. "Oh, you actually thought that I wanted *you*?" He laughed again. "It looks like your face caught fire and someone tried to stamp it out."

Ailsa felt her jaw pop open at the insult.

He leaned forward, regarding her short frame which shook in disbelief and fury. "Ah, I've heard that Eilanmòrians believe that mark means you're a changeling. So, which is it, pet: are you an evil faerie—or are you just ugly?"

She closed her mouth firmly and marched back to the camp, rage boiling in her stomach.

His voice called from behind, getting louder as he followed her.

"Ooh, I think I hit a nerve. Don't they say that changelings kill their human mothers? Is that what you did?"

Ailsa wheeled around. "Watch your filthy mouth. I don't bloody care if you're a captain or a king, I will wipe that sneer off your face with my fist."

Scarsi smirked, his features fully illuminated by the firelight ahead. "If I'd been her, I would have drowned your ugly little body straight away. Better than living with a *parasite*," he spat the word. "Only a simpleton wouldn't have killed you."

"Take that back," she breathed. Pain and wrath crackled in her veins and ears, making her head pound. A gust of wind whipped her hair across her face and the moon and stars disappeared behind heavy clouds.

He gazed lazily back at her, surprised but challenging. "Make me."

Fury exploded inside her.

He clearly wasn't expecting the fist she threw towards him, as it landed square on his jaw, knocking him backwards.

"Bitch," growled Scarsi. He pushed himself up, rubbing his jaw and lunged for her.

He's a good fighter, Ailsa thought as he aimed a sweeping kick at her legs. She managed to knee him in the nose after he missed, causing him to curse again. He grabbed her other leg yanking her to the ground. Trying to pin her, he pulled his heavy body over hers, but this gave Ailsa the ideal angle to bring her knee up between his legs.

Hard.

Scarsi fell to the side moaning and clutching at his

groin. While he rocked himself, she used the opportunity to throw another punch at his nose. Nearby, voices were shouting at them to stop, but the blood pounding in her veins drowned them out.

With a snarl, he grabbed her shoulder and flipped her onto her back, her head bouncing hard off the ground.

Ailsa cried out at the pain.

"What the hell is going on?"

From where she lay on the dirt and grass, she could see that Harris and Angus had finally come to investigate, worry evident on their faces. They'd been followed by the other soldiers, who all looked horrified at their captain.

Scarsi spat at her feet. "Keep your thoughts to yourself next time, filthy changeling." He wiped the blood trickling from his nose and turned back to his troop. Scarsi held his arms out wide, victorious—a shadow with glowing eyes—silhouetted against the fire. The soldiers all stared, open-mouthed, at their leader.

Coughing, Ailsa pulled herself upright. Harris and Angus pushed through the crowd and ran to her. She spotted her axe, leaning against her pack, not a foot away.

Scarsi's laughter rang in her ears as she reached for it gingerly and found the handle.

Standing, she pulled an arm back...

And released the weapon with a howl.

It sailed through the air, right towards the back of his head.

And embedded itself in a tree trunk a hair's breadth to his left.

"Well," croaked Harris, addressing Scarsi, "I guess you've had your warning. Clear off before Ailsa really does put her axe in your skull."

The captain screwed up his face in a sneer. "She missed." He was breathing hard and regarding Ailsa with a wild look in his eyes.

Harris raised his chin. "On purpose. She won't be so merciful again."

Scarsi growled and motioned for his squadron to leave.

"Oh, and Captain?" Angus yelled at his retreating back. "I look forward to seeing you at my brother's coronation."

Scarsi turned, a look of pure dread in his expression. "What? You're—"

"Come on, Captain. We better get out of here," Lieutenant DiMarco urged his leader.

With one last look towards where Ailsa was standing, Captain Scarsi strode off, his soldiers following at a distance.

The silence stretched out as Ailsa stared into the flames of the abandoned fire and said nothing. A hand on her shoulder pulled her from her thoughts.

"Are you okay?" asked Harris. She couldn't bear the concern etched on his face.

"No," she finally answered, letting her shoulders sink, releasing the pent-up tension.

"Here, come and lie down," said Angus "What do you need?"

"Captain Scarsi's brains on the ground," she growled.

"He's a complete asshole," Harris spat. "Probably best you decided not to kill him though, wouldn't want to start a war."

Anger still thundered in Ailsa's veins, threatening to erupt again. *How dare he!*

"I didn't *decide* not to kill him."

Angus frowned. "What do you mean?"

"I missed," she ground out, flexing her hands.

"What?"

"I *missed*," she repeated, staring Angus down. "I wanted to slaughter him. But I missed."

"I know you got into a fight, Ailsa, but it was just a stupid argument," said Angus. "You didn't actually *want* to kill him—"

"You can't just go around killing everyone who insults you—"

She rounded on Harris. "He insulted my mother."

He folded his arms. "Well, the same applies. Sure, if there's an Avalognian raider trying to gut us or some bloodthirsty faerie ready to eat us, feel free to bash all the heads in that you like. But Scarsi is just a pretentious scumbag."

The ground was starting to wobble beneath her.

"You don't know what it's like." Waves of dread were lapping at her feet, reminding her they could sweep over and consume her at any moment. "I have had to live my whole life with assholes like that telling me that I should have died, that my mother should have murdered me. People like that just look for any way to knock you down until they're above you. Until you feel like you wish you had *died*." Her breath hiccupped in her throat. "I am so *sick* of feeling worthless."

Silence followed her words, the weight of them crawling over her skin, making her wish she could disappear. Her mind was blank; everything she'd wanted to say had been said and yet she wished she could take it back.

Both men were statuesque, watching for her next move, no doubt waiting for the next example of her insanity.

She had told them she wanted to murder someone. Ailsa willed away the heat in her face.

"I'm going to sleep on the boat. Don't follow me."

Chapter 44

The girl peeked in the window, staying out of sight. It had become a habit, passing the time between scavenging this way. The children inside were younger than her, still at the age where they didn't have to help around the house.

When her mother had died and her brother had been taken, she'd become her own caretaker; the other villagers were too scared of her to visit. She had been surprised to find a basket of food on the porch a few times, but the mysterious donor never made themselves known. It had been full of fruit, dried meats and—best of all—a mini jar of honey. Her stomach rumbled at the memory and she bent over to muffle the sound.

The children were crowded around an old woman. The scene was familiar, one she had witnessed many times through different windows while journeying. The old matriarchs of each village would tell the children stories designed to entertain and frighten them into behaving.

Little do they know the stories are true. The grim thought came unsolicited as she pressed herself further towards the heat emerging from the cottage.

"Have you heard of changelings?" started the old woman. The girl jumped. She half expected the woman to turn and point at her accusingly, but it was merely part of the story.

The children shook their heads and she continued in a solemn tone. "Faeries like to steal babies. They give them a sickness and if their mothers cannot stay awake, night after night, looking after them, they take the child away, leaving one of their faerie children in the baby's place."

"Why do they want the baby?" asked a freckled boy seated beside the fire.

"Faeries have to pay a tithe to Hell: one child must be sacrificed to the Underworld. They take a human baby as a sacrifice, while their child remains safe. Faerie mothers are also lazy, so they hope that human mothers will look after the changelings. If the human woman is wise though, she will know it is not her child."

"How will she know?"

"There is usually a mark on the changeling. If a babe is sick, then suddenly recovers and has the mark, the woman must kill the faerie child. If she does not, the changeling will grow. It will go on to make the other children sick. When it is older, it will discover its faerie powers and kill any humans it meets." Her voice became serious, a warning. "Changelings are always hungry;

the only thing that sates their hunger is the heart of a human."

The girl in the window shook her head in disgust. She was getting sick of the stupid superstitions. Although she knew the fae were real, she doubted that changelings were. Since she had been called one all her life, she was sure it was just a story. She certainly didn't want to eat the hearts of other humans.

Though, she thought, as she looked through the window, *I do want to eat their cake.* She'd have to wait until they'd all gone to sleep, then she'd sneak in and take some.

The matriarch pulled the children closer to her, her face pale in the firelight. "I am telling you all this because this is our reality." She took a steadying breath, sadness visible on her face. The girl at the window forgot about her rumbling stomach and listened carefully. "I'm afraid that a faerie visited our village last night and took a baby."

The children gasped in horror. The woman ran her wrinkled hands over one of their heads, her eyes filling with tears.

"I'm so sorry, love, but it was your brother." The boy nodded his head slowly, as if he had already known. Perhaps he had known as soon as she'd begun the story. He couldn't be more than nine or ten, yet he accepted the death of his sibling without a word. The girl felt prickling in her eyes but she squared her shoulders.

The old woman sniffed and carried on. "I am warning you because a changeling was left in its place. You may think us cruel," she straightened, "but we must protect the rest of you."

The girl's heart thudded in her chest and icy fear trickled down her spine. She listened with dread as the woman murmured softly to the children around her.

"We had to get rid of it, dear ones. It is always a difficult thing to do, because it looks so much like a baby." She gave the boy's cheek a pat. "Your mother will be upset for a while, but she will soon understand that it was for the best."

The girl backed away from the window in horror. What had they done? Where was the baby?

I'll take it, if they don't want it, she thought wildly as she stumbled through the gloom of the village. She was only fourteen, but she could manage. It would be like having her own brother again.

Then she heard the wailing.

One of the houses at the end of the path had a light lit. She rushed over to the window. Inside, a woman was curled up on her bed sobbing into a pillow while a man rubbed her back. There were a few others in the room with her, each silent and pitying.

A man appeared at the door and gave her husband a nod. He immediately stiffened and the woman raised her tear-blotched face. When she caught sight of the visitor, she began to keen, loudly, her sobs wracking her body.

The girl watched in terror as the other people left the house, muttering condolences. The visitor rested a hand on the husband's shoulder for a moment, then turned to go.

"Wait," the husband called, his voice breaking. "Where did you put him?"

"Hanging in a tree, so the faeries can take him away with them."

The woman's cries rang in the girl's ears as she fled from the house.

What have they done? What have they done? She lurched through the mud, determined to get as far away from this Gods-forsaken village as possible.

Then, as the moon shone through the clouds, she caught a glimpse of a white bundle hanging in a tree and screamed.

Chapter 45

Ailsa awoke with her own screams ringing in her ears. It was still dark, a little before dawn. Cursing her nightmares and the uncomfortable, rigid wood of the boat, she sighed and turned over.

A noise came from her left and she looked into the darkness. The faint glow of the moon outlined a man, strolling down the beach towards her, his hands in his pockets. The flaming, unkempt curls gave away his identity.

"Ailsa?" Harris whispered as he approached. She thought about pretending to be asleep, but was too weary for the bluff.

"What do you want, Harris?" she asked. She placed an arm over her eyes and drew a deep breath. The horror from her dream still clawed at her mind. She felt the familiar prickle of tears in her eyes and willed them away.

Do not cry. You promised.

Harris stopped at the edge of the boat and she was glad for the steadiness of the wood underneath her.

"I wanted to see how you were." She felt the boat creak as he climbed in and sat at the opposite end. "What happened earlier?"

"I got angry." She exhaled.

He came closer, careful of his footing along the narrow boat. She felt his hesitation, but finally he reached out and moved her arm away from her face. She lifted her head to look at him and he gasped.

"What did he do to you?"

"What? I—" She gingerly touched her face, feeling across the smooth flesh of her cheek before finding a graze on her forehead. It was gravelly and sore to touch. She must have received it when they'd been fighting on the ground.

"I'm fine," she answered.

"This is my fault. I should have watched him more closely. When he got up, I assumed he was going to check the perimeter."

"He followed me. Tried to get me to—" She gripped the seat under her fingers. "When I refused, he got mad. Said he could never want someone so deformed. Then he asked me if I had killed my mother." She gulped, swallowing the feelings of hatred and despair that threatened to rise again. "He said she should have killed me when she had the chance."

Harris put his face in his hands. "Oh Ailsa, I'm so sorry. You had every right to want to bash his head in."

"I know that I shouldn't want to kill him. I know that it's barbaric and murderous and horrible. But part of me still wishes I hadn't missed. Does that make me a monster?"

He gave her a level stare. "You are not a monster, Ailsa." He paused, weighing his words. "When I was young, I had everything I wanted. I was pretty spoilt actually. I could go wherever I wanted, do whatever I wanted. When I was nine, I got to go on this big adventure to hide the Stone of Destiny. I thought it would be such fun: sleeping rough, walking around on land.

"Somewhere near the end of our journey, my aunt, our leader, took us to meet some humans. They lived in a tiny cottage and wore rags for clothes. When we arrived, they had set out some food for us—a simple broth. I was so annoyed. I wanted to catch my own food, like we had been doing so far, and I thought they were rude to try to serve us measly soup. So, I turned my nose up at it. Told them I didn't want it." He blew out a breath. "I had never seen my aunt so angry. She explained that these people had nothing. They had so little food that they were slowly starving. And still, they had offered us a meal." Harris bit his lip. "At the time I was angry but now... I can't think about that night without drowning in shame. It makes *me* feel like a monster.

"My point is, Ailsa, nothing for me was very hard, but it succeeded in making me apathetic. I couldn't imagine suffering; I had no empathy. You, on the other hand, have led a very hard life, and it governs everything you do. Whether you realise it or not, it has shaped you into a good person—and it *could* have made you a monster, but it didn't. You know what's wrong and you fight for what's right, despite no one doing the same for you, *because* no one did the same for you.

"While you have your wrath, you also have passion."

Leaning forward, he placed a hand over hers.

"There is a storm beneath your flesh, Ailsa, but it's buried deep under fear and rejection. Only you alone can decide whether to smother it or embrace it."

It was the most earnest she had ever heard him. And yet...

"Storms kill people, Harris. They blow down houses, start fires—"

"They also make way for new life. They heal. All I ask is that you be yourself. That light is worth the dark."

She sat still for a moment, letting his words shield her from the worry and fear inside. His fingers traced patterns on hers, as if willing her to emerge from the darkness. Finally, she lifted her chin and nodded. He smiled at her then, glorious and radiant as the sun, and she couldn't help but return it. A little bit of peace settled back into her soul.

There was a rare moment of openness on his face before it was replaced by that infuriating smirk. Back to teasing.

Well, that didn't last long.

"And you know, just like a storm—" he started.

"Don't say it," she growled.

"You can—"

"I'm warning you, Harris." She picked up her bag and launched it at him.

It narrowly avoided his head and Harris simply grinned and climbed out of the boat. She could hear his laughter all the way up the beach, as she rolled over and huffed. Just when she thought he was being genuine, he had to go and act the fool.

Still, her heart felt a little lighter after their exchange. He had seen the darkest parts of her and hadn't recoiled. Ailsa had been sure when she had stalked off to the boat, that he and Angus would never forgive her. But Harris had surprised her. He had tried to understand.

Once the sun had risen, she approached the campsite with trepidation. She was worried to face Angus again—would he still want to be her friend after last night? But it seemed that Harris had spoken with him. He greeted her amiably and handed her an apple for breakfast. Ailsa let out a breath that she hadn't realised she'd been holding.

After Harris appeared with a couple of flasks of fresh water, they packed up their things and made their way to the boat.

The journey to the Isle of Faodail was completed mostly in silence. This was it. Today, they would find the Stone of Destiny... and encounter whatever obstacles protected it.

Thick mist clung to the water like a second skin, making the crossing treacherous. Ailsa wished they had thought to light a torch before they set off, but Harris seemed to know the route. He sat with one hand in the churning waters and murmured instructions around hidden boulders and against strong currents as Angus and Ailsa took turns paddling.

More than once, Ailsa thought she heard music drifting on the wind but dismissed it. Whenever she had tried to listen, it had faded away and leaving her wondering if she'd imagined it.

She observed her two companions, for they were the only view afforded to her. Angus, although worried, had a way of being centred. There was a quiet diligence in his rowing which told her he was optimistic about what lay ahead.

Harris, on the other hand, had a fierce determination in command of their little vessel. What had his life been like before this? She knew he was charismatic, if a bit of a trickster. She'd imagined his natural habitat was a beach in Struanmuir, where he spent the days lying around. He appeared to have few responsibilities, especially compared to his sister. She was an ambassador and he was... As far as she could tell, his only accolade was being Iona's brother. Yet, he had been the driving force of this expedition. Was it possible he was out to prove himself? If that was true, what would happen if they failed?

A dreamer and a crusader, that's who I'm working with. So what does that make me?

She looked from the two men, to the landmass that was emerging from the mist, and clenched her jaw. Foreboding and unease plunged like stones in her stomach as she beheld the rocky beach ahead and she had her answer.

A realist.

She helped guide the boat onto the pebbled shore and followed her companions onto dry ground, feeling like a child clutching two kites tightly before they could escape and float away into the wind.

Chapter 46

The land beyond the craggy coastline was a wet mess of bogs and marshland that squelched underfoot. They had to fight their way from the shore up a hill, stopping every now and then to extract their legs from the mud. The sky drizzled, the kind of rain that snuck under hoods and clung to skin. It painted a thin sheen of water on the landscape and their faces.

Harris strode ahead purposefully, with Angus following close behind. Ailsa took up the rear, her axe gripped in her hand. When she had drawn it from her belt, they had both given her a look but had said nothing. She was the only one with a weapon at the ready.

They reached the crest of the hill and finally rose out of the mist. Their patch of ground looked like it was floating in a sea of clouds. Ahead, the trio could clearly see the mountain at the centre of the island, it's peak pointing towards the pale-yellow sun glowing through the rain clouds.

"There," said Harris, pointing to a stone path leading to the loch beneath the mountain. "Keep to the pathway," was his only instruction before he forged on, back straight. Behind him, Ailsa and Angus exchanged nervous glances before following him up the trail.

Just as they had reached about halfway, Ailsa spotted a flash of light out of the corner of her eye and gave a quiet yelp of surprise.

"What was that?" she breathed.

Angus turned to stare in the opposite direction. "I saw it, too."

Another flash of blue appeared on her other side and she whipped around, catching the faintest impression of a tiny floating body before it disappeared again. "Harris?" Ailsa called, as the selkie had not slowed down and was oblivious to their fright. He stopped unwillingly and turned back for them.

"It's okay. They're wisps." They watched together as one appeared a little way off, slightly further up the path that they were currently on.

Still bewildered, Ailsa lifted her axe a little higher. "What's a wisp?"

Angus scanned the area, his eyes reflecting the faint turquoise glow of another wisp that appeared closer to them. "I thought they were just a story. They're spirits, sometimes they're naughty and sometimes they're nice."

Harris scoffed. "Maybe in a *faerie* tale. Wisps use their light to trick people into going the wrong way."

"So should we go the opposite way?" asked Ailsa.

Harris pushed her ahead and they continued up the

same path. "Not necessarily. Sometimes they point out the right way to confuse you. Best thing to do is just ignore them." Another wisp appeared in front of him and he swatted at it as he would a fly.

"So, which is it? Are they good or evil?" Ailsa asked. It didn't appear that they were being malicious, but from her experience with fair folk thus far, she was sceptical.

He shrugged and motioned to himself. "Just follow the selkie instead. Chances are he'll either lead you to treasure—or food."

"Look," said Angus, pointing in front of them.

Now that they were at the top of the hill, they could see that the loch ahead was surrounded by a wall of rock, save for in one place, where there was an opening. The water spilled from the fissure, and down into a deep cavern, creating a waterfall. How they hadn't heard it before, Ailsa wasn't sure. It thundered through the crack in the rock.

She stepped off the path to get a better look. The cavity in the ground was about the size of a house. There was a set of stairs running into the hollow and along the sides of the cavern. She could barely make out something sparkling deep underground.

"Look," she called, running forward. "There's a cave..."

A shout from behind cut her off.

Then the ground around them erupted.

"Watch out!"

Ailsa struggled to make sense of what was happening. Around them the earth was breaking apart: clumps were rising and churning, the moist soil like liquid under their feet. They clung to each other to remain upright.

The island seemed to be disintegrating; thick clay swirled in circles, creating large holes which rapidly filled up with brown water. What emerged from beneath made Ailsa feel sick. Hands made of mud grabbed and pulled at her legs, making an awful squelching sound as they moved.

"What the hell?" she heard Angus yell.

She didn't have breath to reply as she was assaulted from all sides by the clawing fingers of mud.

The smell they emitted was revolting—putrid—and Ailsa was trying her best not to throw up as the hands slathered slimy clay in great smears up and down her legs. Another muddy limb managed to upset her balance and she landed on the ground with a squelch, her breath knocked out of her in a *whoosh*. The hands imprisoned her feet, dragging her with them into the mud. From somewhere behind her, she could make out shouts as Angus and Harris fought to free themselves.

She struggled as hard as she could, swinging with her axe chaotically, but she was unable to reach the hands. She had sunk past her knees when a warm palm enveloped hers and Angus managed to pull her free. She crawled out of the muck just as more clay hands grabbed

Angus by the legs.

Now that Ailsa was on her feet again, she swung at them with her weapon, severing several muddy hands at the wrist. They gave way with little resistance, but more appeared in their place.

She freed Angus and whipped her head around to look for Harris. In her struggling, she had moved far from the path and closer to the cavern opening. Back where she had first stepped onto the boggy ground, great clods of mud were swirling around like lava. She wouldn't have known Harris was even there if it hadn't been for a single curl of unsullied red hair. Nearly his entire body had been swallowed by the muck; just the strands of hair and one hand grasping at the air above remained.

"Harris!" Ailsa screamed.

She ran, slipping and sliding through the sludge, with Angus behind her. When they reached him, they grasped desperately at his hand, yanking as hard as they could but their hands slid over his, unable to find purchase. Ailsa dropped her axe to get a better grip. Angus gave a broken sob as Harris's fingers slipped through theirs again.

How long had he been under the mud now?

Harris's hand disappeared under the muck with a wet sound. The other hands around them dissolved too, satisfied with their prey.

Chapter 47

"Dig!" shouted Ailsa desperately as she and Angus began to use their hands as shovels. They soon realised they couldn't win; every handful of dirt they removed was filled again by more oozing in to take its place.

It had been ten long minutes and Harris had still not resurfaced. There was no sound now, save for the squashing of mud and their laboured breathing.

Ailsa leaned back on her heels, her arms aching. A few drops of rain fell from the sky and trailed down her face like tears.

"Stop, Angus." When he continued to dig, she put a dirty hand on his shoulder.

"We need to save him, Ailsa!"

"He's gone," she whispered bleakly, grabbing his arms to force them to stop. His whole body was shaking with effort.

Angus stared blankly at the pool of muck in front of them.

Now, there was silence, stillness.

He's gone.

The thought felt like a bad joke.

Part of her couldn't accept it. He couldn't be dead. She wanted to laugh at the absurdity of it. Yet Angus's sobs beside her conveyed the truth.

Harris was dead.

Harris was dead.

"No..." she whimpered. After all they had been through, he had died before they had found the Stone. They were supposed to find it together. She was supposed to keep him and Angus safe.

"I'm so sorry, Ailsa." Angus reached out an arm towards her and pulled her to his shoulder. He reeked, his sweet, comforting smell gone, but she didn't care as she pressed her face into his neck. She could feel his attempts to swallow his tears as he rocked her slowly. She felt her own eyes prickling, but she couldn't give in. Instead she concentrated on the feel of Angus's pulse to keep her grounded. Thunder cracked in the distance.

"What do we do now?" asked Angus in a thick voice.

Ailsa screwed up her face but didn't part from his shoulder. She hoped it muffled her voice enough to make it sound like she wasn't tearing up.

"We need to find the Stone of Destiny. Eilanmòr needs it."

"But we don't know how—not without Harris," Angus moaned.

She shuddered, willing herself not to cry. It was taking

every ounce of self-control, but she was starting to lose.

Just as she felt moisture gather behind her closed eyelids, she heard a faint sound beside them that had her pulling away.

Squelch.

She looked wide-eyed at Angus, whose mouth had fallen open.

Squelch.

Then the bog erupted, spraying mud everywhere. Something emerged from the sludge and took a gasping breath. Ailsa started to back away, but Angus launched himself at the figure.

"Harris!"

The body took a few more gulps of air and then chuckled. The sound was hoarse and crackling, but clearly belonged to the selkie.

"You can cancel the funeral," he laughed, seeing their faces.

"How?" Ailsa rushed over to help him wipe the grime from his nose and mouth. "How did you survive? You must have been under for more than ten minutes. Are you okay?"

"Ah, nothing to it." Harris pulled a clump of mud from his hair. "Sometimes being a supernatural creature sure comes in handy. Did you know that seals can hold their breath for up to fifteen minutes?"

She was about to smack him for his callous joking,

when a mud coated figure tackled him again and they all ended up lying on the ground. Angus squeezed the selkie's body in a massive hug, all the while telling him how glad he was Harris was not dead.

Ailsa frowned at the display and brushed herself down. "Can the soppy reunion wait? Those things might come back."

"I wouldn't worry about it for a while." The two men disentangled themselves.

"What were they?" asked Angus.

"Bog monsters. They live in the mud and wait for unsuspecting travellers to come by."

She peered at the mud. "What do they look like?"

Harris gave her a strange look. "If a human ever saw their faces, they would die of fright."

Ailsa shivered. "How did you get away?"

"I punched the one holding me in the jaw. They spat me back out when they realised I wasn't going to drown."

Ailsa could still feel the weight of his death pressing on her body. Her head throbbed as if the fright had relieved her of some brain cells. She glanced around, evaluating the threat. If it had been her or Angus, they would be dead. It would be best not to give the Bog Monsters a chance to strike again. They would have to be extra careful on the way back.

"So," Ailsa bent to pick up her axe from where it had landed, "can we go now?"

With a nod from the selkie, they all clumsily got to their feet and made their way over to the edge of the cavern.

Chapter 48

They carefully picked their way down one of the sets of stairs. The waterfall cascading close enough for its spray to wash away most of the muck, leaving them soaked and shivering.

As they descended, Ailsa gasped. She had been expecting to walk down into a dank, dark cave but the sight before her was far stranger. Something glinted in the water, creating shafts of light which reflected reds, blues, greens and purples off the walls. As the trio approached the underground portion of the loch, she realised that there were hundreds of glittering gems littering the bottom like precious seashells.

"The faeries that made this place primarily used it to store their treasure. They were quite secretive; it's why they chose to hide the Stone here," Harris explained as they crept down the rest of the steps. They reached the floor of the cave. Around the circular walls, a series of doorways were carved into the rock.

"And this," said Harris, looking around, "is as far as I got."

"What do you mean?" asked Ailsa. "Don't you know

where the Stone is hidden?"

"Just because I didn't see where it was hidden doesn't mean I can't find it," he replied, pulling out a blanket and a box from his pack. "My aunt told me to look for her mark, a triangle with a wave inside, and then I'll know where it is."

"Well, that's reassuring," Ailsa grumbled.

Harris stuck his tongue out before ripping off a bit of material. He grabbed a stick that had been abandoned nearby and wrapped the cloth around it. Opening the box, Ailsa saw that it carried a hip flask and a box of matches.

"Is that whisky?" she asked, raising an eyebrow.

He grinned before dousing the cloth in the liquid from the hip flask. Then, with a flourish, he lit a match, and with it, his torch. It ignited so quickly that Ailsa was surprised Harris still had eyelashes. The torch's light reflected off his hair, turning his copper curls into flames themselves.

"Okay," he said, straightening, "I'm going to go looking for the symbol, you stay here."

"Can't we come with you?" Angus asked, fidgeting with his sword.

"It's better if you stay here, I'm fairly certain my aunt left traps the last time we were here. Also, I don't know what lives further on inside these caves. You're safer waiting."

Before Ailsa could argue, he strode through one of the stone arches, the light from his torch illuminating the passage. As he went deeper, the light faded until they could no longer see any signs of him.

"Urgh, I hate him," growled Ailsa, crossing her arms.

"He's just trying to protect us."

"He's feeding his ego is what he's doing."

Angus shrugged. "Well if he doesn't find it soon, we can go help." He rolled his shoulders as he walked over to a wall and leaned against it. Or he would have if there hadn't been a door where he'd intended to rest. Angus fell through the opening, landing with a thump.

"Ow, that's embarrassing," he muttered as he rubbed his backside.

"Are you okay?" asked Ailsa, running over to help him up.

"Yeah," he chuckled. "I think I found a secret door. Do you think this is where the Stone is hidden?"

Ailsa eyed the shadowy opening, squinting. "Well if I were going to hide something, it would probably be down there." She stepped forward. "Let's go."

Angus hesitated. "Shouldn't we wait for Harris?"

She rolled her eyes. "He'll catch up." *And, as usual, we'll be doing all the work.*

They didn't have the same supplies as Harris had, so they raised their weapons and let the damp cave wall guide their hands. Soon, the lack of light completely blinded them. Ailsa could only hear Angus's breathing coming from behind her. As they walked, a thin sliver of light filtered in from up ahead, offering the view of a cavern beyond. They stepped out of the small tunnel and into a larger chamber, the narrow cracks in the ceiling just large enough to illuminate it.

No turning back now.

They could barely make out ten half-submerged, white, marble statues of women standing in the loch. In their wavy hair, delicate floral headdresses had been carved. Each looked down at their hands, which were cupping the water, as if examining it. Their chests were bare, but artistically covered by their stone tresses.

Angus clicked his tongue. "Why would someone leave statues in a place like this?"

"No idea but they're creepy. Let's be quick. Where do you think the Stone is hidden?"

"The centre of the pool. Look over there," Angus pointed to a large boulder in the middle of the water. "We must have to swim to it."

"Ok, let's go—"

"No, I'll go. No point in both of us getting wet." Angus pulled off his sword belt and lay it and his weapon at Ailsa's feet. He kicked off his boots, dipped a toe in the water and shivered. "Pretty cold. I better jump in."

Ailsa could almost hear him count down mentally before he threw himself into the pool and landed with a splash. The water rippled making rainbows dance on the ceiling. Ailsa sat down at the edge to wait as Angus slowly pushed himself through the water.

I wonder what's taking Harris so long, she thought. Her eyes felt heavy and it suddenly became clear how hard their day had been. She rubbed her shoulder blade and sighed as Angus paddled further out. *I can't believe after all we've been through, we're going to get the Stone of Destiny without him.*

From where she sat, Ailsa heard the light fluttering of music beginning; women's voices were rising from the darkness in a wordless hum. She scanned around for the source, but couldn't make out any people in the darkness.

Maybe it's coming from outside, she wondered, but batted away the worry that threatened to pull her out of the sleepy contentment she was in. She watched as Angus splashed around and vaguely thought that he didn't seem to be a particularly good swimmer as he hadn't moved far. She noted with disinterest that the water was lapping lazily on the bank of the pool in little waves.

How funny, when we're inside a cave.

Chapter 49

Angus's arms and legs were starting to fatigue as he kicked through the dark water. It seemed that the faster he swam, the further away the boulder was. *Was it magic? Some defence against intruders?*

Angus's strokes became less powerful as he tired. He was breathing heavily and stopped to tread water. Now, with his head fully above the surface, he could hear a faint chanting. He twisted his head around the cave but saw only Ailsa, lying beside the pool, staring sleepily at the waves.

Maybe I should have let her swim out, he thought with exasperation as he continued to search for the source of the music. Finding none, he turned back towards the boulder.

What I need is a good burst of energy.

He threw himself into another set of powerful strokes, his head under the water for the most part, surfacing only to breathe.

Stroke.

Surface.

Breathe.

Stroke.

Surface.

Breathe.

Stroke.

Surface.

A face.

Angus choked in a breath, as he abruptly stopped swimming to behold the woman who was now floating in the water two feet away from him. Her voice was haunting—mesmerising—as she joined in with the music. So pale was she that she looked like all colour had leached from her. Large black eyes watched him as she sang, and he could only stare back, transfixed by her silky voice.

Was this a female selkie? He swam a little closer to ask her what she was doing in the cave and she smiled at him, revealing rows of jagged, pearly-white fangs.

Chapter 50

Ailsa heard splashing and lifted her head slowly from the lapping waves towards the centre of the lake. Slight confusion edged its way through the layers of mist in her mind as she scanned the inky pool. Something was missing. The angelic music lingered but the cave looked strangely bare. *Hadn't there been some statues before?*

Beyond the gentle music, the splashing had stopped. She glanced down at the cool water noticing how mirror-like the surface was; all the cracks reflected from the ceiling, glowing like an expanse of stars in the black of the lake. If she just reached out, she could float amongst them.

A noise from behind her pulled her attention away from the lake. Foggily, she tilted her head towards it. It was Harris and he was mouthing... something... at her. She wrinkled her nose in concentration. *What was he saying?* He was getting closer now. *Why did he look panicked?* It was so strange, he was right up in her face, his mouth was opening as if he were screaming at her, but what could possibly be wrong? It was so pretty in the cave and the singing was so—

He pulled back his hand and slapped her across the cheek.

The sting of the smack cut through the peaceful haze and her hand reached up to hold her face. "What the hell, Harris?"

"Ailsa! Where is Angus?" He was shaking her shoulders roughly and she squinted at him, her brain still slow on the uptake. The music had stopped and she felt slightly clearer with every passing minute.

"Angus?" She looked around saw only the flat black of the lake. "He—He decided to swim out to the boulder. We thought that's where the Stone was hidden."

"Well where is he now?"

"I—I don't know."

Her heart stopped in her chest and cold dread spilled down her back, like she had been doused with a bucket of ice water.

"Harris, there were statues here before..." she whispered. "Where is he? Where is Angus?"

"I have a good guess." Harris pulled out a knife and knelt beside the loch. In one smooth motion, he sliced his palm and held it above the water.

A single drop of blood slid around the underside of his hand before gravity pulled it from him and it landed in the water with a *plop*.

"Harris, what are you—"

"Shh, be quiet and get your axe ready."

"Mmm. Selkie blood," a voice hissed from the shadows. The water rippled and a ghostly white head emerged from the inky pool. The woman still looked like she was carved from marble, save for her eyes which were immeasurable pits of onyx. The hairs on Ailsa's arms stood on end as she beheld the strange creature. Then, rising as if one, more heads appeared from the depths.

"Selkie blood tastes like rotten fish," snarled one to the left.

"That's when they wash in here dead," one of the other women on the right laughed, her voice tinkling. "This one is fresh."

"We've been told not to eat," claimed the one closest, but she continued to devour Harris with her eyes.

"Mermaids?" asked Ailsa quietly.

"*Ceasg*," said Harris. "Different breed. But I don't think now is really the time to educate you in sea creature taxonomy." He spoke to the ceasg. "You took something that didn't belong to you. I want him back."

"Pretty creature, he was."

Ailsa's stomach gave a lurch at the word 'was.'

"Give him back!"

"Who says you get to have him? Maybe I want new pet?" replied the closest, obviously the leader of the group.

Around the cavern, the other women echoed, "*Want. Want.*"

"Or maybe," she spoke again, this time smiling with jagged teeth, "I want a taste."

"Want. Want." The others chanted, splashing around a bit now, excitedly.

"I want him back," said Harris, showing his own teeth.

"But he wants to stay," she grinned. "Want to see?"

A few of the ceasg moved forward, forming a loose circle and raising their hands above the water. From beneath the murky depths, a face appeared. It too looked to be made from marble, but it was not female. If Ailsa had not seen the scruff of beard that coated his face, she would not have recognised him. Angus was motionless, floating corpse-like on top of the water. The only hint that he was still alive was the slow, rhythmic movement of his chest. His eyes stared unseeingly at the ceiling of the cavern, covered in a thick, milky film.

"Give him back. Now!" Ailsa shouted, stepping forward as if threatening to throw herself at the creatures.

The nearest one grinned. "Maybe, I want little girl too."

"Pretty little girl," cooed another.

"I want the selkie."

"Nicnevan wants the selkie. She said if he came here, we had to bring him to her."

Harris baulked. "Nicnevan wants me?"

"You stole something."

"I didn't! I only came with them when they hid it."

"She knows where the Stone is, idiot boy," one hissed. "Thought you would come back for it. Then she could find out where you hid *the baby*."

He laughed, incredulous. "That was definitely not me!"

"All selkies are the same."

"Enough talk," the leader snapped. "I want the girl."

"Here, girly..."

The women started to sing again, but this time, their melody seemed slightly off tune. To Ailsa's surprise, they pulled Angus's body alongside them as they approached the shore.

"Ailsa, get ready," Harris told her, unsheathing his knife.

She clutched her axe and inched closer to the lake. But instead of scrabbling out of the shallows like she had expected them to do, the ceasg floated out of the water on long, ivory legs. As they advanced, their singing grew louder. They raised their arms out towards her opening their mouths wider.

Harris backed up until he was next to her. "There are so many..." His head whipped around when he heard Ailsa chuckle beside him.

"I thought they would have tails. I thought I would have to fight them in the water," she grinned. "On land though? I'd say this makes it a fair fight."

As the first of the ceasg came close enough to reach

out and touch, Ailsa swung her axe down embedding it in her skull. The world was silent for a moment as shock passed over the woman's face, before her body crumpled to the floor, mouth still open in song.

Ailsa looked down at the body. "Well, aren't you accommodating. I thought you would be made of stone too." Her eyes rose to meet those of the leader and she smirked, pulling the axe out of the head to reveal cerulean blood dripping from the blade like sapphires.

Screams of fury possessed the ceasg as they bared their teeth charging up the bank.

Harris stuck his foot out to trip one up, while another fell upon him. He held the woman away from his face by the neck as she gnashed her teeth. Eventually, he kicked her away and sank into a crouch as she advanced on him again, but this time his knife was positioned between their bodies as she lunged.

Another flew at Ailsa, but her axe sliced through the air, catching the woman on the shoulder; blue blood dribbled from the wound as the girl circled her. Suddenly, a pair of pale hands grabbed Ailsa from behind, pulling her to the floor. She wrestled desperately against the marble arms that held her down, as the remaining ceasg approached, licking their lips. One held a clawed hand up, ready to slice through Ailsa's belly, when Harris tackled her to the ground.

Ailsa kicked her legs up into the face of the ceasg who

restrained her, eliciting a guttural cry.

She hauled herself up, before she recovered and let her axe fly. It landed in her captor's neck; blue liquid spurted from the wound and her legs buckled beneath her, eyes closing.

Ailsa saw Harris's torch still aflame a few feet away. She grabbed it before advancing down the bank of the lagoon.

"Give him back, now," she shouted. "Or I'll take great pleasure in cracking every single one of your skulls open!"

The ceasg baulked at the light and backed away, towards the centre of the pool, hands flying up to cover their eyes. They left Angus where he was, drifting face-up in the mere.

Harris appeared beside her, chest heaving as he wiped thick gore from his hands.

"Quick, Ailsa, grab him. I can't go in the water."

She passed the torch and waded into the lagoon. Once she reached Angus, she found his skin surprisingly warm for having been in the cold for so long. She heaved him towards the bank where Harris bent to help.

"For now, you are safe," called the leader as she backed away towards the shadowy reaches of the cavern. "If we find you again, selkie, we will have you."

"Want. Want." The others called, before they vanished beneath the surface.

Ailsa turned her attention from the ceasg to Angus's prone body. Harris rubbed his arms up and down, to stimulate his circulation, but Angus still stared up at the roof, expressionless.

"Harris, what do we do?" Ailsa took one of Angus's hands in her own and held it tightly.

"I don't know!"

"He's starting to get cold!"

They watched the rise and fall of Angus's chest become slower and slower.

"Do something!"

"How does one wake a sleeping prince?" Harris whispered thoughtfully and gave a sheepish smile. He lowered his face to Angus's and kissed him fully on the lips. With a start, the prince opened his eyes to find Harris still leaning over him.

"Our first kiss and I'm unconscious," complained Angus, rubbing his temple with one hand.

"I can do it again if you like?"

Angus let out a snort. "No thanks, you're not my type."

Ailsa, still clutching Angus's hand, gave him a little squeeze. "Are you okay?"

"Stop fussing, it's not like you." He rolled his eyes. "It's not like I'm dying."

"You could have," she said weakly, looking away to hide the unshed tears in her eyes, but he captured her chin with his other hand.

His eyes were soft. "Not your fault." Ailsa nodded and he let go.

Harris clapped Angus on the shoulder. "Can you stand?"

"Yes. Hold on." Through a combined effort of pulling and pushing, they managed to get him on his feet, albeit swaying slightly.

Ailsa hooked his arm over her shoulders to better support his weight and gave the pool a worried glance. "Don't tell me, we have to go back into the water?"

"For what?" Harris examined one of the ceasg's corpses thoughtfully and then reached down to roll her over. Only when he applied a bit more pressure did her body move. She had transformed fully to marble; anyone who visited the cave in the future would truly find them as statues.

Ailsa sighed. "The Stone of Destiny…"

"The Stone isn't hidden in the water, it's up there." He pointed up at the back corner of the cave. There, barely visible against the granite, a number of grooves had been carved deep into the rock. And at the bottom there was a single triangle surrounding a wave.

Chapter 51

Angus and Ailsa followed Harris at a distance, shuffling forward over the rough floor around the lake. As they approached, they saw a wider opening further up the wall. Someone had cut a ladder into the stone leading up to it.

"Do you think you can make it up there?" Harris asked Angus, who eyed the wall with foreboding.

Ailsa gripped his shoulder. "I'll help you."

With Harris in front, leading the way, Angus next and Ailsa last, they ascended the rock wall carefully. The foot and handholds were a little too spaced out for Ailsa, so she had to jump up in a few sections. About halfway, there was a whoop from above as Harris pulled himself over the lip of the biggest cavity.

"I found it! Hurry up!"

Ailsa huffed but pressed on up the makeshift ladder with Angus. Eventually, he heaved himself up over the edge as well, breathing heavily.

"You have to see this, Ailsa!"

"I'm coming!" She reached for the last hollow with her fingertips, but it was just out of her grasp. She braced one foot against the wall directly in front of her and pushed herself up. Then, just as she managed to hook two fingers over, her other foot slipped from its step and her body swung out and away from the rock wall.

Her stomach plummeted to the cave floor below as she dangled desperately by one hand. She tried to call out to the two men above, but her breath wouldn't come.

Her fingers slid slowly over the rough stone, fighting to swing herself back up, but she couldn't quite catch the handhold.

Blood pounding in her ears, she tried one last time.

And missed again.

Her fingers slipped from the rim.

But a hand closed tightly over her wrist.

She let out a faint squeak as Angus pulled her up into the cavern overhead; his face a mask of concern and pain.

"Are you okay?" he croaked, still recovering from his brush with the ceasg.

She lay on her back, panting and nodded her head.

There was a skylight in the small upper cavern, which made the granite walls sparkle. The room was perfectly square, with a dais in the middle, on which stood a modest chest of stained oak. Harris turned around, excitement lighting his features, his eyes twinkling like the treasured lagoon.

"Is that where they hid it?" asked Angus, still crouched

beside Ailsa.

Harris nodded. "I can't take it. Part of the protection is that only a human can retrieve it."

Angus turned back to offer her his hand, "Ailsa, you do it—"

"No," Harris said sharply. "You should stay there and rest. Angus, it's for your family, you take it."

Angus nodded and climbed the stairs, Harris behind him.

"When I was last here, it was the middle of the night. My aunt pulled that box from her pocket and it grew right in front of my eyes." They watched as the prince reached out and felt the smooth wood. Ailsa rolled onto her side to watch as Angus lifted the lid reverently, then gasped. "It's not there."

"You didn't think we would just leave the Stone in an unlocked box now, did you?" said Harris. He waved his hand over the lining, and Ailsa heard an audible click from her position on the floor. Angus's jaw dropped as the selkie stood back from the chest.

From somewhere inside, a fountain of water sprang up, reaching a few feet high before arching to the floor of the platform with a splash. There, suspended inside the water, lay the Stone.

Angus reached his hand in slowly. The water did not change trajectory, instead it parted along his forearm. He hesitated, as if bracing himself for what he was about to do. Finally, taking a deep breath, he closed his fist around the object and pulled it out of the fountain.

"The Stone of Destiny," Harris whispered. Angus held his palm out to Ailsa so that she could see.

The Stone was a lot smaller than she'd imagined, around the size of a strawberry. On one side, it was a dull, grey stone but when Angus flipped it over in his palm, the inside was revealed. It looked as if it had been halved in order to expose the vibrant, purple, crystalline interior. A ring of white crystals bordered the uneven violet quartz, like a night sky with bright galaxies. As light caught the little ridges, they glinted, winking and star-like.

"It's exquisite," Ailsa breathed. Angus nodded and curled his hand loosely around it.

They crouched together for a moment, in silence.

"We did it," Angus whispered. Then, again, a little louder. "We did it!" A laugh bubbled up his throat, echoing around the cave.

Harris joined him in his exultation. Even Ailsa couldn't hold back a bark of laughter.

We found the Stone!

Harris stood up, hands on his hips. A huge smile graced his face, even as he said, "We just have to make it back to Dunrigh now."

That was enough to dull Ailsa's relief. It had been a long journey and it would be a long way back.

Still, thought Ailsa, *we did it. If it makes the people of Eilanmòr feel safer, then maybe it was worth it.*

Harris held out his hand to her as Angus pocketed the Stone. "Come on, if I give you both a boost, we can get out through the hole in the ceiling." He nudged his shoulder into the other man's, as they walked. "Just think of home, Angus." The prince's face brightened a little and he stepped below the opening first.

She watched as the selkie held out his hands for Angus to step up on and felt a niggle of doubt.

"Harris," she murmured as he lifted Angus up. "The ceasg said that Nicnevan knew where the Stone of Destiny was all along, but she was waiting to see if they would claim it."

Harris laughed, elated to have completed their mission. "Well, they didn't catch me, or anyone else, so her trap didn't work."

"So why didn't Nicnevan just take it?" Something didn't feel right.

"Maybe she knew we wouldn't allow her to?" He shrugged. "Maybe she knew it would be protected by strong magic?"

"And now it's in our possession, mostly unprotected." Ailsa's heart sank; she couldn't help but feel they had walked right into a trap.

"Well, I wouldn't say that." He regarded her with a smirk. "Calm down. We'll just need to be incredibly careful on the journey back. I'd say a speedy return is fairly important now." He chuckled to himself and she cocked her head in question.

"Harris? Ailsa? You'll never guess what I can see," croaked Angus up above.

Harris held out his hands for Ailsa's foot. He lifted her up quickly and her fingers found purchase on the mouth of the skylight. Angus's hands hooked under her forearms, pulling her up through the gap. As she rose onto the grassy hill, her mouth fell open in wonder.

They were no longer on an island surrounded by sea, but on top of a hill overlooking a glen. Below them, a grey road snaked its way through the middle. To their right, they could see the miniscule ruin of a house squatting at the bottom of the jagged mountains which towered around them. Further on, patches of forest grew like clumps of hair.

Ailsa laughed out loud. There, to the left of where they stood, the road led to a series of larger hills, and there atop the highest, covered in splotches of bluebells, stood Dunrigh Castle, its flags fluttering merrily in the breeze. Angus gave a shout and fell to his knees on the grass.

"Hello?" called Harris. "Anyone going to help me up?" his voice echoing around the cavern below. Together, they reached back into the hole and pulled him through. Harris eyed the surroundings with a satisfied smirk playing around his mouth.

"You knew?" asked Ailsa "You knew the cave led back home?"

"It didn't before, but that's one of the supposed powers of the Stone of Destiny. When the bearer steps through a portal, wherever they are thinking of going, they suddenly find themselves there. It's why I told you to think of home."

"I guess it's true," muttered Angus in disbelief.

Ailsa grimaced. "You could have just told him, '*Please think of being inside Dunrigh Castle, in front of a log fire.*' He must have been thinking about the Glen of Sorrow."

Angus looked sheepish. "I was thinking how lovely Dunrigh looked as we left. Come on, Ailsa, it's not that far. We're almost at the top of the glen."

"Plus, I'd rather we were able to appreciate the Hero's Welcome!"

"Don't be gloomy, Ailsa" said Angus. "I'll make sure you get a large helping of black pudding when we get there."

She watched the two men, stumble down the hill through the heather in a rush. Up ahead, the clouds were rolling over the sky, tumultuous in the heavy winds. Ailsa breathed in a sigh of fresh air and began the final march that would bring their journey to an end.

Chapter 52

An elegant, red-headed woman sat with her back to the glass as she read aloud to the figure in the bed beside her. The black rot had crept across more of his skin, but his eyes glowed bright as he watched the clouds roll by above. The glass house that was his sick room provided some heat for his weary body as he relived past adventures with the help of the soothing voice of the selkie beside him. His youth had been filled with heroic deeds, mythical monsters and epic romances.

Lady Iona was currently recounting his wedding day. He thought back to how dazzling his bride had been, how he had lifted the veil to reveal her flawless skin, large grey eyes and rosebud mouth. She had blushed when he had run a thumb across her jaw. She had been his light, his beacon, leading him out of the darkness.

The history book that the selkie beside him read left out many of the details. He remembered the day he had told his bride about the terrible mistakes of the past, how he had loved another before her but had been too blind to see the corruption in her soul. How he had had to leave her, only to have her return to tell him she was carrying his child. All of this, his fiancée had accepted with a gentle nod and a kiss to his cheek.

He had not known her, she'd said. She was glad he had escaped. Perhaps one day, they would be reunited with the baby and peace could come to the kingdom.

But then, after a few months of married bliss, he'd had to leave his pregnant wife when a great earthquake struck in the middle of the night. He knew, as he rushed through the corridors, that it was her. Knew he would have to end it, before she broke the country apart.

He rode throughout the night, until finally he came upon her home, tucked deep in the woods. She was frantic, weeping. The golden hair he'd fondly remembered was matted against her head as she screamed orders at the few faeries she kept around her. In front of her, a group of humans and some fair folk sat shivering as, one by one, they were called forward to answer her questions. He had watched from behind a tree as they wept, begging to be set free. She had grown tired of their protests and had ripped them apart like ragdolls.

He knew then, as he had watched the life flicker from a young faerie-girl's eyes, that this was the end. He had to stop her.

He had sneaked up behind her, binding her to the willow tree that sat in the middle of her court, with an iron chain he had carried with him.

The look of betrayal on her face had been replaced by

manic relief as she realised who it was that held her.

"Connall," she had exclaimed. "I knew you would come." Her face turned to anguish. "They took her. They took our daughter," she had grabbed at his jacket then, pleading, "You must find her—you must get her back."

"No!" One of the fae, a selkie, had pushed forward, tears still staining her face. "We took her away. She cannot be raised by this monster." Nicnevan had screamed and thrashed, but the chains had held, limiting her power.

"Please, Your Majesty, she is hidden and safe. When she comes of age, we will find her and she will be the new faerie queen. Do not seek her, you cannot protect her." The selkie had fallen to her knees. "Please, she is our only hope of peace."

He had nodded and turned back to Nicnevan, ready to deliver the killing blow. But he remembered the gentle girl she had been, the one who he had fallen in love with. He'd left her there in the clearing, screaming for him to come back and help her. Since then, Eilanmòr had been at peace.

Now, as he floated in his memories, in the glass house attached to the castle, he wondered what had become of the faerie queen and the daughter he had never known. Did she even know who she was? Tears formed at the corners of his eyes as he thought of all the things he wished to say to her. He had thought he would see her eventually, that she would meet her brothers and they would work together to fully establish peace, forever.

He thought of his wife, gone for thirteen years, He knew she watched over him and still waited for him, beyond death. When he finally let go, she would be there, waiting with open arms, ready to go together into the next world. He imagined how soft her pale skin would be as she held his hand. How her grey eyes would be calm and warm.

He closed his eyes against the sunlight and breathed deeply.

The woman beside him suddenly stopped her reading. He kept his eyes closed, but listened for the reason to her pause. The door to the glass house opened and he heard his eldest son, speaking softly so as not to disturb him.

"Our brothers and the girl are back. I think they have the Stone."

Iona rose from her seat and followed Duncan out of the room. She turned to look at the King before she closed the door behind her and saw a wistful smile painted on his face. She wasn't sure how, but she was struck by the surety that this would be the last time she saw him alive. She closed the door, leaving him his freedom to be at peace.

Chapter 53

The trio were pulled through the gate by waiting arms and passed between people—castle servants and nobles alike—who hugged and congratulated them. It seemed that their journey had not been as secret as they had hoped. Ailsa looked up to see Iona racing down the stairs, her red hair streaming out behind her. Prince Duncan jogged behind, propriety flying out of the window as they both tumbled towards them. Duncan threw his arms around Angus in a back-breaking hug as Iona pulled both Ailsa and Harris towards her.

Angus blinked in shock at his brother's actions.

"Did you miss us that much?"

What a difference from when we left, thought Ailsa, allowing her mouth to pull into a half-smile.

"We all heard reports that something had happened to one of you, that someone had almost drowned," explained Iona.

Ailsa supposed that the rumours had been about her, yet the two men had almost died at various other points too. She marvelled once again at how impossible it was that they'd made it back safe and sound.

Harris ruffled his sister's hair. "Well, we're here now, aren't we?" he said, echoing Ailsa's thoughts.

"Yes," muttered Iona. "And I am most interested to find out how your definition of *stealthy* has changed since I last saw you. Everyone has been talking about some party that you showed up to."

Harris had the decency to look abashed.

"Couldn't be helped," he murmured.

Iona caught Ailsa's eye and gave her a confused look. *What else have they been saying?* wondered Ailsa.

"So, little brother," Duncan asked, clapping Angus on the back. "Do you have it?"

The younger prince laughed and stood back, fishing around inside his pocket. The crowd pressed in around them, holding collective breaths. He revealed it with a flourish, making sure to do his best Harris impression.

"Behold, the Stone of Destiny."

The Eilanmòrians around them cheered and jostled one another to get a better look. Ailsa bit her lip. She didn't like that so many people could see they had found the Stone. *Wouldn't it be better to keep it hidden?* She eyed the people in the crowd with growing anxiety. Any of them could be working for another country—or even Nicnevan herself—waiting for their chance to steal it or sell someone information on its whereabouts. Cold dread clawed at her throat.

Just then, she glimpsed a hooded face in the crowd,

with what looked like gleaming red eyes. She blinked again and it was gone; it was probably just her mind playing tricks on her.

"I'm glad you're home," smiled Duncan. "Come, let's go inside."

Someone was playing bagpipes as they paraded into the castle. Ailsa allowed herself one look back as they ascended the stairs: the castle grounds were alive with summer flowers, but beyond the walls, purple and orange heather covered the landscape. She took in the jagged mountains and boulder strewn moorland they had first travelled through over a week ago. Eilanmòr was wild and dangerous—but it was her home and they had saved it.

Duncan kept one arm around his brother, with Ailsa, Iona and Harris close behind. Lady Moira shuffled ahead, shouting orders at servants to have rooms readied, food prepared and ambassadors alerted that the coronation would soon be taking place. Ailsa realised that Angus's cousin had lost her previously poised demeanor. Ailsa made a mental note to surprise her more often in the future.

The castle was also much busier than it had been when she, Harris and Angus had left. Nobles and guests from around Eilanmòr and neighbouring countries swanned through the halls, like puffed-up pheasants. In comparison, Ailsa felt that they looked like little brown sparrows in their travelling clothes. When they arrived in the main hall, she was happy to see that they'd left the hubbub behind; only a few people sat around the long table, eating their lunch.

She noticed Princess Vashkha huddled over something at the side of the table. As they approached, they heard a gurgling sound and a little hand popped up from the bundle of blankets she was holding.

"Is that?" Angus breathed.

"I'm afraid, brother, that you're *not* next in line to the throne anymore," said Duncan with a pleased smile.

Big, round eyes peered at them with interest when the three leaned in for a closer look. The baby flexed its fingers in front of them.

Angus chuckled, tears building at the corners of his eyes. "They're welcome to it."

Princess Vashkha lounged regally on her seat, surrounded by pillows, like a golden goddess. The baby's jet hair sprouted thickly on his head and she smoothed back a tuft, clearly besotted. The rest of the party, even the soldiers, followed the movement, enraptured. Duncan placed a hand on her shoulder.

"May I present Prince Douglas Visuran MacFeidh."

Princess Vashkha *tsked*, but continued to smile down at the little prince. "My son should have a Visenyan first name."

Duncan rolled his eyes as if they'd had this

conversation many times before. "He is a prince of Eilanmòr. There are no Eilanmòrian names that start with 'V.'"

"Which is why I had to settle for a middle name," she sighed. "It means, *'lucky despite my father not giving me a proper first name.'*"

Douglas stuck a few fingers into his mouth, oblivious to his parents bickering.

Duncan motioned for them to join him at the table and took a seat at the head, all business again. Now that they had arrived in front of the council, the family reunion would have to be called short. Angus did not sit down, instead leaning on his sword, so Ailsa and Harris took their places behind him.

Prince Duncan didn't seem to notice, as he lifted a glass of wine to his lips. "I hope that your journey was less eventful than the rumours would have us believe."

Angus stood up straighter and gave a brief summary of their expedition. He left out any time that they had been in great danger, nevertheless, he was sure to include a quick reference to Ailsa saving his life. At the mention of this, Duncan's eyes flicked over to her, impressed.

Once Angus had finished, Prince Duncan nodded his head and stood.

"I thank you brother, and your companions, Lord Harris and Ailsa." He stopped and his eyes crinkled. "We really ought to give you a title, it will sound better when

I thank you." He began again, in his booming voice. "Time is of the essence. We must inform our guests, and the residents of Dunrigh, that the coronation will take place two days hence, at sundown."

He spoke to General Fraser beside him who, up until then, had been eyeing Ailsa with open contempt. "General, please send out some of your soldiers to nearby towns to tell them they will have a new king by the week's end."

"And what of the old king?" Angus asked, stepping forward. His eyes were eager, but he gripped his sword tightly.

Iona placed a hand on his elbow. "When you returned, I was reading to him."

"Our business here is almost over—let us visit him together," Duncan told his brother kindly. "Lady Iona, could you please escort your brother and Ailsa to their rooms? I believe they could do with a wash and a rest."

Iona led them away through the large doors to the side of the hall. When Ailsa turned to look back, Angus and Duncan were lost in conversation. Without warning, she was struck with a sudden wave of jealousy. How nice would it be to have someone else to share your plans and worries with?

She gave herself a mental shake. Their father was *dying*.

She let Iona push her up the stairs but before she

could follow Iona into their room, Harris pulled Ailsa aside.

His eyes slid over her face but lingered just below her eyes, at the dark circles which must have been blooming there.

"Will you be okay?" The red curls that fell over his brow were in need of a good wash. Her hand itched to push them away, but she gripped the hem of her shirt instead. "Do you need anything?"

She sighed and shook her head. "I just need to sleep for a month. Shame the coronation is in two days."

Harris rubbed the back of his neck. "It's been a long journey, especially for someone who didn't want to go in the first place."

"Well, "she smiled ruefully, "there was this presumptuous selkie who wouldn't take no for an answer."

"I'm glad you were with me, Ailsa." He lifted one of her hands and, despite the dirt caked on her skin, kissed the back of it. "I'll see you later," he said, releasing her and turning towards his room. She stared at the spot he had kissed.

"Okay," she murmured, but he was already gone. Feeling light-headed and tired, she headed to her own chambers.

Iona was there to help her strip off her clothes before Ailsa headed towards the bathroom.

She was scrubbed down quickly by a servant who

could clearly sense that she would fall asleep at any moment. Then, bundled in a fluffy towel, she was dried and pushed towards the bed. They had drawn the curtains to block the sunlight, and a fire burned in the hearth. Once alone, Ailsa managed to change into a robe, before sinking into the soft blanket and falling asleep.

Chapter 54

Later, Ailsa awoke to a muted conversation coming from the main room. She rose groggily and combed her hair out with her fingers; it had become a knotted mess as she'd slept.

Night had fallen but the fire and some candles created a warm glow. Food had been laid out for them but no one seemed to be eating as they talked quietly. Angus was there, sitting on the couch with Iona's arm around his shoulders. Harris was in the process of setting a cup of tea in front of him.

Ailsa took a deep breath. From the look on Angus's face, she knew what he was about to say.

"It's done," he mumbled bleakly. "He's dead."

She pressed her lips together and went to sit in the chair across from him. "When?"

"Sometime between when we arrived in Dunrigh, and when I went down to visit him with my brother." He stared down at his palms, his eyes puffy.

"I'm so sorry, Angus," whispered Ailsa. She was no good with this. When her own mother had died, she had been alone. She hadn't had anyone to share her grief with. She shifted uncomfortably in her seat until finally she did the only thing she could think of and reached for his hand. He jumped when he felt her fingers clasp around his, but he gripped her hand like a lifeline.

"After everything—all we went through—I thought I would get to see him alive one more time."

Iona rubbed his back. "When he heard you had returned, he must have felt he didn't need to worry anymore. He had been holding on so long. You finally brought him peace."

He nodded and took a sip of his tea. Ailsa moved so she could sit on the couch beside Angus and pulled the robe tighter across her body. Of all people, she knew how he felt; Angus was an orphan now, just like her.

At least, she thought, *he has everyone here to help him through this.*

Harris left his seat at the low table to pace across the room.

"How did Duncan take it?" he asked as he set about making another cup of tea.

"When we got to the greenhouse, there were a few nurses there, waiting. They told us he had passed. Duncan... did his duty," he let out a great shuddering sigh. "He walked in, lifted the sheet from my father's face, bent a knee, then left me there. Not even a minute had passed before he was off shouting instructions to staff, arranging his funeral and the coronation." He wiped a hand under his eyes.

"He was trying to be practical," Iona soothed.

"When we were younger, my brother was always laughing, always joking around." He studied Ailsa's hand in his as he spoke. "Then, one day, it was as if he realised the responsibilities that he'd face. They're always at war, the boy and the man. Sometimes, when he forgets that he's going to be king, he's just my brother. I like him better then."

Harris returned from the buffet with a few plates piled high with snacks. He placed one in front of Angus and another in front of Ailsa. She raised her eyebrows but he just flopped down into a stuffed armchair across from them.

"You looked hungry."

Ailsa picked at the food as they all listened to Angus. Iona managed to find a bottle of whisky that had been left in her room and they toasted solemnly.

"To King Connall," said Iona raising her glass.

"And to King Duncan," Angus replied, clinking his goblet against hers. "Long may he live."

They all murmured their responses and took a sip of the amber liquid. It burned Ailsa's throat on the way down, but warmed her belly as she drank.

Chapter 55

They talked long into the night until Angus fell asleep, Ailsa stroking his hair, just like he had done for her during their journey.

She must have fallen asleep too, because when she opened her eyes again, she saw that blankets had been spread out over her and Angus, and Harris and Iona's sleeping bodies on the other seats. She wondered who had done it and whether that person had thought the way their limbs entwined was inappropriate. She quickly dismissed the thought. Impropriety was not the worst thing she had ever been accused of.

She sat for a while, not quite ready to greet the day. Angus's comforting smell rose from his thick hair. As always, Harris's gentle snoring filled the room. *When had this become familiar? When had these people come to feel like family?*

All too soon, the voices of servants in the hallway drifted in to wake the others. They stretched and groaned as they slowly came back to consciousness. Harris gave her a little nod as he went to remake the fire and boil the kettle. Iona slipped to the windows to open the curtains.

No one uttered a word, so as not to break the peaceful atmosphere in the room.

Angus was the last to lift his head, the grief still glazing his eyes.

Ailsa gave his shoulder a squeeze as he sat up, extracting himself from her legs. He nodded gratefully to her. He seemed to give himself a mental shake as someone knocked on the door. Ailsa could see the resolve building in his face as he stood and squared his shoulders. Today would be about saying goodbye to his father and preparing to crown their new king.

Finally, unable to delay any longer, he called to the world outside the door.

"Come in," he croaked.

Lady Moira craned her neck around the door as she opened it. Today she was dressed respectfully in a black dress. Her golden hair was pinned back from her face, revealing dark shadows under her eyes.

"Your Highness, we were looking for you," said Lady Moira as she stepped into the room, her cane making a resounding *clack* in the silence.

Angus shrugged his shoulders. "I fell asleep here."

She approached the seating area and fussed with the blankets they had discarded. Ailsa wasn't sure if she was cleaning up their indiscretion or if she just needed something to do with her hands. "Well, you must come with me and get ready for the ceremonies today."

Iona placed a hand on the back of his elbow. "Don't worry, Angus, we'll be right there."

He forced a half-smile onto his face and nodded. "Thanks. I'll see you all later."

He was led from the room by a kind-eyed maid. He seemed to know her well, as he threw an arm around the woman's shoulder while she patted his back in comfort.

Lady Moira lingered, back straight as she hesitated near the open door.

"The funeral will be quite private. Family, castle staff and high-ranking foreign guests only. Lady Iona, Lord Harris," she nodded to them. "As the ambassadors of Struanmuir, Prince Duncan has asked that you attend." She took a deep breath and turned her disapproving eyes on Ailsa. "He has also asked that you attend, Miss MacAra."

"Me?" asked Ailsa. "But I'm not high-ranking."

Lady Moira nodded once. "He is grateful for the part you played in retrieving the Stone of Destiny. I daresay that Prince Angus would appreciate your attendance also." She turned and let herself out of the room, the door whispering shut behind her.

Iona went to get ready, but before Ailsa could follow, Harris caught her arm, his eyes shadowed. "Will you be alright today?" he asked.

She bit her lip and gripped the folds of her robe in her cracked and weathered hands. She didn't want to go—

there would be so many people—but that didn't matter. She would do this for Angus.

"I'll be fine," she finally said, raising her chin.

He smiled at her then and bent to give her a kiss on the top of her head. "I'll see you soon," he said before letting himself out of the room.

Ailsa closed her eyes as her hand flew to her forehead, right where the brand of his lips was still burning. Something would have to be done about that selkie. She just wasn't sure whether she wanted to hit him—or kiss him back.

Chapter 56

his father's funeral was quiet and refined, not at all like the man he had been. He had been a great explorer and it had cost him his life.

Angus stood before the funeral pyre, where he had been for over an hour as priests and scholars chanted words over his father's body, sending him into the afterlife.

He felt only a melancholy detachment. His father had been a laughing, adventurous and highly-strung man. The body that was spread out, ready to be burned, was not him. Angus closed his eyes for a moment, remembering how he had been when he was alive, before he fell ill.

Although they hadn't agreed on some things, and his father hadn't exactly been accepting of his… desires… he hadn't tried to beat it out of him either. Aside from that, he had been a doting father, if a little easily distracted by distant horizons and curiosities.

He had been a good king too. While the official funeral had only a hundred or so in attendance, he knew outside the castle walls, Eilanmòrians around the country would be toasting his memory.

He risked a glance at his brother, solid and serious as ever. He was playing his part well, but Angus could see the slight way he leaned into his wife. If he treated Eilanmòr half as well as he treated her and their child, the country was in safe hands.

While the priests continued their prayers, he lifted his eyes to scan the crowd. Finally, he caught sight of them. There, nestled amongst his extended family, were Ailsa and Harris.

He felt a surge of warmth. Duncan had allowed them both to come, along with Harris's sister who stood beside them, her hair shining like molten copper in the early morning light. They were all dressed in black, which suited only Ailsa, the contrast against her pale, unblemished skin shockingly lovely. She raised her eyes to his, her dark hair falling away from the left side of her face, revealing her wine-coloured mark. She raised a hand to sweep it back into place, hiding that part of her face, and gave him a tentative smile. She nudged Harris at the same time, his eyes also meeting Angus's.

He felt it then, a bond between the three of them. In his mind's eye, he imagined it, strong and golden, connecting their bodies together with light. *How had he come to love these two people in such a short time?*

He quickly glanced again at his brother, ramrod straight beside him, and then back to his companions. No matter what lay ahead, he had gained a new brother and sister over these last few weeks.

Finally, the chanting came to a stop. Duncan strode forward, ready to complete his duty. After a final blessing, he threw a torch upon the wooden pile, and they all watched as his father's body fed the flames.

Chapter 57

Ailsa watched as the flames from the pyre rose higher. The crowd was silent, listening to the priests and priestesses as they hummed a slow, sombre melody.

Prince Duncan and his wife had stepped forward, ready to receive their guests' sympathies, the very image of a solemn, future King and Queen. He was wearing his family's tartan, while she was clad in an ebony, but heavily embroidered, dress. Angus took one step back into the shadow of the castle towers, his eyes meeting Ailsa's again. Her heart ached for him. After everything, this wasn't how she'd imagined they would end their journey.

The holy men and women stopped their humming, extending their soon-to-be king respect.

"My fellow Eilanmòrians and honoured guests," Duncan began, his rich voice resonating from his spot beside the fire. "I appreciate your attendance here today. We have just said goodbye to my father, a good king. I hope that I can one day be half the man he was.

"As the sun rose today, we prepared to formally end the rule of one king. Before the sun sets tomorrow, I will take his place as the next one. Today we will mourn my father, tomorrow we will celebrate. There is food and drink in the great hall. Please join us."

Once he was finished, he wrapped an arm protectively around his wife and they exited together, stopping only to receive Prince Douglas's sleeping form from a nursemaid. Together, the family disappeared through the large doors followed by a myriad of servants.

The crowd began to depart, some heading straight for the food, others coming forward to offer a more intimate goodbye to the late king. Ailsa scoffed under her breath. If they thought a flaming corpse was going to listen, they were fools.

In their black clothes, everyone looked the same; it was hard to tell nobles from servants, and Eilanmòrian's from foreigners.

It's oddly liberating, she thought as she walked slowly back into the castle with Iona and Harris, *to blend into the crowd.* Here they were just people who were honouring their dead king. No one looked twice as they approached the doors.

She spied Angus leaning against the stone, hands in his pockets, staring wistfully at the cloud-speckled sky. She wondered where he would fit in now that his brother and sister-in-law were to be crowned. *Would he have a role to play? Or would he finally be afforded some of the freedom he desired both in his daily life and romantically?*

He lowered his head when they reached him, his gaze soft. She had expected to find sorrow there, but the desolation from the night before was gone. If she wasn't mistaken, there was now a kindling of hope reflected in his eyes.

"Thanks for being here." He pushed off from the wall and came to join them on their way inside.

"How are you feeling?" asked Iona.

He let out a long breath, the force of it moving the hair above his brow. "Better. I'm glad it's done."

Harris swung an arm around his shoulders, giving a squeeze. "Now to the food!"

"Do you think," Angus began quietly, biting his lip, "We could grab something and then eat it somewhere else?"

"Of course, Angus," Iona said, swatting her brother upside his head, "If that's what you want."

"Thanks." He hung his head. "Hearing condolences, it just makes it harder. I'm glad it's not my duty to stay, I think Duncan is even less thrilled to greet all our guests than I am."

Harris smiled. "The perks of being a younger brother. Do you think you could help me lose my sibling? She's been nagging me since we returned."

Iona let out a harrumph. "Ailsa was probably the only reason you managed to survive the last couple of weeks. I can't imagine how often she had to save your hide." She opened the door to the hall and ushered them inside. The smell of roast chicken and gravy was enough to make their mouths water. They had made it to the food before everyone else; the room was almost empty, save for a few servants who were busy with their tasks.

"Actually," Ailsa said, her lips quirking up, "I think in terms of life saving, we're pretty even."

Iona groaned. "The fact that you had to save anyone's life at all worries me greatly."

"It's like having Mother around," Harris groaned, grabbing a plate and helping himself to a pile of steaming hot food. "When will you be fun again, sister?"

"Oh, just you wait until tomorrow night," she laughed, placing a few parsnips delicately on her plate. "Ailsa and I are going to find some men in kilts to surround ourselves with, right?"

Harris made a choking sound but Ailsa snickered. "Absolutely. Maybe I'll borrow one of your dresses, too."

Iona's eyes lit up. "Oh Ailsa, I have just the one! I've seen how good your legs are in trousers… I'll get them out tonight!"

Sensing that she had dug herself a hole, Ailsa made a noncommittal noise and scooped some haggis onto her plate.

Chapter 58

The next day, Ailsa stood in front of a mirror, examining the gown Iona chose for her.

The dress was fit for a warrior queen. The bodice was made from leather painted gold, cut to resemble the breastplate from a suit of armour. There were no sleeves, but gold chains hung from the neck over the shoulders, creating a waterfall of metal which flowed down her arms. True to Iona's word, there was a flash of leg, where slits in the dress allowed Ailsa to walk freely.

"It's wonderful," she breathed, running her hand over the smooth material. She circled around so that she could see the back. The dress was held together not by buttons, but a row of straps, with Ailsa's skin visible between each one.

"Perfect for a lady and a guard. Possibly even a knight," smiled Angus. "My brother has decided to offer you a job."

Ailsa stopped spinning and stared at her friend as he lounged on the chair by the dressing table. "He wants to make *me* a… knight?"

"Well, why not?" He shrugged. "You saved my sorry

ass and helped secure the safety of the kingdom. I'd say he should give you a castle, but then we'd have to evict someone…"

Ailsa threw herself onto the bed with as much grace as she could muster in the dress.

"Do you really think it will help then? The Stone I mean?"

"No idea," he chuckled. "But if it makes people feel better, I'd say it was worth it." He paused, his face darkening. "I still don't feel right about Nicnevan knowing the location of the Stone. She could have taken it at any point—"

"And if it's so important, why let it go?" Ailsa pulled at a curl that had escaped her up-do. "Something else is obviously more important to her."

Angus nodded. "Her daughter. I wonder what happened to h—"

The door banged open, cutting them off. Harris strode in, carrying three glasses of a sparkling liquid.

"Right lad, and lass, no more moping in here. The coronation is in two hours and I say we should get rip-roaring drunk before then." He handed one to Angus, who placed it on the dressing table.

"I am never getting drunk with you again," stated Ailsa as she stood and brushed her dress off. "You *cannot* be trusted."

I cannot be trusted.

"But Ailsa," he said, his voice like honey as he approached, "The last time we had such fun." His eyes flicked down her body, heating her cheeks. "Nice dress, by the way."

She narrowed her eyes. "You just want an excuse to try to kiss me again."

His grin was feline as he sidled closer, purring in her ear. "One, it was you who kissed me. Two—" He placed the glass into her hand, his fingers brushing against her own. "Two, I don't think I need an excuse."

"Oh, give me a break," muttered Angus. Harris spun around, surprised Angus was still in the room. The prince just shook his head. "I'll see you both at the coronation," he said, doing his best to not look at them, before leaving the room.

"Do you think he'll be okay?" Ailsa murmured. She took a sip of her sparkling wine, needing time to collect her thoughts.

"Well he has us, doesn't he? We'll make sure of it." Harris turned to face her again, his eyes unreadable. "Ailsa, I think we need to talk—"

The door swung open again and the selkie cursed.

"Come on, we need to head downstairs," called Iona. "Harris, someone from somewhere wants to meet you."

He huffed, his eyes still on Ailsa's face. "We'll speak later," he promised. Mischief crossed his face. "I really like that dress. Especially this bit." He reached up and stroked one finger along her exposed flesh between the straps on her back, goosebumps blooming in his wake. Her breathing sped up as she inhaled his sea salt scent. He was so close. If she just raised herself on her tiptoes…

Harris seemed to sense exactly how it was affecting her. "I can't wait to see how you dance in it." And with that he pulled away, giving her one last wink before he went into the hallway.

Ailsa collapsed onto the bed with a groan.

The sun shone shyly from behind a cloud as they waited outside for the coronation. From the corner of her eye, Ailsa admired the selkie beside her. Iona had left her hair unbound and it flowed around her like a living flame in the slight wind. The green dress she'd chosen glittered in the light. It was almost modest, save for the open back which revealed freckled skin all the way down to her—

Iona caught her gaze and smiled.

"I like your dress," said Ailsa, and she meant it. *Maybe one day, I'll be brave enough to wear something like it.*

The selkie gave her a wink, her expression an imitation of the one Ailsa had seen on her brother so many times.

"I may need to kidnap the dressmaker when I return to Struanmuir; his talent is wasted here," she teased.

Ailsa laughed. "You can be a bit terrifying, you know."

"Well, what a pair we make!" She grabbed Ailsa's hand and gave it a squeeze. "A couple of terrifying, magnificent, powerful females," she declared.

Ailsa couldn't help but grin and raise her chin. Perhaps, with Iona's help, she could become that person.

The coronation was taking place behind the castle, on top of an outcrop of land. It faced westward to the hills and mountains, allowing the sun—when it could be bothered to appear—to sink behind, blessing the crowning of the new king.

They made their way over a wooden walkway, which had been placed there to save the ladies' dresses from the damp grass. They soon found some chairs which had been set out for the ceremony. Ailsa and Iona took a couple near the back, saving Harris a seat beside them. Towards the front, the chairs had already been taken. From their regal clothing and poised positions, Ailsa could tell these were foreign dignitaries. Iona saw her looking and quickly set to work telling her who they all were, her knowledge limitless.

"Those two with the embroidered coats are from Visenya. Usually a pretty friendly bunch but do *not* accept a drink from them. They begin drinking gin when they are ten," Ailsa noticed their dress and looks were similar to Princess, soon to be Queen, Vashkha.

"Over there, wearing the silk wraps are the Monadh ambassadors. Their country isn't really ruled by anyone.

Instead, a matriarch runs each village, and every year they gather to have a big old gossip. The ambassadors are usually daughters, chosen at random from a lottery. The Monadhians are neither a threat, nor an ally. They keep to themselves and everyone lets them because their country isn't worth invading. Too many jungles with things that can kill you."

"Remind me not to go there, then."

Iona frowned as she scanned the crowds.

"Of course, there are no Avalognians. Mirandelle has sent someone, though. Ah yes, over there." She waved her hand politely in the direction of some people under large umbrellas.

Ailsa could barely make out the dark, puffed skirts on the women and the pale suits on the men. Her heart stuttered as she scanned the group but there was no sign of Captain Scarsi or any of his soldiers.

"I'll never understand Mirandelli fashion," huffed Iona. "It's sweltering hot there, and humid to boot, but they still insist on wearing heavy velvet dresses with buttons all the way to their necks."

Ailsa laughed behind a hand. "They look like vampires."

Iona gave her a knowing smile. "Between you and me, I've often wondered how they sustain themselves. Apparently, the women never eat in public. Could it be that it's so no one discovers their secret?"

Ailsa grinned. "I could believe anything after these last few weeks."

The seats were quickly filled and any latecomers formed a standing crowd behind. A priest started to walk up the outcrop, swinging ceremonial incense. A hush descended over the guests, watching and waiting.

Where is Harris? Ailsa wondered.

A herald addressed the gathering.

"Please stand for Your Royal Highnesses, Prince Duncan and Princess Vashkha."

Everyone rose from their chairs, watching for the couple.

First came a piper, his instrument bellowing the first notes of the Eilanmòrian anthem. Next came the royal retinue, lords and ladies close to the crown. Angus's bearded face poked up from behind an old man and Ailsa shot him a smile, which he returned when he saw her.

"What did I miss?" asked Harris, sliding into the seat beside her.

"*Harris,*" Iona hissed, furious. "Where the hell have you been?"

He just shrugged. "Some Duke wanted to meet me." He grimaced. "Well, he wanted to pawn his daughter off on me. I barely escaped with my life."

"I can't believe you."

"I can't believe you are talking through this sacred

ceremony, sister," he whispered back. Ailsa could feel the power of Iona's ire and she silently thanked the Gods she hadn't ever been in her bad graces.

At the back of the procession, Prince Duncan and Princess Vashkha glided arm in arm towards the natural dais. Duncan was once again wearing a great kilt in his family's tartan and carried a ceremonial broadsword on his back. His slate grey eyes scanned the crowd, noting those that had come to witness him.

Vashkha's raven hair gleamed in the braids atop her head, as if they were just waiting for a crown. Her red dress flowed out behind her, where two girls were holding the train to keep it from becoming sodden. Behind them, a nursemaid carried young Prince Douglas, cooing to keep him from crying.

They approached the priest, who waved the incense over them. Then they turned, facing the crowd, ready to accept their destiny.

Ailsa searched until she spotted Angus, off to the side, looking on with pride in his eyes.

"People of Eilanmòr," began the priest, his hand raised to hush the crowd, "Friends from foreign lands. We are here today to crown a new monarch."

A young woman stepped forward, holding a golden box. The head priest opened the lid, revealing the Stone of Destiny. He lifted it out carefully, cupping it in his hands and stood in front of Duncan.

Holy men and women in the front began to sing, the sound much different from the sombre tone of yesterday's sermon. The song was joyous, reverent. The priest held up the Stone and its purple interior shimmered in the light.

The sun was beginning to set behind the royal couple. Duncan stood proud and strong beside his wife, but even from where Ailsa was sitting, she could see he gripped her hand tightly. Vashkha smiled at the crowd, already acting like a queen. The sun sank between their bodies and the priest raised the Stone higher.

"Sire, is Your Highness willing to take the oath?" he asked.

"I am," replied Duncan in a steady voice, the sound travelling across the congregation.

"Do you, Duncan MacFeidh, first of your name, solemnly promise to govern the peoples of Eilanmòr, uphold their customs and guarantee their safety?"

"I solemnly do so promise."

The Stone began to glow in the priest's hands, amethyst light shining from within.

"Will you, with the furthest reaches of your power, ensure Law and Justice, in Mercy, to be executed in all your judgements?"

"I will," replied Duncan.

The Stone glowed brighter and Ailsa watched it in wonder. Then, all of a sudden, the light winked out and the Stone was gone. Shocked whispers spread through the crowd. *Was that supposed to happen*? Then an almighty crack split the evening air and everyone gasped. There, in Duncan's outstretched palm, lay the Stone of Destiny, still its mauve light casting shadows across his face.

The priest turned to face the crowd, waving a ceremonial hand. "Then, as representative of the people, I proclaim you Duncan, King of Eilanmòr."

Duncan stepped forward, and the priest placed a crown upon his brow. He accepted it with a solemn nod; Duncan was now King.

Chapter 59

Following Duncan's coronation, Vashkha was crowned as the King's Consort. There were also various readings from high-ranking government officials and clan leaders. By the time Duncan strode off the outcrop and back to the castle, Ailsa's backside was sore from sitting. Angus followed behind his family, to the front of the castle grounds, where the King would greet the people of Dunrigh officially and tie a large purple ribbon to the Peace Tree.

After the royals left, the crowd dispersed, chatting and looking for the food inside the great hall. The sun hovered on the horizon during its final moments, the temperature lowering with it. Some of the crowd was glancing at her and Harris now that the distraction of the coronation was over. Ailsa wondered if they'd heard about their journey to find the Stone. She could feel a few sets of blatant eyes focusing on her face in particular. She clutched her arms tightly around herself, dipping her head to hide her mark.

"Shall we head inside?" she asked Iona and Harris.

Harris ran a hand through his hair, watching a group

of Edessans follow the Eilanmòrian royals towards the front of the castle. One of them, a woman with turquoise braids, turned and gave them all a wink as she passed.

"You go ahead," Harris said with a grin. "I'm going to watch the ribbon ceremony first."

"Well we'll come with y—" Iona started to say, but her brother had run off before she could finish.

Ailsa bit her lip. *What is he up to?* She sighed, trying her best to brush her worries off.

"Come on, Iona. I think I need some wine."

They took each other's arms, muttering curses about boys and the impracticality of heels on grass, and made their way back into the warmth of the main hall.

An hour later, the band was in full swing. Iona had danced to every song and even Ailsa had allowed Angus to sweep her into a jig. They hadn't found Harris again, but Iona just shrugged and explained he was probably getting up to mischief somewhere.

I'd like him to be here getting up to mischief, Ailsa thought with a scowl. She'd thought he might ask her to dance and she had been debating whether to accept or not. It was highly irritating to wait around to rebuff him.

Iona took one look at her, sulking in the corner while the crowd was waltzing, and pulled her to the food table.

"Have you tried the cranachan? I think you need some sugar."

They weaved between the colourful dancers, being careful not to tread on toes. The ambassadors from the different countries were exhibiting various skill levels. While the Mirandellies were doing their absolute best to follow the moves, the Monadhians seemed to be making it up as they went along.

I know who I would prefer to dance with, Ailsa thought, watching a young Monadhian woman spin, her skirts flaring out like an orchid. She imagined spinning with Angus and Harris like they had when they had attended the first ceilidh, but the memory was tainted with her current annoyance for the selkie-man.

Where the hell is he? She scanned the crowd as she accepted two glasses of sparkling wine from a servant's tray.

Iona came back from the table with dessert and they exchanged their offerings. The combination of raspberries and wine fizzed on their tongues. Iona narrated their meal with her ratings on the guests' clothing choices.

"I'm really not sure about that big ball gown Lady Isobel is wearing. She looks like a cake."

"How do they keep them so... *puffy*?" asked Ailsa, watching the Mirandelli Duchess turning red as she attempted to keep up with the dance.

Iona smirked. "There's a theory that they have their servants sit underneath to hold it out."

Ailsa snorted at the impossibility of that and Iona rewarded her with a friendly pinch on her arm.

A deep, male voice caught Ailsa's attention, cutting short her mirth. She knew that voice.

"You would enjoy Mirandelle, M'Lady. Maybe you will visit one day."

"Perhaps I will," answered Lady Moira, a laugh in her voice.

"Perhaps I'll take you with me."

Ailsa's heart stopped as she turned. With Moira's arm in his, Captain Scarsi should have looked like a gentleman. Yet, even now, surrounded by royalty, he had the air of a pub brawler. Indeed, he still sported the faint but unmistakable bruising under his eyes from where she'd kneed his nose. His swaggering was more exaggerated since he had to walk slowly for his companion.

The pair walked close enough to them that Lady Moira clearly thought it impolite to ignore them.

"Lady Iona," she said, and, with a barely hidden grimace, she greeted Ailsa, "Miss MacAra. Have you met Captain Scarsi? He is the leader of King Merlo of Mirandelle's first battalion."

His grin was lazy but rage flared in Scarsi's eyes as he looked Ailsa up and down.

"Soon to be Major Scarsi when we return to Mirandelle. King Merlo thinks the success of my mission here merits a promotion."

"Oh?" asked Iona and his eyes snapped to her, taking in her height, her flaming hair and the barely concealed curl of her lips. "And what mission would that be?"

He placed one hand on his sword as if just shifting positions. "Making new friends of course," he drawled. "Speaking of, I believe I met your brother, Lady Iona."

This threw the selkie off enough for her to show a hint of shock on her face. Ailsa was thankful that she recovered quickly.

"Oh? When did you meet?"

"I am honoured to say that I ran into him and—Miss MacAra was it?—while we were up north a few days ago." He raised his chin. "Why were you up there again?" he fired the questions straight at Ailsa but kept his voice light.

"None of your business," she growled. Moira looked at her sharply, but Ailsa continued to stare him down. A sneer ghosted across his face.

"I always love visiting Eilanmòr," he told his companion. "You are all so... *accepting*." His voice became deathly cold. "Allowing changelings to the King's coronation, for example. In Mirandelle, I'm afraid we are not so tolerant."

Ailsa glowered, but before she could deliver a biting

retort, Lady Moira smoothly placed a hand on his elbow.

"Captain, please indulge me, I would love to go and watch the dancing."

He chuckled: the sound like nails scraping down Ailsa's spine. "Better yet, we should dance together."

Shame had Lady Moira ducking her head, her skin reddening. "I'm afraid… my leg—"

"Don't worry," he grinned. "When you're dancing with me, your foot won't touch the ground." He held out his arm again and Lady Moira took it, beaming.

"Well, until we meet again." He narrowed his eyes at Ailsa before sweeping Moira off to the dancefloor.

"What a prick," announced Iona but Ailsa found she was barely able to handle an answering smile.

"Why was that asshole over here?" asked Angus, appearing at Ailsa's shoulder.

"He was demonstrating how to be an asshole," she replied quietly. She watched as Iona and Angus exchanged concerned frowns.

"Shall we dance?" he asked, giving her a playful shove. She ignored him, still staring after where Scarsi had disappeared.

"I think I'm going to have some more food. You two should go, though," she said, giving Iona an encouraging smile.

"Well…" The selkie looked hesitant. "If you're sure." She grabbed Angus's hand, leading him away. Ailsa realised that Iona was slightly taller than the prince in her heels. Perhaps she would give him a run for his money.

"If you find my brother," called Iona, "Please tell him he is an eejit."

Ailsa nodded, watching as they blended into the crowd of dancers.

Chapter 60

*B*onfires, Ailsa decided, *were beautiful.*

She had been sitting out in the shadows on a balcony that overlooked the gardens. When Angus and Iona had left to dance, she had decided to disappear for a while, grabbing a wool blanket and a bottle of deep red wine. She knew she'd probably regret swigging it from the bottle in the morning but found she didn't really care as she stared into the flames of the bonfire someone had built outside. It was a balm against the civilisation of the dancing hall. Fire felt distinctly uncivilised. Primeval. The revellers who had crowded around were just silhouettes. It made them anonymous. This could have been a party anywhere.

She sipped the wine again and smacked her lips together at the warming liquid. Even with the flames, she could still see the stars above. *What would it be like,* she wondered, *to fly between them? To be free?*

Her mind flew back to the words Scarsi had sneered at her.

Allowing changelings to the King's coronation…

Don't they say that changelings kill their human mothers?

She growled. He was a bully, just trying to upset her. He'd probably said even fouler things to other women who had refused him. And yet, here she was, hiding from everyone downstairs. Squatting on this balcony like a terrible beast in a cave.

Maybe I'll eat some villagers, she thought bitterly, the sarcasm a welcome inoculation against her melancholy. Her eyes swept across the scene below, taking in the merriment and laughter.

She had never felt more alone.

A sudden flash of copper on the stairs below caught her attention. Light spilled from the open doors to the castle, casting a warming glow on those gathered there. She scanned the area again and found the male selkie speaking animatedly with an older Visenyan man. His companion clapped Harris on the back and he responded by throwing his head back in gaiety.

For a reason Ailsa couldn't really understand, the sight had her choking on her wine. She stared as he raised his hands, telling a story, in full flow. The Visenyan called over to one of his friends; clearly whatever Harris was saying was funny enough to share.

To think that only a few days ago, he had been telling her and Angus his terrible jokes as they trudged through the wilderness. *I wonder what the Visenyans would think of him if they were stuck with him for a full week,* she thought.

Despite him being aggravating, flighty and quite useless with a sword, she was proud to know him, to call him her friend.

He laughed again and she smiled along with him.

Here was joy. Here was life. She could see the sheer force of will, the brightness that exuded from this man: he was eternal sunshine.

She leaned over the balcony to call down to him, then hesitated.

Keep your thoughts to yourself next time, filthy changeling.

If he was sunshine, what was she?

A cold hard wind, beating and shoving her way through people before disappearing again.

I am darkness.

The breeze picked up, whipping at the flames of the fire. The evening light vanished as clouds swiftly rolled in overhead, blotting out the stars. Ailsa had been sure it was a clear night before, but it seemed they would be in for a storm.

It was the perfect metaphor for her, she decided: I *am a storm.*

She could barely make out Harris's puzzled features as he looked upwards, taking in the bizarre change in the weather. He seemed to stop listening to the men as his eyes searched the crowd and the castle until, like magnets, they found hers briefly where she was standing on the balcony. Confusion flashed across his features as he took in her face, before she stepped back into the shadows, away from his gaze.

It was time to leave.

Chapter 61

Ailsa made a mental inventory of the meagre belongings laid neatly on the bed. Along with the clothes she had arrived in, she'd been given new travelling clothes before finding the Stone. She'd felt bad for a second about taking them, but since they now had a few holes and stains, she reasoned that no one else would want them. She replenished her toiletries with some pine soap and wondered if she would smell like Angus from now on. The food came next: biscuits, cheese and the apples that had been left out for them in the sitting room she shared with Iona. Then there was her sleeping roll, the money Duncan had given for her time and her mother's box of treasures. This she placed in her pack with the utmost care.

There was a knock at the door and her heart stuttered. *If it was Harris...*

Angus's bearded face appeared as he cracked it open. He paused taking in the room—the clothes and the pack contents strewn everywhere—then he quickly stepped inside, shutting the door behind him.

They stood in silence for a few heartbeats. Angus's

face was unreadable as he explained, "I saw you leave the party."

Ailsa nodded, her body tense.

"You're leaving," he sighed. It was not a question.

She nodded again anyway.

"Why?" he asked simply. His cheek twitched as if he was battling to maintain a neutral expression, and Ailsa had to look away. She returned to her packing and took a deep breath.

"I don't belong here, Angus."

He snorted. "Oh, I know at least one person who doesn't agree."

She carried on folding, ignoring his comment. If she didn't harden her heart, she'd never do what needed to be done. As she threw in an undershirt, he stepped beside her, commanding her attention.

"Listen, it's hard to fit in. I, myself, have had trouble with it." At this she rolled her eyes. He just closed the top of the bag and shifted it behind him. "I've tried to be responsible, sensible, for my brother, but it never worked. I am who I am. And that's okay." He gave her shoulder a squeeze, drawing her closer. "I'm glad we're not the same as everyone else, or the world would be a boring place."

Ailsa's mouth twisted. *Maybe, but probably prettier*, she thought, running a hand over her marred cheek.

He cupped her chin and lifted her face, forcing her to

meet his eyes. There she found sadness.

"Let me make one thing clear," he said, his voice hushed, "You, Ailsa, are beautiful. Not because your face is nice to look at, or you look fair in a dress, but because you are strong and kind and selfless." He sighed. "When did we decide that having an unblemished face was more desirable than being a good person?"

She gave him a weak smile, pulling away. "Thanks, Angus. You've been a good friend these last few weeks. But unfortunately, not everyone thinks like you. Maybe if they did, the world would be a better place."

He sat down on the mattress with a sigh and she took one of his big hands into hers; she still couldn't believe he was younger than her. In this moment, he seemed world weary. She stepped between his spread knees and allowed him to wrap his arms around her body in a hug.

Into his hair, she whispered, "One of the most underrated qualities in this world is kindness. Few people value it, but it's possibly the most important thing of all. I have met many people who have been smart or strong or handsome, but being kind is, in my opinion, the best thing you can be. You are the kindest person I have ever met, Angus. Don't ever change that."

She looked down to see a single tear running down his cheek and into his beard. She pushed down the feeling of discomfort and smiled. "If it weren't treason, I'd even say you'd make a pretty good king."

He wiped at his eyes and laughed. "Pfft. Are you joking? I'd probably blow the place up within five minutes."

"Still," She gave his arm a pat, "Don't go too far away from your brother—he needs you. Eilanmòr needs you too."

Angus nodded, standing to let Ailsa access her bag. "I'm going to miss you. I wish you would stay but…" He blew out a breath. "I know I won't change your mind. Ailsa? Don't give up on the world just yet. And if you ever need someone to get you into trouble—or out of it—just come back. I'll be here."

"Thanks, Angus. Take care."

"You too," he said, and with that he was gone.

Ailsa was just glad he didn't see the way her lip trembled as he closed the door behind him.

Not long after, Ailsa finished packing and had slipped out of her dress into some trousers. She picked up her pack, surveying the room; it had been nice playing at being a lady, for a while. The food, the dresses… the bed! She groaned, realising she'd be back to sleeping on a roll-up mat again. But at least she'd be able to purchase some more home comforts with her money.

Of course, it wasn't just the material things she would

miss. It had been nice to have a female friend, especially one as wicked as Iona. She smiled as she thought of Iona, downstairs dancing in her dress, not caring when she shucked off her shoes or pulled up her hem for better movement.

And Angus? Angus had become a surrogate brother—it had been so long since she'd had that. *Should she stay for him?* To have that relationship again? But Angus already had a brother and a family. He didn't need her hanging around, no matter what he said earlier.

Finally, her thoughts turned to Harris. *If only—*

A knock on the door snapped Ailsa out of her musings. She held her breath as she waited. The candles had burned so low hopefully no one would see the light in the crack under the door.

"Ailsa?" shouted Harris, knocking again, "Are you in there?"

No, she thought, *I'm already gone.*

She heard him grunt from the other side of the door and then his footsteps fell away.

Ailsa gave the room one last glance before heading for the window. She was too much of a coward to risk going back through the castle. She opened the window onto the storm, which was pelting the stone walls, and peered out. She was only one floor up. Ailsa gritted her teeth and made a slow descent, using the spaces between bricks as footholds, before disappearing like a wraith in the night.

Chapter 62

The road was quiet, but in every village she came to, there was merriment. All of Eilanmòr was celebrating their new king. It made it remarkably easy to travel; no one noticed one more stranger among them. If Ailsa kept her hood up and her hair swept over her left eye, she blended in as well as the next person.

On her second night, she arrived at a village decorated with bunting. It flailed in the wind, dancing to the music emerging from the local tavern, despite the rain. The smell of freshly baked pastries wafted from inside, the temptation too much to resist.

If I just sit in the corner and keep quiet, I won't be bothered, she told herself, motioning to the barman for a drink and some food. Her stomach rumbled as she peered around the room, watching the locals enjoy their dinner. A half-hidden table at the back beckoned her over, and she slid into the shadows with a relieved sigh.

Dinner and that's it, she promised herself as she settled into the leather armchair. She was surprised to find she was quite content to listen to the idle chatter of those around her.

"I heard her dress was stunning—"

"—Demons up north—"

"—I *swear*, he was healed, it was a miracle—"

"—the Stone of Destiny—"

Ailsa's ears pricked up and she leaned her head in the direction of the couple sitting to her right, as the barman brought over a pint.

"—hidden somewhere, but some soldiers were sent to retrieve it," the man was saying as he munched through the mashed potato on his plate.

"No," his partner, a pretty blonde with glasses, argued. "I heard they weren't soldiers, they were fae—"

"Fae? Who's been filling your head with that nonsense?"

"Kennie—"

He laughed. "Kennie is a drunk."

She pouted, annoyance creeping into her voice as she replied, "Well, *yes*, but he worked at the castle during the coronation. He said that Prince Angus went to find the Stone of Destiny and two fair folk went with him."

"The prince would never be allowed to do that, it's too dangerous—"

"Well, he's a spare, isn't he?" she muttered.

Ailsa fought to control the growl under her breath.

"And that's why the fae got sent with him. A selkie and a changeling."

"A changeling?" The man looked around the room,

as if to check for anyone listening to their conversation. Ailsa narrowly missed meeting his eyes, ducking her head just in time. Her cheeks burned as she continued to listen.

"Don't changelings eat people?" he asked.

"You're a bampot. Changelings are good luck," the girl stated, primly sipping on her wine. "Faeries leave their children in place of dying babies so that the mother doesn't have to lose a child. When they grow up, they grant their parents' wishes."

Ailsa wasn't sure whether to snort at the absurdity or to stare in awe at the young woman. *Changelings are good luck?* That was certainly a refreshing opinion.

"Anyway," said the girl, "I heard that Prince Angus fell madly in love with her."

"Who?"

"The changeling."

Now Ailsa did snort, drawing the attention of the young couple. She coughed into her hand, pretending the beer had gone down the wrong way.

Her and Angus?

She could imagine his face, as clear as if he were sitting beside her. Her heart sank at the image, remembering too late what she had left behind.

The couple's conversation moved on to the boring topic of their future wedding and Ailsa stopped listening. She ate her food in silence—cullen skink with crusty bread—and when she was finished, she deposited the plate and her glass at the bar. The barman gave her a warm smile.

"Want a room?" he asked, nodding to the stairs at the back.

She hesitated, fingering the strap of her bag. She had planned to camp tonight, but a sudden clap of thunder made her change her mind. She reached inside her pack and brought out a few coins, being careful to ensure no one saw the bulging purse she carried. The barman smiled again and swapped the coins for a key.

"First door on the left."

She gave him a nod of thanks, doing her best to keep her face covered, and walked towards the stairs.

The room was plainly fitted and smelled of soap. Half an hour later, she had managed to start a fire in the grate and had shed her outer clothes, leaving on only her undershirt and leggings. She lay on the double bed, allowing the heat to penetrate her skin, listening to the sounds of people in the tavern below. Slowly, the sun's light faded outside, replaced by a veil of darkness, the moon and stars covered by the thick clouds that had been lingering all day. She closed her eyes and allowed herself to drift into a dream—

Tap, tap, tap.

A knock at the door had her flying upright.

She ran a hand through the hair that had managed

to knot around her face. She must have been asleep for a while, although it didn't feel like that long. There was another tap and she rolled her shoulders.

"Who is it?" she shouted, cursing under her breath.

The barman had probably realised he had a changeling under his roof. Maybe he had come to tell her she couldn't stay here anymore, she thought glumly.

But it wasn't the barman's voice that answered.

"It's Harris. Open up, Ailsa."

Chapter 63

Judging by the wet hair plastered to his forehead, it was still pouring outside. For some reason, he had not bothered to raise his hood against the elements. Raindrops clustered on his eyelashes, sparkling like diamonds in the firelight.

"All the way here I rehearsed what I was going to say when I saw you, but..." he rubbed his neck in consternation. "It seems like my mind has gone blank."

"Well," she mumbled, "I guess you had better start by coming inside."

Relief passed over his face before he stepped in and threw the door shut behind him. The lock clicked into place and he turned to examine her.

"I brought you this," he murmured, pulling something out of his pocket. He opened his hand to reveal a tiny white flower and Ailsa's breath caught in her throat.

"Like the one in the story," he whispered, his lips tilted up into a half smile.

"I know," said Ailsa, forcing her face to be impassive. "Why are you here, Harris?"

"You left without saying goodbye," he said in place of

an explanation. His tone was easy, calm, but from the way he was clenching his hands, he was anything but.

"I thought it would make it easier," admitted Ailsa.

"Why? Because you knew it would be too hard to leave me?"

There it was, the joking again. This wasn't a game. A growl came into her voice as she said, "I'm leaving Harris. The journey… It was fun, but I'm supposed to be back home, on my beach."

He stepped forward, eyeing her like a dangerous animal. "I want you to stay."

"Why?" Her lip curled. "You've only known me for less than a month."

He let out gasping laugh, running a hand through his hair. She watched the action, her fingers itching.

"A day would have been enough. I like you Ailsa. I've known that from the begin—"

"Don't you dare!" She thrust a finger in his direction, stepping forward until she was right in front of him. "Don't you dare tell me you like me. I can't stay Harris. I don't belong here—"

He cut her off. "Neither do I!"

She threw her hands up. "Of course you do! Look at you," she grumbled, gesturing in his general direction. "You fit in. You're only going to make this harder—"

Now he was angry. His eyes thundered as he ground out, "Good. You are being a coward." He reached out and squeezed her shoulders. "You are being a coward and I'm not going to let you. You could go back home and then what? You'll be alone for the rest of your life. And one day, when you're old, and wrinkly and *dying*, you're going to think of my face and get so pissed off because we didn't do this more." He pulled her roughly to him and captured her lips with his in a searing kiss.

As soon as it had started, he pulled back. She was panting but he continued speaking, still holding her shoulders tightly. "And I don't want you to feel pissed off when you think of me. I want you to think *'wow, we had a wonderful time together.'* Or better yet, you won't even have to try to remember me, because I'll be right there with you, holding your hand."

He kissed me.

Ailsa fought to collect herself. "Harris, I can't—"

"Don't you want to know how things could be, if we were together?" he growled.

"But what happens when I'm old and I look horrible? And you're sitting there, still looking the same, feeding me soup because I've lost all my teeth?"

He smiled. "I wouldn't care. Besides, we could die before then." Her brow furrowed and his grin stretched wider. "I know that sounds harsh, but the thing is, we don't know what's going to happen. We could have sixty years together—or six. Shouldn't we make the most of every moment we have?"

"I don't know, Harris."

He let her go, allowing her the space she had been craving. It was easier to think when he wasn't holding her.

"We could at least try?" he pleaded. "And if you don't think it's working out then that's okay…" He paused and her eyes snapped to his again. "Don't you like me?" he murmured.

She bit back a laugh. This was ridiculous. "Yes, you idiot, but—"

"Please, Ailsa," he said quietly, evenly.

"You might regret it…"

"Never," he vowed, his voice hushed. "I will never regret any time I get to spend with you. Please. Come back with me, Ailsa." He held out a hand, like a question. "Just say yes."

She hesitated, the sound of their breathing filling the silence. "Yes."

"Good." His face brightened. "I'm going to kiss you now," he told her.

Now she felt unsure. "But you just did—"

He stepped closer and she could feel the heat of his body. "That wasn't a real kiss." His voice was husky and the sound warmed her cheeks.

"A real kiss?" Ailsa felt faint. He reached out a hand to finger a lock of her hair lying on her shoulder.

She backed away, until her heels hit the door.

As Harris approached, she smelled his familiar, citrus and sea salt scent, enveloping her like a cloak. *Just like the beach.* He rested a hand on her shoulder and the breath hitched in her throat. His emerald eyes locked on hers, holding them in place as he leaned in. Wrapping one arm around her waist, the other around her shoulders, he pulled her into his warm body, just embracing her. Her breath left her in a *whoosh* as she realised this was all he would do for the moment.

They stood like that for a while, just breathing each other in. Ailsa wondered how she felt to him. *Was she soft or hard like he was? Did she feel tense?* She thought about her body, attempting to unlock the muscles from her feet to her neck, as he rubbed her back in soft strokes.

"I'm going to kiss you now," he repeated in a murmur. This time it wasn't a command, but a warning. She could pull away if she wanted to. He wouldn't stop her.

Slowly, she lifted her head from where it had been leaning against his shoulder and gazed up at him. Inside his eyes she found barely concealed excitement.

He gave her a tentative smile.

Closing her eyes, she tilted her head back slowly. Harris rubbed a thumb over her jaw, coaxing her slightly higher so that she stood on her toes. She felt his hot breath, first on her chin, then her cheek, then her forehead as he planted a soft kiss there. He moved his mouth further down and kissed her on her eyelids, her nose, finally biting the delicate flesh of her ear. As his teeth grazed her skin, she let out a low moan.

The sound snapped the leash he had on himself and his lips crashed down upon hers. Her pulse pounded through her veins as he pressed himself more securely to her body and moved his mouth over hers.

The kiss felt like a claiming, like a contract. They had danced around this for weeks, but finally their intentions were laid bare. With each push of his lips on hers, a tiny bit of granite tumbled from the stone wall around her heart.

Deepening the kiss, he licked along the seam of her lips, delving his tongue in when she opened to him. She lifted her hands to twine in his flaming hair.

Playing with fire, she thought and inwardly winced at the absurdity of it. She felt giddy; unhinged. When the hand on her back drifted further down, sense all but fled from her mind.

Harris broke the kiss, but his mouth lingered on her face, kissing around and down, lower, under the hollow of her jaw.

"I've been wanting to do this since before we got to Dunrigh," he chuckled, and she felt the curve of his mouth against the skin of her neck. "I've been waiting to hear all the noises you'd make..." As he finished, he bit down on the skin between her shoulder and her collarbone, eliciting a groan from her lips.

"What noises can you make?" she wondered, and he raised his face, the grin wiped away. "I wouldn't be so sure you'll have the upper hand, Harris." He stared at her for a beat, taking in the smirk she was valiantly trying to keep in place, despite her heaving breathing.

"Oh Gods," he whispered hoarsely, before claiming her mouth again. She allowed him to back her up, gasping when her heels hit the wall. He pushed her into the wood, pressing his body around her small frame.

He leaned his forehead into hers, with his eyes closed. One finger slid rapidly against her hip bone in time with his breaths. "I think I could die from this."

"Stop talking," she growled, pulling his lips back to hers.

More, more, more, her thoughts chanted as their tongues fought for dominance. Now was not the time for words.

Harris's hand stroked down her back, leaving sparks in its wake. She gasped a little into his mouth as he quickly caught her behind her knee and hooked her leg over his hip, angling his body so that it fit between her limbs. With a smirk, she pulled his hair, drawing from him a few choice curses between kisses.

One of Harris's fingers slipped around the waistband of her trousers, and between the heated gasps, Ailsa wondered how far she would let this go. At some point she would have to put an end to this. *Wouldn't she?*

She was saved from her inner debate by an insistent knocking at the door. She lifted her face to peer over Harris's shoulder, but he grumbled, capturing her ear again between his teeth.

The banging grew louder.

With a groan, Harris shoved himself away from the wall, releasing her body. The air from the room cooled her fevered skin, making her shiver.

He stood before her, breathing heavily, hands clenched into fists.

"This isn't over." He promised, the crack in his voice betraying his emotion. He pinned her to the wall with his gaze. She nodded and he turned to open the door.

As his fingers clasped around the handle, the thumping got louder still, as if the visitor would break down the door, had it not been locked. A sinking sensation hovered in Ailsa's chest and she took a step forward.

Something was wrong.

Too late, Harris's hand turned, releasing the lock on the door. It exploded inward, under the weight of the other person's fist, sending splinters everywhere. Harris was thrown back, landing first on the bed, then bouncing to the floor.

Chapter 64

A ilsa was frozen, her eyes round with shock.

A tall, muscled figure stalked into the room, the lamplight illuminating their features.

Or it would have done they hadn't been wearing a skull mask.

Ailsa gasped and reached for her axe, but she was pushed to the bed before she could react. Strong hands held her stomach down against the mattress. The stranger lifted a knife to the side of her face, parting her hair with the blade to reveal her mark.

"Ailsa!" Harris cried, rising from the floor and running at her assailant. She watched in horror as the knife swept up, cutting him on the shoulder.

"No!" she struggled to get free as blood spilled from Harris's wound. He held a hand to it and charged again. This time, the Avalognian landed a hard blow with the hilt of the weapon to the side of his head. Harris's legs crumpled under him and he sank to the floor, eyes rolling back into his head.

"I remember you," said the raider. Ailsa lay on her back, her torso exposed and vulnerable. The stranger lifted a hand to her own face, and pulled the skull mask away, revealing mahogany skin, a curled lip over sharpened teeth and brown eyes full of hate and recognition.

It was the raider she had fought with on the beach.

"I was in that boat for two days before anyone found me. No food, little water. And would you like to know what I did to pass the time?" The woman grabbed the front of Ailsa's tunic and pulled her to her feet, her face inches from her own. "I thought about how I would pay you back." She smiled cruelly and pushed her towards the door. Ailsa's gaze slid from Harris's broken form to her axe, sitting beside the hearth, useless now.

As they left the room, they heard a cry. An elderly man, clearly someone who worked in the inn, leapt in front of them brandishing a wooden chair. The raider growled, before shoving Ailsa to the floor and pressing her boot hard into her back. She watched from under her hair as the Avalognian grabbed the chair from the man and, without any preamble, plunged her knife into his neck.

Ailsa felt the raider moving in slow motion as she waited one beat, two beats, before withdrawing her blade and watching the man sink to the floor. He groaned and clutched his wound as he fell, his face landing inches away from Ailsa's. She watched as bubbles of blood formed around his lips, his mouth opening and closing like a fish, as his life force seeped out of his body. His eyes met hers, empty and unblinking. Before she could watch him die, she was pulled to her feet again.

"Move." The woman commanded, before shoving her roughly towards the stairs. She chanced a look over her shoulder, but the man was no longer moving.

The scene downstairs was so different to the previous afternoon that Ailsa felt she had walked into another world. The tables had been overturned and there were mugs and plates shattered everywhere. The people around the room fell into three categories: raiders, the people they had captured, or those that had fought and whose bodies now littered the floor.

As if moving through honey, Ailsa's eyes found the corpse of the blonde girl, her glasses askew. Bright red blood leaked from her neck wound—her fiancé was nowhere to be seen.

They were planning on having a summer wedding...

The woman pulling her along stopped in front of the group of terrified Eilanmòrians and pushed Ailsa's head down so she had to kneel with them.

Her voice came out whip-like and loud. "Report."

A hulking figure stepped forward, his face still covered in his skull mask. "Nine bodies in here, twelve out in the village." Bodies? With a start she realised he was referring to their captives as if they were nothing but meat.

"Resistance?"

"Just what you see on the floor." He gestured to the corpses and smiled. "Plus a few locked in rooms upstairs."

"Good. We're leaving. Burn this place to the ground."

"But Brenna, what about plunder?"

"Twenty-one slaves are more than enough plunder," she growled. "Now turn this place to ash before I lock you in one of the rooms with the rest of the scum."

Rough hands grabbed Ailsa and forced her arms painfully behind her back, so they could bind her hands with rope. She watched as they did the same to the people around her: the barman, some musicians, a little girl who was sobbing and desperately reaching for one of the figures on the floor.

Ailsa was pulled to her feet and shoved through the front door and out into the night. The fresh smell of saltwater hit her, and she thought of Harris back up in her room. *Is he dead? Wounded? Will he get out before the inn was incinerated?*

She watched helplessly as the last of the Avalognians left the building, carrying a lantern and half a bottle of whisky. The man grinned at the weeping crowd before turning and smashing the bottle onto the wooden floor, followed by the glass lantern.

No, Harris!

The alcohol immediately roared with flames, which licked at the wood underneath. In a few breaths, the fire was consuming the room, aided by all the bottles of spirits and flammable furnishings. They waited a while and Ailsa wondered why, until she heard the first screams coming from inside the building. Ailsa craned her neck, desperately looking for anyone who might escape. Every crumbling beam of wood looked like a figure, until it was eaten by the flames. The Avalognians around seemed satisfied and finally pressed them on, towards a larger group of raiders and their captives.

Her stomach heaved as she staggered forward. *He'll be okay, you'll see. He'll get out.* Believing otherwise was not an option.

The homes and shops they walked past had also been set alight; it was a massacre. The crackling of the buildings was drowned out by the wailing of the other Eilanmòrians, whose lives, loves and freedom had been snuffed out in one night.

As they were pushed out of the village and towards the path, Ailsa caught sight of a slight figure darting between the buildings. It seemed that not everyone in the village had been captured. She watched as the child crept through the shadows, following the progress of the captives. *Maybe their family has been captured?* Before they cleared the ruined village, the group was halted.

"I think we left someone behind." The man from earlier strode towards the nearest building and pulled the child out from behind it. The boy's tiny fists pummelled the large man's back as he was thrown over a shoulder.

One of the captured women gave a sob.

"Room for one more?" asked the man, walking back to his fellow Avalognians. Though he addressed all of them, it was clear he was waiting for the woman, Brenna's, response.

She crossed her arms and regarded the little boy as he struggled. His sandy blonde hair flopped back and forth across his head as he struggled to pull himself free.

"I think we have enough. Kill him."

Horror froze Ailsa's throat. She threw herself forward, but her captor held onto her wrist bindings tightly. The woman beside her howled and Brenna's attention snapped to her.

"Does this one belong to you?"

"Please—" she sobbed. "He's my son!"

Brenna showed her teeth in a smile.

"Good." She knelt before the boy, cocking her head. "Boy. You will come with us and work hard. If you don't, your mother will die. Understood?"

Screaming. All she could hear was screaming.

The boy whimpered but stopped struggling and he was deposited beside his mother.

The noise in Ailsa's ears suddenly stopped and a strange sense of calm washed over her. Despite the confusion and terror—despite the gnawing loss and emptiness—one thing was clear: she would make these Avalognians pay.

Chapter 65

The slave caravan slowly worked their way towards the coast, further away from hope. They had been marching south since first light, working their way between abandoned farms and smoking villages. The Avalognians had already been through here.

They hiked over a hill and Ailsa fought the urge to be sick.

In the glen below, hundreds of raiders were converging, all pulling captives behind them. They had congregated in a camp of sorts, turning the landscape to mud beneath their feet. The cold afternoon air was punctuated by screams.

Her captors led her group into the rabble, pulling on the ropes that bound them and laughing whenever anyone fell. *How far had they walked now?* Ailsa tried to calculate it in her head. With their slow pace, six miles last night? Maybe ten today? Her hips ached from the marching and cramps.

They had killed off one of the older musicians this morning. He had sustained an injury from the carnage and was starting to show signs of fever. The raiders had neither the time nor the patience to heal him.

The others had pushed on after that, fear snapping at their feet, but their tiredness bled through. The young girl who had been hysterical earlier had stopped crying, her tears mostly dried up, but every so often her body was wracked by involuntary sobbing noises. Ailsa heard her fall to the ground behind her for what seemed like the hundredth time.

"Get up," snarled one of the Avalognians, a towering brute of a man.

"I can't," she moaned. "My legs—"

The leader, Brenna, turned from the front of the group and stalked back to where she lay. "You get up," she snarled, "Or you die."

The girl broke into fresh keening as she attempted to pull her legs underneath her. She slipped around in the mud, failing to stand.

"I guess you die," voiced Brenna, raising her knife.

"No," shouted Ailsa, stepping between them as best she could with her hands still tied to the group's rope. "She'll stand." *She just needed time.*

"Oh?" asked Brenna, her lips pulling back from her pointed teeth. "And what of you, girl? Do I have to kill you?"

Ailsa stood straighter, staring the woman down as she listened to the child slip in the mud behind her. If she could just keep them talking…

"You won't kill me," she told her with more confidence than she felt. "You want me to suffer more than that."

Brenna stepped forward, crowding her. She still held the knife in her hand.

"You're right," she finally said with a wicked grin. She raised the knife and cut through Ailsa's bindings. "I think I'll start now."

Brenna dragged her down the hill and into the camp. Instead of taking her into the heart of it like Ailsa thought she would, she was brought to a tent, tall enough to stand up in, and was shoved inside. Ailsa landed hard on the ground, which was covered in bamboo mats. Brenna followed, pinning her down with a knee on her stomach.

"And how should I start?" she crooned, lifting her knife again. "Perhaps I should remove your lips? Or..." she smiled. "I could carve out a piece of flesh for every one of my brethren who has been killed by your people."

Ailsa curled her lip. "If you didn't invade us, we wouldn't kill you," she said sweetly.

In answer, Brenna slammed Ailsa's head into the ground, causing stars to appear in her vision. She slid her knife to Ailsa's mark, contemplating the red skin there.

"The Eilanmòrians are scared of people like you," said the raider. "They say you are a changeling," she grunted. "Superstitious sheep. You are just a girl with an unfortunate birthmark. There is nothing special about you, except a good throwing arm. And you don't have your axe anymore."

She moved the knife from her left cheek to her right; to the unmarked skin.

"I said I wanted you to suffer and suffering is for the living," Brenna snorted a laugh. "And I'm going to make sure you have a long life, girl. You'll work for me and I'll put those muscles to good use. Chopping wood, cleaning clothes. Maybe if you're lucky, I'll let you inside every now and then to gut my kills?" She looked her up and down. "But you are an awful sight to have around the house. That mark is fairly distracting." She eyed Ailsa's left cheek. "I think you need to be evened up."

She pressed harder on the knife and Ailsa could feel blood trickling down her cheek. Pain lanced through her and, as the knife cut deeper, she struggled to hold in a scream. Her hands clawed at the bamboo under her fingers. Finally, after she felt like her whole face may have been sliced off, the knife was lifted away from her skin.

"There, much better." Brenna grinned sadistically. "But we can't let that get infected. You're no good to us dead, after all." She held Ailsa's head down and poured from a flask at her side. Salt water. This time Ailsa did scream.

Finally, Brenna let her go. It took a moment for the

burning to subside but when it did, she looked at the raider, who had rocked back on her heels to survey her handiwork. With a final smirk, she stood and made to leave.

"Thank you," croaked Ailsa.

Brenna stopped and turned, looking at her incredulously. "What the hell for?"

Ailsa raised herself up so that she was leaning on her side. Drops of blood fell on the ground beside her hand.

"Now, when I look at myself in the mirror, I'll remember how I survived this. I'll know that I'm strong and that is *infinitely* better than beautiful. But mostly, I'll remember how it felt to kill you. To see the light drain from your eyes. So, thank you." She spat into the sand.

"Big words. We'll see what you say when you've lost all of your fingernails from scrubbing." Brenna narrowed her eyes and stalked off, allowing some guards from outside to take her place.

In the middle of camp, the other prisoners were thrown into wagons which served as cages on wheels; it seemed that they would no longer be walking.

Ailsa was jammed in with fifteen other people, all with rope binding their ankles. Some of them were older than her, but none looked beyond middle age. Most were younger, nothing more than terrified children. One boy had begun to cry when the wagon shuddered forward, but after a few hours, his sobs were silent. They were pulled along by cattle, clearly stolen, and it felt like the stink of sweat and manure permeated every pore of her body by the time they were halted for the night. The raiders left them in their prisons while they set their fires and made camp.

When the call for food started, some of the wagons were opened and Ailsa watched in terror as some of the children were pulled out.

Avalognians were cannibals, she remembered.

But the children were merely shoved in front of the fires, given pans and sacks and told to make dinner. The adults left in the cages watched in a mixture of worry and hunger as they cooked. Ailsa didn't think she or the other captives would be offered any. She closed her eyes in an attempt to sleep, trying to forget her pain and grief.

The sun was about an hour from setting when she was pulled from her dozing by a hand on her shoulder. She jumped, expecting to see Brenna or another raider, but instead met the gaze of a petite woman.

"That mark," she whispered, eyeing Ailsa's left cheek in awe.

Ailsa's hand flew to the side to her face. "Who are you?" she asked.

The woman was a slight creature, with eyes that seemed

far too big for her face. Her strawberry blonde hair was knotted and messed from walking and labouring. The Avalognians must have mistaken her for a child, but her face and the pain there were almost ancient.

"You're a changeling," she said, and Ailsa frowned. She was *done* with people telling her that.

"You were left by the faeries."

"And how the hell do you know?" snapped Ailsa.

Surprise flickered in her unfathomable eyes for a moment, before she lifted a hand slowly from her side, to sweep back her hair. Ailsa watched as she revealed her ears, which were almost normal, save for the way they pointed at the top.

A faerie.

A real faerie.

The woman blushed but continued. "I can feel the power contained inside you." She raised her hand to touch her arm again. "It wants out."

"And what power would that be?" Ailsa asked, watching her warily.

The faerie looked to the sky and at the last rays of sun. "I can feel your magic wanting to reach up there." She fixed her with a glare. "It has been sneaky, trying without your permission. You have to control it."

"What do you mean?" Ailsa tried to pull away, but the faerie just gripped her arm tighter, her little fingers sinking into her skin.

The woman tilted her head. "See that cloud up there? Move it."

Ailsa's found the fluffy cloud she'd indicated, the sun's rays turning it a golden rose.

"That's impossible."

"Silly girl. Do it now," commanded the faerie.

Ailsa gave her one final scowl and then turned her gaze to the sky. She concentrated hard on the puff of pink. She screwed up her eyes and directed her thoughts at the cloud: *move*. The wisps of water vapour stayed where they were. Ailsa wrinkled her nose and lifted her chin. In her head, she pulled together all her anger and commanded: *MOVE*. Still the cloud didn't move an inch.

From beside her she heard a cackle. Ailsa grunted in frustration.

"Not like that," the faerie huffed. "You would think you'd have some brains. How can you move something without giving it a *push*?"

"What like this—" Ailsa stopped and stared at the sky in shock. She had merely lifted her arm and poked her finger in the direction of the cloud—and it had moved. Not far, but it still *moved*.

She tried again. Reaching up, she lifted her pointing finger in front of the cloud. Then she dragged it to the left. The cloud moved along with her finger! It didn't move quickly and felt heavy.

She turned to the woman in surprise, but the faerie

was already moving away from her.

"Wait," called Ailsa, but the faerie carried on. Ailsa returned to moving the cloud, watching in wonder. She moved her fingers around in bigger strokes, marvelling at the way the clouds were pulled slowly across the sky, just as if they were moving through thick treacle. She collected them to her right, in a cluster of wisps, marvelling to herself.

How was she doing this?

How could a human do this?

The answer came to her gradually and then all at once: a *human* couldn't.

The clouds above her suddenly darkened.

She wasn't human.

She wasn't human.

Changeling they had called her.

And they had been right.

How could she not have known this?

Her blood felt like ice in her veins. Half remembered words, said in the cover of night, rang in her ears.

There's a storm beneath your skin, Ailsa. A storm.

Harris had known.

Nausea roiled in her stomach and she had to angle her head out of the wagon. A few of her cellmates voiced their half-hearted complaints as she threw up whatever had been left in her stomach. And through it all, the truth made her insides clench.

Harris. He had looked right at her and understood.

She was the one changing the weather.

She wasn't human.

It all started to make sense. Harris must have assumed she was human at first—that was why he wanted her to go with him to Dunrigh.

Because he needed a human to open the box containing the Stone of Destiny. But when he had discovered she wasn't human, then he knew, he *knew*, she couldn't be the one to open it.

That was why he had brought Angus along. He needed a human.

And Angus, he had offered to let her open it. Harris had stopped her. *You should stay here and rest. Angus, it's for your family, you take it.*

She felt a wave of heat spreading from her toes, up her body, to the crown of her head, along with one word.

Changeling.

Chapter 66

Thoughts muddled Ailsa's brain, like a mass of snakes, slithering and hissing in all directions; certainties and questions, following each other around relentlessly.

She was not human. Harris had known this, but had never mentioned it directly. Why hadn't he told her? Had Iona known too? Somehow, she didn't think so. Harris had been playing a game, keeping his thoughts to himself. But to what end?

It doesn't matter, she told herself. Harris could be dead, and she was worrying about his motives. *He's not dead, I would know it.* She had to believe that, or she wouldn't be able to carry on. And when she found him again, she would be sure to ask him herself, right after she kissed him senseless.

Ailsa stayed awake all night, listening to the shuffling of other people—of the humans—who surrounded her. She replayed moments over and over again inside her head in which Harris featured heavily, but so did her mother and brother. Maybe Cameron—if she could even find him—would have answers for her.

Most of the Avalognians had bunked down for the

night, while an unlucky few still guarded the camp. She did her best to seem unconscious when they passed. When they weren't there, she stared at the clouds through the slats of the wagon.

Raising a hand, she scrubbed at the sky, pushing cloudy wisps off to the edges of her vision, until finally she had a patch of clear; the stars shone brightly through the gap and she allowed herself to truly study the sight. She had sometimes wished that she could fall into the stars. Perhaps one day, now that she knew she was *other*, she could. Perhaps there, in the sea of twinkling lights, she would find peace.

A little after dawn, a horn sounded, rousing the camp and pulling Ailsa from her thoughts. She hadn't slept at all. Every time she closed her eyes, she saw Harris's shocked face as the door flew open. *He's alive*, she told herself for the thousandth time. It was inconceivable that such a light had been extinguished forever. Even if he had lied to her about her heritage, he was still a part of the strange, new family she had found.

The camp was dismantled and the wagons shuddered into motion again. *They couldn't be far from the coast now*, thought Ailsa, sure that she could already taste salt on the breeze.

Around midday, they were handed food, bread and fruit the Avalognians had likely plundered. The sight of another burning village confirmed Ailsa's theory; they hadn't paused long enough to take survivors.

Finally, the sea became visible on the horizon and what she saw made her choke. Squatting in the water were huge ships, five of them: this was how the raiders had arrived in Eilanmòr—and this was how they would leave.

She watched with unease as those ships sailed closer and closer. If only she could move the sea, like Iona, and send them flying into the ocean without their crew.

A few hours later, they reached the beaches, the wagons finally coming to a halt on the sand. The door of hers was thrown open and two Avalognians began to pull out the inhabitants, throwing them down on the wet sand.

"Now you," one grunted and dragged her out by her ankles. She managed to land a kick to his stomach before he deposited her on the ground in a heap. The man cursed.

"You'll regret that," he grunted, but before he could land a blow, a shout had him reaching into the wagon again to pull another person out. Still, she could feel him hovering close, waiting for his revenge.

Raising her head, Ailsa could see the other captives were getting the same treatment. There must have been at least sixty people. She scanned their faces for the faerie from last night, but found only terrified humans.

A hush broke like a wave over the crowd and she had to crane her neck to see why. From the other end of the group of captives, a tall man came strolling across the sand. His black hair fell in a curtain around his shoulders, dusting the cape harnessed there. He was mask-less but a jewelled headdress sat on his brow, increasing his height and marking him as someone important. He surveyed the captured Eilanmòrians as he went, a cruel sneer on his lips. The Avalognians watched him with a mixture of tension and reverence.

"My," he boomed. "What a plunder. So many strong slaves to bring back home." He smiled. "Brenna, you have done well."

The female raider stepped forward and placed a fist on her chest. "Thank you, Ivar. The Gods have smiled upon us."

"It is indeed a gift. One we will have to thank them for." He stopped in front of the captives. "Before we head back home, we will need to make a sacrifice." His eyes gleamed as they raked over a woman clutching a child at the front of the group. Ailsa shivered as she beheld his bloodlust.

"We must sacrifice one of the prisoners to please the

Gods," he continued, seeming to relish the sharp intakes of breath his words drew. "But whom to choose?" Ailsa sneaked a look at the man from beneath her lashes as he sauntered along the line of people. "Who will make a good offering to see us off back to Avalogne with our bounty?" He raised his eyes to the raiders standing strong and tall amongst the prisoners, and then they fell on the man to the side of Ailsa, the one she had kicked.

"Ollin, you have served me well during this journey." He smiled. "You choose."

Ailsa didn't need to look to feel the man's gaze fall on her like a brand.

"This one."

Chapter 67

The hairs on Ailsa's scalp were pulled painfully as she was yanked upright. The huge man forced her to the front of the crowd, where terrified eyes met hers.

"Behold, our offering to our mighty Gods, who have led us across the ocean to take what we need." Ailsa was pushed down onto her knees, her hands bound behind her back. "We ask you to bless us again with safe passage back to your kingdom." From the corner of her eye, she saw another raider walking towards them, carrying a heavy-looking wooden club. She started to struggle in earnest as a meaty hand pushed her head down into the sand.

"We spill this blood for you to drink, to quench your thirst so you need not drink from us." said Ivar, arms stretched as he addressed the heavens.

Her breaths came out in gasps which disturbed the clumps of sand beside her face. She struggled to rise but couldn't move an inch under the weight of the person on top of her. He moved his hand from her head to her shoulders as the raider with the club lined himself up beside her.

"Now swing true," ordered Ivar "and bring us a safe journey."

Ailsa closed her eyes and felt a single tear escape down her face and onto the beach below. Thunder rumbled in the distance.

Too late, she thought.

"Not that one." Ailsa's eyes flew open to find Brenna standing in front of the crowd. She had her arms crossed over the furs on her chest. The hands holding Ailsa relaxed their grip ever so slightly.

"But we must have a sacrifice." Yet the priest's voice held slight hesitation.

Brenna just *asked*. "Pick another."

The holy man regarded her for a long moment, but she didn't tear her gaze away. They seemed to fight a silent battle.

"I will trust your judgment in this, Brenna," he relented finally. He grabbed the club from beside him and Ailsa sucked in a breath, before he swung it down, not on her head, but on the skull of man beside her. She let out a squeak before backing away as she was released. The man fell forward from the force of the blow and tried to speak before the club was brought down upon him again and again. Finally, all that was left of the man was a body and a pile of oozing flesh where his head had been. Ailsa willed herself not to throw up where she sat.

"Up now," Brenna pulled her by the arm and threw

her towards the boats. "Time to go."

"Why did you save me?" Ailsa felt the bite of frigid sea water as she was forced to wade through the waves. Strong arms lifted her up and into one of the smaller boats that would take them out to the ships.

"My property is not to be damaged." Brenna hopped over the side and kicked Ailsa so that she fell into the bed of the raft. "Don't worry, little girl, you'll soon be wishing that you had been sacrificed back there. Better to die free than to wish for death as a slave." She sat at the helm of the boat, fixing her mask back onto her face. "You should watch the coast as we sail away. You'll never see it again, I guarantee."

The light rain did nothing to deter the raiders as they pushed the boat out into the breaking waves. No one paid her any heed as she gripped the side of the boat and closed her eyes. She braced herself as they rowed away from the beach while the same thunder rumbled off in the distance.

She opened her eyes to a flash of lightning and counted. One... Two... Three... Four... The thunder boomed again, too far away. The waves around the boat tossed them about but they ploughed on.

Eventually the craft bumped up against the hull of the first ship. Ailsa was pushed up the rope ladder. When she reached the deck, her legs gave out, but no one seemed to care, not even Brenna who marched off shouting orders as soon as she boarded.

Ailsa dragged herself up to see over the edge. The other ships were also being loaded and readied. Her only hope was to go with the Avalognians and try to get hold of a weapon when they arrived in Avalogne. Then she would have to escape the village, or wherever they were taking her. She could steal a boat. Avalogne and Eilanmòr weren't *that* far apart.

She watched as the crew set began to unfurl the massive sails. *This will be the last time I see Eilanmòr.* If only someone knew where she was. For all she knew, Harris was dead and her trail would be cold by the time Angus and Iona found out what had happened. Her ears pricked again and she kicked the side of the boat in frustration.

Warriors nearby were making the last checks and shouting to each other in their thick dialect. Rain began to fall from the sky, and Ailsa turned her face so that each drop was a kiss on her skin. Now that she understood, it was as if she could hear the intentions of the wide space above her. The wind blew through her hair in a gentle caress.

You will be alright, it whispered. Soothing. Motherly. If only she knew how to speak back. More than moving a few clouds, she wished she could tell the sky what she wanted. Then maybe she could save herself.

I could just jump in, she realised. She glanced

around but everyone seemed to be preoccupied with the approaching storm. Before she could second-guess herself, she swung a leg over the side and got ready to pull her body over.

"Where the hell do you think you're going?"

Brenna appeared beside her and pulled her violently back onto the deck. Her forehead hit the wood as she went down and her vision swam. Above her, Brenna stood with three other warriors, all holding spears.

"Looks like you were about to abandon us." One of the men beside Brenna pressed his boot to Ailsa's shoulder so that she couldn't move. "I thought you could behave yourself for the journey, but it seems I was wrong. I'll just have to keep you in chains until we reach Avalogne."

The lightning flashed closer as Ailsa met her eyes. Maybe it would help. She spat in Brenna's direction. One of the other men beside her stomped on her stomach, knocking the wind out of her.

"I wouldn't do that if I were you," Ailsa wheezed.

"And why not? I would get used to it if I were you, slave." Brenna had to shout the last few words as the thunder threatened to drown her out. Gusts of wind were pulling at their clothes and Ailsa was distantly aware that the rowers were struggling to keep the craft under control.

"Because this," her eyes flicked to the storm, "is my doing. And if you don't let me and the other prisoners go, I will sink every one of these boats." It was a bold threat—one Ailsa hoped she could actually carry out.

"I don't believe you. And I am getting tired of your bullshit." Brenna pulled out one of her knives and weighed it in her hand, as if contemplating whether to end Ailsa there and then.

Suddenly, Ailsa knew. Knew that she was the only person who could save her now. Knew that she had to gain control.

From deep within herself, she whispered: *now, now, now.*

She closed her eyes, focussing on the thundering beat of her heart. Distantly, she heard the female raider asking her what she was doing. Still, Ailsa pressed her eyes tightly shut and searched for that hammering inside her chest. With every clench of her heart, she chanted: *now.*

Chapter 68

*N*ow. Now. Now.

She felt it then, the electricity under her skin. She sensed the power as it coursed out of her and when her eyes flew open, she watched as the lightning nearby was pulled from the sky, over and down—right onto the head of the man standing next to Brenna.

The bolt hit him with a deafening crack, from his skull, right through his left boot. He fell where he stood; the pungent smell of roasted flesh emanating from his shocked corpse.

The world paused. The people around her blinked down at the man, then slowly their gazes turned to Ailsa where she lay, incredulous at what she had just done.

"Well…" said Brenna slowly, "I believe you now." Then she turned to the two other men. "Get her up!"

She was hauled to her feet as everyone on the ship crowded round the dead man. The rain still pounded down on them, drowning out their murmuring.

Brenna fixed her with a steely grin, clearly unfazed by what Ailsa had just done. Instead, she seemed excited, her expression possessive and calculating. The plan to keep her as a house slave was obviously no longer relevant. Now, those eyes told her the truth. Brenna would carve that power out of her and then, if Ailsa were still alive, she would be sold to the highest bidder.

"Rope. Now," she shouted, but her orders fell on deaf ears and she turned, wrathful.

"You are not giving orders this time, Brenna," the priest interrupted, stepping out from between two warriors. He lifted his skull mask to sit on top of his face as he addressed her. "This girl is no longer your possession. We cannot have her on this ship. It's too dangerous."

Finally, Ailsa thought as the hands on her arms loosened ever so slightly. *Now they'll let me go.* She turned her face back towards the beach, which was still within swimming distance. Something was moving over the headland that she couldn't quite make out. The rain was letting up around her and a thin ray of sun shone on the sand.

The priest looked at Ailsa gravely as one of the men picked up the club that had been used to make the sacrifice earlier. Brenna launched herself towards Ailsa but was pulled back by two, heavy-set raiders. They held her as she snarled at the priest to stop. Ailsa was hauled to the side of the ship, her body bent over the side of the wooden vessel.

"Once we kill you, our journey will go smoothly." The priest's voice floated to her ears as her stomach dropped.

"Goodbye, storm girl."

The heavy footsteps of the executioner sounded behind her as Ailsa raised her head towards the dying beam of light.

Harris was standing on the beach.

Barely audible over the crashing waves, his shout nevertheless grabbed the attention of the raiders around her. Lifting their heads in confusion at the noise, they took their attention off Ailsa.

Now, she thought again, swinging her head back so it collided with one of the men that held her. He released his grip, and she managed to pull his sword from his belt, swinging it up through the air, just like Angus had taught her. The blade connected with the soft side of the other man, and he let out a shriek before falling over the side of the ship.

Brenna snarled in fury but didn't come any closer. The priest nodded to the executioner who lifted his club again.

"I wouldn't do that if I were you." Ailsa raised the sword out in front of her, despite the pain in her side. "See that storm? One thought from me and you'll be electrocuted."

"She's bluffing. She wouldn't risk setting the ship on fire."

"I can swim. Try me." From the corner of her eye, she scanned the beach, but Harris had disappeared. She had to get off this boat.

"Enough of this nonsense. Kill her."

The time for thinking, for wondering, was over. Ailsa looked up at the sky and simply *willed* it. *Here, now*, she commanded, as if the sky was no more than a disobedient dog. It built slowly. She could feel the energy behind her, then inside her.

Then a voice whispered in her ear, ancient and knowing.

Take it, the voice encouraged, *it belongs to you*.

The executioner stopped in his tracks, mouth falling open.

Brenna backed away, her need for self preservation winning out over her greed.

The priest just gaped at her, words eluding him.

Ailsa fixed her eyes upon him, still concentrating on the force behind her, and grinned. She knew that her white teeth were the only spot of lightness against the impending tempest.

Fire, lightning hot, coursed through her veins, while ice formed over her skin, turning it hard and unyielding like crystal. She raised a hand, marvelling at the change, though she felt no pain.

She *was* the storm. She could command it because it was part of her in the same way she could wave her hand or wiggle a toe.

Yes, murmured the voice.

"Turn the boat around or I'll kill you all."

"You'll kill everyone? Even the slaves?" shouted Ivar.

They don't believe you, thought the voice. *Time to show them what you can do.*

Ailsa unclenched her first and swirled it in circles at her side. She felt the air stirring around her, whipping her hair and sending goosebumps down her arms. From the look on the Avalognian's faces, she could tell that the storm was building behind her. She didn't dare turn to look.

Yes, said the voice. *That's it.*

With an upwards sweep of her hand, the air rose like a wave. She felt the boat momentarily levitate above the water, before she twisted her hand to the side and the boat landed back in the sea with a splash. Raiders were thrown from their feet, landing in sprawling masses across the deck.

The priest and his soldiers gaped at her as she stood firm upon the wood, her body perfectly still even as they were battered by the high winds.

"Kill her now." The priest shouted, spittle flying from his mouth as terror overtook his composure.

One of the soldiers sprang towards her, but a lift of her hand tore him from the boat with a gust of wind, depositing his body overboard.

The remaining Avalognians hugged the timber of the boat as it rocked up and down precariously. No others dared to follow the priest's orders.

Show them more, the voice urged.

Ailsa swept her hand up again, but this time at the boat next to them; the vessel was pulled from the sea and then thrown back into the waves. From across the water, she could hear screaming.

Icy clarity ripped into her mind. *The other prisoners. I need to stop, before I kill them too.*

But as she fought to pull away from the power, the ancient voice hushed her. *No, don't let go. You are the storm. Destroy.*

Her other arm raised involuntarily above her head. She watched in horror as her hand clenched and a bolt of lightning struck the mast of the nearby ship.

It immediately caught fire and the smell of burning wood drifted over the air whipping between the crafts.

"No," she whispered, her voice feeling raw in her throat. She had to stop this before she killed all the other prisoners.

Her ears rang with phantom laughter as she felt the power erupting from her body, charging the air around her. The nearest Avalognian, a barrel-chested warrior, threw himself forward to grab her legs. One touch of her skin sent him flying backwards, zapped by the electricity. Her hair stood on end as she the smell of burning flesh mingled with the sea-salt-tinged wind.

The ship that had been struck was slowly being

engulfed by flames. Despair tugged at her, threatening to pull her under. She knew that if she lost herself to the storm there would be no coming back.

As she fought to control the movements of her arms, she caught a glimpse of something silver swimming beside the burning ship.

Her heart paused.

The seal raised its head from beneath the waves and fixed her with his shiny black eyes. Even from a distance, she could understand their message.

Save them, it said. *I believe in you.*

With monumental effort, Ailsa turned her body so that it was angled towards the flames. Her breath was laboured as she concentrated on the storm, on the power she held so tenuously.

Now, she thought at the maelstrom.

She waited a moment and then like a groaning beast the tempest reared back, assessing her command. She stared right back into the middle of the swirling wind and rain, unflinching despite the intense pressure in her head. Something hot and wet dripped from her nose but she didn't dare lift a hand to wipe at it.

Then, when she couldn't hold on any longer, she felt the storm's submission. Ailsa thought she heard a hiss of displeasure, then the voice inside her head whispered a dejected, *yes.*

Without hesitation, she swept her arms up to swirl

the wind towards the boat, sending a shower of rain over the fire. The flames died down with the water, but she still heard screaming from the ship. Fanning her hand in front of her, she pushed the wind in the direction of the beach, making a wave which carried the boat closer to land. She watched as the vessel was lifted by the water and deposited near the shore. Ailsa could just make out figures jumping from the deck and wading through the shallows towards safety.

Raising her gaze towards the three other boats, she did the same, sending them hurtling towards the beach in a crest of saltwater and wind.

"Ailsa?" a voice called from over the prow. A head of copper curls peeked up over the side before a familiar, concerned face appeared.

"Harris!" she shouted, unable to move from her position on the deck without losing her hold on the storm.

Despite the worry etched into his features, he did his best to pull on a smirk. "I told you that you were a force to be reckoned with."

A sob broke in her throat. He vaulted over the edge and hugged her. He was still wearing the same clothes from the inn, which looked even more dishevelled from the raging wind.

"I can't control it for much longer, Harris. You need to get away." Lightning crackled overhead but Ailsa managed to throw the electricity further out to sea.

"Did I ever tell you I think that you're striking?" He smiled at her, and in that moment, against the backdrop of the churning sea, he looked the least human she had ever seen him.

Suddenly, Ailsa was thrown from her feet as something solid and colossal impacted with her ship. The wood under her groaned from the impact, buckling and sending her body flying. She landed heavily on her back and grimaced at the pain.

Over the ringing of her ears, she heard music rising from the sea, and underneath the melody came the piercing, wailing cry of '*want*.'

"*Want. Want.*"

"Harris?" cried Ailsa before she was again pitched to the side by another impact. She rolled towards the boat's edge, expecting to see his red hair nearby, but he wasn't there anymore.

"Pretty little selkie," cackled a voice. Ailsa managed to raise herself to her knees to peer over into the water. The sight made her stomach drop.

Harris was encased in white arms, as strong as marble. Despite being back in the water, he hadn't turned back into a seal. Instead his body hung limp from the ceasg's embrace. Surrounding him, five more ceasg drifted around, creating a tight circle. The one who held him grinned menacingly up at her.

"Look what we caught," crowed another.

"Told him we'd catch him."

"Shouldn't have come here."

"Now he's ours—"

"—but not for long."

"Give him back!" Ailsa screamed, barely managing to hold on to the side of the boat. The winds still whipped around, rocking the ship from side to side.

"I want girly," said one, baring her teeth at her. The one holding Harris slapped a hand out and pushed her sister away.

"Not now. Soon. Goodbye, girly." She smiled sweetly and then sank under the waves. The other ceasg disappeared behind her but she could still see their white bodies under the water. They darted under the boat and a second later, Ailsa felt the biggest impact yet hit the side. The whole vessel capsized into the water and she had just enough time to take a deep breath before she was plunged into the sea.

Chapter 69

The water's cold hit her skin like a thousand needles. She forced her eyes open to look for the ceasg but saw nothing but chunks of debris and other people, some alive and some dead. The force of the sinking ship sucked her deeper under water and she watched as both Avalognians and Eilanmòrians were pulled down with her into the freezing depths.

How many times had she almost drowned now?

She knew she'd prefer that today remained an 'almost.'

Forcing her tired arms and legs to power her forward, Ailsa moved through the murky water slowly. Her lungs began to burn with the effort of holding her breath.

From the corner of her eye, she could see a dark shadow moving towards her quickly. For one fearful second, she thought of sharks, but then there were whiskers and flippers.

Her heart leapt. *Harris?*

But the seal swimming to her was smaller. It hesitated momentarily before prodding her side with its nose. She wrapped an arm around its neck and it propelled upwards, faster than any normal seal could.

Finally, her head broke the surface of the water with a gasp. The air that whipped her face was frigid but mercifully calm. The storm had ended. Bits of star-speckled sky could be glimpsed through the thinning clouds. Cheering could be heard from the beach. Ailsa couldn't tell which side were celebrating until she heard an Eilanmòrian shout, "*Soarsa!*"

Freedom.

"Harris?" she whispered to the waves, waiting for him to raise his head from the water. She almost cried out when she caught sight of a mop of red hair emerging three feet away. The figure turned around and her heart sank.

"Are you okay?" asked Iona, swimming closer to where Ailsa treaded water.

Ailsa took a gulp of air and tilted her chin up. "How did you find me?"

"We heard about the raids along the coast and then Angus told me where you'd gone."

"Angus is here?"

Iona nodded. "We found Harris outside the inn, attempting to put out the fire. Then we followed the trails, trying to catch up to you."

She felt her eyes burning, but Iona gave her a little shake and Ailsa blinked them stubbornly.

"Ailsa," Iona asked, her voice deadly quiet, "Where's my brother?"

Chapter 70

"What happened?"

Iona had dragged Ailsa's half-frozen body through the water and up onto a deserted part of the beach. The Eilanmòrians had landed half a mile away and were quickly dismantling the ships to make large bonfires to keep them warm. Any Avalognians that had been on board had obviously died or had escaped into the night. Ailsa's own boat had sunk, pulling many people down with it, but a few survivors were still being washed up, having followed the glow of the flames. Every time a new one was found, the Eilanmòrians would let loose another round of cheers.

The giddy high of celebration did not reach the stretch of sand they were on. Instead, worry permeated the sea air.

Ailsa sat curled up on the ground, while Angus rubbed feeling into her stiff limbs. When Iona had pulled her from the surf, he had engulfed her in his warm arms and had not let go as she coughed up saltwater.

Iona stood a little way off, watching the waves roll in and the stars glitter from their reflections on the calm ocean.

At first, Ailsa couldn't speak and Angus did his best to lend her his body heat.

"It was my fault," she finally said when the shivers in her body had died down. "I did this. I tried to get free, and in the process, I let Harris get captured."

Angus held her tighter. "How Ailsa?"

"Ceasg."

He froze, his gaze leaving her face and going out to sea.

"I just—I lost control. I was trying to save the people on the boat, while he was trying to save me."

"I don't understand."

"She made the storm." Iona turned around towards them. In the moonlight, her white skin and red hair made her look ethereal and otherworldly. Ailsa couldn't tell whether she was surprised or not; her face had been schooled into neutrality.

Angus's, on the other hand, was incredulous. "How could she make a storm?"

"She's not human."

He sank back on his heels, relaxing his grip on her. Though the action was small, deep down Ailsa felt the rejection and it hurt.

She swallowed thickly and nodded. "I made the storm come, but I lost control of it. I set one of the boats on fire but then I managed to get them to safety. Ours was the last one out at sea when Harris climbed on. We were attacked—" Her voice cracked, and she paused for a moment before continuing. "Then Harris got captured. The ceasg had warned him that they were looking for him, that they'd take him to Nicnevan."

She felt Angus withdrawing from her, so she turned her attention to Iona. "Nicnevan has him. What are we going to do?"

"She was never really that interested in the Stone of Destiny."

Angus ran a hand through his hair, as if unable to process the situation.

Ailsa's head was spinning. She thought she saw something move out of the corner of her eye, beside the trees that pressed up against the beach, though when she looked there was nothing there. Fatigue was taking its toll.

"What does she want with him?" Ailsa asked while she massaged her temples.

Iona stepped closer and dropped down into a crouch in front of Ailsa. "I doubt that she thinks he was the one who stole her daughter, but he's pretty useful anyway."

"How? Revenge? Blackmail?"

"Exactly. Either she'll kill him immediately or she'll use him, hoping that someone with knowledge of her daughter will strike a bargain. But her daughter's whereabouts have been kept a secret. I don't know who took her. She could be anywhere."

"Or she could be right in front of you," croaked a voice from within the trees. Ailsa felt a chill creep over her skin as she turned to look at the owner of the new voice.

There it was. It had finally found her.

It towered above them, with grey skin and red, glowing eyes. It was all she could do not to turn and run, just like she had done that first day in the woods outside her home village. Just like she had done every day of her life.

The monster gripped the trunks of the two nearest trees, which splintered and groaned under his mighty hands. Finally, she could see what it was she had been running from.

With a growl, she pulled the dagger from Angus's belt and braced herself to throw, aiming right between the creature's eyes. She pulled the weapon over her shoulder and started to swing it forward—

It stepped forward out of the shadows and her heart seized in her chest.

"Gris?" Ailsa breathed.

Chapter 71

The knife fell from her hands and embedded itself in the sand beside her. Her eyes traced over the man in front of her, but her mind was blank. Questions would float to the surface—*What was he doing here? Why does he look like that?*—but they would sink quickly again into the mire.

The monster held his hands up. "I'm sorry, Ailsa," he said.

"What the hell is going on?" demanded Angus from beside her. She turned her head, as if in a dream, to find he had drawn his sword and was baring his teeth at the creature.

Iona took a step towards him.

"He's a Fear Laith," she explained, staring in wonder. "A Grey Man. Ailsa, do you know him?"

Her own voice came out in a whisper. "He's the soldier who trained me." It had been two years since she had last seen him. Or had it? Her gaze flicked over the sharp teeth, the red eyes… Was he the monster that had been following her? *Oh Gods*, had he been following her since she was a little girl?

"What do you want?" she croaked. She was starting to feel sick.

"I can explain," he said slowly like he was talking to a frightened animal.

Ailsa raised her fists in front of her. "You had better."

"What does it mean?" Angus interrupted. "*Fear Laith?*"

"They're found all over the world," replied Iona, "But they're rare."

"We're forest guardians," explained Gris. "But that's also my curse. I'm bound to the forest."

"You weren't before," Ailsa argued. His jaw hardened. "When I found you, when you were attacked, I don't even think you realised how badly you were hurt. You were *dying*." His voice broke on the last word. "We're allowed five months and a day every ten years to leave the forest and appear human." He closed his ruby eyes. "I had to use it to save you."

"Why?" she asked, barely able to breathe. "Why did you save me? Why have you been following me?"

He opened his eyes and gave her a fierce look. "To keep you safe. I've been your shadow all your life, trying to protect you," he said, taking another step towards her. "I brought you to your mother, the woman who raised you."

Ailsa's head was reeling. "You need to explain. Now."

He stepped forward and she flinched.

"You don't need to fear me, Ailsa," he said. With a deep rumbling sigh, he lowered himself to sit in front of them, leaning against the trunk of an ancient tree.

"Before anyone launches into long histories, I think we need a fire," proclaimed Angus. "You must be freezing, Ailsa."

She nodded woodenly, never taking her eyes off the monster in front of her. She barely noticed when Iona summoned the water from her skin and clothes, the droplets shimmering in the starlight before being flung off to the side in a wave.

"I've been protecting you your whole life. At first, from a distance. I used to stand in the woods beside your adoptive mother's cottage, before she died and you had to leave. Then when you were by yourself, I tried to watch you to make sure you were alright."

"She wasn't my adoptive mother. She was my mother. We had the same eyes—"

"The same eyes as everyone in Eilanmòr, near enough. It's not uncommon to have blue eyes. In fact, Nicnevan's eyes are blue, if I recall."

"But she looked after me—"

"After her own daughter died."

"I'm not listening to this. This is ridiculous, and quite frankly it's poor taste to imply she wasn't my mother when all she ever did was care for me."

"She looked after you because she loved you. Just like

she loved her other daughter. I'm sorry, Ailsa, truly. But you may be the key to ending Nicnevan's tyrannical rule over the fair folk. Humans might be safe right now, but as long as she remains uncontested, you won't get your friend back.

"Just over nineteen years ago, I was guarding my forest when I heard crying. When I searched, I found a faerie, an arrow through her heart. In her arms was a baby. You.

"I did what I thought was best. You stopped crying when I held you and so I carried you through the woods. I knew that without food, you would die, so I went looking for something for you. When I stumbled upon the cottage, I was just going to take some honey and then take you back to my home. But when I opened the door, there she was, your mother. Asleep in a rocking chair. Tear marks staining her cheeks. She had obviously stayed awake most of the night, nursing the baby in her arms. But the child was dead. Pneumonia, I think. She looked like such a good mother. It was so sorrowful. So, I lifted the bundle from her arms and swapped the corpse with you."

"So, you stole her dead child? You didn't think to wake her up?"

"I didn't want to scare her! I watched from the window till she stirred. At first, she was confused. I'm sure she thought her baby had miraculously recovered.

But then I saw realisation dawn. She knew you were not hers, that you had been left in place of her child, and yet she rocked you in her arms and went to fetch you some food. I knew you'd be safe in her hands."

"She must have been disgusted. Imagine, one minute you're fighting for your daughter's life, then you wake up and she's gone, replaced by a stranger." "I assure you, she did not feel that way. After I had buried the body, I returned and kept watch over both of you. Never was a girl loved so much by her mother as you were."

"And then she died."

"I spoke to her, you know. The day before, she came to the window and shouted for me. 'Beastie' she called me and waited, staring into the trees. You were away, collecting medicine for her. I emerged and she smiled. She thanked me for bringing you to her. She told me she was dying and that I was to look after you again. She loved you so much."

"But I didn't want to frighten you. I gave you a few months, making sure to leave food nearby. I'll admit, you were good at keeping house, for a girl of fourteen. I was away when the villagers came and trashed the cottage four years later and you had already left by the time I arrived. I looked for you. When I found you, you were a mile away, in the next settlement. I tried to catch you, to take you away but you ran. I'm rather slow, I'm afraid, heavy feet. So you disappeared. Every time I thought I had found you again, you bolted. Then you started avoiding the forest all together. I can't leave it for too long, or I will wither and die."

"So why do you think Ailsa is Nicnevan's daughter?" asked Angus.

"She's the right age," said Iona. "And it was a group of faeries who stole her. Also, now I think we can all be fairly sure she isn't human."

"I'm not a faerie princess."

"Obviously." Angus motioned to her mud-coated clothes.

"Maybe it doesn't matter. Maybe the only person who needs to believe you're her is Nicnevan." Iona's eyes were sparkling.

Ailsa frowned. "What was the girl's name?"

"Eilidh, I think."

"Eilidh?" She certainly didn't feel like an Eilidh.

"Don't you see, Ailsa," Angus came closer to grip her shoulder. "If we pretend you're Nicnevan's daughter, maybe we can get close enough to free Harris!"

"How will I pass for a faerie? I don't even really know how to use my power. Surely the daughter of Nicnevan would be good at magic?"

"We can teach you," Iona offered. "We'll coach you along the way. By the time we reach her court, you'll be a master."

"Well, I guess we have to try. How long will it take?"

"You'll need to go slow, my feet…" Gris said.

A shiver ran down Ailsa's spine. "You're coming with us?"

"I've been with you almost your whole life, I'm not leaving you now. I've watched you grow into a strong young woman." Grey eyebrows framed his red eyes. "Please, let me help you."

"Fine." *She would regret this later.* "I suppose you'll be dragging yourself into this too, Angus?" Ailsa asked, rounding on him.

"Wouldn't miss it for the world."

"You'll probably die, you know," Iona cautioned. "Nicnevan does not like humans."

"I'll win her over." Angus turned, giving Ailsa a tired smile. "Besides, now I can be *your* bodyguard."

Chapter 72

It was a strange world, Ailsa thought.

A month ago, she had been on a beach, quite content in her loneliness. Now she was on a mission to rescue a selkie, accompanied by his sister, a Prince of Eilanmòr and the monster who had haunted her nightmares. She touched the mark on her left cheek. And maybe, just maybe, she would find out where she came from.

They reached the top of the hill and were met with a sight that previously would have made Ailsa's blood freeze: a sea of trees. The spaces between the tree trunks appeared pitch black despite the morning sunlight.

She stared into the darkness, on the edge of a new life. To her right, she saw Angus stop Iona and Gris with a raised hand. He knew this needed to be her decision.

Ailsa fished out a leather cord from her pack and hesitated only a moment, before pulling her hair off her face and tying it back. Fear was the real monster who had hounded her steps all these years. Now was the time for courage.

Be brave.

Head held high, and back straight, Ailsa MacAra

stepped into the forest, searching for a selkie, a faerie queen—and her past.

Chapter 73

The young woman wrenched her knife out of the faerie's body at her feet and cleaned it on her dress; it was already covered in the creature's thick, black blood anyway. She would need to burn it along with the corpse. That had been too close. The creature had almost made it to the house. She let out a huff of breath as if to slow her heart rate.

It wasn't easy, killing. Every time she did it, she worried that they took a little piece of her to Hell with them. Still, she would keep doing it if that's what it took to keep her mother away from her.

She heard Maggie's cries from the house, but she knew the baby was being taken care of. Nanny Agnes had looked after her when she had been that age and now the woman would trust no one else to look after her daughter. Agnes knew the risks as well as she did. They could never be found.

The woman set to work making a fire, right where the faerie had died. The job had to be done quickly before other creatures smelled the blood and came looking. As soon as it was hot enough, she threw the body in, along with her dress, leaving her in her underclothes.

The flames rose higher, the crackling now the only sound as Maggie had been quieted. The woman watched the light dance on her skin, content for the moment that she had protected her loved ones. Her hands brushed absently against the skin on her elbow, where she knew the reminder of her inheritance and escape rested. She was lucky that it was so easy to hide the mark with long sleeves. She knew other changelings were not so fortunate.

With a grim smile, she turned away from the fire back towards the house. Tonight would not be the last night she would need to fight the creatures—she would need to fight them for the rest of her life.

After all, Nicnevan would never stop sending them to search for her daughter.

The End

About the Author

Caroline Logan is a writer of Young Adult Fantasy. *The Stone of Destiny* is her debut novel, and is the first in *The Four Treasures* series.

Caroline is a high school biology teacher who lives in the Cairngorms National Park in Scotland, with her fiancé. Before moving there, she lived and worked in Spain, Tenerife, Sri Lanka and other places in Scotland.

She graduated from The University of Glasgow with a bachelor's degree in Marine and Freshwater Biology. In her spare time she tries to ski and paddle board, though she is happiest with a good book and a cup of tea.

Follow Caroline online:
Instagram: @bearbooksandtravel
Twitter: @bearpuffbooks

Acknowledgements

This feels a bit like a cross between writing an Oscar's speech and a report card. I never thought I'd be typing this, and the fact that I am is a testament to the support and faith of so many people. I truly am lucky.

First, to you, the reader. Thanks for getting your hands on a copy. Hopefully you've enjoyed the book and you're now planning on passing it on to a friend, writing a glorious five star review, or placing it right in the middle of your coffee table.

Colossal, gigantic and tremendous thanks to Anne Glennie at Cranachan Publishing for seeing the potential in my story.

Thank you to Kelly Macdonald, also at Cranachan. I am super glad I came to chat to you at Waterstones that day!

Speaking of, thank you Merryn Appleby for encouraging me, when I first arrived at Kingussie High School, to start my wee book group. Who'd have thought it would have led to a dream coming true!

Thank you to all of my fellow #clancranachan authors, especially my Twitter pals: Ross Sayers, Joseph Lamb, Barbara Henderson, Lindsay Littleson, Annemarie Allan, Joan Haig and Helen MacKinven.

Thanks to my Mum and Stepdad, and my Dad and Linda, for giving me life and raising me. Not many people are lucky enough to have even one parent that they can count on, and I have four. Also, thanks to my sister, Rachel, for wiping my tears when we watched sad movies and never letting me forget the time I gave you brown sauce instead of medicine.

Thanks to Diane Proctor, Martin Proctor, Blair Proctor, Neil Phillips and Winter for welcoming me to your family and supporting me.

To Loli Cummings, David Walsh, Martin Kinnear, Cara Donald, Alan Steen, Calum Nicolson, Craig Smith, Eilidh Milligan, Kirstin Norman, Carine Cairney, Rachel Henry, Emmy McCrow, Callum Arthur, Rachel Richards, Laura Peters, Balazs Magyar, John Watson, Laura Watson, Jimmy Anderson, and Greig Walker—thanks for being my pals and celebrating my achievements. (Oh god, I've probably forgot someone. I'll sort that out in the next book, promise.)

Cheers to my online friends—especially Kayla Duff, Alex Micati, Christopher Drost, Sarah Audrey Young—for keeping me sane through writing and edits.

It wouldn't be fair of me not to acknowledge all of the pupils I've taught over the last seven years. I have loved being your teacher. Here's to many more years. I'd like to especially thank my book group—Nicholas Macdonald, Iona Craig, Sasha Bailey, Charlotte Fraser, Nayeema Sultana and Connall Drummond.

Thanks to Jenna Moreci, for starting it all.

Thank you to Ranger Danger, the tripod dog. You're a really good boy.

Finally, I wouldn't even be here without Vince Logan. I'm pretty sure I love you more than anyone has ever loved anyone else in the history of the world. Thank you isn't enough.

Coming Soon

A Four
Treasures Novel

The Cauldron of Life

Book 2

CAROLINE LOGAN